THE
Pearl
OF THE
Antilles

Bilingual Press/Editorial Bilingüe

General Editor
Gary D. Keller

Managing Editor
Karen S. Van Hooft

Associate Editors
Barbara H. Firoozye
Thea S. Kuticka

Assistant Editor
Linda St. George Thurston

Editorial Board
Juan Goytisolo
Francisco Jiménez
Eduardo Rivera
Mario Vargas Llosa

Address:
Bilingual Press
Hispanic Research Center
Arizona State University
P.O. Box 872702
Tempe, Arizona 85287-2702
(480) 965-3867

THE Pearl OF THE Antilles

ANDREA O'REILLY HERRERA

Bilingual Press/Editorial Bilingüe
TEMPE, ARIZONA

ISBN 0-927534-95-9
Printed simultaneously in a softcover edition. ISBN 0-927534-96-7

Library of Congress Cataloging-in-Publication Data

Herrera, Andrea O'Reilly.
    The Pearl of the Antilles / Andrea O'Reilly Herrera.
    p. cm.
    ISBN 0-927534-95-9 (alk. paper) — ISBN 0-927534-96-7 (pbk.: alk. paper)
    1. Cuban American women—Fiction. 2. Mothers and daughters—Fiction. 3. Women—Cuba—Fiction. 4. Exiles—Fiction. 5. Cuba—Fiction. I. Title.

    PS3558.E734 P43 2000
    813'.6--dc21   00-060876

PRINTED IN THE UNITED STATES OF AMERICA

Acknowledgments

Partial funding provided by the Arizona Commission on the Arts through appropriations from the Arizona State Legislature and grants from the National Endowment for the Arts.

Rough years I've had; now may I see once more
My hall, my lands, my people before I die.
—*The Odyssey*

And if I whistle, then, hum a little ditty,
Just a tune to charm and drug sleep off,
Oh, it turns into a dirge for this stricken house—
So gone down, so fallen from its governance.
How I wish there'd come at last a happy end to the strain!
Oh make the bonfire blaze
Good news upon the gloom.
—*The Agamemnon*

Gracias to Teresa Alvaré-O'Reilly, Hubert O'Reilly, Carlos Alvaré, Maggie Bryan-Peterson, Bob Deming, Jan Fairbairn, Carl Smith, Candice Brown, Vivian García-Conover, Joan Burns, Nancy Bates, James Burns, Larry Arrigale, Tom Keels, Anna Leadem, Jorge Guitart, Delia O'Hare, Barry O'Reilly, Phil O'Reilly, Rob O'Reilly, Chris Dunkerley, Angela Herrera-Martin, Ron Ambrosetti, Pauline Caras, Jeff Rubin-Dorsky, Elaine LaMattina, Dennis Maloney, Pablo Medina, Judith Ortiz-Cofer, Heberto Padilla, Alvina Quintana, Cruz Stark, Jan Stryz, and Helena María Viramontes for your encouragement, suggestions at various stages, and support of many kinds over all of these years; to Delia Poey and Virgil Suárez for giving me a first chance; to Alicia Ostriker and Fred Chappell for giving me confidence; to Karen Van Hooft for believing in me; and to my patient editors Linda Thurston, Barbara Firoozye, and Thea Kuticka; to Alex Herrera for the amazing orange tree; and to Niki and Marty Herrera for your excellent suggestions and your willingness to read and listen to draft after draft; tres mil gracias to Lourdes Gil, Marjorie Agosín, Vivian de la Incera, Efraín Ferrer, Judy McKelvey, Steve Warner, Paul Harvey, Jan McVicker, Bill Spanos, and Ruth Shokoff for your insights, guidance, and wisdom; and to my husband Martin, for your inspiration and, most of all, your unflagging faith.

The voices of multitudes sound through this single throat.

Para mis tres cielos Alex, Niki y Marty
y mi querido compañero Martín,
con mucho cariño y amor.

Separated from the world below, the old woman sat upright and motionless, rooted into the side of the mountain. Her crossed legs were folded beneath her and the flattened palms of her hands rested on her knees. Her silvery hair and indigo-colored skin seemed to drink in the colors of the earth and the sky that spread out around her, and her eyes were filled with movement and desire, like the ever-changing forest and the sea. From a distance she might have appeared to be part of the landscape.

The air was unusually still and silent, except for the eternal roar of the sea and an occasional cry that sounded from the deep recesses of the forest and caught on the breeze. The ancient one, as the townspeople had taken to calling the old woman, bent her eyes toward the place on the horizon where the violet light had slowly begun to gather into a dome. Though the sky was clear and the sea breeze mild, the muffled hush of the forest and the uninhabited skies signaled to her the approaching storm. As the sun began to push its way above the horizon, she broke into a low, quivering chant that seemed to quicken the dawn like the polishing of a stone.

Despite the serenity that came with isolation, the old woman could not quell her unease. Perhaps she should have listened to the mulata after all. The child had begged her not to go to the mountain, though she could not find the words to explain why. Cupping the palm of her hand over her brow, the old woman scanned the horizon for fishing boats, but a gauzy mist clung like netting to the surface of the sea. As though she were caressing a familiar face, her gaze swept across the tourmaline sea until it ran up against the ribbed pink-and-white sand, which bled into the raw, red earth and the deep green foliage that surrounded the little town at the base of the mountain upon which she sat. She always positioned herself in the same place—beneath a crooked thorn bush—knowing that there the view was most expansive. From this place she could look down the side of the mountain, beyond its jutting precipices into the town below, though from that distance it lost its particularity.

Looking down from her height, the old woman's gaze rested on the tall spires of the cathedral, which lay at the heart of the town. She cocked her head sideways, blocking out the entire cathedral with the palm of her hand. As she turned her eyes toward the interior of the island, before her spread a great expanse—fields of white lilies, tobacco and cane, surrounded by groves of wild fruit trees and thickly tangled vegetation that formed a skirt around the amphitheater of blue mountains that rose up in the distance.

Bending her eyes downward once again, she could see from her vantage point that all of the streets in the town led to the large, rectangular plaza across from the cathedral, like the inter-woven branches of a great river emptying into the sea. A steady flow of people coming from all directions were making their way toward the plaza. Those who had already arrived formed a kind of living barrier around a wooden cart that stood near its center. The tall palm leaves that they held in their hands fanned the air above them like feathery plumes.

Sitting motionless on the mountain, the old woman became conscious of her own heartbeat pounding in swift rhythm with the movement of the crowd, which shifted impatiently from side to side like a great, swaying beast. Though the townspeople appeared to be indistinct shapes in the distance, she knew they had gathered to draw the wooden cart that would bear the carved and gilded image of the Virgen through the streets to the sea. She recalled at once that it was the sixteenth day of the seventh month, for every year on the same date the townspeople gathered together in the plaza to escort the statue to the water's edge. She had witnessed the ritual a thousand and one times before.

The ancient one watched in silence as the cathedral doors swung open and the statue of Nuestra Señora was carried down the steep marble steps and placed on a dais, which was lifted high above the crowd and then carried to the wooden cart. Then the priests emerged from the cathedral like dark-winged birds, cut-ting a path through the crowd that formed a wall around the statue. They were followed by a ragged band of women dressed and veiled in black. Although the strain of their voices was washed out by the distance that separated them from the old woman on the mountain and drowned by the sea, she knew that the townspeople were reciting with one voice the prayers that were composed especially for the feast day of the Virgin, whom they had adopted as the patroness of their town. Her lips began to move in unconscious rhythm with theirs, and the soft sounds that she whispered slipped over her tongue like gliding serpents.

As the bells in the monastery that stood behind the cathedral began to sound, the ancient one closed her eyes and saw in her mind's eye the procession, which had begun to wind its way toward the sea. As though conjured out of air, a vision suddenly sprang up before her like some unbidden dream:

A group of twelve—hooded in white robes like orishas and wearing telling beads around their necks—passed before her eyes like a carnival. They followed a man who looked like some ancient priest dressed in a dark green habit. He carried in one hand a crooked staff, and in the other a broom. There were wings on his boots, and his face was partially concealed by a flowing beard. A large cat-shaped amulet hung from his neck.

Up the side of the mountain they rose, stepping to the beat of batá drums that sounded beneath the callused heels of their hands. From the distance came the soft pounding of other drums, calling out from all directions and echoing in the mouths of the mountain caves. When they reached the top of the mountain, they formed a circle around a group of gaily dressed people. As the air began to thicken and swell with the sound of the drums, the twelve began to dance around the crowd. Soon the people were swept up in the swirling motion of the dance like black-and-white and caramel-colored leaves gathered up by the wind and pulled into the circle as though by some unseen current. Baring themselves to their waists, the women bent their knees and slowly swung their hips from side to side. With parted lips and parted legs, they rolled their eyes in their heads and moaned and chanted aloud, while the men shouted and whooped and jumped into the air around them, bending their supple bodies into a thousand fantastic shapes. Losing themselves in the rhythm of the dance, it was as though their feet had been given voice.

For a brief moment the crowd moved together in perfect rhythm while the initiated danced in pulsing circles around them. Then seven claps of thunder sounded and the sky rolled back, emptying its womb of hail the size of small stones. As though given a command, the robed figures threw off their white garments, exposing to the people faces shaped like crows'. Over their shoulders hung bayonets, and in their hands some held whips and sickles, and others silver crosses and jewel-encrusted scepters of Incan gold. The humming of the sickles and the lashing of the whips drowned out the joyous laughter of the people; then all was left to silence and fear, except the sound of the sea crashing upon the shore.

The people seemed to recognize them at once, though no one dared to call out their names. One by one, they fell to their knees and beat their fists and their foreheads against the earth, staining the ground beneath them with their mingled blood. And though the people cried out with anger and despair, the crow-faced men and women continued to dance in a wild frenzy around them in an unbroken circle like a serpent with its tail in its mouth.

With one voice, the women in the crowd pleaded for the lives of their children, whom they'd concealed in the folds of their skirts; and the men begged them to spare their honor. Without a word, the bearded priest pointed toward the sea, prompting the women to gather their children in their arms. They wrapped them, cocoonlike, in layers of tender green skeleton leaves and the juices that ooze from trees, then pushed them off the edge of the mountain. In silence they watched as a warm tropical breeze carried them—children without shadows—across the water to a land that had two walls. Many from the crowd followed in their wake, throwing themselves like wriggling insects into the waves. Those who remained behind called after their children, only to be answered by words that clanked and drummed against their ears like silver coins dropped to the bottom of a tin. At that moment the earth began to tremble, the wind to blow, and the mountain island upon which the people stood began to uproot and split apart. A small piece broke loose and sailed across the sea toward the place on the horizon where the children had vanished from sight.

Who will bear the blame? the priest cried out, pointing one by one at the richly dressed people in the crowd. His voice echoed like a trumpet through the canyons of the mountain. And then the words became a *flock of great black birds that swooped down upon the unarmed crowd, pecking at the men's genitals, robbing them of their futures and their pasts, and plucking the jewelry from the arms and the necks and the fingers of the women. When they had finished stripping the people, they carried in their beaks the gold rings and bracelets, silver crosses, and strings of pearls across the seven seas, and dropped them into immense, bottomless nests. When they returned, they perched on the shoulders of the bearded priest with claws like scarlet sickles. He nodded his head with approval, and at that moment the people found that their feet and hands were chained together and a great wall of fire was rising up around them. Twice the circle of fire that hemmed them in began to contract, shrinking the plot of land beneath their feet.*

Bent with age and half ravaged by the cannibal hidden within him, the priest smashed a great red conch shell beneath his heel. Then he turned his back on the people and began to wave his arms above his head, seeking absolution from a crowd that was not there. Gradually, he withdrew from sight followed by no one but a boy who had lost his mother at sea.

The mountain valley that he had abandoned was a crucible of seared vegetation, and the air was filled with the smell of burnt sugar and flesh. The Poet is dead, someone called out as the false dawn lit by the wall of fire broke all around them. Suddenly a great roar arose from the crowd; the distant hills took up the sound and carried their hollow, ancient cry across the sea until their children rose up on a distant shore, barking out harsh-sounding words in response that took flight from their lips like a cloud of doves.

As she opened her eyes, the old woman tried to recall the first time she had seen the vision. Over the years, from her place on the mountain, she had seen so many visions. This was not the only one. But from her height, she lost all sense of time—confusing the past with the present and the future with the past. To her, time seemed to be moving in a restless circle that turned in on itself like a dog frantically chasing its tail. With a heavy sigh, she recalled the times she had tried in vain to warn her people about the horrors to come. Shaking her head in sorrow, she thought of the words that every generation had scrawled in wiry letters across the waxy leaves of bushes and trees and the peeling paint of yellow walls—**Never Again.** Even now, they refused to listen to her, just as she had ignored the mulata's warning.

The snakelike movement of the procession as it wound its way toward the sea caught the old woman's attention and drew her back to the drama taking place in the little town below her. From such a great distance the townspeople looked small and insignificant, like the painted figures on an urn. While the procession arrived at the water's edge, a group of men lifted the statue of the Virgin from the cart and placed her in one of the larger fishing boats. After they had secured her onto the bow, an armada of small skiffs escorted her to a floating platform anchored just beyond a thin strip of land that jutted out of the mouth of the bay into the sea. Meanwhile the fishermen and devoted townspeople followed in her wake, scattering flower petals into the water from the backs of their boats.

The old woman watched in silent detachment as the bobbing knot of fishing boats launched across the bay. With her eyes she traced the haphazard pattern of the crowd, spread out unevenly across the shore. Some waved their straw hats and red bandannas over their heads, while others waded through the water after the fishing boats, as the flower petals undulated around them like colorful wreaths. Having lost sight of the statue, the crowd gradually broke off into smaller groups, making their way toward the deserted town. She knew that most would return to their homes—the women to begin making pasteles and natilla, and the men to take refreshment and rest.

The ancient one resumed her vigil on the top of the mountain. Once again, she allowed herself to be swept up in the vision, but the dance was suddenly interrupted by the certain knowledge that something irretrievable had been lost. "He perdido una perla—la he perdido en el mar," she whispered beneath her breath. An unexpected void opened within her like a wound, causing her to rise from her place and make her way through the rain and the darkness that had suddenly swallowed up the sun, along the steep path that sloped down the side of the mountain toward the town.

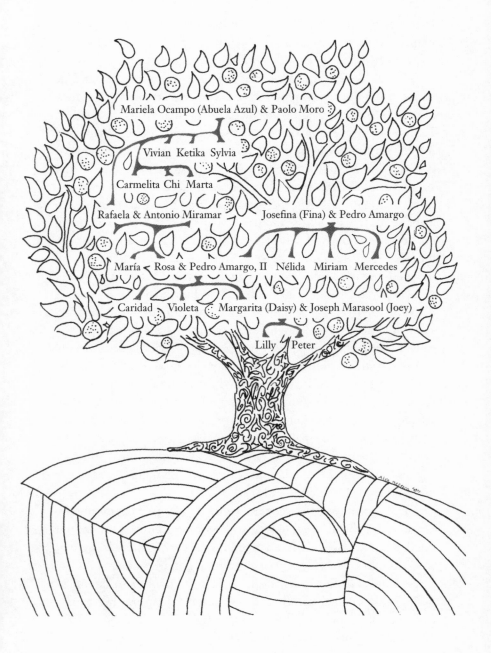

Part One

May 1949

Although he never once mentioned her refusal, Rosa knew that her husband would never forgive her. Pride and thick-headedness, she convinced herself, stood in his way. For almost three years Pedro had traveled back and forth between Cienfuegos and Havana at least twice a month to manage his widowed mother's affairs. In between his visits Fina wrote faithfully to her son. In her long letters, which were filled with trivial details that she extracted from the society section of the newspaper (such as who attended the opening matinee of La Bohème at the Jardín Miramar, which was a grand success despite the fact that it had been delayed almost forty-five minutes by the rain), she always remembered her two granddaughters and closed her letters by reminding Pedro to attend to the small matters (which he had somehow overlooked during his last visit) that came to her attention. She never asked after her daughter-in-law, even on her death-bed. In her own mind, Rosa had ceased to exist.

Upon their mother's death, Pedro's sisters, Nélida and Miriam, inherited all of Fina's clothing and jewelry, except for her immense diamond engagement ring and wedding band, both of which she left to whichever one of her granddaughters married

3

first. In her will, Fina also left her silverware and china to her two eldest daughters. The youngest, Mercedes, who was in a perpetual state of disgrace in her mother's eyes, received Fina's worn leather prayer book, a scapular bearing the back-to-back images of la Virgen de la Caridad de Cobre and Our Lady of Mount Carmel, and a glass rosary with a large silver cross, which she had watched her mother roll on the back porch every afternoon at three. Bebita, who had cared for Fina from her birth, received a bottle of holy water from the shrine at Lourdes and a rosary ring that Fina insisted had been blessed by the pope during her visit to Rome. "The house on la Calle de la Semilla, along with all of the furniture, carpets, window dressings, and the oil painting of Fina and Cuca (the Amargos' lap dog), which hung above the mantelpiece in the front parlor, is left to Pedro," Don Pedro's former law partner Arturo Rodríguez announced, with his reading glasses balanced on the tip of his nose, to the family members who had gathered in his office to hear the reading of Fina's will, "being that he is Doña Josefina and Don Pedro's only living son." Though the news of Fina's death had already been announced in the papers, the details regarding her son's handsome inheritance graced the front page of the society section of *El Diario de la Marina*. The article also revealed that Fina had stipulated in a codicil that in the event of her son's premature death, her house and all of its contents would go to Nélida and Miriam. Should they survive their old aunts, her "adoring" granddaughters, "who resided in Cienfuegos with their father," stood to inherit their grandmother's estate. Nowhere in her will did Fina mention her daughter-in-law, an omission which caused a stir among her friends and neighbors.

Upon his return to Havana, following the reading of his mother's will, Pedro insisted once again (this time at his sisters' request) that they move into the house on Calle Semilla. Although she knew in her heart that she could not refuse her husband's wishes a second time, Rosa attempted to change his mind, arguing that ever since her grandparents had moved to Cienfuegos, all of the women in her family (for there had been no sons), including their two daughters, Caridad and Margarita, had been born and raised at Tres Flores.

"Tres Flores was built by my grandfather," she reminded Pedro one afternoon as they sat at the wrought-iron table on the balcony eating their merienda, "when he first arrived in Cienfuegos with Abuela. She was only 19 at the time."

"I know. I know," Pedro sighed, "and Paolo was only 21. I've heard this story a thousand and one times, Rosa."

"It was the other way around, Pedro," Rosa corrected him. "Abuela was two years older than my grandfather, though she swore until the day she died that she was two years younger."

"You're making it sound as though I'm asking you to move to the ends of the earth," Pedro continued, uninterrupted. "For God's sake, we'll only be a few hours away from Tres Flores, Rosa. We can come back whenever you want."

From across the table, Rosa frowned at Pedro, though he was staring down at his plate, carefully avoiding her eyes. Nothing in his Havana, she thought as she watched him spoon natilla into his mouth, could compare to Tres Flores.

"You have to give Havana a chance, Rosa. My mother's house is just as beautiful as Tres Flores," Pedro told her in exasperation, as though he had read her thoughts. Knowing that she was unmoved by his argument he added, "If things don't work out, we'll move back to Cienfuegos. I promise."

"Once we leave Tres Flores, you know as well as I that we'll never move back, Pedro. Never."

"Yes, we will," he insisted with renewed energy, upon hearing the note of resignation that had crept into her voice. "Besides, I'll have to return to the plantation at least twice a year." Rosa raised her head and gazed at Pedro with empty eyes. "Even though we'll be living in the city," he continued, ignoring the pained expression on her face, "I'm still going to have to oversee the cleaning of the fields and the planting and harvesting of the cane. You'll learn to love Havana, mi amor. I promise," he added, knowing that he had broken a chink in her wall. "Don't you remember what my father always said?" Rosa, who was at that moment pretending to be occupied with piercing a thin slice of ham and a wedge of melon onto the end of her fork, shook her head. "One night in Havana—three in Paris."

"Pedro," she said with a sigh, raising her eyes to meet his, "shouldn't we be thinking about the future?"

"The future?" Pedro repeated with a puzzled look, as he unfolded a corner of his napkin and smoothed it across his lap.

Rosa could tell by the tone in his voice that her husband was genuinely perplexed by her question. "Yes, the future," she said, nervously fingering the fringe of the tablecloth as she watched him split open a fresh melon and scrape out the seeds before cutting himself a slice. "We could sell the house on Calle Semilla and invest the money in sugar cane. My mother always said that land was the best investment. Your sisters could come and stay with us whenever they wanted," she quickly added, cutting him off before he had a chance to speak. "It would do them good to get out of the city once in awhile. The fresh country air would do them wonders."

"Sugar cane?" Pedro repeated between mouthfuls. "What do we want with more sugar cane, Rosa? As it is, your father has already left us three warehouses, a sugar mill, and a plantation half the size of Cienfuegos."

Rosa gazed across the table, knowing that he was right. When her grandfather had first settled in Cienfuegos their land grant had been just under five hundred acres—fifteen caballerías read the framed document, with the red wax seal and the blue ribbons, that still hung in Paolo's study. Over the years, as the cane flourished and her family prospered, the plantation had almost tripled in size.

In silence, Rosa noted that though he continued to chew his food in his usual slow, methodical way, the veins in Pedro's neck had grown taut and his throat and cheeks had begun to color. She knew that she had angered him by suggesting that they sell his mother's house.

"If you're so concerned about the future," Pedro finally said in a low voice, breaching the wall of silence that had thrust itself up between them, "why aren't you a little more concerned about the welfare of *your* two daughters?"

"What do you mean the welfare of *my* two daughters?"

"You know perfectly well what I mean, Rosa. We've discussed this before. Cienfuegos is no place to raise the girls."

"No place to raise the girls?" Rosa repeated in astonishment. "No place to raise them? This is the first time I've heard *this*."

"That's just not true, Rosa. We talked about *this* when my father died—the *first* time that I asked you to move to Havana."

Prompted by anger and guilt, a plume of color flashed across Rosa's cheeks. It was the first time that Pedro had openly acknowledged her refusal to move to the house on Calle Semilla.

"Don't forget, Señor, that like it or not, your wife was raised in this town."

"Oh, I see," Pedro scoffed, with his fork poised in midair, "if it was good enough for you, it's good enough for Caridad and Margarita . . . is that what you're saying?" Noting the way that her eyes flashed and the threatening manner in which Rosa knit her brows, he hastily added, in a notably softer tone, "The city will offer the girls opportunities that they will never have here, mi vida."

"Like what?" she asked in a dull voice, with her eyes fixed on the orange tree her grandfather had planted in the far corner of the courtyard over a half a century before.

"Like good families from their own class, to begin with." As he spoke, Rosa absently touched the silverware that was lying alongside her plate with her fingertips—silverware, she thought, that had been passed down to her grandmother, Mariela, from her great-grandmother, Milagro, and carried with her across the ocean. She knew by the triumphant tone in Pedro's voice that she could not hold out against him much longer. Soon, the walls would come crashing in and the fortress she had guarded so jealously would yield like a sand castle to the flood of words. She knew she had already lost the battle.

Turning in her seat, Rosa fixed her eyes on Pedro's. They were her only weapons. He was sitting across from her, passively

7

returning her gaze as he slowly twisted the waxed end of his mustache with his fingertip. It was a habit that signaled to her that he might strike out at any moment, like Niño, the ginger cat in the kitchen who warned his prey with the impatient thumping of his tail.

Too irritated to be intimidated, Pedro laid down his fork and they stared at one another in awkward silence. "Forgive me, mi amor," he said in a caustic tone, recalling his father's insistence that a house was destined for ruin if the man allowed a woman to wear the pants in the family, "forgive me for not wanting my daughters to marry guajiros with dirty fingernails, who work in their father's fields."

Instinctively lowering her eyes, Rosa flushed at the mocking tone in Pedro's voice. She quietly cleared her throat, allowing herself a moment to collect herself before responding. She knew that if she did not master her emotions, she would lose her chance to be heard. Long ago she had vowed that she would never give *her* husband the opportunity to accuse her of being irrational—of being hysterical—as Fina had given Pedro's father.

"Por Dios, Pedro," she said in an even voice, slowly raising her eyes to meet his once again, "Caridad just turned ten and Margarita is only eight years old. I think we have a little more time before we begin worrying about whom the girls will marry."

Pedro drained his coffee cup and slammed it down on the porcelain saucer. "Excuse my impertinence, Señora, but didn't your mother teach you that it's a wife's duty to respect and obey her husband's will? Don't forget that you already refused me once," he added, wagging his index finger at her, "when Mother was so ill."

"I couldn't leave *my* mother, Pedro. Don't forget that I lost *my* father, too. What was I supposed to do?" Rosa retorted, turning down her mouth like a child who had been scolded. Shaking her head, she recalled that after Don Pedro's death, Fina had invented a long list of mysterious illnesses that even the most skilled doctors in Havana could not cure in order to keep her son at her side. She wrote at least once a week, telling Pedro that her heart would give out if he didn't move to Havana, even though everyone—including her servants—knew that she had a heart as strong and spiny as an artichoke. In truth, Fina had never dreamed that her husband, who had died so unexpectedly, would leave her without warning to manage his affairs (not to mention the myriad problems that arose on a daily basis, such as the leak that developed over the mantelpiece, which Don Pedro had promised to attend to) alone. Rosa almost laughed out loud at the memory of her mother-in-law, who periodically proclaimed that she was knocking on death's door but miraculously resurrected to comb out her hair, powder her face, and apply a fresh coat of coral-colored lipstick to her lips before greeting Dr. Incera, the family physician who paid her a house call every other Wednesday. It was a performance that even Pedro had witnessed one too many times to believe his mother's complaints. (When La Pelona finally came for her, Fina received her alone, for her daughters had disregarded her complaint that her heart was aching and went to the yacht club to watch a boating race. But as luck would have it, she passed on a Sunday, the day when the Blessed Mother allowed borderline cases to sneak in Heaven's back door.)

"¡Qué va!" Pedro snorted, "Your mother didn't need you to look after her."

"It doesn't matter what you think. I couldn't leave her. Besides, you and I know perfectly well that Nélida could have taken care of your mother without your help. She's more than capable when she wants to be. And don't try to tell me that she had other responsibilities, either. Por Dios, Pedro. She was over fifty years old when your father died. It still amazes me how helpless your sisters can be when they want to be."

"Your mother has been gone for almost six months now, Rosa. Stop using her as an excuse for why you won't move to Havana. If it's not one thing, it's another. What is it with you? I turn myself inside out trying to please you and this is all the thanks I get. Maybe I made a mistake. Maybe I should have stayed with Mother and the girls. At least they appreciate all that I have done for them."

9

Rosa winced at the bitter aftertaste of the words that passed over her lips without her consent. Rarely did she speak so openly, so spontaneously, to anyone—especially Pedro. Drawing her breath, she waited for him to roar back at her, then realized, to her great relief, that he had spoken over her and drowned out her voice, a strategy he exercised on the rare occasions when they got into a verbal argument.

"If I leave now, what will happen to María and Tía Marta?"

"Your sister and your aunt can take care of one another. They're not *your* responsibility, Rosa. As far as I'm concerned, this conversation is over," he said, scraping back his chair in anger. "If you refuse to come with me," he added, snapping out his napkin and then throwing it on his plate, "I will leave without you, and mark my words, this time I will not return."

"I couldn't leave her," Rosa whispered after him, though he had already left the room.

* * *

That day, though she refused to admit it even to herself, Rosa submitted to her husband's will, and the ground she had fought so hard to defend shrank beneath her feet. What she hadn't realized at the time was that her greatest disappointment was lying just ahead of her, for only a few days later, on the morning of their departure from Tres Flores, she learned that her old nursemaid, Tata, refused to accompany them to Havana.

"I'd die in the city, mi cielo," the old woman said, as she snapped shut the clasps on Rosa's steamer trunk. "Besides, everyone knows that you can't pull a stubborn old weed like me out by its roots. But you know that I will never abandon you. I will always be waiting for you and the girls when you return to Tres Flores. Siempre, m'ija."

Knowing that it would be useless to argue, Rosa sat on the edge of her mother's bed in silence as Tata knelt on the floor, cording together hatboxes. When she had finally agreed to move to Havana, the possibility that Tata would stay behind had never entered her head. Despite the constant presence of her mother and her grandmother throughout her childhood, Rosa's first memories were of Tata. For as long as she could remember, the old woman had been standing beside her, and as far back as anyone could recall, Tata had always been at Tres Flores.

Soon after his marriage to Mariela Ocampo, Rosa's grandfather Paolo decided to lay claim to the land grant his wife's family had been awarded by the king of Spain for their loyalty and service to the crown. Being the youngest of twelve brothers, Paolo knew that he would have to find some way to make his fortune. From the time of his birth it was made clear to him that none of his father's wealth, substantial as it was, would be his. After receiving a letter from Mariela's cousin, Nemesio Gutiérrez de la Concha, which described the great fortunes that the Spanish colonists who had migrated to the islands after the fall of San Dominigue were amassing from their sugar crops, Paolo announced his decision to move to the tiny island. Despite Mariela's protests and tears, the young couple left the small port town in the north of Spain, where most of the tombstones bore the names of their friends and relatives, and traveled across the ocean to the island that they would call, from that time forth, home.

Upon their arrival they discovered—much to Mariela's discontent—that they would have to travel on horseback from Havana to Cienfuegos. Deciding that it would be best to leave his young bride behind in the city with her cousin and his wife, Paolo set out for Cienfuegos alone, taking with him nothing more than a large valise.

When they reached the place where the dirt roads ended, the guide Paolo had hired in Havana gathered together several guajiros who were willing—for a certain sum of money—to walk ahead of Paolo's horse with machetes to clear a path for him through the thick tropical undergrowth that grew in the forest. After three arduous days and nights, Paolo arrived in Cienfuegos. Though the little town was located in a remote and undeveloped region, several small sugar plantations had already

11

been established and a Jesuit priest, Padre Rabia, had erected a church and was petitioning the patrones of the neighboring plantations for contributions so that he could build a cathedral dedicated to Our Lady of Mount Carmel, and a monastery for the nuns, whom he had brought with him from Spain.

The morning after his arrival, Paolo went to the mayor's house to show him the declaración authenticating the Ocampo's right to the land. Convinced of its authenticity, the mayor, Vincente Sosa, agreed to accompany Paolo as he surveyed his property. To his great dismay, Paolo discovered that most of the territory included in the land grant was covered by a dense forest and that the open land was inhabited by several families. Among them was an old Englishman and his wife. With the mayor's assistance, Paolo set about the business of repossessing his land. Together they went from finca to finca, offering work to anyone who wished to help clear the land and evicting those who refused. Much to his surprise and consternation, the Englishman, who was known to be as greedy and stubborn as a tick, refused to leave without at least some compensation, for he had cleared several acres of Paolo's land at his own expense and had planted tobacco. Realizing that the old man would not be moved by words alone, Paolo offered him a small sum of money for his house and his slaves. After much bickering, the Englishman reluctantly agreed to sell the house, but he refused to sell the slaves, for he was convinced that they would fetch a better price at the market in Havana. Among his slaves was Tata.

As the time drew near for her departure, Tata refused to go. Though the Englishman slashed her across the legs with his bullwhip, she remained unmoved, her face as expressionless as parchment. Recognizing some of his own willfulness in the old woman, Paolo tripled the price he had originally offered for her. Unable to refuse, the Englishman accepted Paolo's offer. As he counted out his money, he told Paolo that when he had first arrived in Cienfuegos he, too, had purchased Tata—along with two other slaves, three mules, twenty-three chickens, two calves, and the house with the thatched roof and the whitewashed walls—for she had refused to leave the land where, he presumed, she had been born. It was the Englishman who first began referring to her as the ancient one, a title that stayed with her for the rest of her life.

Over the years, Tata had nursed back to health and quickened the births of three generations of Rosa's family, with her bags of herbs and the sweet-smelling salves and ointments she concocted with her mortar and pestle from flowers and roots that she gathered from the fields and the garden. They had fed on her milk for generations. When she was just a child, Rosa recalled, several women from the neighborhood—led by Doctor de Silva's mother, Pilar—had gone to Padre Rabia to complain about the old woman. They claimed that she was a cimarrona and asked the priest to banish her from their town and send her back to the mountains where she belonged. Others were convinced that she was of Indian stock, descended from the Taino or the Ciboney. Pilar's sister, Asela Martínez, who starched and pressed Padre Rabia's vestments and altar cloths, swore that Tata was a bruja. She claimed that she had seen her change the color of her skin like a chameleon, and insisted that the palms of the old woman's hands had been scorched and turned gray from holding burning embers.

At first, Padre Rabia ignored the old women's petitions, claiming that the Moros were pious and respectable people who had generously donated great sums of money toward the building of the cathedral and the monastery in Cienfuegos. Seeing that the women remained unconvinced, he paid a visit to Tres Flores. After speaking at great length with the couple, he assured the old women who gathered in the vestibule the next morning that Paolo would have been the first to kick Tata out if he was even the least bit suspicious of her character. Resigning themselves to the fact that the priest would not take their side, the women in the neighborhood sent their children to the Moro's gate to call Tata names and pelt her with pebbles and nutshells as she swept the portico. But soon they discovered that their insults failed to disturb the old woman—for the words they shot in her direction and the objects they threw at her back bounced off of her old, leathery hide like rubber arrows.

13

Although the women appeared to direct their hatred at Tata, Paolo and Mariela were convinced that at least some of their ill will was intended for them, for ever since the time that they had first arrived in Cienfuegos, they had been shunned by most of the townspeople and treated as outsiders. Paolo was convinced that Mariela's obvious refinement and culture had stirred the jealousy of the wives of the other plantation owners, not to mention the fact that she had arrived in a lavish, horse-drawn carriage followed by an entourage the likes of which had never been seen before in Cienfuegos. Her insistence on having her privacy, which the women took for snobbery, made her an object of public scorn and wild speculation. Despite the townspeople's obvious resentment of the Moro family's presence, Padre Rabia showered his attention on the couple and praised them whenever he was given the opportunity. (He could also be found sampling pasteles at their table almost any given Wednesday afternoon.) Following his example, even the most haughty women gradually began appearing at Mariela's door to taste Tata's pasteles, and before long it was as though the Moros had always been in Cienfuegos.

* * *

As Rosa recalled the story, the thought of being alone in Havana—the thought of abandoning Tata, of leaving the old woman behind in Cienfuegos—brought salty tears (that Mariela had taught her to hold back by biting her bottom lip) to the rims of her eyes. Later that same night, as she sat by Fina's bedroom window listening to the unfamiliar noises of the city, Rosa admitted to herself what she had known all along. Tata had been right—her spirit would weaken in Havana, like the iridescent colors of the fish she had seen the pescadores pull from the safe, dark waters of the ocean into the air.

She might have adjusted, Rosa thought, in a halfhearted attempt to console herself, but she would never have been happy. When it came down to it, she honestly could not imagine the old woman anywhere but at Tres Flores. In her mind at least, Tata was Tres Flores.

12 July 1954

"It keeps him occupied," Rosa explained to her three elderly sisters-in-law, as she sat like a Madonna between tall, potted ferns on the veranda at the Havana Yacht Club. Her sister, María, who had agreed to stay with Rosa until Pedro returned from Cienfuegos, sat to her left, while Margarita knelt on a small cushion at her feet. Caridad had been invited to a classmate's fifteenth birthday celebration, otherwise she, too, would have been at her mother's side.

Even though they hadn't asked, Rosa knew that Nélida, Miriam, and Mercedes all wondered at the idea that Pedro had left her, so far along in her pregnancy, alone with them in Havana. Ever since Rosa and the children had moved from Cienfuegos to her mother-in-law's house on Calle Semilla, they had always left the city at the end of June to spend two weeks at the sulfur springs at San Miguel de los Baños, and then they traveled on to Cienfuegos for the clearing of the fields and the planting of the sugar cane at Treinta Sierras, the family plantation. For the first time in almost five years Pedro had decided—without consulting his wife—to leave them in the city, fearing, he had told her, that she would give birth to their third child during the long, hot train ride to Cienfuegos. He had insisted, despite her protests, that if he had anything to do with it, his son wasn't going to be born next door to a boxcar filled with cackling old women carrying chickens under their arms and baskets full of yuca and malanga at their feet. (He had whispered these words into her ear the morning of his departure, as he crouched by the edge of their bed. When he had tried to kiss her good-bye, Rosa turned onto her side without a word and closed her eyes to shut out his gaze.)

"No need to explain, dear," Nélida consoled her, "we understand. Don't forget, we *all* know how Pedro can be. He's just like our father. He *always* had his way," she added, with a quick glance at Miriam and Mercedes, who both nodded in agreement.

From her place on the floor Margarita watched her tía lean forward and pat her mother's hand. Perhaps because she was the eldest, Nélida always spoke for her sisters, as though she had been chosen by some unspoken agreement. From where she sat, Margarita could smell her old tías' violet-scented cologne. Gazing across the tiled coffee table at the three of them bunched together on the glider, she noticed that they all wore the same face powder—the crushed-pearl powder in the floral-patterned cardboard box that Margarita had watched Fina pat on her forehead and chin with a soft, round puff until all of the shiny spots on her face disappeared. All three women had painted plumes of rouge on their cheek bones, and despite the black eyeliner that caked in their tear ducts and the rose-colored lipstick that smeared onto their teeth, their mouths and their eyes seemed to be receding into the wrinkled webs of their faces. Sitting together, the three old tías looked like a garish bunch of knotted flowers.

Pedro's sisters had been born only a year apart from one another. (Her son had been a surprise, Fina always said, arriving almost twenty years after Mercedes.) Nélida was tall and slender and had a face like a prune. Her silver hair was always pulled back into a tight bun and secured with fan-shaped combs, which she nervously touched with her fingertips from time to time when she spoke. Her neck was covered with dark brown moles, which she insisted were beauty marks whenever she caught her nieces staring at them. Pedro's second sister, Miriam, was short and plump. Even though she, unlike Nélida, was always smiling, she could not mask the sorrowful expression that always lingered around her eyes. As Margarita gazed at Miriam, she recalled having heard that she had been left at the altar by two different men. All Margarita could see of her third tía was the thin oval of her face. Although age had not robbed her of beauty, Mercedes hid her thick, chestnut-colored hair—which she had vowed never to cut again the moment that her husband died (and Bebita stilled the pendulum in the grandfather clock on the landing)—with a long, black veil. Regardless of the occasion or the weather, she always wore the black embroidered mantilla, which she had worn when they first began courting and insisted be draped over her husband's casket during his funeral mass, and a gray high-collared dress that concealed her throat and had long sleeves that buttoned at her wrists. Aside from an occasional afternoon at the club, Mercedes lived like a Carmelite, cloistering herself in the back bedroom of her mother's house. Despite the fact that her husband had been dead for nearly three decades, she kept perpetually lit a candle in front of his portrait, which she had placed on a batiste oval on the night table next to her bed.

Though only Mercedes had actually married, everyone had taken to calling the three sisters the Señoras after their mother had died, out of respect for their wisdom and age. Over the years, as she knelt by her mother's feet or sat by her side listening in silence to the women's conversation, Margarita had managed to piece together Mercedes's story.

In deference to Nélida and Miriam, whom everyone expected to marry before Mercedes (because they were older), she had turned down a host of suitors. The most delicate and elegant of Don Pedro's daughters, she had always attracted the most attention. Even as a small child, people would turn their heads to gaze at her as she passed them in the park, something Don Pedro never failed to notice. (His daughter's unearthly beauty caused him such consternation that he threatened to give her a chastity belt and a necklace of garlic cloves for her quinceañera in order to ward off her admirers.) Despite Don Pedro's efforts, Carlos Luis Cuevos, an accomplished musician who walked the promenade in the park every Sunday, discovered Mercedes.

Mercedes, too, had discovered Carlos, and on one particular Sunday her willpower failed her. Miraculously evading her mother's prying gaze, Mercedes slipped her ivory-colored calling card into the pocket of Carlos's linen suit coat and that very same evening he serenaded her from beneath her balcony as the sun went down. Certain that the young man had come to claim Nélida, for her balcony window was next to Mercedes's, Fina regarded his advances with calm amusement until it was too late. As far as Margarita could make out, it was Bebita who first discovered that Mercedes had disappeared—when she arrived in the girl's bedroom with a tray full of pasteles and a cup of café con leche, the old woman found Carlos's guitar, rather than the Amargos' youngest daughter, reclining under the cut linen sheets. Rumor had it that Mercedes had climbed down her mother's rose trellis in high-heeled gold lamé shoes—nearly breaking her beautiful, swanlike neck in the process—and the couple had eloped, causing a scandal that took most of Havana, not to mention Fina and Don Pedro, by surprise.

Although it took the Amargos several years to get over the idea that their youngest daughter, who had always been so mild and obliging, had disgraced them, they eventually accepted Carlos into the family on the condition that he and Mercedes agree to live under their roof. (When Mercedes and Carlos failed, after several years together, to produce any offspring, Fina and Don Pedro found consolation in the possibility that the couple had never fully consummated their marriage and lived together in a chaste union—a charge that Mercedes privately denied, to her sisters' horror and dismay, by claiming that she and her husband had simply chosen not to have any children. Though Mercedes and Nélida longed to know exactly how they did this, neither one dared to ask.)

* * *

"I'm not trying to make excuses for him," Rosa explained, reading the worried expressions on her sisters-in-laws' faces as they nodded and smiled with sympathetic eyes. "Pedro had to go," she added, wondering to herself why she always ended up defending him, when in truth his decision to leave her behind in Havana made her furious.

"I really don't understand why he doesn't just hire someone to oversee Treinta Sierras," Nélida commented. In response, Rosa just rolled her eyes, for she had suggested the same thing to Pedro a thousand and one times before, though he refused to listen to her.

"That's exactly what I told her, Nélida," María broke in. "But men are all the same. My father didn't trust anyone with overseeing Treinta Sierras, either. He had to do everything himself."

"It keeps him out of trouble," Rosa whispered in a barely audible voice, for she had caught the sullen tone in María's and guessed that her sister would never forgive Pedro for getting her pregnant again. Her sister and Pedro had both been in the room when Doctor de Silva warned her that after three consecutive miscarriages her body, let alone her heart, couldn't bear the strain of carrying and giving birth to another child.

Feeling the weight of her sister's eyes upon her, Rosa raised her head and met María's imperious gaze.

"He should be here in Havana with you and the girls, Rosa."

"Your sister's right," Nélida agreed.

"And what would you suggest that I do?" Rosa snapped back at María in a voice that surprised even her.

"Go to him," María responded. For a brief moment the two sisters locked eyes, and then they turned away from one another once again.

"That's probably not such a good idea, dear," Nélida broke in, exchanging a nervous glance with Miriam. "Pedro probably had his reasons for leaving you with us. And besides, he's the man of the house now. You don't want to go against him, do you?"

Noting the pained expression on Rosa's face, Nélida lowered her eyes to her lap and began touching the combs in her hair with her fingertips. In awkward silence, the three sisters fixed their gaze on the points of their shoes, while Rosa twisted her sandalwood fan in her hand and María pretended to be absorbed in tracing circular patterns onto the surface of the fabric cushion on her chair.

Grateful for the unexpected pause in the conversation, Margarita listened to the sound of the waves pounding against the sea wall. She wondered why she and Caridad were expected to come to the club with their mother and their old tías every Thursday afternoon. Not one of them ever bothered to include the girls in their conversation. They only talked about them, as though they were not present. Besides, didn't they all live in the same house together? Didn't they see one another every day? Why couldn't she and Caridad have some time alone with their mother? Why did the tías always have to come?

With envy, Margarita thought of her sister, who was probably enjoying herself at that moment at Elena Hernández's birthday party. She had grown tired of asking her mother when she, too, would be allowed to attend parties and tennis matches and boat races like the ones Caridad was invited to. But Rosa always delivered the same mechanical reply when she asked—When you're older, querida, when you're older. Patience is a virtue.

Margarita looked toward the sea, at the place where the gulls rose and fell between the tourmaline furrows of the waves. In silence, she watched as they carelessly dipped their sharp beaks just below the surface of the water in search of fish and then glided on the back of the wind. How free they seemed compared to her, in her straw hat and stiff patent leather shoes. How happy and free, she thought.

* * *

Unable to bear the silence any longer, Nélida quietly cleared her throat and shifted in her seat. As though given a cue, María spoke:

"Did anyone see the story in *El Diario de la Marina* this morning about the girl who was buried alive?" she asked, reaching for the newspaper that was lying half-open on the coffee table in front of her.

"No," Nélida responded eagerly, grateful for the opportunity to steer the conversation away from her brother and the plantation. It was a conversation that always ended in an argument.

"It's unbelievable!" María said, taking up the newspaper and handing it to Nélida. "I think it's on page seven."

"¡Madre de Dios!" Nélida gasped, as she adjusted her reading glasses, which hung from a silver chain around her neck, on the bridge of her nose. For a few moments the women were silent again, as they watched Nélida leaf through the paper to find the second half of the article. Their attention was fixed on her as she scanned the narrow columns of print with raised eyebrows.

"Read it out loud, Nélida," Miriam said, unable to suppress her curiosity. "We all want to hear."

"Buried Alive," Nélida began, as her eyes, magnified to twice their regular size by her glasses, leapt from side to side. "The beautiful María Teresa Hidalgo, the only daughter and heir of Doctor Rudolfo Hidalgo de Alcalá and his late wife, Catalina.

". . . a beautiful girl, whom men traveled long distances to court," Nélida continued, jumping to the next paragraph. "She had vowed never to marry, a friend insisted, but after having rejected a countless number of suitors, all of whom were quite eligible, her father decided upon a handsome, well-respected lawyer, Señor Gustavo Ramón Gómez de Ferrer.

"After the young man had successfully petitioned for Señorita Hidalgo's hand, her father warned him that his daughter had a condition, of which no one but himself was aware, that he needed to be mindful of. Without advance warning, she fell into a comalike state. Her heartbeat would slow down and her temperature would drop. Her pulse and her breathing virtually ceased. Even the most sophisticated medical instruments, the doctor warned his future son-in-law, failed to detect the living spirit within her.

"As fate would have it, Doctor Hidalgo passed away less than a month before María Teresa's wedding day. Despite her grief,

21

the young girl was determined to honor her father's memory by fulfilling his will, and so, she insisted on going forward with their wedding plans, much against her family's advice. At the last moment, however, she almost changed her mind, her friends later revealed, for when she woke up the morning of her wedding day it was raining—a very bad sign for a bride, Señorita Hidalgo's cousin, Aurora Menecal, insisted.

". . . the wedding was like something out of a storybook. Señorita Hidalgo wore the same gown her mother had worn almost twenty-five years earlier to the day. . . . When the couple reached the Havana Yacht Club, where the reception was to be held, Señorita Hidalgo, perhaps out of grief and fatigue, collapsed. Unable to revive her after several hours, Doctor Juan José García, a close family friend of the Hidalgos, pronounced her dead. Ignoring the tradition that mandated that she be buried within twenty-four hours after her death, Gustavo Gómez held a vigil at his young bride's side for three days and three nights, but Señorita Hidalgo remained cold and still. Before his eyes, Señor Gómez confided to his friends, his beautiful bride turned into an old woman. Her hands, which clasped her mother's prayer book and crystal rosary, withered and dried; her cheeks turned pale; and even her lips lost their luster. 'She looked as old as Eve,' the young man said.

"With great difficulty, Señor Gómez's family and friends convinced him to begin making the preparations for the girl's funeral. He insisted that his bride be buried in her white wedding gown and wear the large diamond ring he had placed on her finger less than a week before. Only then would he allow her to be buried in the cemetery between the doctor and his wife.

". . . The evening following the burial, the police were called to Doctor Hidalgo's house—one of his neighbors had reported a disturbance of some sort. When the authorities arrived they found, to their horror and surprise, Señor Gómez's bride on her hands and knees scratching at her father's door like a wild dog. Her veil was torn and the front of her gown was covered with her own blood and dirt. When she arrived at the clinic, the doctors who attended to her discovered that the finger on her right hand, where Señor Gómez had placed her wedding band, was missing.

"Months later a man whose identity is being withheld by the authorities was caught trying to sell María Teresa Hidalgo's wedding ring in a pawn shop on the east side of Havana. While questioning the suspect the police discovered that he had been present in the crowd the day of the girl's funeral and had seen the large diamond ring on her finger. That same evening, after the gates of the cemetery had been closed, he climbed the fence with a small spade in his hands, opened up her freshly dug grave, and exhumed her body. He said he remembered tugging on Señorita Hidalgo's ring, but the girl's finger had swollen with the heat. At that very moment, feeling the cool night air upon her cheeks, she began to revive. Frightened nearly out of his mind, the thief sliced off her finger with a knife that he carried in his boot and fled from the graveyard.

"After she was released from the clinic, Señorita Hidalgo refused to return to her husband, insisting that death had dissolved the ties that bound her to him. Upon hearing that the thief who stole her wedding ring had been caught, she had her father's chauffeur drive her to the courthouse where she petitioned for the man's release. She argued that he had saved her life in more ways than one.

" 'Me ayudó a vivir,' she told the judge. Much to everyone's surprise, he granted her request. After the trial, Señorita Hidalgo sold her father's house and vanished from Havana. No one has heard from her since."

"Qué barbaridad," Miriam cried, throwing herself back on the glider.

"It's quite a story, isn't it?" María laughed.

Suddenly Nélida, who had continued reading the newspaper, broke into the conversation. "Did you say that Caridad was invited to Elena Hernández's quinceañera today?" she asked, lowering the newspaper.

"Yes. Why do you ask?" Rosa responded in surprise. Nélida held up the paper and pointed to a short column announcing the names of all of the young ladies who would be celebrating their fifteenth birthday that week. "Soon Caridad will be celebrating her own."

"¡No me diga!" Nélida gasped, clapping her hand over her mouth. "Caridad—fifteen already?"

"Impossible," Miriam sighed. "How quickly time passes. Before you know it, Caridad will be engaged and Margarita will be celebrating her own quinceañera."

"She still has two more years to go," Rosa said, patting the top of Margarita's head.

"Do you remember the story Tía Marta used to tell about her quinceañera?"

"You're not going to repeat that one, are you?" Rosa sighed.

"Of all of the stories Marta told, this was the best," María began, with a quick glance at Margarita, who had risen from her place on the floor and, sauntering across the veranda, appeared to be lost in thought. "And Tía always told it with such pleasure and delight."

"Much to Mami's dismay," Rosa chimed in.

Ignoring her sister's words, María began:

"All of Cienfuegos seemed to be caught up in the preparations for Paolo and Mariela Moro's eldest daughter's introduction into polite society. It was rumored that many of the cakes and the chocolates that would be served that day had come from as far away as Vienna, and Abuelo had commissioned a full string orchestra from Havana to entertain his guests. Tía was instructed to make her entrance down the long marble staircase at eight o'clock sharp. (For weeks beforehand Abuela had made her practice each morning by balancing a leather-bound copy of *Don Quixote* upon her head as she walked down the steps with her hands extended from her sides.)

"As the hour grew near, the guests began to stir with excitement. The sense of expectation, Tía assured us, was almost palpable, for it was a widely known fact that the dress she would wear that day had been custom ordered from a famous department store on Fifth Avenue in New York City. Just as the clock in the entrance hall began to chime, the orchestra took its cue and began to play a selection from Tchaikovsky's *Sleeping Beauty*. All eyes turned to the top of the staircase, where Tía stood stark naked, with a lit cigar in her hand, wearing nothing more than the pearl necklace her mother had loaned her for the occasion and her father's black leather riding boots.

"With a collective gasp the guests, which included Padre Rabia, stood mesmerized as they watched Tía Marta gracefully float down the staircase—blowing smoke rings through the air—and disappear into the shadows of the corridor that led to the kitchen. As though time had stood still, everyone remained motionless and silent. You could hear an embroidery needle drop. Less than ten minutes later, Tía Marta appeared at the top of the staircase once again, wearing the ivory-colored gown with the seed pearls sewn in a latticelike pattern into the bodice. For the second time she glided down the staircase and greeted her parents and their guests with the grace and serenity of a princess receiving her subjects.

"Although the party was apparently a grand success, the story of my grandparents' humiliation spread like wildfire through the town. Anxious to still the wagging tongues of his neighbors, Abuelo considered the possibility of asking Carlucho de Silva to speak on their behalf, claiming that their daughter had gone temporarily mad. Taking an alternate course, Abuela insisted that they should act as though nothing had happened.

"'If we keep denying that it ever happened, eventually every-one will believe that it never did,' Abuela assured him. 'People do it all the time.'

"For weeks afterwards the neighbors exchanged the stories Abuela had confided to them like trading stamps—stories which seemingly confirmed the fact that a streak of madness had riven a deep gash in the Moro's family tree. (Among them was the one about our great uncle, Carlos Roberto, who was invited to feast at the king of Spain's summer palace. Rumor had it that he rode through the front entrance of the royal palace on a white horse, followed by a guajiro riding a donkey. He was fully attired in military gear, complete with a ruffled collar and a lance. When the guardia tried to throw him out of the palace, he claimed that he was San Martín de Tours, and the guajiro was a poor beggar whom he had discovered on the side of the road.)

"As the months passed by the townspeople's gossip grew more and more outrageous. They nevertheless failed to provoke a response from my grandparents, for they had thrown up a thorn-covered wall of silence around them—a wall, they hoped, that some young prince would have the courage to scale in order to save their eldest daughter, whose reputation appeared to be dead. Eventually, even the calambucas grew tired of reciting Tía's scandalous tale and everyone became half-convinced that their eyes had played tricks on them that day. However, no one—much to Marta's relief—came to beg for her hand in marriage."

At María's last words Nélida, followed by Miriam and then Mercedes, burst into laughter. The sound of their laughter pulled Margarita's attention back to their conversation. She had been thinking about María Teresa Hidalgo and the mysterious *condition* that caused her family and friends to think her dead. Margarita's gaze then settled on her mother. As she studied Rosa's pregnant form she was reminded of the conversation she had overheard only the day before between her mother and her aunt. Rosa had been talking in quiet tones to María about her own *condition*, a word that had translated in Margarita's mind into something like a wound that would not heal. The idea that she, too, might inherit her mother's *condition* filled her with terror.

Later that same afternoon, Margarita gathered the courage to ask her mother, who was in the sewing room with María, if she was going to die from her *condition*, but Rosa, pretending to be busy with her embroidery, acted as though she hadn't heard the question. When Margarita asked a second time, Rosa bent even closer over her work. With her hands folded in front of her, Margarita watched in silence while her mother stretched a piece of linen across a large wooden embroidery frame with expert skill, pulling at the edges of the fabric until it was as tight as the skin of a drum. Then she began pricking a pattern into the fabric with one of the oversized needles Bebita had threaded for her earlier that morning.

Glancing at her mother's face, it struck Margarita that she looked almost angry, though her downturned eyes and the color that rose in her cheeks suggested otherwise. Then Rosa cried out, startling both María and Margarita and drawing Bebita from the entrance hall, where she was dry-mopping the marble floor.

"What's wrong?" María asked, pulling Rosa's finger from her mouth.

Bebita stood in the doorway behind Margarita, leaning heavily on her mop. "Didn't I tell you to let Mirta take care of that dress for you, Señora? If you would only show a little patience. Her son comes by every Tuesday and picks up the sewing."

"See what you made me do, Margarita?" Rosa broke in, ignoring Bebita's comment as she released her hand from María's. At her words, Bebita let out a long sigh and spun around on her heels.

"You shouldn't allow Bebita to talk to you that way, Rosa. She's only a servant," María chided her, in a voice loud enough to reach the old woman's ears. "Besides, you weren't even working on your dress. She's a meddlesome old lady, Rosa, who has her nose in everything now that Fina is gone. You really need to put her in her place."

"I know, I know. Pedro says the same thing. He's always scolding me about making the servants into familiars. Maybe he's right. But it's not as though I treat them as equals—I don't," Rosa protested, in response to the skeptical look on María's face. "I only try to show them a little kindness—they are human beings, María."

"Oh no, my embroidery!" María called out with obvious distress. At her aunt's words, Margarita noticed the red blossom of blood that had bloomed next to the rosebud María had begun to stitch onto the fabric that lay across her lap.

"It's all your fault, Margarita," María said, sending a withering glance across the room at her niece.

Filled with an inexplicable sense of guilt, Margarita stood in the doorway in awkward silence, with her hands still folded together in front of her.

"Well," María continued, "don't you have anything to say for yourself?"

Perhaps out of nervousness, Margarita posed her question once again: "Can you die from a *condition?*"

At her daughter's words, Rosa sighed and turned her attention back to her embroidery, refusing to raise her eyes until Margarita finally left the room.

"That child had the indelicacy to ask not once but twice," María whispered, unaware that Margarita lingered in the hallway just outside the room.

"Three times. She asked me three times."

"I've never seen anything like her, Rosa. Never. Caridad would never have asked. Never," she repeated, shaking her head a second time. "How can one be so quiet and obedient and the other be so . . ."

"She's only thirteen years old," Rosa broke in, growing annoyed with the manner in which her sister spoke about Margarita. "She's still a child, María."

"That's old enough to know better."

"Then why didn't *you* answer her question?"

"Me? Why should *I* be the one to tell her? You're her mother."

"And you're her madrina! Besides," Rosa continued, "Mami never told us anything."

From the hallway Margarita could hear her tía whispering something to her mother, though she could not make it out, and then the two sisters broke into waves of laughter that filled Margarita with humiliation and, once again, an inexplicable feeling of shame. With tear-filled eyes, she ran to the front parlor and closed the French doors behind her, certain that no one would find her there, since the tías only used the parlor to entertain special guests. Hidden in the dark crawlspace behind Fina's blue velvet sofa, Margarita listened as her mother called out her name from the second floor. (Rosa must have realized that Margarita was standing outside the sewing room.)

Hoping to punish her mother with her silence, Margarita did not answer. After a few moments, she heard Rosa's retreating footsteps—then the parlor doors swung open and Bebita's feet appeared at the end of the sofa. Bit by bit, she coaxed Margarita out of hiding by offering her a triangle of fried batter dipped in warm, clear syrup. The old woman, like Tata, always seemed to know where she was hiding. As she wiggled out from behind the sofa on her belly, the first thing Margarita noticed was the portrait of her grandmother staring down at her from her place above the mantel with apparent disappointment, as she held her lap dog, Cuca (who, in Margarita's view, looked like one of Mariela's French end tables) in her arms.

* * *

"Let's see," Miriam murmured half aloud, counting on her fingers with raised eyes, "Caridad is going to be fifteen, so Margarita is just about to turn thirteen. Is that right, Rosa?"

"She already turned thirteen, remember?"

"Then she must have had her amiguita by this time?" Miriam asked, lowering her voice to a whisper that caused her two sisters to furiously fan their faces and titter. Margarita watched their faces as they responded to the private joke they obviously shared among themselves, sensing all the while that they were amusing themselves at her expense.

"Not that I know of," Rosa whispered, as a flash of color rose in her cheeks. Miriam's question had taken her off guard. Perhaps age, she thought, gave her sister-in-law the liberty to speak so openly about private matters in such a casual, immodest manner.

"Pobrecita," Miriam said, pointing toward Rosa's distended belly, "she doesn't know what she's in for!"

Miriam's words confirmed Margarita's worst suspicions and fears and recalled to her mind Tía María's ominous words to her when she followed Bebita out of the front parlor:

"It's a small sacrifice, dear niece, that all of us must learn to accept. You'll understand when you get older," she added, as she adjusted the brim of her hat in the hall mirror one last time before leaving the house for her daily walk along the sea wall that bordered the harbor.

Now, sitting among the circle of women, who insisted upon talking in riddles, Margarita felt more confused than ever, and Tata wasn't there to explain. Imprisoned in her stiff shoes and her starched dress, Margarita could not help but think how miserable she was, and how much more she preferred the long, balmy evenings at Tres Flores when she and Caridad, along with Tía María and her mother, would sit in a circle listening to her great-aunt, Tía Marta, tell stories. Although it had been years since Tía Marta had left them, and they now lived in Havana with her father's three sisters, Margarita had never grown to love her old tías the same way that she had loved her grandmother's eldest sister.

As Margarita knelt at her mother's feet on the veranda at the yacht club, she recalled the way that Tía Marta would kick off her two-toned leather pumps after they had eaten their evening meal together and perch herself on the edge of her father's over-stuffed leather armchair in the parlor. Sometimes Margarita and Caridad would balance themselves like bookends on the arms of Paolo's chair to listen to Tía Marta's soft, singsong voice. All the while, she rubbed spirals into their backs with her finger-tips. Other times, Tía Marta would sit in the armchair, knitting a throw, which she used to cover her legs when the evenings were cool, or embroidering labyrinthine patterns onto the fabric that lay draped across her lap as she recited the tales that her own mother had carried with her across the sea. While she spoke, the fabric sprouted and bloomed beneath her needle like a tropical garden. Suspended in the air, her tiny feet, which were disfigured with corns and calluses, swung from side to side like a pendulum, as though they were keeping beat with her words. Margarita recalled that she always wore the same chipped red nail polish on her short fingernails and toenails, and opaque silk stockings with crooked black seams in the back that bagged at her ankles and were knotted just above her kneecaps. (To her sister's scandal, Marta refused to wear garter belts and corsets, insisting that they cut off her circulation and made her short of breath.)

Night after night, as the warm summer breeze gently lifted the sheer curtains behind her, Tía Marta spun out her tales. Caridad would insist that she repeat the folk tale about the cuckoo, who laid her speckled eggs in other birds' nests, and her sister, the pelican, who tore open her own chest with her beak in order to give her blood to her thirsty children. Even though it left her feeling melancholy, Margarita preferred the story of the little nightingale and the emperor, a story that Tía Marta reenacted with great passion and histrionics.

". . . While drinking from a jewel-encrusted goblet and eating from a plate of solid gold," Marta would begin, tilting an invisible cup to her lips and dropping make-believe handfuls of silver-skinned fish into her throat, "the emperor listened to the song of the nightingale. But one night, to his great displeasure, the little bird failed to appear at the emperor's window. Filled with impatience and anger, he commanded his servant to capture the nightingale. With great difficulty the servant caught the little bird in a gold mesh net. When he returned to the court with her, the emperor demanded that he clip the nightingale's wings and impale her on the thorn bush that grew just outside his window. Only then, he argued, could he hear her sing whenever he wished. Hanging his head in sorrow, the servant did as he was commanded, though he had grown to love the little nightingale. And from that day forward, the sad little bird spent the rest of her life impaled on the fiery tip of a dark thorn, dreaming of the days when she came and went as she pleased, soaring through the air, from the emperor's casement window to the chinaberry tree that grew just beyond his courtyard wall, where she had built her nest."

Recalling Tía Marta's story sent a sharp pang of sorrow and regret through Margarita. If only she had listened more carefully. If only there had been more time. Except for those moments that had caught in their collective memory, and the green notebook her mother filled with newspaper clippings and the record of significant moments in their lives, Tía Marta's stories would remain unrecorded, and the world that she had created and recreated for them countless times—the world that they could only catch a glimpse of in Rafaela's photo albums—was gone.

As her gaze fell on her mother's thickening waist once again, Margarita noted that Rosa had grown almost as large and round as her sister. (Even though Rosa was nearly seven months into her pregnancy, María was still much larger.) Margarita laughed inside herself at the sight of her tía's soft, pleated chins and her plump hands. She had always noticed hands, and María's looked as though they would burst out of their smooth, translucent skins. Her fingers were like chorizos.

How can one be so slim and the other such a gordita? Margarita wondered, as she gazed at her mother and her aunt. It was only in silhouette—something, perhaps, in the curve of the nose or the cut of the chin—that one could tell that the two women were sisters. Maybe one of them was adopted, Margarita pondered, as she took account of Rosa's dark, olive-colored skin.

Margarita's attention was caught by the quick movement of her mother's hands. Rosa had the habit of gesturing wildly as she spoke, as though she were embroidering her words with her hands, stitching herself into a pattern. María's profile came into focus at the same time, partially eclipsed by the silk flowers fastened onto the brim of Rosa's straw hat. Even though her mother's skin was darker, she had always seemed to Margarita so much more delicate and elegant than María. As a child, Margarita had always associated her mother with the graceful movement of sheer curtains, softly breathing in and out of open windows. In her eyes Rosa was a garden—a goblet—a cut crystal vase filled with newly gathered flowers.

*   *   *

As the women continued to talk among themselves, Margarita's eyes wandered around the enclosed veranda seeking the opening that led outdoors. Her attention was drawn to a group of men in pale linen suits and straw boaters who had emerged from the white stone clubhouse. She watched them as they sauntered across the lawn and casually leaned against the sea wall, leaving thin, filmy trails behind them as they smoked their thick black cigars. They reminded Margarita of the men who walked the promenade in the park near the house on Calle Semilla every Sunday in hopes of meeting eligible young women.

Occasionally Margarita and Caridad would accompany their old tías on their walk to the park where they took the fresh air. Together with Nélida and Miriam, they sat on a park bench watching the elegant young women strut past them in their magnificent plumage—some with their arms entwined around the coat sleeves of men wearing immaculate white suits and Panama hats and others escorted by matronly chaperones. As Margarita observed the parade of people passing before them in the park, she was always reminded of a painting she had once seen in a book of French artists lying on Fina's coffee table.

It seemed to Margarita that all of Havana underwent the ritual of walking the promenade on Sunday afternoons. Oftentimes she and her sister and aunts arrived in the park when there were only two or three couples. As the crowd began to gather, all of the unattached women, with their painted faces and tight corsets and their pointy, high-heeled shoes, began walking in one direction, as though drawn along by some unseen current. The young men strolled by them in the opposite direction, chatting among themselves, though their eyes remained fixed upon the young women who strolled by them. Forming a kind of barrier around the gaily dressed crowd, the elderly matrons, who had come along to chaperone the young women, seated themselves together on the stone benches that encircled the park, strategically placed beneath the palm trees. Though they talked together, exchanging meaningless gossip, their attention was fastened upon the young women, who gracefully paraded around the promenade conscious of the young men gazing upon them, though their eyes were lowered to the ground. Only the married couples or, occasionally, those who were officially engaged, openly strolled arm in arm together. Some were followed by servants pushing hooded baby carriages that were draped with filmy netting, or nursemaids who led small children by their hands. As the day wore away the young men who were unattached gradually paired themselves off with the single women and led them, trailed by the matrons, around the loop. By the end of the afternoon, nearly all of the chaperones had been asked by at least one gentleman or another for permission to call upon their young charges at home.

The memory of the men in the park recalled to Margarita's mind her father, whom she hadn't seen for several weeks. She could not erase from her memory the pained expression in his eyes as he left for Cienfuegos, all because her mother had refused to speak to him when he announced that he would travel to Tres Flores unaccompanied and that she should complete her confinement in the city. Withdrawing her gaze from the men at the sea wall, Margarita looked at her mother once again. For days before Pedro left for Tres Flores, Rosa had punished him with her silence, treating him as though he were invisible. Although Margarita had never heard her mother raise her voice or openly display her feelings toward her husband, she knew that Rosa's silence was the weapon that she employed when she was angry. In a way she understood her mother's response, for she, too, felt abandoned by her father. But as she listened to the drone of female voices on the veranda, it occurred to Margarita that perhaps her tía was right, even if her suggestion that Rosa go to Tres Flores was partly motivated by her own desires. (When she had first arrived in Havana—at Pedro's request—María didn't attempt to mask her annoyance and displeasure at the *extreme* inconvenience the unexpected trip to the city had caused her.) Perhaps her mother should have spoken out for once, Margarita thought, and insisted that they accompany her father to Cienfuegos. She could not imagine how her mother could stand to be apart from him—how she could endure the company of the old tías with their tiring conversation for another moment. In Margarita's eyes her father's sisters seemed ancient and withered compared to her mother, like a plate full of wizened fruit. Somehow Rosa did not figure into the pattern the old women cut with their lumpish figures and their gnarled feet. After all, hadn't her mother always insisted that she preferred the company of men, with their talk of politics and literature and art, rather than the idle gossip of the women?

As she sat at her mother's feet gazing at her face, Margarita searched in vain for the fleeting expression, the small gesture that would betray Rosa's desire, her longing to escape from her sisters-in-law's company and join the men smoking their cigars at the sea wall. But she could only find the shadows that always lingered at the corners of her mother's mouth and in the depths of her eyes.

Just at that moment, as though she had divined her daughter's thoughts, Rosa turned in her seat and looked into Margarita's eyes, and she felt herself rising up from her chair . . . she felt herself unpinning her straw hat, and pulling off her shoes, and walking . . . running . . . barefoot through the thick, matted grass toward the men leaning against the sea wall smoking their black cigars. Feeling as though they were bound together in a secret tryst, Margarita returned her mother's gaze, and a smile slowly spread across both of their faces.

Rosa's attention was drawn back to the veranda by her sister's laughter. "What's so funny, María?"

"I don't know what made me think of this, but I was just remembering when Pedro brought his parents to Tres Flores to meet Mami for the first time."

"¡Ay Dios mío! I'll remember that day as long as I live," Rosa said with a smile, seemingly forgetting the angry words that had passed between her and her sister.

"Tell us, Rosa," Nélida pleaded, "we've never heard the whole story. All I know is that Mother and Father left for Cienfuegos in the morning and returned, with long faces, later that same evening. Mother refused to tell us what happened, and none of us dared to ask. All she said was that your father had insulted them."

Rosa and María exchanged astonished glances at Nélida's words. "*My* father insulted *your* parents? I think it was the other way around," María responded, accompanying her words with a shake of her head.

"That's not the story *we* heard," Nélida said, arching her eyebrows. "Why don't you tell us your side of the story." Sensing Rosa's hesitation, Nélida pleaded a second time. "Don't forget, Rosa, we're all family here," she added in a confidential tone, sweeping the circle of women with her eyes.

"We're all family here," Miriam echoed. At her words the three sisters leaned forward on the glider, bending toward Rosa like flowers following the sun.

"Only if you promise not to tell your brother that you heard this from me," Rosa said, shooting an angry look at María.

"Of course," Nélida promised, turning her eyes toward Miriam and Mercedes, who both nodded their heads in agreement as they pretended to zip shut their mouths. "Our lips are sealed."

"Well, I suppose it's all right, now that Maria told you the story about Tía Marta."

"Trust us," Nélida assured her, patting Rosa's hand once again.

With a short sigh, Rosa began: "Even though Papi had already arranged our marriage with your father, he insisted that we wouldn't have his final blessing until Mami had given Pedro her approval. He said that Pedro would have to ask her for my hand, even though we all knew that everything had already been settled and that Mami would never go against his wishes once he had reached a decision."

"It was a game they always played," María added, rolling her eyes.

"Tía Marta and Mami worked for days preparing the house. They polished the silverware and the candlestick holders and washed Abuela's crystal at least three times over until everything was spotless. Ordinarily the servants would clean the house, but Mami said that she didn't trust anyone but Tata and Graciela with Abuela's things."

"She wanted everything to be perfect for her little girl," María said with a sour smile.

Ignoring her sister's interruption, Rosa continued. "The day of your parents' arrival my mother had every room in the house filled with flowers from the garden."

"Tata refused to help her," María added.

"But why?" Nélida asked.

"I'm not really sure," Rosa shrugged. "Sometimes she's like that. She just makes up her mind that she's going to be a majadera. Anyway, Mami went to an awful lot of trouble. She even had Graciela prepare bacalao."

"Father's favorite dish," Miriam said.

"Uh-huh," Rosa confirmed with a quick nod of her head. "Papi's chauffeur, Francisco, picked up your parents at the train station around midday. They spent the early part of the afternoon resting in the guest room. It was an unusually hot day—so hot that not even the chameleons were moving in the courtyard."

"But not as hot as it would get at the dinner table!" María laughed.

"You can laugh now, María," Rosa said, "but nothing seemed very funny at the time."

"¿Qué pasó?" Nélida asked. "Tell us what happened."

"After your parents had rested a bit, Mami paraded your mother around Cienfuegos and then took her to meet Padre

Rabia. They seemed to be getting along famously. Meanwhile, Papi took your father on a tour of Treinta Sierras. Everything was going perfectly until we sat down to dinner."

"And . . . ?" Nélida asked impatiently, as she rocked back and forth on the glider.

"Well, Papi was sitting at one end of the table wearing his beret," Rosa said, gesturing to her right, "and your father was sitting at the other end. No one spoke for awhile. It was very awkward. So, to break the silence Mami told your mother that she and Papi had both agreed we would make a wonderful match. She promised that they would treat Pedro like the son they never had. Those were her exact words."

"She didn't!" Nélida cried, wringing her hands.

"Oh, yes she did," María responded. "That was her first mistake!"

"I guess she just wasn't thinking," Rosa broke in. "She knew better than anyone else how sensitive Papi was about not having a son. He always said that a marriage wasn't consummated if there wasn't a boy."

"Whenever he would say that," María interrupted, "Tía Marta used to love to annoy Papi by telling him that he had it all wrong. A marriage wasn't blessed, she always insisted, unless there was flan."

"That Marta certainly was a bird," Nélida smiled.

"She was a real character," María agreed.

"Anyway, to make matters worse," Rosa broke in, gesturing toward Nélida with her head, "your father—who also knew full well how sensitive Papi was on the subject—started going on and on about what an exemplary son Pedro had always been. No one was more surprised than Pedro—it just wasn't like your father to go on like that."

"You're right about that," Nélida agreed. "Father rarely praised us, even when we deserved it. He insisted that too much praise would give us swollen heads."

"That's just not true, Nélida," Miriam broke in. "Father always praised Pedro. He was the favorite."

"Well," Rosa continued, noting Nélida's ire at having been contradicted, "your father went on and on . . ."

". . . and on and on," María added.

". . . about Pedro."

"It was almost as though he was trying to provoke Papi," María interrupted a second time. "And, as if *he* hadn't already said enough, your mother punctuated your father's comments by telling Mami what a wonderful catch Pedro was and that he could have married almost any girl he wanted in Havana. Meanwhile, Mami kept nodding and smiling, and clearing her throat, and smiling . . . but her eyes were fixed all the while on Papi's face which was, by that time, purple."

"She was probably afraid of what he might say," Nélida volunteered in a gay, falsetto voice.

"*Might* say?" María called out, unable to suppress her laughter.

"With good reason, Nélida, with good reason," Rosa chimed in, shaking her head and raising her eyes to the ceiling fan that slowly revolved above her head. "She knew exactly what was coming, so she tried to distract your mother. But how do you stop a hurricane? It was only a matter of time before Papi started."

" 'Don Pedro,' " Rosa said, folding her arms across her chest and lowering her voice in imitation of her father's, " 'do you mean to tell me that you traveled all the way from Havana to insult my wife?' "

"Even though his face was absolutely expressionless," Rosa continued, settling back in her chair, "Papi's eyes were flashing and the tone of his voice was imperious. I was sure that at any moment tongues of flame were going to shoot out of his ears and his mouth."

"How did my father respond?" Nélida gasped.

" '*I* insulted *your* wife, Señor?' " María answered, taking up Don Pedro's part in the conversation.

" 'You heard what I said,' " Rosa answered, " 'insult my wife. Do you realize that in less than twenty-four hours you have not only managed to attack Rafaela's reputation, Señor Amargo, by insinuating that she cannot produce a son, but you have also managed to insult my honor, as well.' "

" 'I hardly think *that* is what I intended to do, Señor Miramar.' "

" 'On the contrary, Señor Amargo, I think that's exactly what you meant to do,' Papi said. Just at that exact moment—probably out of sheer nervousness—Mami and Tía Marta both started laughing at the same time. And when I say laughing, I mean laughing. Tears were rolling down their cheeks."

"Papi went insane," María said, throwing her hands above her head.

"Insane isn't the right word," Rosa corrected. "Berserk is more like it. He started screaming at the top of his lungs, ordering your parents to get out of the house. You would have thought that he was talking to one of the servants. Mami begged him to stop."

"Yes, and without even thinking," María joined in, "Papi told her to shut up." At María's words Nélida drew in her breath and Miriam began clucking her tongue against the roof of her mouth and shaking her head. "He definitely wasn't thinking."

"That's the first time that I ever heard him speak to Mami that way. What was worse was that it was in front of company. Mami was so shocked she didn't say another word."

"For a whole month," María shouted with laughter, causing all of the old women to smile.

"She was almost in tears," Rosa added. "And Papi was furious. He really felt as though your father had attacked his honor."

"With all due respect, Nélida," María added, "your mother sounded like a parrot in the background, repeating the same phrase over and over again: 'Pedro, please, remember who we are!' "

"Then Papi stood up like this," Rosa cut in, rising to her feet before Nélida had a chance to respond to her sister's comment. "He threw his beret at your mother's feet like a gauntlet, leaned across the table, and began to scream again, '*If* your son is fortunate enough to marry our daughter, Don Pedro, he will have to learn—for once in his life——to work for a living. Here there will be no handouts—no sitting around the house on your fondillo eating pastelitos and reading the society section of the paper. There is real work to be done—real work to be done on land that has been passed down through almost three generations. And don't you forget, Señora,' Papi added, shaking his finger at your mother as though she were one of the maids, 'my wife's family also came from Spain and settled here long before yours. She can trace her family roots back to the eighth century. The eighth century! ¿Qué les parece, señores? ¿Qué les parece?' "

" 'Is that so, Señor Miramar? Well, I have something to tell you,' your father said in a voice that made Papi's face turn black with anger. 'I think that you and your wife ought to be grateful that our son could be convinced to take one of *your* daughters off your hands. Considering that you live in the country among guajiros, this may be your only opportunity to marry Rosa off to a decent young man.' "

"Father didn't say that," Nélida gasped with disbelief. Both Rosa and María nodded their heads in unison. "¡Ay Dios mío, qué roña!"

"That was the absolute end," María said. "Being as proud as he was, Papi could not allow your father to have the last word. I was sure that he was going to run Don Pedro through with that old rusty sword hanging over the breakfront."

"If they had lived a century earlier," Miriam said, "my father would have had your father in the streets, challenging him to a duel."

"I'm sure you know that they had always been rivals," Nélida added, in a subdued tone, "even when they were in grammar school together."

"We know!" Rosa nodded, exchanging a quick glance with María.

"Then what happened?" Miriam asked.

"Papi pushed back his chair," María responded, rising from her own chair in imitation of her father's movements, "threw his napkin on the floor on top of his beret and began shouting all kinds of insults at your father."

"¡Qué barbaridad!" Nélida said loudly. The others just stared at María.

"Thank God Graciela arrived with the bacalao—by that time they were both standing on their feet, leaning across the dining room table, shaking their fists at one another and carrying on like two children. The smell of the food seemed to calm them both down."

"That was no mistake, María. Mami rang for Graciela with the service bell underneath the carpet by her feet."

"I didn't know that. I thought it was just a stroke of brilliance on Graciela's part."

"Hardly! Papi had a terrible temper," Rosa admitted, with a shake of her head, "one minute he was laughing and as docile as a lamb, and the next he was roaring like a madman. We never knew which way the wind was going to blow with him."

"So did my father," Miriam volunteered.

"They both did," María corrected. "My father was so angry that night he didn't even notice that his pants were undone."

"What?" chorused the three sisters.

Rosa and María started to laugh at the shocked expressions on the old women's faces. "Papi always undid his belt buckle and the top button of his pants before sitting down at the dinner table," Rosa explained. "He insisted that that way he could eat and drink as much as he pleased without feeling too full."

"He loved to eat," María added. At her words the three sisters shifted uncomfortably in their seats.

"It's true," Rosa laughed. "Mami was horrified when she realized he was standing, undone, right in front of your mother, although I really don't think your mother noticed. Her mind was on other things!"

"And . . . ?"

"They continued to call one another names and shout across the table, batting insults back and forth like a tennis match. Papa had the habit of pounding his fist on the table whenever he shouted. You know how it goes," Rosa said, banging the palm of her hand against the arm of her chair, "the more noise you make, the better the argument. At least that's what Papi thought. I can still hear him now: '¡Ladrón!' ba-boom, '¡Hedonista!' ba-boom."

"But Señor Amargo was insulting Papi, too," María cut in, lowering herself into her chair, "at the top of *his* lungs. Your father," she continued, pointing her finger at Nélida, "was pawing the floor with his foot like a racehorse and calling Papi a campesino. I thought Papi was going to break a blood vessel when your father accused him of having prostituted himself to the American borrachos who distilled rum from his molasses."

"¡Ay, Dios mío!" Nélida and Miriam cried in unison.

"Yes, but don't forget, María," Rosa broke in, "that Papi had told Señor Amargo that lawyers like him were nothing more than a pack of thieves who would sell their own mothers for a peseta. We didn't know where to put our eyes," Rosa blushed, shooting a quick glance at Margarita, who, she realized, had been following their conversation.

"How did it end?" Nélida asked, as she picked a sprig of hierbabuena from her iced tea and raised her glass to her lips.

"Papi pounded so hard on the table," Rosa responded, "that one of Abuela's cut crystal water goblets danced off the edge and shattered on the floor."

"No one said another word after that. (Actually, I think Mami was angrier at Papi for telling her to shut up and then breaking the goblet than she was at your father, though she never would have admitted it.) Your father pushed in *his* chair, pulled out your mother's, and then escorted her out of the room."

"You mean Señora Amargo sailed out of the room ahead of him," María corrected.

"They packed their bags . . . one, two, three . . . and returned to Havana on the last train out of the station."

"It's a miracle that my father allowed Pedro to go through with the wedding," Nélida observed, with a shake of her head.

"Are you kidding?" Rosa said, throwing back her head. "Your father was even prouder than my father."

"I'm not so sure that that's true," Nélida said in an icy tone, which caused Rosa to lower her eyes.

"It's true," Miriam laughed, fanning herself with a handscreen she used to eclipse the angry look Nélida was sending her. "Father couldn't lose face and go back on his word. He would rather have died. Besides, he really cared for you, Rosa. He always said you were one of the most beautiful women he had ever seen. He thought you were exotic. Plus, how could he turn up his nose at your father's plantation, Americans or no Americans?"

"Regardless of who was prouder, you know the rest of the story," Rosa interrupted, in an attempt to redirect the conversation. She was visibly embarrassed by her sister-in-law's compliment. "But I'll never forgive either one of them for refusing to attend our reception."

"The only reason Papi went to the wedding was because there was no one else to give you away," María added.

"Sin vergüenzas," Miriam muttered, clacking her tongue against the roof of her mouth once again. "That explains it. They both should have been ashamed of themselves. Pobrecita," she added, patting Rosa's hand, "you must have been mortified."

"¡Qué pena! ¡Qué barbaridad!" joined in the others.

"I didn't know that Abuelo had such a bad temper," Margarita burst out in surprise, with her eyes raised to her mother's face. The entire time that the women had been talking, she had sat at Rosa's feet, silently listening to the conversation. She found it hard to believe that the frail little man who, she remembered, always smelled like cigars and allowed her to sit on his knee and dip her little finger in his thimble-sized glass of anís when her mother wasn't paying attention was capable of such harshness. Every time she saw him, she recalled, he would press a silver coin in her palm and ask her to remember him in her prayers.

At the sound of her voice the tías all turned their eyes on Margarita. She'd been so quiet they'd forgotten that she was there listening.

"Hasn't your mother ever taught you that little girls should be seen and not heard unless they're invited to speak?" María snapped, throwing Margarita a scorching look that caused her to lower her eyes to the ground. "En boca cerrada nunca entran moscas." Meanwhile, the three old tías gazed at their niece with silent disapproval.

As the conversation among the circle of women struck up once again, Rosa reached down and pressed her daughter's hand in hers. Margarita knew at once that her mother was trying to compensate for María's sharp words. Her touch, gentle and soothing as lemon balm, stirred Margarita's memory—the memory of her mother's hands that came, when she was sick, out of the night, pressing like a cool cloth against her fevered brow.

Despite her mother's touch, Margarita was still sore at María. Her tía had no right to talk to her that way, purposely humiliating her and her mother in front of everyone. It was something that she apparently took great delight in doing, for she did it every chance she got. For some unknown reason that Margarita hadn't quite figured out yet, María had taken a strong disliking to her, and she made her preference for Caridad obvious to even their most casual acquaintances, for they often made comments about it. All of her affection seemed to be reserved for Caridad— the only *good one* in the family, María always reminded her.

As she gave her aunt a sidelong glance, the words of the story María used to tell them whenever she and Caridad played by the tiled fish pond in the courtyard at Tres Flores came to mind:

". . . and for the third time the greedy sister refused to share her cheese sandwich with the little fish. She shook her head back and forth, causing the long black ringlets of hair that hung about her shoulders and down her back to sway from side to side, and shaped her lips into a circle, 'No.' "

"At that moment a stream of thin green serpents and scaly reptiles slithered over her tongue and out the corners of her mouth. Her fair-haired sister, who had willingly and unselfishly shared her meager lunch with the little fish, began to scream in horror. Though no sound came from her throat, a shower of precious stones and gold coins fell from her lips into a pile at her feet."

Though her aunt always made it clear that the story was meant for her younger niece, Margarita could not help but think that the moral better applied to María. Everyone knew that her tía was jealous of her mother, not only because of Rosa's beauty but because she had been the one to marry her father and have his children. María, she thought, as she gazed at the wrinkles that fanned out from her tía's eyes and the mottled liver spots that covered her throat and her arms, had always been the selfish one, and she had projected her anger onto her, rather than Caridad, perhaps because Margarita resembled Rosa.

Turning her head in order to avoid María's prying eyes, Margarita stared sullenly at her old tías from her place on the floor, though they did not seem to notice. They were so caught up in their conversation that Margarita had become invisible to them once more. As Margarita glanced at Nélida's hands it struck her that they looked like the gnarled roots of the orange tree in her great-grandfather's courtyard at Tres Flores. They seemed to be growing together in her lap. Something about them reminded her of Tía Marta once again.

* * *

Gazing blindly at Nélida's hands, Margarita pictured Tía Marta waiting for them on the portico at Tres Flores with Tata and María. Rosa would send her aunt a telegram days in advance announcing the exact date and time of their departure from the sulfur springs at San Miguel so that the servants could begin preparing the house. As their motorcar pulled into view of the family compound, Tía Marta would spring out of the bentwood rocker Pancho had carried for her from the back porch. While Luciano swung open the tall wrought-iron gates and Francisco pulled into the circular drive, Tía Marta would stand at the front door waving both of her arms above her head just in case they hadn't seen her and jumping up and down like a child.

As their mother embraced Tata, Tía Marta would coo nonsense words into their ears while Margarita and Caridad attempted to climb out from the back seat of the motorcar:

"Riquísimas. Bellísimas," she would twitter like a bird, "qué niñas tan ricas y bellas. ¡Qué niñas tan graciosas!"

She would pinch their cheeks all the while until they burned, and squeeze their faces with her tiny hands, which were mottled and gnarly and covered with ropy, blue veins. Then she would smother them with kisses and hug them tightly against her chest, while they inhaled the familiar scent of perspiration, dusting powder, and cologne that was always about her.

As Nélida's hands came into focus once again, Rosa recalled the morning in early spring when they left the house on Calle Semilla unexpectedly and returned to Tres Flores. Although her parents refused to tell her why they were going to Cienfuegos, she knew before they arrived that Tía Marta was gone. In her dreams the portico was already empty.

With Carlucho de Silva and Faustino Aragona's help, Pedro placed the satin-lined mahogany coffin that contained Tía Marta's childlike frame on a table in the front parlor. Because Margarita was only nine years old at the time and Caridad eleven, they weren't permitted to hold vigil with the body—a rite reserved for the older women, her mother told her. After hours of thrashing around in her sheets, Margarita crept down the back staircase and hid herself behind an immense potted plant that stood in the corner among the shadows of the entrance hall.

From her place she watched her mother arrange a glass rosary in Tía Marta's hands while Tata and Tía María lit the tapers that were placed like a glowing halo around the casket. As the women from the neighborhood arrived one by one, María greeted them at the door and pointed them toward the parlor. After expressing their condolences to Rosa, they seated themselves in the high-backed chairs that the men had arranged in a semicircle around Marta's coffin.

Tía María and her mother sat like sphinxes at opposite ends of the room. María, being the eldest of the two, began the recitation of the rosary once all of the women were seated, followed by Rosa. The others waited out their turns, alternately announcing the mysteries and beginning the call and response of Padre Nuestros and Ave Marías. Without prompting, each took her part, leading the others in prayer. As she listened to the women praying in one voice, Margarita sensed that the room was filled with other presences—as though a great ancestral crowd reaching back through the ages had gathered in the front parlor to lift and embrace Tía Marta's spirit and guide her on the long journey home. Among them, she felt certain, was her grandmother Rafaela.

In counterpoint to the women's voices were those of the men, who spoke in hushed tones on the back patio as they smoked their cigars. Somehow the familiar smell of the cigar smoke, combined with the women's prayers, acted like a soothing balm to Margarita's aching heart and made her feel less alone.

They buried Marta the next morning. Although Caridad was allowed to accompany her parents and her aunt, Margarita was left at home with the servants. She could still recall the moment when she realized that she would be left behind. No one had bothered to wake her from her sleep. Starting from her bed, Margarita reached the second-floor landing just as her father slammed the front door shut. The thought that her mother and her sister and her aunt would soon be returning after the service at the cathedral—for none of the women was permitted to attend the burial in the cemetery—brought her little consolation. She hid behind the sofa so that no one would find her crying; with great difficulty Tata convinced her to come out of hiding.

Turning her eyes toward the sea once again, Margarita saw herself following Tata into the kitchen. The old woman sat her at the marble-top worktable where she and Graciela always rolled out dough together. From her place she watched as Tata poured out for herself a tall glass of aguardiente she had made from Pedro's sugar cane and Margarita a tumbler of fresh goat's milk. Then the old woman filled a plate with guava-filled pasteles, the sight of which brought Margarita immediate consolation. As she fed Lobo crusts of bread beneath the table and Margarita drank her milk, Tata answered all of her questions about death.

At first, Margarita insisted upon knowing what Tía Marta's last words were, filled with the hope that her great-aunt had left for her some secret message or advice that she could carry with her for the rest of her life. To her great disappointment, Margarita learned that Marta had only asked for some liniment and a jigger of rum. Then Margarita asked Tata if she would recognize Tía Marta if they were to meet in the next world.

"The next world?" Tata had laughed. "Por qué a next world? Let me tell you something, m'ija, Lobo probably knows more about death than you do."

Rosa looked skeptically at the old dog, who was drooling incessantly at Tata's side, leaving a great pool of spittle at her feet on the kitchen floor. She laughed inside herself as she recalled the afternoons she had commanded the old dog to lie quietly in the corner of the kitchen so that she could play dress-up with him. She would wear her mother's dresses, hiked up at the waist, and a pair of high heels, which she had selected from one of her mother's shoe trees while rummaging through Rosa's closet. The poor animal would remain perfectly still for hours at a time, with Rafaela's sewing glasses balanced on the tip of his nose, while Margarita adorned his neck with strings of glass beads and artificial pearls and filmy silk scarves, and fitted onto his head her mother's old sun hats, which Rosa had banished to the back of the closet once they were no longer in fashion.

"But I'm afraid. I'm afraid that I'll forget what she looks like," Margarita suddenly burst out, returning her gaze to Tata's face once more.

"Only those who believe that life is everything and death nothing fear to die, mi vida. Life is only a thin skin, corazón, drawn tightly over sorrow and sometimes despair. When you return to your grandmother's house in the city tomorrow, don't forget to look into the night sky. The moon that rises above the palmeras will tell you everything you need to know."

Margarita knitted her brows together at the old woman's words as she washed down a bite of her pastry along with her tears, with a gulp of warm, frothy milk.

"The slice that appears in the sky is death, m'ija," Tata explained, etching the moon into the vacant air above her head with her hands, "and the part that is hidden in shadows is life. Only those who choose to live among the shadows are easily fooled by the dark side of the moon. They are the ones who refuse to believe that the moon is full and round simply because they cannot see the other half. Life and death are a web that has no weaver."

Margarita shrugged her shoulders and helped herself to a second pastel. As she did so she recalled her father's insistence that her mother return to Tres Flores after Tía Marta's funeral mass. "Why aren't Mami and Tía María allowed to go to the cemetery with my father?" she asked, with her mouth full of pastry.

"For the same reason that Graciela cuts the head and the tail off the fish before frying it in the pan."

"What do you mean?" Margarita asked in a puzzled tone.

"Every cook who has fried fish in this kitchen—beginning with the first, Manola—has cut off the head and the tail. Manola started this tradition because the cast iron frying pan she was using was too small for the fish she bought from the street vendors. After Manola died, Graciela took over her frying pan. Even though that pan is long gone, and the one Graciela uses is twice its size, she continues to cut off the fish's head and tail without even knowing why."

"Oh, come on," Margarita laughed, "tell me the truth. Why isn't Mami allowed to go to the cemetery?"

"Because men like your father believe that women are too delicate to handle la muerte," Tata answered. "What he doesn't realize is that every woman who has carried a child has ridden on La Pelona's shoulder. And since when do you talk with your mouth full of pasteles?" Tata added. "You know better than that."

"Do you agree with him?" Margarita asked, ignoring Tata's comment.

"Of course I do," Tata laughed, tossing the dog the last crust of bread and taking a sip of her aguardiente. "Ask Lobo."

At her words, both Margarita and Tata turned and looked at the old dog, who had swallowed the bread crust with one gulp.

Though he was almost completely deaf and blind and had lost nearly all of his teeth, Lobo never missed a handout from the kitchen table. Somehow sensing that their eyes were upon him, the dog reluctantly returned to the corner of the kitchen near the stove with his tail tucked between his legs and curled up beside the oven. And though he appeared to be sleeping, he continued to lick the last remnants of breadcrumbs off his muzzle and his dark, rubbery lips, as if he were dreaming of eating.

Margarita returned her gaze to Tata's face, and when their eyes met they both began to laugh. She knew, at once, that the old woman wasn't telling the truth. In fact, everyone in Cienfuegos knew that Tata had buried Graciela's brother, Pito—with Rosa's consent of course—in the family cemetery just outside of town. Despite Rosa's petitions, Padre Rabia would not permit her to bury Pito in the parish cemetery because, he argued, the boy had refused to convert. "Pagans," he insisted, "could not be buried in consecrated ground." And so, Tata had buried him in a simple pine box that Pancho and Luciano had hastily nailed together and blessed his unmarked grave during the night so that no one would see her. (Years later Margarita learned that Pito had converted on his deathbed. Rumor had it that he had been banned from the parish cemetery not only because his family had no money, but because he was a mulato.)

After the women returned from the cathedral following Tía Marta's funeral service, Margarita rejoined them in the front parlor. The first thing she noticed when she entered the room was Tía Marta's immense blue-and-green throw, which was cascading like a great woolen waterfall over Paolo's armchair and onto the floor. The sight of it sent a sharp pang through her heart. For what seemed to be an eternity, they sat in silence in the parlor, listening to the soft bustle that came from the dining room as Tata and Graciela, along with Señora de Silva and Señora Aragona, set out trays filled with bocaditos and pasteles that several of the women in Marta's rosary group had prepared and sent over when they heard about their friend's death. Margarita's gaze was fixed on her mother's face. Lavender semicircles were etched beneath her eyes and Margarita could tell that she had been crying, for her eyes had grown very small and her eyelids were still swollen and red. In contrast, María's were as dry as sand.

Glancing around the room, Margarita's gaze settled upon the curio case in the corner. Among a set of miniature teacups and a collection of porcelain thimbles of various shapes and sizes lay what Marta crossed her heart and swore was Maita's (the nickname she and Caridad had given Rafaela) bun.

"During all of the years that they were married," Tía Marta would tell them, "your grandfather refused to allow my sister to cut her hair. He had always said that Rafaela was his queen and that her long, chestnut-colored hair was like a crown. The day after your grandfather was buried in the family plot, Maita summoned me to her room, asking that I bring with me a sharp pair of scissors and a comb. When I arrived at her bedroom, she insisted I shear off all of her hair. Convinced that my sister had poured an extra gotita or two of rum in her café, I refused. Only after she had walked a straight line with her arms extended outwards and touched her nose with her fingertip did Maita convince me to comply with her request."

"Old age had turned my sister's hair white—it was as fine as an angel's. And when I combed it out it reached all the way across the bedroom to the dressing room. Then I began to cut and cut," Marta would say, shaping her own fingers into scissors that cleaved the air like the mouth of a crane. When I finally finished, we spun my sister's hair into a bun and put it in the curio case for everyone to see." At that point in the story, Marta would grow silent and point her finger, followed by her eyes, toward the gilded case in the corner of the parlor that housed their grandmother's hair like a relic.

The first time they had heard the story she and Caridad had been filled with amazement, though Margarita secretly thought that her grandmother's hair looked more like an over-sized bird's nest than a bun. By the third time that she had heard the story, Margarita began to grow skeptical, for each time Tía Marta recited the tale Maita's hair grew at least a foot longer. By the fourth time, she entertained the possibility that their great-aunt had conjured up the whole story, and that it was no more real than the tale of the nightingale. Finally, Margarita became convinced that the hair in the curio case had actually been taken from their old dog Lobo's back. But then Tata confirmed the story—admitting that Tía Marta had only embellished the tale here and there—so Margarita knew it had to be at least partially true.

As Margarita's eyes wandered listlessly around the room, they fell upon Tía Marta's throw once again. The metalic crocheting needle that Marta always used was stuck in a skein of blue wool that lay in a workbasket alongside the armchair, as though at any moment Marta might enter the room and take up her place by the window with the throw covering her lap. For as long as Margarita could remember, her tía had worked on the blanket, claiming that it, like the Sagrada Familia, would never be complete. Suddenly she was struck by the possibility that only a few hours before, Tía Marta had probably held the needle in her hands—hands, Margarita realized in that moment as her eyes rested on Nélida's once more, that she would never hold again in hers.

"And if this one's a boy will you name him after his father?" Nélida's loud, quivering voice scattered Margarita's thoughts of Tía Marta.

"*If* it's a boy?" María called out, in a voice made shrill with anger. "It had better be a boy this time, or Pedro will divorce her. 'Bring me an heir, your husband needs an heir,' he always tells her."

Rosa winced and looked away from her sister, recalling Doctor de Silva's words the night before she miscarried for the third time:

"With all due respect, Señores," he had told them, though his eyes and his words were toward Pedro, "if Rosa doesn't bring you a boy this time you'll have to be satisfied with three girls. Some women are just not meant to have a lot of children."

Though the old doctor had obviously offended his pride, Pedro did not respond. But the expression in his eyes—an almost imperceptible flash that Rosa alone could read—betrayed him. Rosa knew instantly that he had been insulted. That same night, Pedro shrugged off the doctor's warning, reminding her that the old man had said the exact same thing before Margarita was born.

"The old man's crazy," Pedro had scoffed, "women are made to carry children. This convinces me more than ever that de Silva's only an old guajiro whose grandmother claimed that she knew how to cure a few ailments and relieve a few aches and pains with her bag of weeds. I'm certain that the doctors at the clinic in Havana would laugh the old man right into the street. Besides," he assured her, kissing the base of Rosa's neck before mounting on top of her, "I dreamed that this one would be a boy the size of three green melons."

Rosa didn't have the heart to tell him that dreams were sometimes like mirrors, offering up images that were turned inside out.

Though nothing was ever said afterwards, the following morning, when Rosa awoke in a sea of blood, Pedro nearly lost her, along with their child, whom they named Mariela in memory of her grandmother.

"If women are so worthless," Mercedes suddenly broke in, drawing Rosa back into the conversation, "who will men find to give them sons?" It was the first time, Margarita noted, that her tía had spoken all afternoon.

Rosa shrugged her shoulders. "They never think of these things, do they, Mercedes? Anyhow, to answer your question," she responded, directing her gaze back to Nélida as she rubbed small circles over her own stomach with the palm of her hand, "if it's a boy he will be named after his father. Pedro wouldn't have it any other way. And contrary to what my sister thinks, your brother won't divorce me if I bring him another daughter. As long as she's healthy, he won't care."

"If he were still alive, Papi would be disappointed to hear you say that," María shot back, wagging her finger at her sister as though she were scolding a small child. "When Rosa was carrying Caridad," she explained to the Amargo sisters, who had all turned their attention to her, "he told Mami that if he ever had a grandson he wanted him to be named Antonio, after him, not after Pedro or his other grandfather."

"As though it was his son!" called out Mercedes, clapping her hands together. "Oye muchacha, your father was really a majadero, wasn't he?"

María looked at her sister and burst into laughter, but Rosa's face remained expressionless. Meanwhile, Nélida scowled at Mercedes until the smile disappeared from her sister's lips.

"You shouldn't be talking like this in front of Margarita."

"¡Qué va!" María responded, waving her sister's words off with a nonchalant flourish of her hand.

"But I guess it's ridiculous of me to expect you, of all people, to understand, since you don't have any children of your own," Rosa returned, regretting the words the moment they slipped over her lips, but refusing to take them back, despite the injured look in María's eyes.

Rosa's words were like an unexpected slap across María's face, causing her cheeks to glow with humiliation and anger. If her sister only knew how often she had lain awake at night—

staring into the darkness—tormented by the thought that she would go to the grave alone and childless. Practically all of her school friends had moved away from Cienfuegos—the only person who occasionally dropped by to see her at Tres Flores was the blue-eyed priest, Padre Morales, though he always seemed a bit distracted when he came and insisted that they sit together in the back courtyard, rather than in the front parlor as María preferred, where they could watch the maids performing their chores. Though the priest was handsome and young, she knew that he was beyond her reach. Even though she had given up the hope of marrying long before, every time she saw her sister with her children the old wound was reopened and she was reminded of her grandmother's words: "A woman without a husband and children is no woman at all."

"I'm certain that it's a boy," Rosa said, steering the conversation back to Nélida, though she was conscious of the weight of her sister's eyes upon her.

"I'm sure, too," agreed Nélida. "Look at the way you're carrying that child. He's sitting on your lap like a melon."

"I hope you're right," Miriam joined in, "the Amargos need a boy to carry on our name, otherwise the family line will die out with Pedro."

"The last time we were at Tres Flores, Tata told me that there might be two."

"Do you really think so, Rosa?" Nélida asked.

"She has yet to be wrong, Nélida." After the words had escaped her lips, Rosa grew quiet. She wasn't exaggerating—Tata was never wrong. Hadn't the old woman known even before they were conceived that both Margarita and Caridad would be girls? When Rosa asked her how she could be so certain, Tata told her that she had seen the color of their water in her dreams. The last time that they had been together, as Rosa reclined in the warm soapy waters of the claw-foot tub in the bathhouse and the old woman combed out her hair, Tata announced, like an angelic messenger, that she could already read the thin brown line that divided her belly in half and see the dark mask that had begun to shadow her face. "You will carry once more," she had said, "like the flower that carries two blossoms on a single stem." As she spoke, her voice seemed to catch on the words and her eyes were dark and empty.

*   *   *

"¡Qué va!" Nélida snorted, "from behind no one would ever guess your condition." As Nélida pronounced the word, Margarita turned toward her mother, but Rosa refused to meet her gaze. "You're too small to be carrying one, muchacha," the old woman continued, "let alone two. Besides," she added, "your hips are too narrow for you to be giving birth to more than one at a time."

"Nélida's right, Rosa," Miriam agreed, "it's a miracle that you managed so well with Margarita and Caridad."

"Leave her alone," Mercedes joined in unexpectedly. "Caridad and Margarita were both easy births for her. They just slipped out like little rose-colored fish."

"That's true," Nélida conceded. "I'd forgotten all about that."

Unable to listen to another word, María pushed back her chair and announced that she suddenly felt light-headed and thought it best to return to the house.

"Ven, m'ija," Nélida said, rising from the glider and waving María toward her, "we'll take a walk around the grounds together. There's nothing like the salt air to revive the spirits. Besides," she added, "my knees are getting stiff sitting in one place for such a long time."

"Nonsense," María responded, brushing the old woman off, "I'll be fine if I just lie down for awhile." Sensing that Nélida's suggestion was prompted by her own concerns, María added, "It will only take Manuel a minute to drop me off at the house— then I'll send him back to pick you up. Besides, he's just sitting there waiting for us in the parking lot. This will give him something to do."

Reluctantly, Nélida conceded, and the three old tías bid María farewell. She turned on her heels and left without a word to her sister.

After María had gone, the old women decided to take a stroll around the grounds, accompanied by Margarita. Declining their invitation, Rosa remained on the veranda, lost in thought. She tried to brush off María's suggestion that she follow Pedro to Cienfuegos, but her sister's words continued to sting her like a thorn. Perhaps María was right after all, Rosa considered. Perhaps I should have insisted and returned with him and the children to Tres Flores.

Though she was filled with apprehension, Rosa made up her mind to take Margarita and Caridad to Cienfuegos without Pedro's permission so that they could all be together—so that their first son would be born in her mother's bed, just like his sisters before him. She considered telegramming him with the news so as not to catch him by surprise. But upon second thought, she decided that it would probably be best to simply show up at the door. If she gave him the chance he would tell her not to come. Besides, she convinced herself, the thought of her and the girls traveling alone on the train would cause him unnecessary worry. She knew that Pedro would probably be angry with her at first, but when he saw them all standing on the portico at Tres Flores with their valises in their hands he would have to forgive her, wouldn't he?

13 July 1954

Upon hearing that Rosa had decided to follow Pedro to Cienfuegos, Nélida took every opportunity to dissuade her sister-in-law from making the trip. Convinced that Rosa would not heed her warnings, Nélida announced that she and her sisters would spend the remainder of the summer in Varadero until their brother returned to the house on Calle Semilla. Leaving Bebita to oversee the closing of the house, Nélida, Miriam and Mercedes insisted upon being dropped off at the yacht club with Margarita and Caridad, while Manuel chauffeured Rosa from house to house so that she could deliver the hastily scribbled notes, which she had written out the night before, declining the dinner invitations and luncheons extended to her by the wives of Pedro's friends and foreign business associates who purchased his sugar and molasses to make their rum. With great dismay she had discovered that upon her return to the house the previous afternoon, María had packed her bags and gone, without so much as a word to anyone, to stay with an old schoolmate who had long since moved to Havana with her family. (Rosa had learned her sister's whereabouts from Manuel—in spite of his promise to María to keep them secret—for he, at her bidding, had dropped her at her girlfriend's house before returning to the club.)

While her mistresses were out paying their calls, Bebita packed their valises with the assistance of several of the other servant girls. Meanwhile her grandson, Mariano, spread camphor balls across the Persian carpets that were scattered throughout the house and rolled them into funnels that he pushed up against the walls. The servants in the kitchen, under the direction of Concha and Lucía, were busily emptying the pantry shelves of perishable items while Magda and Eulalia mopped the tile floors and the marble staircase with lukewarm water. Although the house would remain vacant for several weeks, at Rosa's insistence the housemaids washed and rehung all of the curtains and starched and pressed the bed linens before remaking the beds. Then they drew the persianas and covered the furniture and the paintings, including the portrait of Fina and Cuca, with old sheets that were stored in the cedar closet on the third floor when they weren't in use.

Working on the second floor, Bebita jammed frayed valises and steamer trunks with all of the things Rosa might need once she arrived in Cienfuegos, a task which she had performed countless times. In a separate bag she placed the things that her mistress would probably want on her trip, along with several items from the new baby's layette.

The Amargos made the trip to Cienfuegos so often that Bebita felt as though she could have packed blindfolded. Over the years she had developed a system: first, she stacked Rosa's hats, one on top of the other, in round boxes that she corded together with hemp. (She was clacking her tongue against the roof of her mouth all the while after she'd noticed that most of the hats still bore their tags and had, she assumed, never been worn.) After she had finished with the hats, she began the task of gathering together Rosa's toiletries: lavender soaps; bath gels and soft, silver-backed brushes; brown-and-yellow sponges; two gray pumice stones; a hot water bottle; an ice bag; dusting powder; castor oil; cologne; a roll of cotton; and gauze. Bebita organized all these things at the bottom of the steamer trunk before she threw open the large, walk-in cedar closet where Rosa's dresses hung side by side on wooden hangers. Her canvas shoes, sandals, and pumps were arranged in matching pairs on several shoe trees at the back of the closet and her handbags were lined up on the shelves that hung above them. Bebita folded more than a dozen dresses into a neat pile before opening Rosa's drawers, from which she selected several embroidered handkerchiefs and chose a kerchief for breezy days, a black mantilla for the evening, and a veil for church. She also packed nearly a half-dozen camisoles and corsets, assorted cotton undergarments, three pairs of silk stockings, and several garter belts, a scapular and a hand-carved coral rosary, a pair of wrist-length gloves, several loose cotton nightgowns, and a parasol to protect her mistress from the ravaging midday sun.

When she had finished, she lined Rosa's belongings against the wall in the bedroom so that Manuel and Paz, who also helped tend the gardens, would know what to take when they were ready to load the motorcar. Then she went to Caridad's and then Margarita's rooms to make sure that the other housemaids were packing all of the belongings the girls would be needing as well. She had nearly completed her tasks when Rosa returned to the house with her sisters-in-law and her two daughters. As soon as they arrived, they all took a light merienda together consisting mainly of fruit, cheese, and café con leche. By the time they were finished eating, Mariano and Paz had the car ready and Manuel was waiting patiently in the entrance hall with his old straw hat in his hands. Though Rosa knew that Manuel did not approve of her plans, he had politely offered to accompany them to Cienfuegos on the train. Mariano had agreed to take them to the station so that he could drive the car home.

"Please forgive me, Señora, but I feel it is my duty to intrude," the old mulato began in a timid voice, as Rosa was stepping into the motorcar. "Perhaps I am a bit old-fashioned, but in my time ladies never traveled alone. I think the Caballero would be very displeased with me, Señora, if he found out that I allowed you to make the trip unescorted."

Though she would have preferred to travel without him, Rosa knew that she could not refuse Manuel's offer.

Margarita watched out the back window of the car until the house on Calle Semilla was cut from sight, first by a Royal Palm and then by a bend in the road.

The large white houses and the tall palms and ceibas and banyan trees that lined the streets spun past her as the motorcar sped toward the train station. When they arrived, Rosa paid for their boarding passes—she reserved an entire compartment to accommodate their luggage—and then they waited on hard wooden benches for the train that would take them on the long, hot journey to Cienfuegos.

When it came time to board the train, the conductor refused to allow Manuel to sit with them in their car. Despite Rosa's protests and her insistence that he had no right to ban the old man from riding with them, she finally gave in and purchased a separate ticket for Manuel.

16 July 1954

Though Paolo had decided to settle in the country so that he could oversee the clearing of the forest and the planting of the cane fields, he knew he could not bring his young bride to live in the house with the thatched roof that he had purchased from the Englishman and his wife. After much thought and deliberation he determined to build a stable next to the thatched house and hire a guajiro to assist him in overseeing Treinta Sierras (the name he had chosen for his plantation because, he boasted, it would take thirty years to saw down the trees and the thick undergrowth that covered his vast property). After purchasing more than fifty slaves to clear the land, Paolo divided up his property, designating a third for tobacco and the rest for sugar cane. Then he bought a large plot of land near the center of town for the house that he and Mariela would live in, and another on the outskirts of Cienfuegos for the family cemetery.

Without fail, he wrote to Mariela every day, assuring her that he had begun to civilize the place and gradually establish some kind of order in preparation for her arrival. He told her that when she arrived in Cienfuegos, she would think she was home, for their "island palace," as he called it, would be a replica of the

Ocampo family's ancestral estate. "Cienfuegos is the pearl of the south, mi vida," he assured her. And so the house, which Mariela suggested be called Tres Flores, was modeled on the French neo-classical architecture that was so common in the town where they had grown up in the north of Spain.

The portico at the front entrance was a columned arcade supported by two flanking pairs of Doric pillars. Above the front entrance was a balustrade richly ornamented with relief work. All of the windows on the first floor were protected by thick wrought-iron bars and every window on the second floor opened onto a balcony. Paolo personally designed a courtyard for his wife that was sandwiched between the family compound and the barracones—the slave quarters where all of the domestic servants, except for Tata, slept. It was complete with labyrinthine paths, a wrought-iron gate—with a rambling rose pattern, which Paolo had commissioned by mail at Mariela's request and had shipped from Spain—a fountain complete with a lion's head that spit a stream of water into a tiled basin filled with colorful fish and water lilies, and an immense hive-shaped cage, which was placed at the center of the courtyard and housed parrots of many shades and a variety of wild tropical birds with painted wings and faces.

Under Paolo's explicit directions, the courtyard was filled with carefully manicured beds that overflowed with fragrant and colorful flowers, some of which were imported from the north of Spain and others that could be found growing wild on the island. In addition to the neatly clipped hedges and the azalea bushes that bordered the winding paths, the garden was filled with jacarandas and ceibas, a row of stately palm trees laced with orchids and poincianas, which blossomed with lavender and purple blooms that were shaken loose and carried by the breeze, forming a carpet on the back balcony that faced the courtyard. A variety of trained vines climbed up the tall white walls that separated the garden from the outside world, and in the corner of the courtyard Paolo planted an orange tree.

When the building of Tres Flores was completed, Paolo sent for his wife. In no time at all word of the doña's arrival spread around the town. Peering out from behind parted curtains, the women of Cienfuegos watched with amazement and curiosity as Mariela passed by their houses in her volanta, followed by a long procession of carts that wound like a carnival through the streets of the tiny town. Assisting his wife down from her carriage, Paolo escorted Mariela to the furthest corner of the courtyard, where he pointed out to her the orange tree that he had planted, he announced, as a symbol and a reminder of their proud Spanish heritage, and in memory of his grandmother, who had been born in Valencia.

*   *   *

On the morning of the fiesta just before the sun had begun to rise, Margarita crouched behind Paolo's orange tree, digging a hole with a large serving spoon from her great-grandmother's silver chest. Dull elastic pains wrenched her stomach muscles and shot up her lower back as she buried the white cotton nightgown that the nuns at the monastery had embroidered with pink satin thread. Fortunately, she had managed to strip off the gown before the dark, sticky liquid that had wept down the inside of her thighs stained the linens on her bed. Somehow she had been wounded during the night, she thought to herself as she dug into the earth, though she could not imagine how. All Margarita could remember was that something had awakened her from her dreams. When she switched on the lamp on her nightstand and saw the amber-colored blood on her legs, she was gripped with fear. She was certain that she had contracted the very same *condition* her mother and aunt had spoken about in whispers.

Margarita dug as fast as she could, knowing that her father would soon be rising. Moistened by an early shower, the reddish-brown soil yielded easily to her touch. As she turned it with the silver spoon she recalled the time that Tía María had caught her eating fistfuls of dirt out of the flower bed. Her tía frightened her so completely with the idea that worms the size of anacondas would grow in her stomach that Margarita even stopped biting her fingernails, a habit she had adopted when she gave up sucking her thumb. (She stopped sucking her thumb after María told her that her grandfather had caught her grandmother sucking both of her thumbs on her honeymoon night—an event that would haunt Rafaela for the rest of her life, for Antonio teased her about it until the day he died.)

Having finished burying the nightgown, Margarita moved to another spot in the flower bed to bury the heavy serving spoon with the rambling rose pattern. Her mother would never miss the nightgown, for Margarita's drawers were jammed full with them, but it was only a matter of time before she would discover that the spoon was missing, for Checha counted out the silverware every evening.

As she dug into the flower bed, Margarita unearthed a small doll. Its dress was soiled beyond recognition by the dirt and its hair was shaved down to the scalp. Thinking it best to leave the doll in its burial place, Margarita covered it up once again and began to dig in a nearby spot. While laying the silver spoon in the freshly dug hole, she recalled the story she had once overheard her mother telling her father about the day Mariela, her great-grandmother (who for some reason or another her mother and Tía María always referred to as Abuela Azul), discovered that a gravy ladle was missing from her silver chest.

Early one morning, as the servants were quietly going about their chores, Mariela sailed like a dark cloud past the front parlor where her daughters were reciting their French lessons after their tutor. As the girls soon discovered, she was on her way to Paolo's study to tell him about the stolen ladle. From the parlor they and their tutor, Señor Menéndez, could hear Mariela's screeching voice rising and falling. She demanded that he handle the situation immediately, for her heart could not bear the strain of having to deal with such matters. Although he knew that his wife had a heart as strong as an avocado seed, Paolo agreed to settle the matter. With his usual brusqueness, he ordered the housemaids outdoors and lined them up in the courtyard, threatening to dismiss all of them unless someone came forward and confessed. With lowered eyes and hands folded in front of them, the women stood in silence against the courtyard wall. As he passed through the kitchen on his way to the parlor where Mariela sat waiting in his favorite armchair (wringing her hands in her lap all the while), Paolo forbade Graciela and Tata from giving the women any food or drink.

Before taking their merienda, Paolo and Mariela retired to their bedroom to say their rosary together and nap. Although all of their daughters were also supposed to be resting, Maita (who had passed the story down to Rosa) slipped out of her bedroom and watched from the balcony as Tata placed the tinajones, the ceramic jars that were used to catch the rain, in the four corners of the courtyard and filled each one with water that she carried back and forth from the well in a clay pitcher. When she finished filling the jars, she began sponging down the women's bodies with the water and rinsing off their feet. Then she quenched their thirst with pieces of pan dulce that she moistened in the cool water from the tinajones. (Several of the women later claimed that the bread tasted as though it had first been soaked in rum.) All the while, the women stood very still in the scorching sun, their eyes hollow and dark, as though they had detached themselves from their surroundings.

Paolo waited until the noon shadows had stretched across the courtyard for one of the housemaids to come forward, but none came. In an effort to pacify his wife, he sent them to their quarters, where they were each flogged several times with a thick joint of sugar cane that left a cross-hatch pattern on their backs and their legs.

"It's in their blood to steal," Mariela told him later that same afternoon, as she knitted furiously in her rocking chair. She was surrounded by her daughters, who were working in silence on their embroidery. "You just can't trust any of them," she continued, "not for one minute."

"They are like children, mi corazón," Paolo agreed, without lowering his newspaper. "I was afraid that something like this would happen when we gave them their freedom."

"Well, perhaps some good will come out of this after all," Mariela responded with a sigh of resignation, as she pulled out a row of knitting she had meant to purl. "Hopefully all of the other servants will benefit from their example. But if it happens again, I'll have their heads shaved and branded and make them stand in the street for a whole week like common whores."

Later that same evening, shortly after Mariela had retired to her bedroom, Graciela found the missing ladle as she swept the cobwebs from beneath the breakfront in the dining room. When she told Tata about the discovery, the old woman went to Paolo's study, for he had stayed up past his usual bedtime in order to catch up on the work he had missed the previous day. In silence Tata laid the spoon on his desk. Unwilling to lose face in front of a servant, Paolo unlocked his top drawer and placed the silver ladle in his desk. Then he sent the old woman from the room. As far as he was concerned, he told her, the silver ladle had never been lost. The matter was closed.

The next day, at Mariela's request, Paolo asked Tata to count out the utensils in the silver chest. When she refused to blindly follow his request, claiming that Paolo would have to find another way to test her loyalty, he reported back to his wife, who was also rebuked by the old woman when Mariela burst into the kitchen like a tropical storm and made the same demand. Mariela then ordered Graciela—who was supposed to oversee the kitchen anyway—to undertake the task of counting out the silverware, after she'd put away the last of the cazuelas and the dinner dishes and wiped off the tile countertops. Miraculously, to everyone's great surprise and relief, Graciela discovered the missing ladle in the chest. Despite the discovery, the old woman was charged with counting out the silverware, in order to prevent another theft, her mistress told her. And so, each night thereafter Graciela sat at the kitchen table after everyone else had retired and separated the serving spoons from the soup spoons and the ladles, the teaspoons from the demitasse, the four-pronged dinner forks from the three-pronged salad forks—which were not to be confused with the dessert forks, Mariela reminded her every evening—the butter knives from the cutting knives, and the cutting knives from the steak knives. When she had finished laying out the other miscellaneous utensils in the chest, she'd stack the silverware in neat piles and begin counting them with the help of an old wooden abacus that had once belonged to Paolo when he was a child. After Graciela grew too old to do anything other than make a sofrito or sit on a stool in the corner of the kitchen with Lobo and suck on maté, her niece, Checha, took over the responsibility of sorting and counting out the utensils, though by that time most everyone had forgotten why she was doing it in the first place.

After she had buried the silver serving spoon, Margarita crept soundlessly across the courtyard in her bare feet, past the dome-shaped cage where the parrots huddled closely together on the bars. Reentering the house through the kitchen door, she climbed the back steps that led from the pantry to the servants' quarters and walked slowly past Tata's door, one foot after another—toe to heel—for the old woman had the ears of a lioness. Her door stood slightly ajar. Margarita paused for a moment, recalling the night she had fled to Tata's side during a storm. As the lightning flashed, illuminating the entire bedroom, Margarita found the old woman staring at the ceiling speaking in a foreign tongue she could not decipher. At first she was certain that Tata was awake, for her eyes were open and they moved wildly from side to side, as though they were following something invisible to Margarita's sight. When she called the old woman's name and Tata failed to answer, Margarita knew that she was still sleeping.

Now, as she stood before Tata's door, Margarita was struck by the silence and the absence of soughing and snoring. Then the thought occurred to her, as it had the night of the storm, that perhaps Tata was dead. Drawing in her breath, Margarita swung open the door and discovered that the old woman's room was empty.

Tata's old iron bed was pushed into the corner of the room. A large mahogany crucifix with a tortured Christ—with real hair—hung above it. A wooden rosary with a silver death's head at the place where the nuns at La Sagrada Familia, the private school she and her sister attended in Havana, had taught her to recite the Padre Nuestro, was draped across her pillow.

Margarita passed through the doorway to inspect the nightstand by the bed. There Tata had made a kind of makeshift altar. Tall cylindrical candleholders bearing the colorful images of saints were carefully arranged on a batiste cloth alongside a painted plaster statue of Santa Bárbara. At her feet lay apples and plátanos, a crudely carved amulet shaped like a cat, a scapular with a picture of la Virgen Loreto on one side and la Virgen de la Caridad de Cobre on the other, and the butt of one of Graciela's cigars. On the floor just in front of the nightstand was a porcelain bowl filled with water and bicania.

The only other piece of furniture in the room, aside from Tata's bed and nightstand, was a case filled with an odd assortment of colored glass vials. Margarita opened the door of the bookcase and selected one of the vials. It was filled with what looked like dried herbs and insect wings, which floated in a green, viscous liquid. As she drew out the cork, the room began to fill with a putrid smell that caused Margarita to quickly stopper the bottle and return it to its place on the shelf.

The top of the case was covered with photographs. One was of an infant—Maita perhaps—simultaneously sucking her right thumb and her left fist, most of which was in her mouth. She was propped up on a sea of pillows on the caoba bed in Margarita's parents' bedroom. The infant wore a cloth diaper and a sleeveless linen shirt tied at the collar with a satin ribbon, and her feet were encased in woolen booties. She also wore a pair of pearl earrings in her tiny earlobes and someone had tied a wide ribbon around her head like a hair band—though she had almost no hair to speak of. The bow fell across her forehead and one eye. Beside the photograph of the child was a postcard of her mother and father on their wedding day. They were standing next to a fountain Margarita didn't recognize, and her mother was cradling a spray of loose lilies in her arms. Her father, with his pencil-thin mustache and clenched jaw, was wearing a sprig of orange blossom in the top buttonhole of his guayabera.

In another photograph Mariela, Maita, and Tía Marta were posed in the courtyard in front of the dome-shaped birdcage, wearing ankle-length dresses and wide-brimmed hats. Tía Marta's hat had cherries stitched onto the side and Maita's and Mariela's had silk flowers. Even though the photograph was taken in black-and-white, Margarita could tell that Tía Marta wore dark red lipstick and she had brushed a plume of rouge on her cheekbones. Much to the family's scandal, she also insisted on having her picture taken with a lit cigarette in her hand, though privately she always said that she much preferred the taste of cigars. Maita's eyes were half open and her lips were shaped in a circle, suggesting that the camera had caught her off guard, and Mariela's mouth was pursed shut, as though she had swallowed a lemon whole. Standing beside the three women, Antonio held Rosa, who was just a baby, in his arms. She was dressed in a long white gown and a bonnet, which she was desperately trying to tear from her head. María, who looked as though she were six or seven, stood as stiff as a Beefeater in front of Mariela, whose gloved hands were resting on her shoulders. She was wearing a hat with a chain of daisies strung across the brim. The unnatural curve of her frilly taffeta dress suggested that she wore a crinoline slip underneath. Graciela and her sister, Carmencita, who had long since passed away, stood off in the background, wearing kerchiefs on their heads and matching white aprons, with their hands folded behind their backs. Margarita guessed that it was her mother's christening day.

The last two photographs on Tata's case were formal portraits of Margarita and Caridad in their First Communion dresses, taken at a professional studio in Havana. Margarita lifted her own photograph off the case and examined it closely. In it she wore a starched white satin dress and a long tulle veil stitched to a silver tiara that cascaded over her shoulders and nearly reached to the back of her knees. A small diamond-studded crucifix, which Margarita still kept in a jewelry box from El Encanto, hung around her neck. (Though the jewelry box was somewhat childish, Margarita still loved to watch the tiny ballerina that spun around to music when she opened the lid.) It was the only piece of jewelry that she wore, except for the pearl earrings her mother had given her. Someone had dry-brushed her lips red—a color she never would have chosen for herself, let alone have been permitted to wear—and painted her brown eyes green like her mother's. Her face was piously raised toward a luminous crucifix that was superimposed on the photograph and looked as though it would burst into flames at any moment, and her gloved hands were pressed together at chest level in prayer.

"Like the wings of the Holy Spirit," Madre Escaño had told them, as they practiced taking the host with pieces of unblessed bread that tasted like cardboard, though no one dared to say so out loud.

Although she could not recall having had the picture taken, Margarita remembered the events surrounding her First Communion day in perfect detail:

It was early in May—the month of Mary—just before her mother announced that they would be moving to Havana. The night before, Tata laid out her lacy white ankle socks and her underclothing on the cedar-lined hope chest that stood at the foot of her bed. (Just before her death, Rafaela had begun to embroider tiny pink rosebuds on the socks and the white underpants and the cotton slip that she would wear for the first time with her Communion dress.) As Margarita watched in silence, she noticed that Maita had left one of the rosebuds half finished. Tata put her veil and her dress on satin hangers, which she hung from the top of the closet door. Then she scratched deep lines with the sharp blades of her scissors on the bottom of Margarita's new patent leather shoes so that she wouldn't slip on the marble floor in the cathedral.

The old woman woke her early the next morning with a scalding glass of café con leche. As Margarita sipped the café, Tata chafed her with a warm, wet washcloth until the skin on her nut-brown cheeks glowed. When she had finished, they began the ritual of dressing. Margarita felt like a bride preparing for her wedding day.

A great party was planned in her honor—Rosa had invited half of the neighborhood to make up for the fact that Rafaela would not be there. As Margarita dressed, Graciela and Checha busily filled Mariela's crystal dishes with bite-size pieces of turrón de Alicante and Jijón and laid out trays of pasteles and bocaditos. Then they arranged in neat rows creamy breaded croquetas made with ground chicken and ham, which they had prepared with Tata's assistance the day before. Margarita had watched as the three women made the pastelitos. Tata had allowed her to help stuff the crescent-shaped pastries with spicy meat or guava paste. Next, they prepared the filling for the little sandwiches, dotting the chicken salad with pieces of hard-boiled eggs and pimientas and mixing mayonnaise into the ham and the shrimp and the lobster Tata had shredded in the grinder. Meanwhile, Graciela creamed asparagus into a paste and Checha mashed a bowl full of almonds with a wooden spoon and then mixed them together with sugar and milk to make horchata, Margarita's favorite sweet. After all of the sandwiches were made, Tata expertly cut off the crust and shaped the bread into triangles and circles and squares. Then she layered the remaining pieces of bread in ribbons and pinwheels, which Margarita helped her frost with cream cheese and decorate with sliced olives, pimientas, cilantro, or short sprigs of parsley that Tata grew in the courtyard. When they had finished, the kitchen table was a sea of multicolored geometrical shapes.

Knowing that Tata was occupied with other things that morning, Tía Marta and Tía María volunteered to set the dining room table with Mariela's linen tablecloth and napkins and her best china dishes—the ones that María reserved for the times that Padre Rabia and his assistant, Padre Morales, joined them for meals. While they arranged the silverware on the table, Rosa filled every room on the first floor with freshly cut roses Pancho and Luciano had gathered for her that morning from the garden.

As she stared at her photograph, Margarita could still recall the fluttering, spidery sensation that seemed to blossom in her stomach while she and her classmates waited in the vestibule for the signal from Madre Escaño's wooden clapper to begin processing to their assigned places. (She was to sit with her family in the pew that they occupied every Sunday.) She could still remember thinking that if she opened her mouth to accompany her classmates in singing the songs they had practiced for their Communion day, a cloud of yellow butterflies would escape from her churning stomach and fly through the air above her head.

When the time finally arrived for her to receive her first host, Margarita stepped into the center aisle with her classmates. Signaled a second time by the sound of the clapper, they moved toward the main altar and waited for a third clap, which told them to kneel as one person at the altar rail. She could still recall the feeling of the cold, hard marble on her bare knees. Perhaps it had been the weight of her dress, or maybe it had been the sweltering heat, combined with the sickeningly sweet smell of the incense that burned in the gold censer the altar boy swung back and forth from a chain—either way, when Padre Rabia and Padre Morales approached her holding the host above the silver chalice her great-grandparents had donated for their golden anniversary—followed by Madre Escaño, who held the Communion plate—she vomited on the priests' shoes and proceeded to pass out at Luis Villareal's (the boy who knelt beside her at the altar rail) feet. The last thing she heard was her aunt gasping aloud from the pew. María was scandalized.

The trip back to Tres Flores seemed endless at the time, though the house was located only a few blocks from the cathedral. Her father carried her on his shoulder, followed closely behind by Tía Marta and her mother, who led Caridad like a pull-toy with one hand and held a bottle of smelling salts, which she applied to her nose from time to time, in the other. (At the last minute Tata had decided not to accompany them to the ceremony, arguing that Graciela needed her help in the kitchen. Perhaps she had known all along what was going to happen.) Though she had already regained consciousness, Margarita buried her face in her father's shoulder and squeezed her eyelids shut, partly out of shame and partly to avoid her tía's eyes. (She knew for certain that María was glaring at her with disapproval.)

After her father had covered her with a comforter and quietly closed the bedroom door behind him, Margarita opened her eyes and stared up at the ceiling, praying that she would go into a deep coma and never wake. Then, and only then, she convinced herself, would Tía María take pity on her. With great disappointment, however, Margarita woke up the following morning to the growling of her empty stomach and received the news that Padre Morales was waiting for her in the front parlor. Padre Rabia had sent him to Tres Flores to give her her First Communion. And so, Margarita received her first host from the young priest's hands, while Caridad, Tata, and her mother stood at her side and her father held the Communion plate beneath her chin. Rosa could still recall the mixed expression of amusement and pity in Padre Morales's pale blue eyes as he held the moon-shaped host above Paolo and Mariela's silver chalice.

For days afterwards, Margarita prepared herself for the verbal lashing she was sure to receive at María's hands, but much to her surprise, her tía didn't say a word to her. As the days passed without event, Margarita reviewed in her mind the various punishments María might threaten her with in order to make her into a lady. The possibilities were limitless. After more than a week of silence, Margarita's terror mounted and peaked. Allowing her imagination to run free, she envisioned herself abandoned in the forest, left to be eaten alive by a swarm of large red ants. (Caridad added to her list of possibilities by suggesting that perhaps Tía

María might tie her to a chair and torture her, Chinese style, to the point of madness by dripping drops of water in steady rhythm on her forehead, or force her to shove sharp pieces of bamboo up her fingernails until she bled to death. Judging by the sober expression on her sister's face, Margarita could not be sure as to whether or not she was serious.)

To Margarita's great surprise, her punishment turned out to be relatively benign compared to the ones she and Caridad had conjured up together, for María only took to pinching the tender spots under her arms—places on her body her mother surely wouldn't notice—when she wasn't paying attention to Padre Rabia's endless sermons. After weeks of silent torture, and several indigo-colored bruises, Margarita realized that nothing in the whole wide world was preventing her from yelling out when Tía María pinched her. And so, she finally did so, causing all of the altar boys, including Luis Villareal, to laugh and Padre Rabia to glance in her direction and mournfully shake his head. From that time thereafter, María resorted to sending her withering looks that Margarita learned to ignore by simply turning her face away or pulling her veil down over her eyes.

* * *

Margarita placed the oval frame that held her portrait back on Tata's bookcase and looked around the room, noting that it was nearly bare. It reminded her of the narrow cells where the nuns slept at La Sagrada Familia. Of course none of the students was actually permitted to see their rooms, but one of the older girls who boarded at the school had discovered quite by chance that the cloisters emptied out when the nuns were at matins. And so those who were both courageous and curious traded their best holy cards and an assortment of small trinkets with the girl to go on a guided tour, during which they stole quick glances at the nuns' scrupulously clean bedrooms. To Margarita's great disappointment, she discovered that all of the rooms were identical—one after another had the same whitewashed walls and contained a washstand with a white porcelain basin and pitcher, a single bed, a portrait of the Holy Family, and a statue of la Virgen Loreto on a shelf which hung precariously above the door frame.

Sweeping Tata's room once again with her eyes, it occurred to Margarita that Tata, too, owned next to nothing, excluding the photographs, books, and the few items on her night table. She could almost count the old woman's possessions on two hands. There wasn't even a chest of drawers in her room.

Margarita crossed toward the closet and swung open the door. It too was bare, except for a white cotton robe that looked to Margarita like a bedsheet, and the pink-and-ivory cardigans with pearl buttons and sequined appliqué butterflies that Rosa had given to Tata over the years for her feast day. The cardigans hung, apparently unused, from the crooked shoulders of wire hangers that had rusted in the salt air, for Tata seldom wore anything other than a plain linen housedress and a starched white apron tied around her ample waist.

Though she had seen her the night before, Margarita knew that Tata's room had been unoccupied throughout the night. She was certain that this was so, for the loamy scent that was always about her was barely perceptible in the air. Standing at the closet door, Margarita recalled that Tata had come to her room the previous evening to wish her good night. She had sat on the edge of the bed singing softly into Margarita's ear as she scratched out mysterious words on her back with the callused tips of her fingers.

"¿Y tu abuela dónde está?" she had trilled into her ear with her dark brown voice—a warm marmalade voice that had rolled over her and soothed her to sleep for as long as Margarita could remember. While she sang her song, Tata rubbed a sweet-smelling mixture, which she had specially prepared from oils, herbs, and coconut, into the curve of Margarita's back. "You'll need this for tomorrow, mi amor," the old woman had whispered before kissing the tip of Margarita's ear.

Tata covered her with the comforter and sheets. While the old woman tucked in the edges, Margarita amused herself by making mountains beneath them with her bent knees. Inhaling the sweet scent of the ointment all the while, she studied her old Tata's face. Over the years it had remained virtually unchanged. Her hair was silver and violet, and she always wore it twisted into a swirling knot, which she pinned to the back of her head with wavy black hairpins. Sometimes her skin was the color of whipped chocolate, sometimes it was the color of saffron, depending on the hour of the day, but most of the time it was blueberry and plum. The undersides of her palms were gray and white, as though they had been rubbed in ashes, and the shadow of a mustache curved over her lips. Her father had always said that Tata's face had the features of a great baroque cathedral he had once seen in Spain, and her skin looked as though it had been cut from the ancient, leathery hide that stretched across the ceiling above the main altar. And though her eyes were soft and rheumy, they were still the eyes of a young girl, filled with movement and desire. Yet something deep within them suggested that she had witnessed many things—lived many lives.

As Margarita looked into the depths of the old woman's eyes, she recalled the day she had asked Tata where she'd come from. Tata was paring a mound of dark brown malangas, slicing the rootlike tubers into even halves with a sharp kitchen knife. Without raising her eyes from her work, the old woman told her that she had been a wedding gift from her great-grandfather to his bride when he first brought her to Cienfuegos, confirming the story Margarita had heard, and that Mariela had left her to Rafaela in her will.

"By the time you were born," she laughed, "I had already been given my freedom, but I chose not to leave Tres Flores."

"Why?" Margarita had asked.

"Because this is my home, corazón."

"But you were free. Why didn't you go?"

"If you look at it that way, none of us is really free, m'ija. Not you or I or even poor Lobo," Tata said, gesturing toward the flea-bitten dog, who waited patiently under the kitchen table for a morsel to fall to the ground.

"Which Lobo?" Margarita asked with a laugh, knowing that every dog that found its way into the courtyard at Tres Flores automatically bore the same name.

"All of the Lobos," Tata responded, playfully swatting Margarita on the head. "Take, for example, Graciela," she said, pointing to the old mulata, who stood at the stove frying dough in a skillet. "Her mother was a slave on her father's plantation. A part of her is free, and the other part remains enslaved. Like it or not, that's the way it is for you and me too, mi vida. No matter how you look at it," she said, pinching up the skin on her arm, "you and I are both prisoners as long as we have to carry these old hides around on our backs. But you know, m'ija, there's a part of you that always remains free. Something that none of us can name or put a finger on."

"I would have left," Margarita responded.

"You don't understand, m'ija. I chose to stay at Tres Flores. No one forced me to stay here. There's a big difference between choosing for yourself and being told what you can and cannot do. Life will offer you many choices, mi cielo, like a drawer filled with hair ribbons or a basket of yarn. Not that terrible things won't happen, which you won't be able to change or control. But the trick is to know the difference between when you are choosing for yourself and when you are allowing others to choose for you. Always remember, only you can choose to be happy, m'ija."

"But I'm afraid . . . afraid of losing you."

Tata laid the paring knife on the table, then reached to grasp Margarita's hand in hers. "Never be afraid, mi cielo. I'll always be with you. Besides," she added, patting Margarita's head, "nothing is ever really lost."

"But how about Abuelo and Abuela?" Margarita asked, recalling her grandparents, who lay buried side by side in the family cemetery on the outskirts of Cienfuegos.

"Don't you know that just because you can't see someone it doesn't mean they're not there with you?" Tata said, studying Margarita's face. "Why, at this very moment I can see your great-grandmother's nose and your mother's ears." The puzzled expression on Margarita's face caused Tata to smile. Margarita shrugged her shoulders and began arranging the spiral-shaped peels of skin from the malanga in mazelike patterns across the tabletop.

"Did you know that my name wasn't always Tata?" the old woman asked, causing Margarita to raise her eyes. "When your grandfather first bought me," Tata continued, glancing at the girl from time to time to see her reaction, "my name was Nácar. Your great-grandmother, Mariela, decided to change it because she thought that it did not suit me."

"Doesn't it bother you that she changed your name?" Margarita asked, leaning toward Tata with her elbows resting on the table.

Tata shrugged her shoulders, and without raising her eyes from her work confessed that she was grateful that at least Mariela hadn't named her after some obscure saint who had died on a pyre of burning embers, or some martyr with an arrow through her head, or after some remote Spanish pueblo.

Unable to see Tata's eyes, Margarita could not tell whether or not she was joking. She remained silent for quite awhile, thinking about all of the things the old woman had told her, when she suddenly burst out, "Tata, how old are you?"

Tata smiled and nodded her head. "Older than you can imagine, m'ija. Older than the number of beads on your great-grandfather's toy over there," she added, gesturing toward the ancient abacus Checha used to count out the silverware every evening.

"Like how old?" Margarita asked in a skeptical voice.

"So old, m'ija, that my bones have already begun to turn to sea salt and my hair to banana leaves," Tata laughed. "Long ago I lost count of my age, like all the others."

"All the others?" Margarita asked.

"Neither I, nor Graciela, nor Checha, nor Pancho really know how old we are."

"What do you mean? How could you not know how old you are?" Margarita asked with amazement, thinking of the three-tiered cakes and the fancy organdy dresses, the stiff, patent leather shoes and lacy ankle socks, and the pile of packages wrapped in brightly colored paper and ribbon, which the girls opened in front of all their friends at the elaborate birthday parties their mother organized for her and Caridad each year.

"There are no papers—no documents—to prove that any of us were born, let alone to find out how old we are."

"So in a way, you don't exist?"

"In your world, mi amor, none of us really exist."

Sensing Margarita's bewilderment, Tata continued. "When Graciela finishes frying her dough ask her how old she is. I bet she will tell you she was born the year that the lemon grove on her father's plantation was flattened by a hurricane. If you ask Pancho the same question, he will say he was born only a few days after the great wall of water swept all of the houses in his village into the sea."

"If that was true, he'd be dead too."

"No, m'ija," Tata said, shaking her head slowly back and forth. "Blasa, Pancho's mother, dreamed about the storm just before he was born. In her dream, she saw her brothers and sisters standing with her parents and her husband around the banyan tree that grew in front of their house. Their hands were clasped tightly together like the roots of the tree. Although she could not hear their cries, their mouths opened and closed like a fish struggling to catch its breath out of water. Unable to reach them, she helplessly watched their bodies bend and sway back and forth as they tried to hold out against the wind. Blasa said that purple fish and red conch shells rained down on them from the sky, and the earth around them turned from green to indigo. She woke just at the moment that their hands were torn apart and the circle was broken."

"So what happened?" Margarita asked impatiently.

"Pancho's father refused to put any stock in her dream, so he stayed in the village like a stubborn mule along with the rest of Blasa's family. And so, she and her three daughters fled to the mountains, where she gave birth to Pancho. When she and her children returned to the place where the village had stood only three days earlier, the ground was carpeted with dead fish and broken shells. Not even the banyan tree had been spared from the fury of the sea."

"So when were you born?"

"¿Quién sabe?" Tata laughed. "Probably when the mountains pushed their bald heads out of the boiling sea."

As Tata bent over to kiss her, Margarita wove her arms around the old woman's neck and pulled her ear close to her lips. "I wish you were my mother," she whispered.

Tata didn't answer right away. Instead, she looked at Margarita searchingly with loving eyes. "Do you know that your mother said the very same thing to me when she was just about your age?"

"And what did you say?"

"I told her the story that *my* tata told me long ago."

"Tell me," Margarita said, patting the edge of the bed in hopes of prolonging the old woman's stay.

"Once," Tata began, settling on the edge of the bed again and pulling herself into an upright position, "there was a woman who lived all alone, surrounded by a labyrinth of mountains. The mountain where she lived was separated from the sea by a great desert, a wasteland of sand and rock and stone. Day after day the old woman watched the sun rise over the sea—night after night she saw the moon climb across the dark back of the sky. Then one day she suddenly realized that she had grown tired of living all alone. It wasn't so much the silence that bothered her. In fact, it wasn't the least bit silent where she lived. From her mountaintop she could hear the sound of the waves breaking on the shore in the distance and the wind sweeping across the surface of the sea. In the evenings she listened to the music of the planets and the moon spinning above her in the sky. She was bothered because she was alone and had no one to share her happiness with. So the old woman plucked twelve whiskers from her chin," Tata said, pointing to the wiry white and black hairs that grew beneath her own chin, "two of each color. The first pair was red; the second yellow; another was blue;

the fourth was green; the fifth orange; and the last violet. She held the little hairs in the cup of her hand and began to blow upon them ever so gently. Soon she was surrounded by twelve boys and girls of varying shapes and colors. Then the old woman plucked several hairs from the top of her head. Once again she blew on the hairs, and all of the animals and all of the plants and all of the flowers and the trees of the world sprang up around them. With great joy and celebration she paired the children together in various combinations and sent them off in the four directions."

"In no time at all the valleys below the mountain where the old woman lived filled with churches and roads and schools and houses. The old woman was happy when she saw what she had done. She saw how good it was. And so she spent the rest of her days traveling from town to town visiting her children and grandchildren. And never again did she feel alone."

"So maybe you are my mother after all?" Margarita had asked her with a laugh that turned into a yawn. Tata only smiled back at her and closed Margarita's eyes with her thumbs. Then she whispered into her ear the prayer they recited together every night:

"Cuatro pilares tiene mi cama,

Cuatro angelitos que me acompañan."

The last thing Margarita remembered before she sank beneath the surface of consciousness was the sound of the breeze whispering through the screen of palm leaves outside her window.

* * *

Shrugging her shoulders, Margarita closed Tata's bedroom door behind her, recalling that the old woman often disappeared without explanation, sometimes for several days at a time. This was nothing new or unusual. She always returned with dark blue circles beneath her eyes—darker than her plum-colored cheeks. It was as though she hadn't slept for centuries. Even Tía María knew better than to ask Tata where she'd been.

Following her return, the old woman would spend the entire day in the kitchen, humming and swaying her hips back and forth as she heated coconut milk, together with cinnamon sticks and sugar, in a medium-size saucepan for coco quemado. When she had finished, Tata would carve out the insides of halved oranges from Paolo's tree for natilla. Margarita loved to watch her pour sugar over the sweet custard and then press it with an iron that had been heated over the coals in the oven. When she had finished, she began shelling almonds that Margarita would later press into the soft centers of her famous sugar-coated sweet rolls, which were rising in a large porcelain bowl the old woman had covered with a dishcloth. Tata seemed unaware of Graciela's sour looks or the way she stormed around the room, slamming cabinet doors, sighing loudly, and making a dry, clacking sound against the roof of her mouth with her tongue in order to signal her displeasure at the fact that the old woman had invaded her territory and taken over her kitchen. But soon the smell of almonds and burnt sugar baking in the oven soothed even Graciela and made her forget that Tata had dirtied so many dishes and pans and scattered flour across her countertops and her newly mopped floor.

Margarita passed the walk-in linen closet and then paused for a moment to listen at her parents' bedroom door. Feeling certain that they were still sleeping, she crossed the hallway to her own room, which was diagonal to theirs.

Once in her bedroom, Margarita became conscious of the dull elastic pain that had begun to fan out from her lower back and knot the muscles below her stomach into fists. She also noticed that her button-sized breasts had grown sensitive and sore, her waist felt thick, and her legs were as swollen and heavy as pillars. Feeling uncomfortable and unclean, Margarita washed herself with warm soapy water and placed a terry cloth washrag between her legs in order to catch the thin stream of blood that continued to flow from her wounded body. After she had finished, she sat on the hope chest her grandmother had begun filling for her when she was first born, and dusted her neck and her stomach with powder. Then she dabbed cologne behind her ears, recalling that Maita had always insisted that ladies should powder their bodies, perfume their hair and the creases on their arms and behind their knees so that men would think them gardens filled with opulent-smelling flowers.

"When I was a child," Rafaela once confided to her granddaughters, "my grandmother told me the same thing. For months I walked around carrying a bouquet of flowers in my arms with the hope that I would be taken for a garden. Everyone in the neighborhood started calling me 'la floridita.' "

As Margarita recalled Rafaela's words, it occurred to her that wherever she went her grandmother always carried with her a linen handkerchief dampened with scented water, which she tucked into her sleeve and held to her nose from time to time.

Suddenly Margarita recalled the wound she had received in the night. Perhaps this was the great sacrifice, to which Tía María had referred, that she would have to endure. But, she wondered with mounting alarm, would she have to sacrifice her own life? What if she bled to death?

Margarita's thoughts were interrupted by the muffled pat of her father's footsteps, which sounded from across the hall as he moved around the dressing room. At the sound, she lay back on her bed and watched the dawn split open like an overripe fruit outside her window.

Just as the first rays of light began to thin out the darkness, Pedro awoke with a start. Without opening his eyes, he listened for the almost imperceptible noise that had awakened him to sound once again. Although the bedroom remained silent—except for the quick, uneven breathing of someone beside him—he sensed with great uneasiness that something stood just outside of his bedroom door. After a moment he turned onto his side, convinced that he had imagined the sound. It was then that he recalled that his wife lay next to him, fitted into the curve of his side, as though she were joined to him at the ribs. He leaned over and pressed his face into her hair, taking in her soft warmth and the fragrance that was, after all of their years together, unmistakable to him. It was the scent of jasmine and sandalwood that he would always remember her by.

Rosa had kicked off their purple comforter during the night. Her legs were carelessly splayed open across the bed like a pair of wings, in a position she never would have assumed had she been conscious. In the dim morning light Pedro noticed that the cloth-covered buttons on her nightgown had nearly all come undone. He ran his eyes freely over her body, pausing at the caramel-colored ovals of her breasts, the soft curve of her swollen belly, now divided by a thin brown line, and the dark tangle of hair between her thighs. She would never have allowed him to gaze at her this way, he thought to himself. Though they had been married nearly sixteen years, she was as shy and modest in his presence as a virgin bride and would only allow him to catch fractured glimpses of her naked body as she undressed behind the rosewood screen in their bedroom. Over the years, he had memorized her changing scents, like a man who was half blind, and the various shapes that her body took as she lay prone beneath him in the darkness.

Pedro gazed at his wife until the morning light that entered the room through the tilted shutters gave definite shape to the furniture and the vendors began calling out like night birds in the street. Then he raised himself into a sitting position on the edge of the bed and glanced around the bedroom his in-laws had insisted that they take over on their wedding night. Rafaela had once told him that all of the Moro and Miramar children had been conceived and born in the hand-carved caoba bed that her father had commissioned for his young bride when they first arrived in Cienfuegos, and she was determined that her grandchildren would not be the exceptions.

Gently covering Rosa with the purple comforter, Pedro went into the adjoining room to dress. There the mulata had already laid out his clothing and filled the washbasin on the marble-top stand with water from the well. According to his precise instructions, she had polished his tall black riding boots the night before and stood them in the corner of the room alongside his chiffonier. Standing in the doorway, Pedro stared absently at the roses that were carved into the legs of the furniture. But instead of seeing them, he was thinking about all of the things he intended to accomplish in the cane fields over the next few days before returning to Tres Flores.

Bending over the washbasin, he splashed his face with water and then began chafing his cheeks briskly back and forth, causing the course black hair to stand upright. With a camel-hair brush that had once belonged to his father, Pedro methodically lathered his throat and his cheeks with the stiff white cream the mulata had warmed for him in the coal oven. He stared at his reflection in the mirror, noting that even though he was well into middle age and growing visibly older (and perhaps had gained too much weight), he had still managed to retain his good looks.

"Qué guapo eres, caballero," he murmured to his reflection in the mirror, as he scraped a straight razor down the side of his cheek and then wiped the hot, peppered lather onto a green-and-white cabana towel that hung over his shoulder. "You can still turn the girls' eyes in your direction." Stretching his neck forward like a tortoise from its shell, he passed the sharp blade over the soft, fleshy folds of his neck, leaving a trail of bloody beads in its wake.

Pedro hung his father's shaving mirror on a nail above the washbasin and turned his head sideways in order to better inspect the underside of his chin. His mother had always told him that in profile he looked identical to his father. Standing before the mirror with the razor pressed against his neck, Pedro recalled the many times he had crouched in the corner of the bathhouse that adjoined the house on Calle Semilla. From his hiding place he would watch his father perform the very same ritual that he was now performing—a ritual Don Pedro undertook with his wife's assistance every morning.

Unaware of his son's presence, Don Pedro soaked in the slipper-shaped metal tub in the bathhouse. He always smoked a cigar and read the newspaper while Fina squatted on a low stool behind him, scrubbing his back and his shoulders with a coarse sponge which she occasionally lathered up with a cake of black soap. The room, Pedro recalled, was like a Turkish bath, filled with a soupy gray mist that rose in a cloud from the scented waters of the tub. Together his parents would sing "Ciboney" as his mother washed his father's hair and then shaved his face with the same razor Pedro now held in his hand, carefully maneuvering around the lighted cigar that he clenched between his teeth. When she had finished, she would pour clean, warm water from an earthen pitcher onto his head and pat dry his face and his neck with a hand towel before applying lotion to his cheeks and a styptic pencil to the places where she had nicked him. Sometimes Don Pedro stayed in the bathhouse for hours afterwards, insisting that he, like his idol Napoleon, did his best thinking in the tub.

Though his parents never knew it, Pedro thought to himself as he began stropping his father's straight razor, he had witnessed many things—many things, such as the time he had caught them dancing together in their bedroom late at night—his father pantless and wearing a ribbed T-shirt and Fina in her cotton slip—to a rumba their old Victrola scratched out in the dark. The memory of his parents gliding across the room cheek to cheek—with their arms extended like wings and their toes pointing out—as the stylus dragged across the record, brought a smile to his face.

The sound of the mulata arranging the breakfast dishes on the glass-top table on the balcony drew Pedro's thoughts back to the dressing room. He hastily splashed his face and his armpits with the gray water from the basin and then dressed in the shifting shadows that entered the room from the balcony. After he had pulled on his riding boots he selected an extra pair of pants and several shirts from the drawers of the chiffonier, which he folded and placed in a small canvas backpack. Usually he spent several days at Treinta Sierras, sometimes sleeping on a blanket beneath the night sky with Tomás, the old guajiro who oversaw the plantation in his absence, or in the house with the whitewashed walls and the thatched roof. Lifting his hat from a peg on the wall he paused for a moment in order to choose a thick black cigar from the wooden humidor on his dressing table.

*　*　*

The smell of burnt sugar and almonds was brushed thickly onto the breeze. As Casandra rolled up the rattan screens that hung from the ceiling of the balcony, Pedro stood at the doorway taking account of her shape, which was partially visible beneath the loose-fitting shift she wore to conceal her thickened waist. She seemed unaware that her swollen breasts wept, causing dark blossoms to unfold across the front of her dress. Though she was only fifteen, she had the features of a Mayan goddess carved like sacred inscriptions on some ancient stone. Her skin was light brown, her cheeks were thick and pronounced, her nose wide and flat, and her generous lips were the color of the soil in the cane fields where Pedro had first taken her.

Conscious that his eyes were upon her, the girl spun around and met his gaze before disappearing into the shadows of the house. Though she was no longer in view, Pedro continued to shift uneasily in his seat. Her eyes. Somehow the look in her eyes made him feel as though he owed her some age-old debt which he had somehow overlooked or failed to pay—something more than the small tokens and silver coins that he offered up at her altar from time to time. It was a look that he could never quench or satisfy. And so, when he came to her in the evenings, he had always made sure to draw the mosquito netting that hung from her bedpost over her face like some unholy bride, for the way she stared up at him in the darkness with her stony, hollow eyes made him doubt his own abilities.

As he waited with mounting impatience for the mulata to return with his food, Pedro examined the thin, hair-fine cracks that spread out like delicate webs across the surface of the mint green porcelain plates. He took up the knife that lay alongside the plate and rubbed the silver handle between his thumb and forefinger, across the place where the rambling rose pattern had already begun to wear smooth. The silverware had been passed down to his wife from her mother, who had, in turn, received it from her own mother. It had crossed the ocean, Rafaela once told him, encased in gray flannel pouches with blue piping and satin ties. Mariela had chosen the rambling rose pattern as a symbol of the pain and the beauty of life. Before Paolo built Tres Flores, she requested that the pattern be repeated throughout the house. And so it was inscribed on the caoba set in their bedroom and dressing room, stenciled onto the mirrors and the walls, woven into the woolen carpets, carved into the trim in the dining room and the parlor, and wrought into the iron gates on either side of the circular drive and in the courtyard.

Pedro tapped the silver knife against the side of his plate as the mulata stepped onto the balcony carrying an octagonal metal tray decorated with large cabbage roses which Rosa had hand-painted herself along with the small oval mirror that hung beside her writing table.

"¿Caballero?" she asked offering him a platter of vaporous sweet rolls coated with burnt sugar and almonds. Fixing his gaze in another direction, he nodded his head in his usual brusque manner as the girl placed two rolls, which had knit together while baking in the oven, on his plate with a pair of silver tongs that looked like lions' claws.

As he snapped his rose-colored napkin open and spread it across his thighs, Pedro could feel the girl's eyes upon his back.

Her insolence made him flush with anger. Thinking that she ought to be domesticated, he had brought her out of the fields to work at Tres Flores. The results of his good intentions, however, had been more than disappointing, for shortly after her arrival she became another person. Not only did she avoid his company during the daytime when they happened to be in the same room together, but she also seemed afraid and only responded when she was spoken to. Though she continued to rebuff his advances and had taken to locking her bedroom door at night to keep him out, Pedro demanded that she serve him his morning meal, which he always took alone on the back balcony. It seemed as though the more she spurned him, however, the more obsessed he became. Night after night as he lay alone in bed, he thought about this girl, whom he had first seen bending over a pile of cut cane with her shift riding up her brown thighs and her rounded, untouched breasts swinging freely like pomegranates from side to side. In his daydreams she lay naked beneath him, her mouth wide open with desire. She was the one who demanded that he break her, as he rocked on top of her and nursed on her firm, ripened breasts, causing her to give out small animal cries. She was wild and unbridled, bursting with a fiery passion that he alone could quell. Perhaps he had made a mistake bringing her to the house, he chastised himself as he stole a quick glance at the girl, taking her out of her natural environment.

"¿Ya, Caballero?" the mulata asked, suddenly interrupting his thoughts.

"¡Basta, niña!" Pedro answered gruffly, gesturing her away with a quick nod and covering his plate with his hand. As the girl covered the remaining rolls with a checkered cloth and placed the basket back on the tray, he pushed his coffee cup to the edge of the table and rang it several times with a spoon. At the sound, she lifted a silver pot that had also belonged to Mariela from the serving cart and began pouring out the steaming liquid within, partially filling his cup. Then she mixed the coffee with freshly boiled milk, which overflowed into the saucer as she poured it out.

"¡Basta!" Pedro called out with an impatient flourish of his hand, causing the mulata to move away from the table with the saucepan of boiled milk. Without a word she backed into the shadows and stood against the wall with her hands woven together behind her. Her dark, scarablike eyes, which appeared to be lidless, were fixed all the while on his boots.

Pedro spooned a generous helping of sugar into his café con leche. My sugar, he thought with pleasure, as he stirred the grainy crystals into his coffee and then tore the sweet rolls on his plate apart and smothered them with runny clots of slightly rancid butter. He dunked the rolls into his coffee cup, causing the foamy brown liquid to overflow into the saucer once again. As the bread soaked and bloated like a sponge, the butter began to shimmer like gold on the surface of the café.

When he had had his fill of the bread Pedro drained his coffee cup, leaving only the pale white skin of boiled milk clinging to the porcelain rim. Then he sucked the sugary coating from the sweet rolls off his fingertips, cleared his throat loudly, and spat over the balcony railing. As though she had been given a command, the girl immediately began clearing his dishes away, leaving only his coffee cup and the silver spoon. He watched her stack them in an uneven pyramid and vanish into the house with the metal tray balanced on one hand over her shoulder.

After a few minutes she reappeared in the courtyard below him wearing the Spanish mantilla and the ebony combs Pedro had brought for her from Havana in her hair. The early morning sun played off her head, making the highlights in her long, coarse hair appear to be bluish green. Pedro leaned forward in his chair with his knees slightly parted and his elbows resting on his thighs to get a better view of the girl.

The color of the waves, he thought to himself as he admired the cape of hair that hung down to her waist. Absently rubbing the insides of his thighs, he wondered whether the infant he had seen her carrying in her arms when he first arrived at Tres Flores was his own. Yet the child's eyes were as blue as the sea, he recalled. To the best of his knowledge it was a color that no one in his family shared. Who knows, he thought, shrugging his shoulders, perhaps some long-lost relative from generations back had blue eyes. Who knows?

Pedro knew that his unexpected appearance at Tres Flores had caught the mulata by surprise, for she had disappeared from the room when she saw him, allowing him only a momentary glimpse of the child, whom he had yet to see a second time. Afterwards, he dared not inquire about the child's origins, and the mulata, who rarely spoke directly to him anyway, volunteered no information. Nevertheless he felt certain that the child was his, for despite its dark skin and pale eye color, he imagined that he could discern their resemblance to one another. In addition, Pedro thought to himself with a flush of jealousy, she wouldn't dare give herself to another man in my absence.

Knowing that one day he would have to give her up, Pedro considered the possibility of confessing, but in his heart he knew only too well that he would never gather up the courage. Besides, he argued with himself, both of the Padres would recognize my voice at once, even if I tried to disguise it.

Casandra moved toward the dome-shaped cage and swung open the heavy door. From the balcony it looked like a giant hive. She placed several white saucers—some filled with water and others with slices of overripe fruit—on the bottom of the cage. From Pedro's vantage point the fleshy pink-and-red fruit looked like bloody wounds splayed open on the plates. Reclining back in his chair, Pedro casually pared his fingernails on the balcony and observed with detachment the mulata, who was performing what had become for her almost a sacred rite. It occurred to him as he watched her that he had never bothered to ask her her real name. He had always called her Flor and she had always answered. It was as simple as that.

Conscious that her patrón watched her, the girl lifted her thin arms into the air and began clapping her hands together and making a sound, which came from somewhere deep within her throat, like dry rattles. Upon hearing her voice, the huge tropical birds rose to the top of the cage with an agitated beating of their moss-colored wings. From his height Pedro witnessed the spectacle—a carnival of flashing color, creasing and bending and folding before his eyes. He watched until the birds settled on the bottom of the cage once again and began tearing apart the fruit with their sharp beaks. By that time the girl had disappeared into the shadows of the courtyard.

Pedro looked into the sky and knew by the position of the sun that he should have been well on his way to the cane fields. He was certain that Francisco had already pulled around his motorcar to take him to the stables at Treinta Sierras where Tomás awaited his arrival. (He had already sent a tearful Manuel back to Havana, threatening to dismiss the old man when he returned to the city for having allowed his mistress to travel to Tres Flores in her condition.) Placing his folded napkin on the glass-top table, he started from his chair.

Her whole body glided weightlessly just beneath the pale milky skin of the sky, and the sun—unlike any she had ever felt before—pressed like hot polished stones against her eyelids and warmed her dark, blisterless skin. She was surrounded by a ring of dolphins arching in and out of the waves, and then her legs knit together and turned the color of mother-of-pearl, and her hair blossomed around her like a flower, the way it used to when she would lie back in the bathtub as a child pretending she was a mermaid. Old Chang sat across from her, cross-legged in a bed of waxy pink-and-red flowers, laughing like some toothless Buddha as he combed out her long opal-colored hair with a conch.

Turning onto her side, Rosa awoke with the sensation of drowning. She ran the palm of her hand over the empty space beside her on the bed, knowing that it hadn't been long since Pedro had risen, for the pillow still held the hollow curve of his head. Closing her eyes once again, Rosa recalled the dream that still lingered just beneath the surface image of Chang. It was a recurring dream that she had had since she was a child. Often it divided itself up into consecutive nights.

At first she saw herself as a young girl walking past Chang, the old Chinaman who sold fruit-flavored ice cream and orange granizados on the street corner across from the cathedral. Then her legs carried her without her consent to a narrow alley where the darkest shadows gathered ominously together in thick, oily pools. As she approached the alley she became filled with some nameless fear as though something that had sprung full-blown from a dark corner of her memory—with head, hands, feet, and wings—was pursuing her. It was as though she had taken a wrong turn somewhere and had somehow lost her bearings. She knew that she was moving in the wrong direction, though she could not stop her forward motion. Thinking that it would be best to retrace her steps, she turned her head around only to find that the mouth of the alley had sewn itself shut behind her. She searched in vain for an outlet—an opening—but there was none. Knowing she had no choice but to keep on running forward, she continued down the alley. As her speed increased, the street began to tilt and slope and buckle beneath her and the walls on either side of her narrowed to a point of violet light at the end of the alley. The sound of her feet hitting against the pavement slapped a wild hubbub around her. Suddenly the street fell away from her and she was facing an insurmountable wall stained with black blossoms of blood. At the center of the wall was a red wooden door through which only a child could pass.

As always, the dream ended at the red door and Rosa was drowning in a liquid pool that was her own.

A sharp, exquisite pain that slowly bloomed through her body caused Rosa to draw in her breath. She knew from its intensity that within hours the child would come, nearly a month ahead of time. Perhaps it had been the strain of the trip to Cienfuegos, or the fact that she had insisted upon lifting her carry-on bag by herself, rather than allowing Manuel to handle it. Perhaps she should have stayed in Havana as Pedro had wanted. If anything happened to the baby he would be the first to tell her that she had only herself to blame.

Although the bedroom had already grown quite warm, Rose found herself trembling uncontrollably at the thought of what lay ahead. The idea of giving birth again filled her with fear. Somehow it didn't matter that she had already gone through it twice before.

A passage through the vale of death, she heard a thin blue voice call out in her head. *Each pain brings you closer to her.*

At that moment the child dug its heels into her side and twisted about, causing the soft brown rind of her stomach to rise and fall.

"You are impatient, my son," Rosa whispered aloud, lightly running the palm of her hand across the ridge of her belly. "But if you must come, then come, Pedrecito." It was then that she noticed that most of the buttons on her nightgown had come undone.

Fingering the flowers carved into the caoba bedpost, Rosa was reminded of the night she had first submitted to her husband. She had never known another man before him. Recalling their wedding night, she could see herself propped up on the pillows like an invalid, watching Pedro pull off his riding boots in the next room. She switched off the light on the nightstand and slid under the purple comforter while he washed his face in the water basin and dried it with a hand towel. As she listened to the plashing sound of the water, it occurred to her how very strange it felt to be lying in her mother's bed—the bed she and María had jumped on in their stocking feet when Rafaela wasn't watching and had hidden under as they played hide-and-seek together— waiting for a man who was almost ten years older than she. A man who was now her husband of almost sixteen years, she had thought, raising her right hand to inspect her wedding band. A man, she suddenly realized at the sight of her ring, whom she barely knew.

When Pedro reentered the bedroom the moon, which seemed to sympathize with her plight, disappeared behind a cloud. He rolled her onto her back in the darkness and roughly pulled her white nightgown above her waist. Thinking that it would be wrong to resist, Rosa submitted to his touch, allowing her body to become as pliant as moistened clay. When the moonlight swept through the bedroom once again, she fixed her eyes on the red fringe that hung from the shade of the lamp on her mother's nightstand. For what seemed to be an eternity, she watched the beaded silk threads tremble in silhouette in the breeze. She could still recall the crushing weight of him as he moved on top of her. After he had finished, he kissed her forehead, turned onto his side, and fell asleep almost instantly.

Only after she was certain that Pedro was asleep did Rosa feel her way to the dressing room where she purified herself, in the moonlight, with the water from the porcelain basin where he had washed. When she returned to her place at his side, she realized that Pedro had stretched himself out, taking up more than half of the bed. Perched onto the edge of the mattress, she stared at the spot on the back of his head where his hair had already begun to thin. As she traced the slope of his shoulders with her eyes, it struck Rosa that from behind Pedro resembled her father.

With bended knees, she thought, she had taken part in the cosmos that first night—the great plan, as Rafaela used to say. But even now she still held the memory of the pain and the loss. Somehow she had imagined—somehow she had been made to believe—that their first night together would be like the unfastening of the heart-shaped silver locket that her mother had given her for her fifteenth birthday. For years she had prepared herself for that moment, but it had been more like the sudden flight of expectation she'd always felt as a child after she'd torn open the last of her birthday presents and discovered that she had not received the thing she had failed to ask for but really wanted. It had not been anything at all like she had supposed it would be. The only memory that lingered the next morning was the thought that she had been wounded, the feeling that she had been spoiled and made unclean. No one had prepared her for the disappointment and regret. No one. She realized now that although she had been nearly twenty years old at the time, that night marked the moment in her life when her youth began to slip away and something inside her cracked like a rib of ice.

If only he had spoken to me, Rosa thought to herself. If only he had uttered a single word of love or consolation. But perhaps words should have been unnecessary. Perhaps *she* had gotten it all wrong after all. Perhaps she should have asked. Nevertheless, she had wept through her wedding night, with her head buried in her pillow so as not to wake Pedro—so as not to allow him to see her cry.

"Never let them see the seams in the garment," the nuns at the convent school had taught them, as Rosa and her classmates sat side by side in a sewing circle.

"Ladies never raise their voices. Ladies never cry aloud. Never," Rosa whispered. She knew the words by heart. They had rung out in her head on her wedding night, and then rung out nine months later as she lay stretched across her mother's bed, with clenched teeth and hands wrapped like the rambling roses around the caoba bedpost, soundlessly giving birth to Caridad.

Even back then, when she and Pedro lay with their arms wrapped tightly around one another, she had had only her own thoughts, only her own foolish dreams and desires. But she was certain that Pedro knew nothing of her thoughts, though his seemed so transparent to her. Despite Tía Marta's claim that women's intuitions were superior to men's, she could not help but feel somewhat envious of her husband, for he always seemed to need so much less than she did. His needs were so easily satisfied, almost like a child's.

From time to time, Rosa tricked herself into believing she could leave him, knowing all along that she never would, for life and circumstances beyond her control had left her totally unprepared to stand alone. So over the years, the losses they had sustained together (not to mention the children) bound them together. First, her own father died unexpectedly, causing her to miscarry their second child. Then Don Pedro and her mother left them, then Fina, and finally, Tía Marta. In the years that followed, they shared their memories together and retraced the sacred grounds of their pasts. And so, though the thorn-covered wall that had existed between them from the start still remained, their lives had become intertwined like fine silver chains in a polished box.

Maybe it's all my fault, Rosa chastised herself, while shifting onto her side and adjusting Pedro's pillow under her belly for support. Maybe I'm the one who's failed. For years now, they had sailed on a fragile, glassy blue sea, avoiding confrontation and open conflict; but suddenly something had come between them. A stone thrown carelessly in the middle of the path. It was something that Rosa feared to name or put into words, though she knew it existed, for she could feel it in her husband's embrace, feel it in his irritation and impatience and in the way that he avoided her eyes.

"Maybe I should never have married him in the first place," she murmured. At that moment the packet of letters, which she had tied together with a grosgrain ribbon after the birth of their first child and buried at the bottom of a drawer in her escritorio, nudged its way into her thoughts. She recalled the image of Fernando—a scarcely recognizable shape partially concealed in the shadows at the back of the cathedral the day she married Pedro. She would never forget Tata's words to her as the old woman pinned down her veil—the same veil her mother and her grandmother had worn on their wedding days—and fastened the satin-covered buttons that ran all the way down the back of Rosa's gown:

"There are three men in a woman's life: her first love, her true love, and her husband."

"And which one is Pedro?" she had asked sarcastically, unable to suppress her annoyance at Tata's poorly timed commentary.

"You tell me," Tata had responded, with a hairpin clenched between her lips. Rosa was taken aback at the old woman's words, for she suddenly realized that Tata had known about Fernando all along.

As she watched Pedro slip the silver band on her finger, Rosa could not help but recall Tata's words. And though she was standing at the altar rail as motionless as a statue at Pedro's side—as though she had temporarily ceased to breathe—she felt a part of herself breaking loose and running down the aisle toward the place where she was certain Fernando watched her exchange vows with a man, he had warned her, with whom love might never come. As they knelt at the front altar with Mariela's mantilla draped over their shoulders and Pedro lifted her bridal veil to give her a kiss, she suddenly sensed Fernando's absence. She knew that he had left the cathedral and that she would never see him again.

Weeks later the story spread that Fernando had joined the navy and left the island. Then Amparo Aragona told her at a dinner party that he had run off to Italy, abandoning a girl they had both known in school with his child.

"Didn't it strike you as odd that Ana Mari just disappeared with no explanation? Well, I'll tell you, querida, she wasn't just spirited off by goblin men. Fernando was a womanizer," Amparo insisted in a casual, offhand way, which nonetheless betrayed the obvious pleasure she took in breaking the news to her friend. "He made eyes at all of the daughters of his mother's rich clients. Didn't his mother make dresses for your mother and your grandmother, too?" Amparo asked with an innocent air. "She was really quite a seamstress, don't you think? Anyhow," she continued, picking up the thread of their conversation once again, "he used to send all the girls scented letters that professed his eternal love. I'm sorry, I thought you knew," Amparo said with a laugh, as she noticed the plume of color that had risen up Rosa's neck. "I thought everyone knew. But of course, the innocent are always the last to find out. Did you know it was rumored that his mother was married to a mulato, though no one actually saw him, for he died long before Fernando was born? Anyhow, it's neither here nor there," she added with a wave of her hand that caused the large diamond ring on her finger to sparkle, "we're both spoken for now, aren't we?"

That was the last that Rosa ever heard about the shy young man who used to deliver the hand-sewn linen dresses her mother and her grandmother always wore. Over the years, during the still points of her marriage when she was filled with doubt and desires Pedro could not seem to quench or extinguish, Rosa's thoughts had always turned toward Fernando, despite Amparo's claims. Though she was certain that he had long since ceased to resemble the boy she had once known, the memory of him came to her every now and then during the quiet afternoons when the girls were in school and she passed the time rearranging her past and imagining another life for herself.

Turning onto her back, Rosa pictured the wild expression on her father's face when she had teasingly told him she wanted to marry Fernando instead of Pedro.

"And then the next thing you know, you'll be bringing me grandchildren with cloven feet and curly tails and dirt under their fingernails!" he had shouted with unexpected anger. "That's exactly what would happen if a young girl like you—whom we have tried to raise, I might add, with a sense of pride and respectability—married below her rank."

The memory of her father's face twisted and deformed with emotion frightened her even still. As she adjusted the purple comforter around her legs, Rosa assured herself that she had made a wise decision by agreeing, without any argument, to marry the man her father had selected for her like one of the cigars from his humidor.

"It never would have worked, Fernando," Rosa whispered in a barely audible voice, as though he were standing nearby. "Papi never would have allowed it. And even if we had gone ahead . . . against his will . . . he would have treated you like one of his hired hands . . . as someone beneath him. It's best that I married Pedro instead of you."

S uddenly conscious of the scuff of footsteps in the hall just outside her door, Margarita opened her eyes. She didn't remember having fallen back to sleep. A soft, diffused light filtered into the room, slowly spreading its pale fingers across the marble floor. Margarita rose from her bed and crossed to the French doors that opened onto the balcony.

The first shadows of the morning had begun to withdraw into the mouths of the alleys and the gated courtyards, and the sound of church bells echoed through the air. The street in front of Tres Flores was filled with activity—a great, living river of people, pulsing and pulling and shoving their way toward the plaza. Women wearing brightly-colored bandannas and skirts, who shepherded their children down the avenida past the iron gates that separated Tres Flores from the commotion of the crowd, hurried past the fruit vendors who lined the streets. At first Margarita wondered at the sight, but then she remembered that it was the morning of the fiesta, something she had completely forgotten in her distraction.

Margarita saw Pancho swing open the gates for her father's motorcar. Though she did not dare go out on the balcony, from her place she could see the tilted silhouette of his hat through the back window of the car and the waxed handles of his mustache. She watched as Francisco slowly pulled the old Buick out into the avenida and was swept away by the swift-moving current of people.

Knowing that her father would be gone for several days and that her mother would probably remain resting in her bedroom for most of the morning, Margarita decided to venture out on her own without her parents' permission. She and Caridad were forbidden to take part in the carnival because, their father insisted, the guajiros and the mulatos had turned the Virgin's feast day into a pagan bacchanal. (Though their father never knew it, Rosa had agreed—after days of listening to Margarita whine and complain—to allow them to drag their chairs to the windowsill after Pedro had left the house and watch the revelers parade down the street.) As Margarita watched the throng of people moving down the street, it occurred to her that the fiesta was one of the few occasions when the citizens of Cienfuegos joined together in celebration. Whenever there was a party in the neighborhood, she recalled, la soga always made its appearance, like a silent chaperone. Though it was never discussed, the rope still served as a visible reminder of the differences that separated the blacks and the mulatos from the whites.

After she'd pulled on her canvas shoes and selected a felt hat from her closet shelf—with a floppy brim, she noted in the mirror, that partially concealed her face—Margarita slipped down the back stairs to the kitchen. She crept soundlessly by Graciela, who was bent over the stove, slowly adding minced garlic and finely diced onions to the sofrito that was simmering in her black skillet. Margarita knew that she could pass through the kitchen without attracting the old woman's notice because only the day before she had discovered, quite by chance, that Graciela had begun to lose her hearing, for the crash of a large clay plot that fell into the courtyard from the balcony railing failed to interrupt the quick rhythm of her fingers as she sat on a stool near the hive-shaped cage sorting out a sack of red beans and lentils into separate bowls.

As she carefully pushed open the screen door, Margarita's gaze fell upon the young women who came to Tres Flores twice a week to wash the laundry and assist with the household chores. The older women who accompanied them squatted with their backs against the courtyard wall. Tata ordinarily sat among them. Margarita noticed at once that her place was unoccupied, for the women left open a space at the center of the wall where Tata usually sat. A semicircle of barefoot girls also worked in the courtyard near the dome-shaped cage. As Margarita walked past them she recalled that most of the girls bore her great-grandfather's name—Moro—a vestige from the days when their own grandparents were slaves on his plantation. Many, like their mothers and grandmothers before them, were named Mariela or Rafaela after Margarita's great-grandmother and Maita, much as one might name an infant after a favorite saint.

When Margarita was younger, Maita used to tell her that Mariela always regarded it her duty as mistress of Tres Flores to civilize and look after the girls.

"For some reason—perhaps because so many were named after her—my mother felt responsible for them," Rafaela always said. "Mother always made certain that the girls who came to work for her at Tres Flores, pobrecitas, learned to be useful with their hands. They were taught to cook and sew, and your great-grandmother instructed them herself in embroidery and needlepoint, arts that she learned long ago from the nuns who ran the boarding school she attended as a child in Spain. My mother loved to read to them from the Bible in the front parlor as they did their needlework, and she taught them the hymns that we sang every Sunday at mass. She even started teaching them the proper way to set a table and how to hold a knife and fork when they were cutting meat. From time to time she sent them home with breads and fruits from her pantry and clothing that we had outgrown. You can be sure that there was always something to spare or pass down, since I had six sisters. At the end of the summer my mother gave the girls the long-haired ponies that my father kept in the stables at Treinta Sierras. He purchased them," Maita would add, "at the beginning of the season for our amusement, even though my mother always insisted that it wasn't ladylike for us to ride."

* * *

The girls looked up momentarily as Margarita passed through the courtyard. The women, who were sitting against the courtyard wall like a mirage, had their eyes bent over their work. Though a hot ribbon of fear—tempered by guilt and excitement—passed through her, she headed toward the wrought-iron gate that fed into the avenida. It was almost as though someone else had taken control of her body, for her legs seemed to move forward mechanically without her consent. When she reached the arch, Margarita glanced up at her mother's bedroom window, which looked out onto the back balcony and the courtyard. Noting that her shutters were still closed, she unhooked the gate with the rambling rose pattern and stepped out into the street, losing herself in the cavalcade of people who were making their way to the plaza.

As Rosa's thoughts turned back to Pedro, she recalled the queer expression on her husband's face when he met her and the girls at the front entrance of Tres Flores:

They had arrived from the station filthy and exhausted, for the train had stopped twice en route—once for a herd of cattle wandering unattended across the tracks, and a second time for no apparent reason at all. As Pancho swung open the wrought-iron gates and the taxi they had hired at the station pulled into the circular drive, Rosa noticed Tata at once, standing on the portico with her hands planted on her hips, waiting. Somehow she had known that they were coming.

"Porquería," she had murmured aloud, as she watched Manuel and Pancho unload the trunk of the motorcar and process back and forth like giant ants, carrying corded hat boxes of varying sizes and shapes, steamer trunks, valises, and canvas bags, until the entrance hall—which she had just finished mopping—was full. Rosa threw her arms around Tata's neck and pressed her lips against her cheek, completely ignoring the old woman's sullen expression.

"The lighter the shell that you carry on your back," Tata had whispered in her ear with her eyes fixed on Margarita, who was standing at her mother's side, "the easier it will be to move from place to place. The more one gathers and collects, mi cielo, the harder it becomes to leave it all behind when the time comes to go. Soon we will all have to learn to live provisionally—to improvise and inventar, so that we do not forget."

Rosa released her hold and looked into Tata's face. She could tell by the expression in the old woman's eyes that she was happy to see them, despite her knitted brows and the turned-down corners of her lips.

As she walked into the entrance hall with her arm wrapped around Tata's, Rosa's eyes met Pedro's. Without a word of welcome or condemnation, he stepped out of the shadows and brushed past her, slamming the front door behind him. Now several days had already passed since their arrival, but Pedro—stubborn as a cork stuck in a bottle—had yet to say one word to her. He had taken a vow of silence, which Rosa (who was equally stubborn) refused to encourage him to break, for she knew that what bothered him wasn't so much that she had broken her confinement, but, rather, the idea that she had completely ignored his wishes. Though she, too, remained silent about the matter, Rosa was filled with regret. She could not help but think that her own childish disregard for his authority had, once again, spurred his ferocious temper, the consequences of which all of them would be made to suffer.

Rosa turned restlessly once again, wondering if perhaps she should send Francisco or Pancho to call for the doctor. The last time she had been through this—with Margarita—she had foolishly waited until it was too late. Even though the old doctor had delivered over half of the children in Cienfuegos, he had nearly lost both mother and child that day, for Margarita had decided to come in a hurry and enter the world heel first and bawling—a sign, Tata later predicted, that she would experience great sorrow in her lifetime.

But maybe this one will be like Caridad, Rosa considered, who had made everyone, including Carlucho de Silva, wait almost twenty-four hours before she decided to make her quiet entrance into the world. (She sucked contentedly on Tata's breast and didn't utter her first cry until Tía Marta pierced her earlobe with a silver embroidery needle she'd sterilized with rubbing alcohol and the blue light of the fire.)

El pobre, Rosa thought, recalling the dark rings under Doctor de Silva's eyes on the day of Caridad's birth. The old man was already on his eighth tasita of café when the midwife who had come along to assist him saw the child's head crowning and called him to the bedroom.

The thought of her long labor and delivery prompted Rosa to decide against calling for the old doctor and rousing him needlessly from his sleep. Besides, she reasoned, her large belly suggested that her son would not come quickly. A child that size would surely take his time.

Thinking it best to get as much sleep as possible while she still had the chance, Rosa closed her eyes and listened to the soothing sound of the breeze fingering through the leaves of the palm tree just outside her window. As she began to drift into sleep, she saw herself as a young girl once again, approaching the blood-stained wall with her arms extended before her, as though she were playing blindman's buff.

Once she had passed through the archway, Margarita leaned against the courtyard wall and slipped off her shoes. She concealed them behind a large, waxy plant with leaves shaped like outstretched hands so that no one would find them. She would put them back on when she returned.

Unpinning her hat, Margarita shook loose her thick black hair and then threw it behind her so that the sun could caress her shoulders and her neck. Walking down the avenida toward the plaza, she stared defiantly into the faces of the old matrons who passed by her. Much to her chagrin, however, she spotted her mother's old schoolmate and friend, Amparo Aragona, and her nauseatingly perfect daughter, Isabelita, moving toward her. The black leather prayer books in their hands told her that they had just come from the early mass in the cathedral. Margarita hastily clapped on her hat and pulled it over her eyes, but she did so too late, for Señora Aragona had already seen her. As they passed she overheard her mother's friend issue a sharp warning to her daughter about wayward girls, while she chastised Margarita with her eyes. Without considering the possible consequences, Margarita stuck out her tongue, causing Amparo's mouth to drop open as though it had been weighted.

Without a word, Señora Aragona angrily wagged her finger at Margarita. Then she turned her back and spirited away her daughter, who stared over her shoulder at Margarita.

As she watched the pair press down the avenida against the crowd—Amparo would never have dreamed of permitting Isabelita to take part in the carnival—Margarita knew that the first chance she got, Señora Aragona would be at Tres Flores paying her mother a call. She would probably bring Doña Perfecta (the nickname that she and Caridad had given Isabelita) along.

"By the way," Señora Aragona would say in an offhand way, once she had finished off a plate of Tata's pasteles, "on our way home from church Isabelita and I saw your daughter walking unescorted in the street on the day of the fiesta—without a hat or shoes." Then she would pause to see Rosa's reaction. "I realize that it's none of my business, but I also know that you and I happen to feel the same way about these things. We know how easily a young girl's reputation can be ruined. And once it's gone, it's gone."

"Really?" Rosa would respond, containing her horror and throwing Margarita a look that could send her to the moon.

"I don't want to intrude," Señora Aragona would break in, "but you can never be too careful these days."

"No, no," her mother would say, "I'm glad you told me."

Of course Margarita could be certain that everyone in the neighborhood, including the servants, would already have been exercising the story on their tongues—by the time it reached Rosa's ears it would be yesterday's news. She pictured Señora Aragona running from house to house spreading the story like butter on hot rolls among her mother's friends. They, in turn, would blame Margarita's rebellious nature on the fact that Rosa had allowed herself to be influenced by the imported foreign ideas (not to mention the gadgets and the gizmos) that she brought with her every summer from Havana.

Margarita could still recall the jealous looks on the neighbors' faces when Rosa returned to Cienfuegos after their first winter in Havana with an electric mixer—a useless piece of junk, Graciela had proclaimed, which sent Lobo running from the kitchen like a whirlwind with his tail tucked in between his legs. Not long after its arrival the ornery old woman hid the mixer in the dark corner of a cabinet filled with scorched frying pans and pots with broken handles that she had refused to throw away—a place that nobody thought to search the day Rosa had invited her friends over to watch Tata make meringues. The following year the Amargos arrived at Tres Flores in a red Buick with chrome-colored trim and a horn that sounded like the braying of a sick donkey. It was an event that had burned itself into Margarita's memory and was documented by Caridad's new Brownie camera. In the photograph, Tía Marta was stretched out like the *Maja Vestida* across the hood of the brand new Ford motorcar, sporting a red feather boa and a cloche Rosa had bought her at El Encanto. Pedro stood stiffly at her side, wearing a frown upon his face. Hanging like a dog's ear from the top pocket of his double-breasted suit was a silk handkerchief that matched Marta's boa, a detail Rosa had added at the last moment, as she posed the pair for the photograph. Back then her mother had seemed so lighthearted and gay, characteristics that had long since disappeared, Margarita thought.

"Qué moderna eres, Señora," Emilia Ramos, Amparo's mother, had said to Marta in a loud voice meant for Rosa's ears, as she and a few other women from the neighborhood gathered around the car and fingered the red boa.

Even though the women attributed the change in Rosa's attitude to her move to Havana, the truth was that her behavior had always shocked them. In one way or another Rosa had always given them something to whisper about, such as the time she took it upon herself to dismiss the wet nurse Dr. de Silva had sent her after Margarita's birth. Her insistence on nursing her daughter herself left the women in the neighborhood reeling and speechless.

Now it's my turn to give Señora Aragona something fat and juicy to chew on with her friends, Margarita thought as she pulled off her hat once again. After weighing the possible punishments she might receive for her blatant disobedience, she halfheartedly convinced herself that her mother, who wasn't speaking to her father and was obviously preoccupied with other things, might dismiss the incident as the least of her concerns. But it wasn't her mother's reaction that worried her—it was the thought of her father's temper. Though it was long ago, she could still recall the day he had caught her in the courtyard playing in a rain puddle with Graciela's nieces and nephews. She couldn't have been more than five or six at the time. Margarita still wasn't sure what had irritated him more—the fact that she had trampled her sun hat and soiled her dress, or the idea that she was making mud cakes in the dirt, barefoot and hatless, with his servants' children, delicacies that they had all intended to feast on together.

"Only common people allow their children to run wild in the streets like gypsies," he had scolded her mother, while Rosa spanked the dirt from the back of Margarita's dress. "Only peasants allow their skin to burn and calluses to form on their feet."

113

"Por Dios, Pedro," her mother had sighed with obvious exasperation, "you make it sound as though the child is a little creature. The next thing you know, you'll have her spitting and hissing and eating small animals that she catches with her teeth and claws. Honestly, Pedro, the older you get, the more you sound like your mother."

Margarita recalled her mother's response with amusement, but beneath her laughter she cringed at the thought of her father's anger—how he would boil over when he learned that his daughter had disobeyed him. Perhaps Tata would intercede, Margarita thought with hope, and convince Rosa not to tell him just this once.

* * *

The sight of the crowd gathering in the plaza as she approached the mouth of the street focused Margarita's attention back on the fiesta. Though she was certain that a thousand eyes were upon her, she continued to elbow her way down the avenida, deflecting the matrons' piercing gazes and trying to swallow the barb of fear that had lodged itself at the back of her throat.

When she reached the plaza, Margarita paused at the ice cream cart that stood on the corner of the street beneath a palm tree that looked to her like a giant pineapple. It was shaded by a large pink-and-red umbrella and mysterious words were scrawled in a shaky foreign script across the side of the cart:

Ayúdame a vivir.

A Chinese man stood behind the cart calling out the same words—help me to live—into the crowd that passed him by. He spoke as though he were crying out in his sleep. Margarita saw him each Sunday morning on her way to the cathedral. He always had on the same baggy pants cuffed several times over at the ankles, as though they had been made for someone twice his size. He wore soft cotton shoes with rubber soles that looked to Margarita like bedroom slippers, and a stiffly starched guayabera that nearly reached down to his knees. There was always an oily smell about him, and he had a certain way of shuffling his feet, as though he were dancing to the rhythm of some unheard music. And the deep wrinkles and creases on his face—etched by some foreign sun—and the curving gashes that were his eyes made him appear to be laughing even when his mouth was turned down.

While the Chinese man was filling her cup with mango-colored ice cream that had already begun to melt with the heat, Margarita gazed at him with pity. He seemed so forlorn. And to think that there were so many just like him—they lined the back streets of Havana.

The Chinese man handed Margarita the cup of ice cream and, in exchange, she pressed all of the loose change she had shaken from her bank into his outstretched palm, wishing all the while that she had thought ahead and brought something extra to give him.

"Demasiado," he said in a reedy voice that betrayed no emotion. Margarita shook her head.

"Too much," he repeated, and as he said the words a second time Margarita imagined him kneeling at the altar rail in the cathedral before the shrine of an unfamiliar god, muttering the same phrase over and over again: Too much. Too much.

She shook her head from side to side once again, exaggerating the gesture in case he hadn't understood her meaning the first time. In response Chang—the name, she recollected, her mother had called the old man as they passed by him one morning—accepted the extra change and bowed stiffly from the waist, bobbing his head up and down.

As Margarita crossed the street, heading toward the stone fountain at the center of the plaza, she turned around and glanced at the Chinese man, whose head continued to bob as though it had come unstrung.

S tanding at the foot of the caoba bed, Pedro gazed at his wife. Her hair was loosely spread out in fernlike tendrils across her pillow and her pale, lavender eyelids looked to Pedro like the tiny shells that Rosa collected from the shore and arranged on the night table next to their bed in Havana. In the dim light, her face looked like a luminous flower floating on blue-black vines. He had never seen her look so lovely; the sight of her sparked his desire. Rosa seemed to glow with the child inside her, despite her awkward, swollen form. Perhaps his father was right after all. "Women are always at their best," he used to say, "when they are carrying their husbands' children. There is nothing more becoming," Don Pedro would insist, "nothing more natural."

As he gazed at her face, Pedro recalled how striking Rosa had looked when she was pregnant with Caridad and Margarita, but this time she seemed transformed with unearthly beauty. It was almost shocking.

If only she carries our son, he thought as he bent over to kiss her. For weeks now he was unable to suppress the thought of the nagging absence he knew he would feel if she gave birth to another daughter. But as he gazed at her he felt assured, convincing himself that only a son could bring out his mother's beauty in such a way.

Pedro closed his mouth over her lips, gently drawing her warm breath into his lungs. Half wishing to wake her, he brushed her forehead and her eyes with his tongue, but she did not stir beneath the comforter. He knew that this time he had gone too far—he had been too harsh and unyielding, especially in light of her condition. Her feelings were so delicate—so fragile now. But she had taken him by complete surprise, arriving from the station so unexpectedly with the two girls. Who would blame him for reacting the way he did?

As he pictured the scene of their homecoming in his head, the smoldering ashes of his anger stirred up within him, but they were soon quelled once again by the sight of her, for she looked so defenseless and vulnerable, so innocent in her sleep, like an unsuspecting child. Shame and regret flooded over him once more, and he made a silent promise to make it all up to her when he returned to Tres Flores in a few days.

As he leaned over her sleeping form, the memory of their first meeting came to him—a timeless image captured in a photograph he always kept on his night table of a young girl wearing a blue linen sundress, sitting as gracefully as an early spring blossom on a dark bough in the shade of a framboyán tree:

Rosa had traveled to the city accompanied only by her father on the train. They were to be introduced at a tennis match at the Havana Yacht Club. Long before Don Pedro had arranged the match with his longtime rival and friend, Antonio, over tall beaded glasses of rum and thick black cigars. The two men had studied together as boys at a Spanish boarding school run by the Jesuits. Over the years, they had lost contact with one another, for life had pulled them in different directions. Just by chance, they became reacquainted at a charity dinner that the priests at the boarding school had organized to raise money for their missions in South America. They spent that evening reminiscing and reclaiming their memories together (such as the time they had stolen out of the dormitory window after their companions had fallen asleep and swum naked in a nearby lake that was said to be filled with snakes and crocodiles). After that night they met for dinner once a month in the city. During one of those evenings they agreed that their children should marry. At first Antonio insisted that Pedro court María, since she was his eldest daughter, but when Don Pedro saw the girls' photographs, he insisted that Rosa was better suited for his son. After a lengthy discussion and several glasses of rum, Antonio realized that his old friend would not be persuaded otherwise, so he agreed that Pedro and Rosa would make a perfect match. In light of his concession, he insisted that the couple live with them at Tres Flores, where Pedro could learn to run the plantation. At first Don Pedro hesitated, knowing that Fina would be inconsolable, crying for weeks on end when she heard the news that her only boy would be leaving her, but bit by bit Antonio managed to coax Don Pedro by assuring him that his son stood to inherit all of his land, being that Rafaela had failed to provide him with an heir.

When Don Pedro returned home from the club that evening—with watery, bloodshot eyes and reeking like a mountain lion—he told his wife about the conversation with Antonio Miramar. Pedro woke to the sound of his father's voice booming behind his parents' bedroom door:

"Enough already, Josefina. Enough. The boy will never amount to anything unless we push him. He's almost thirty years old and he still has no direction. For the life of me, I just don't understand it, but there it is. Sometimes I feel that I've failed with him. But then other times a part of me is half convinced that if you hadn't allowed him to stand in your skirts, listening to women's conversation and doing women's work . . ."

"Por Dios, Pedro," Fina had responded in a voice made shrill with anger, "are you suggesting that just because I allowed him to hold a skein of yarn around his wrists once or twice while I wound it into a ball, our son will be a failure in life? Or maybe something worse? You make this whole thing sound like it's a business proposition. But it's not. We're talking about Pedrecito, our son."

"Antonio Miramar has given me his word that he will leave Treinta Sierras to Pedro in his will. He has no sons, Fina. He is offering the boy a future. He is offering to make him into a man."

Although Pedro had seen a photograph of Rosa, he had never met the girl who was destined to become his wife until the day of the tennis match. While his father waited at the outdoor bar for their refreshments and Pedro stood in his shadow holding a plate full of sliced fruit, he searched the grounds for the mysterious green-eyed girl with the thick black hair.

There were many young women at the club that afternoon. It seemed as though all of Havana had come out for the match. The women decorated the terraces and the lawns like brightly colored nosegays of hibiscus and bougainvillea. Though most stood in silence, beating the cool sea breeze around them with their fans and sipping iced drinks against the wall, their hand-screens seemed to be communicating back and forth in coy, mute whispers to the young men who circled around them like the old women who purchased fruits and vegetables at the market. Seated in lawn chairs that were scattered across the veranda were the thick-waisted matrons who had come to chaperone the young girls on their outings.

Rosa sat apart from the other women. When his eyes lighted upon her, Pedro recalled his father's words at the breakfast table earlier that morning as he contemplated her photograph and Don Pedro sliced open a melon with his knife:

"You will recognize her the moment you see her, m'ijo. She is the pearl of the Antilles." Without responding, Pedro watched his mother scoop out the seeds of the melon Don Pedro had flayed open with the butcher knife. Meanwhile his father, who had taken his seat at the other end of the table, consumed a sweet roll which he had smothered with a pat of butter made slightly rancid by the heat and sprinkled with sugar.

As Pedro approached Rosa, he noticed that she had taken off her cumbersome hat and her pumps and laid them at her side. Her hair was pulled back off her face and knotted into a chignon that hung loosely down her back. Two red roses blooming from a single stem were pinned to the collar of her dress. Lost in her own thoughts, she seemed quite unconscious of the fact that the group of men surrounding her—laughing too loud, gesturing too widely—were competing for her attention. Her mercy. They in turn were unaware that she was now an unattainable object. In Pedro's own mind, she already belonged to him.

Their eyes met for only a moment, and Pedro knew in that instant that she had recognized him too. Rosa quickly averted her gaze, tucking her chin into her shoulder like a swan. Her lashes were lowered beneath her dark, triangular eyebrows—brows that arched over almond-shaped eyes and joined together at the bridge of her nose like a bird taking flight. Pedro watched as she pulled back her head with a jerk, as though she were in pain, and held her chin in the cup of her hand. He seemed to be the only witness to her agony. And then she raised her eyes to meet his and looked at him as though he had wounded her.

Crossing the lawn that stretched like an emerald-colored sea between them, Pedro offered her his handkerchief in silence. Although she was visibly embarrassed, Rosa accepted it with a nod of her head. She moved her hand away from her face as she reached for the linen, and only then did he notice the jagged thread of blood, etched by a single thorn, across her skin. Forgetting himself, he knelt beside her and took her hand in his. Then he kissed her perfumed glove and her soft brown wrist. As he did so, he inhaled for the first time her scent of jasmine and sandalwood. Reclining back on his elbows, he selected a ripe strawberry from his plate and pushed it against her lips until she yielded with a laugh that sounded like a small child's cry.

They were interrupted by Don Pedro who, having turned around at the bar with two glasses of minted tea, discovered that his son had wandered from his side.

"I see that you have already found each other out," he had laughed, breaking the spell between the couple.

"And so have we," Antonio chimed in, coming up behind his old friend and slapping him on the back. "But it looks as though our business is finished here, Don Pedro. Our children are getting along famously without us." At his words the two men clinked their glasses together and drained them of tea.

"Go stand beside her," Antonio said, motioning Pedro and Rosa together. "I want a picture of the happy young couple."

* * *

Pedro tenderly grazed the base of Rosa's neck with his lips once again, sucking on her soft, warm flesh as though he intended to consume her. He searched her sleeping face for its hidden youth and could almost see the young girl once again in the dim half-light, for the shadows in the room softened the lines and creases around her mouth and blended the dark lavender circles that arced beneath the rims of her eyes. Brushing a few wavy threads of black hair from her forehead, he kissed her lips once again. "Wake up, sleeping beauty, mi rosa de oro," he murmured in her ear, but she lay motionless beneath the purple comforter, remote from him and folded away in what appeared to be a dreamless sleep.

Pausing on the threshold with his canvas bag slung over his shoulder, Pedro gazed at Rosa's face. Her hair swept like a widow's veil across her eyes—and in that moment, Pedro imagined her standing over his grave, her slim shoulders bent with sorrow and grief. "The pearl of the Antilles," he whispered as he turned his back on her.

While he walked down the back staircase, fitting his hat onto his head, he could not shake the feeling that he should have kissed her once more—he should have woken her and told her that he loved her. But in all the years that they had been married, they had never openly spoken about their love for one another. It just wasn't his way, he reassured himself. Besides, who could change an old perro and teach him new tricks?

Of course she knows I love her. How could she not know? Pedro thought, as he absentmindedly selected a ripe guava and a stalk of sugar cane from the newly purchased pile of fruits and vegetables that Checha had spread out on the countertop in the kitchen.

"Hasta pronto, Graciela," he called behind him as he kicked open the screen door, knowing all the while that the deaf old woman would not respond.

As he headed toward the side gate that led to the front drive where Francisco was waiting with the motorcar, Pedro passed the servants' quarters. Attached to the building was a large room with a cathedral ceiling hung with fans that lazily batted the hot air around the room. There a group of girls, some of whom came from neighboring towns seeking work, assembled every Wednesday and Friday to launder the family's linen. Passing by the door where the washbasins stood, Pedro looked in on the mulata, who was pressing the guayabera he had worn the day before, along with his imported cambric handkerchiefs and his cotton underclothing. She seemed unaware of his presence.

As he passed through the wrought-iron arch, Pedro glanced up at Rosa's shuttered windows. It was then that he noticed that the sun had already climbed almost halfway up the spires of the cathedral. He knew that he would have to hurry to make up for the time he had already lost.

Margarita perched herself on the cool, wet lip of the fountain. While she spooned the yellow ice cream into her mouth, she gazed up at the naked stone women who danced with joined hands in a watery circle at the center of the fountain. Then her eyes wandered across the plaza and she felt suddenly alone, like a spectator—silent and detached.

The streets surrounding the plaza were filled with motion and sound. A saffron-skinned woman shaped like an ample pear swept empty bottle tops and jumbled bits of colored glass across the pavement in front of a large pink marble house with a walled-in courtyard and a gated arch. The woman moved her hips in rhythm with the drums that sounded faintly in the distance, while another washed down the sidewalk behind her with a bucket filled with soapy brown water. Across the street a shopkeeper drew up the jalousie in his front window. As it slowly ascended, rows of dried fish with skin the color of mother-of-pearl appeared. They were strung across the shop window, suspended above a mound of freshly baked sweet rolls, piles of ripened fruit, and several wheels of cheese. A young boy with ochre-colored hands and a red bandanna tied around his neck scattered sawdust across the clay tile floor of a nearby bodega with a broom, while the bartender dusted and rearranged the bottles of rum on the back counter next to the cash register.

Margarita's attention turned back to the pink house on the corner diagonal to the ice cream cart. A group of men in immaculate linen suits and wide-brimmed Panama hats emerged from the dark entrance into the sunlit courtyard. They were escorting several young women—with painted faces and soft pastel dresses—who hung on their arms like clinging orchids. They reminded Margarita of the men who stood in the vestibule of the cathedral while Padre Rabia celebrated Sunday mass. As they waited for their wives and children, the men talked quietly among themselves about politics and sugar cane and tobacco. Margarita knew that this was true, for she had stood there with her father one morning to get fresh air after the incense that burned on the main altar made her stomach—which was empty with fasting for an hour before taking communion—churn. Just as the old Jesuit began the blessing of the Sacrament, the men unfolded their white handkerchiefs, which were tucked away in their back pockets, and spread them at their feet across the tiled marble floor. Margarita watched with fascination as they knelt upon the linens during the blessing of the host, beating their breasts with closed fists each time Padre Rabia uttered the Lord's name. They spread out the handkerchiefs, her father later explained, so as not to soil or wear out the knees of their trousers. She could still recall the scent of their pressed Irish linen and the particular way that it creased at their elbows and knees.

As the couples crossed the street, they passed a bevy of old women who looked, in comparison, like a trampled bouquet. Margarita guessed, from the rosary beads and the missals they carried in their hands, that the old women, like Señora Aragona and Isabelita, had just come from the chapel in the cathedral where Padre Morales celebrated the early mass each morning. She watched as they paused to purchase from the vendors, who dotted the sidewalks and circled around the plaza with coiled baskets on their heads.

Bearing armfuls of flowers, tortas, and fruit, the old women wove their way through the crowd of people throwing streamers and confetti into the air above them and dancing in the streets to the sound of guitars and drums. Then they crossed the avenida and were swallowed up by the shadows of the pink marble house. Margarita knew that they were going to pay their respects at the altar of the Virgin. Throughout the year, during ordinary time, a plaster miniature of la Virgen Loreto housed in a tall glass case with blue satin lining was escorted from home to home. Each week a different family had the privilege of acting as her host. (Though most people had to wait several years for the honor, Maita successfully petitioned Padre Rabia for the statue and received the Virgin into her home at least twice a year.)

With her eyes fixed on the entrance of the pink house, Margarita recalled the busy flurry in the kitchen at Tres Flores as Graciela and Tata prepared for the Virgin's visit. Luciano and Pancho would clear the front parlor of all but a few chairs and the family Bible, which was propped open on a rosewood stand. There in front of the marble mantelpiece—whose function Margarita could never determine, for it was always hot in Cienfuegos—Maita would prepare an altar consisting of one of her best linen tablecloths, which was draped over a steamer trunk, and several cardboard shoe boxes, which she stacked one upon the other like stairs. After adjusting the tablecloth so that it concealed the trunk and the boxes, Maita adorned the altar with tall votive candles, which she kept burning throughout the week, and an array of flowers that Graciela had gathered from the courtyard. The kitchen counters were lined with trays filled with tempting pastries, which Margarita and Caridad were strictly forbidden to touch, for the hosting family was expected to open their doors and their kitchens to those who came to show their devotion to the Virgin. (Afterwards, Maita always insisted that at least half of those who appeared at Tres Flores actually came to sample the pastries and gawk at her knickknacks and furniture.) The visitors, in turn, offered flowers and assorted fruits and cakes at the Virgin's altar, most of which Lobo pilfered when no one was watching and carried to his corner in the kitchen.

* * *

Just as Margarita spooned the last of her ice cream into her mouth, the front doors of the cathedral swung open and a group of young men, many of whom she recognized as the sons of her parents' friends, emerged bearing a life-size statue of Our Lady of Mount Carmel. Each year on the same date the statue was taken from its base and carried on a dais to the seashore, where a large fishing troller waited to transport it to a floating platform anchored in the bay. The statue was left on the platform until the last day of the month, when it was returned to its shadowy nave in the cathedral.

As the statue rose above the plaza a hush fell on the crowd. It was apparent by the expressions on the townspeople's faces that they revered the Virgin. In their eyes she was a symbol of holy womanhood—a symbol of self-sacrifice and submission. The young men carried the statue on their shoulders toward a large wooden cart that stood at the center of the plaza. From her place on the fountain Margarita could see the perspiration pouring down their cheeks and the water stains that formed dark flowers on their shirts.

Pushing her way through the crowd until she was within arm's reach of the carts, she watched as the women arranged small caskets encrusted with semiprecious stones and containing the black splinters of sacred bones and swatches of cloth that had once touched the skin of saints around the Virgin's feet. The caskets were scattered among fruit, and flowers, and spindles wrapped with pale linen thread. The Virgin's robes were painted robin's-egg blue and gilded with gold trim. On her head she wore a crown of fresh flowers and someone had placed a single white lily in her outstretched hand.

While studying the serene expression on the Virgin's face, Margarita thought of the thousands of times she had prayed to the Little Flower asking her to send a bouquet of roses as proof of her faith. As a child, she had longed to receive the stigmata— a sure sign, the nuns at the convent school told them, that she was chosen above others to endure suffering and pain. Laying her empty cup and spoon on the ledge of the fountain, Margarita searched for the sign of Mary on her palms. (Stretching the girls' fingers backwards toward their wrists, the nuns had also told them that a spidery *M* was etched into every girl's palm as a sign that she belonged to the Virgin, a notion Tata contradicted by insisting that the *M*s on her palms and the jutting shape of her knuckles when she pressed her hands into fists were reminders of the mountains that surrounded Cienfuegos.)

Unable to withstand the press of the crowd any longer, Margarita returned to the fountain and balanced herself on its lip once again in order to get a better view of the procession. In the harsh sunlight the statue of the Virgin looked stiff and lifeless, whereas in the cathedral her features were softened by the candlelight and her face animated by the flickering shadows that danced on the wall behind her. While she sat in church, absentmindedly listening to the drone of Padre Rabia's voice, Margarita often imagined that the statue's lips were moving, mouthing words to her as the Virgin had to the children at Fatima or the dark Madonna at Guadalupe, who spoke to Juan Diego in his native tongue from a pillowy white cloud.

Just at that moment, the bells in the spire of the cathedral, whose tongues had been silenced when the statue was taken from the nave, began to peal once again, signaling the priests waiting in the sanctuary with the Bishop, who had traveled—at Padre Rabia's request—all the way from Havana to celebrate the fiesta. Dressed in black cassocks with satin sashes tied around their waists and wide-brimmed hats on their heads, they emerged from the cathedral like blackbirds. Led by Padre Rabia and Padre Morales, they took their places around the statue behind the Bishop, who stood at the front of the crowd like a band leader, bearing his crosier and wearing his damask miter. The priests were closely followed by the calambucas, as Tata called them—the old women who cleaned and swept the cathedral every morning following the early mass. Together they carried an oversized rosary with hand-carved ebony beads the size of clementines. From where Margarita stood the beads looked like shrunken heads. The women's downturned faces and bent heads were covered with long black mantillas that trailed behind them like widows' veils, smoothing the dusty street into soft brown ribbons as the procession began to move out of the plaza.

A young girl, probably close to her own age, walked alongside the Bishop, smiling and waving at Margarita when she passed, as though she were in a parade. She reminded Margarita of the poor children she saw from time to time as they drove through the barrios on the outskirts of Havana in their brand-new chrome-covered American car. Despite her father's insistence that there was no poverty in Cuba—"it's a paradise," he would insist whenever she questioned him—Margarita could not shake herself free of the memory of the children by the side of the road—with their bare feet and large, distended bellies—though they seemed to be invisible to everyone but her.

The girl was pulling a small fawn-colored goat by a rope. Its flanks were dressed in a jasmine garland. Frightened by the noise and the movement of the crowd, the animal dug its hooves into the ground. Now and then it raised its head and bleated sadly at the cloudless sky. The girl frantically whipped it with a thorny branch until it began to move a few paces, then it stopped and wailed again.

Margarita joined in with the crowd as it pressed toward the water's edge. There, with the sound of the waves pounding in the background, the priests took out their worn leather missals from beneath their cassocks and began to pray in one voice while the statue was secured like a figurehead to the bow of a fishing boat with thick hemp ropes. Then the men began loading baskets of rose petals onto an armada of smaller boats that were docked on the beach. (The previous day Margarita had seen the women in the courtyard at Tres Flores stripping long-stemmed roses of their petals and leaves.) As the boats pulled away from the shoreline, the fishermen began emptying their cargo into the bay. The women and children, who remained behind, watched in silence, waving palm leaves and the thorny stems of the roses like green wands above their heads.

After the boats had nearly vanished from view, Margarita turned and followed the unpaved road back to the town, picking large trumpetlike lilies that grew wild along the way. Moved by the ritual she had just witnessed for the first time, she decided to offer the flowers at Our Lady of Mount Carmel's now-vacant altar. But before entering the cathedral, she paused to pin on her hat, suddenly recalling the stern warning issued by the nuns at La Sagrada Familia against entering God's house with uncovered heads. Even she dared not break this rule. She hoped that the cathedral was empty so that no one would see that she wasn't wearing shoes.

The wooden door was woven into the wall by a thick, gnarly vine bearing luminous sweet-scented flowers that burned despite the gloom of the alley. Shafts of almost blinding, sublime sunlight pierced through the chinks in the door. Rosa saw herself wedging her long, thin fingers—piano fingers Mariela always told her, though she never had the least inclination to play the upright piano that stood unattended and silent in the front parlor—into the jamb, but the red door was securely knit into the wall by creeping vines. Pressing her face against the door and cupping her hands over her eyes, she looked into the garden that lay beyond the wall as she had done so often as a child, peering out the gates of Tres Flores into the street. At the center was a fountain that branched into four streams, surrounded by beds of exotic wildflowers of almost unearthly beauty and fringed by crowded groves of ceiba trees and royal palms and framboyanes with frilly skirts of red and purple and orange—an anarchy of colors and smells that drowned Rosa's senses, for she had never seen or experienced anything like it before. As she gazed longingly through the chinks in the red door, she felt as though she would burst—she felt as though she had supped on a sumptuous meal, though a sudden appetite grew within her, filling her with untold desires—the desire to smell to taste to see to hear to feel everything in the garden without restraint. And so she pressed her face even closer to the door and gorged herself on the opulence and the incense until she perceived a disturbance in the peaceful order of the garden—an almost imperceptible shifting of light and sound which became the shadowy form of a woman shrouded in layers of black who wove through the marble shadows of the garden toward a door in the wall across from where Rosa stood watching. The woman pushed herself against the door with all of her weight until it began to revolve and as it swung around, Rosa noticed that a large basket woven out of yarey leaves was fastened to the back of the door and above it were large painted words that she could not make out. Then the woman lifted the hem of her skirt and removed two shapeless bundles. As she lay the first bundle in the basket, the earth began to shudder and dilate, then it parted open and swallowed the second. In despair, the woman reached out her arms as though to reclaim what she had placed inside the basket, but instead, she pushed closed the door, causing it to swing back into the gray interior of the wall. And as the door swung shut, Rosa closed her eyes and listened to the sad unearthly music that issued from behind the wall. When she opened them once again, she was facing the woman of the shadows, whose hair was the color of the sea and skin was as pale as an angel's, though she had the features of a Mayan goddess. It was a face that she studied for what seemed to be an eternity until the woman reached out and touched her cheek. And though she wanted to cry out, Rosa's tongue lay thick and heavy in her mouth like the iron tongues of the bells she heard tolling in the distance marking the tropical noon, which the woman apparently heard as well, though no one would have been the wiser, for her mouth was stitched shut, as though she had taken an eternal vow of silence, and her eyes were vacant and red and wandered wildly in her head, but they still seemed to express to perfection the sorrow that Rosa felt inside and a knowledge of the suffering she had endured, which was summed up even more palpably in the long pausing kiss the woman planted on her lips . . .

. . . and woke her from her sleep.

It seemed as though her very spirit had been sucked from within her. Rosa opened her eyes and looked around her bedroom in disbelief. It had all been so real, she was certain that it couldn't have been a dream. She could tell by the shifting of the shadows and the intensity of the shafts of light that pierced the closed shutters that Checha would soon come to her door with a glass of scorching hot café con leche and a slice of melon. With her eyes fixed on the corner of the ceiling, she suddenly realized, with mingled fear and relief, that she had dreamed out the dream.

"It is finished," she whispered, suddenly conscious of the sound of silverware chiming against the dishes that issued from the balcony where Pedro always took his morning meal.

The cathedral was noiseless except for the occasional breeze that caught in the deep recesses of the ceiling vaults, mocking the almost inaudible rhythms of the empty structure. Although it had grown quite warm outside, the church, with its massive stone walls and marble floors, remained pleasantly cool.

Margarita knelt in the long wooden pew where she sat every Sunday with her family. (Long before, her great-grandparents had paid for the honor of permanently reserving the pew in their family's name.) During the mass she memorized the words on the rectangular brass plaques mounted beneath the stained glass windows that lined the walls. They bore the names of the wealthy families in Cienfuegos who had donated the glass when the cathedral was first built in memory of those who had gone before them. Inscribed somewhere in the church beneath a statue of a saint whose name she could not recall, were her great-grandparents' and her grandparents' names. Perhaps one day when she was long forgotten by the world, a child such as herself would pass the time reading her name—preserved for eternity, Margarita thought, on the walls of the cathedral.

Margarita's eyes wandered to the stone angels supporting the immense multicolored columns that held up the vault over the main altar. How effortlessly they seemed to bear the strain, Margarita thought, with mixed admiration and skepticism, while gazing at their impassive faces. They embodied an ideal of patience, strength, and tolerance which she had been encouraged—both at home and at school—to emulate. It was an ideal that Margarita often found difficult, if not impossible, to model herself upon, for even though she dared not say it, she thought it far more natural to act on her desires and openly express her feelings and attitudes—behavior which she knew without being told was unacceptable for a little girl.

As her eyes settled on the murals of painted saints on the ceiling above her head, she thought about Tata and about the fact that the old woman never accompanied them to mass. Every time Margarita begged her to come with them, the old woman stubbornly refused.

She said that she preferred to pray at her place on the mountain, rather than in a building carved out by human hands like a hollow gourd. The clouds were her cathedrals, she insisted.

"Looking only in places that men have shaped with their crab-claw hands and their simple tools," Tata told her as she combed out and plaited Margarita's hair one afternoon, "is like looking for a shadow under a red rock, mi corazón. Men's eyelids are too narrow to see, their tongues too loose to hear, for their ears are too filled with senseless roaring."

"But if you don't come with us, you'll go straight to you know where," Margarita said pointing her thumbs downward, "along with Graciela. You'll be lost, Tata."

"But maybe down there is really up there or over here," Tata said, swirling her finger through the air around them. "Who's to say, m'ija? Anyway, if Graciela comes along too, I'll have good company, won't I?" the old woman laughed, as she tied a satin ribbon to the end of Margarita's braid. "By the way, who's filling your head with these ideas?"

"Padre Rabia," Margarita responded, recalling the sermon the old Jesuit had delivered from the pulpit only the week before, causing everyone, including Padre Morales, to shift uncomfortably in their seats. According to him, no one could be certain of the hour when La Pelona would arrive. "Only those who are prepared," he had said in a booming voice filled with emotion and stern conviction, "only those who have been baptized and attend weekly mass (and confession, he added) and say their daily prayers, will pass through the pearly gates of heaven. All of the others will suffer indescribable pain—pain that comes from the four corners of the earth—pain that is beyond human comprehension. Nevertheless, their bodies will remain unconsumed in the eternal flames of hell." As she recounted the priest's warning, Margarita could see by the expression on the old woman's face in the mirror that Tata was unmoved by her words.

Heavy white cloths embroidered in blue and silver by the Carmelite nuns who resided in the monastery adjoining the cathedral covered the main altar. At the center was an immense gold tabernacle shaped like a Gothic church, which housed the chalices and the plates Padre Rabia and Padre Morales used to serve Communion. (When Margarita was a child, Maita had told her and Caridad that God resided in the tabernacle, an idea that fascinated the two sisters, though they eventually agreed that it was highly unlikely that someone as big and great as God could be squeezed inside a box.) A series of slipper-shaped windows bearing the signs of the four Evangelists—each representing one of the four directions, Tata had once told her—divided up the wall behind the main altar.

As she gazed at the Evangelists pieced together with bits of broken glass, Margarita laughed within herself at the recollection that as a child she had thought that the halos over their heads were silver platters. (For years she wondered why they wore plates on their heads, and when she finally gathered the courage to ask the nuns at school, her question earned her a thrashing across the palms of her hands with a rubber-tipped pointer.) The stained glass filtered and diffused the sunlight that spread its thin, rosy fingers through the cathedral, softening the sacred gloom that gathered in the corners and the recesses and washing pink-and-red the marble floors and altars.

"Tata is wrong. God is here somewhere," Margarita whispered aloud, though she still could not make herself believe half of what the padres and the nuns at La Sagrada Familia told her. She had first begun to have serious doubts about some of the things they said the day that Madre Juan José tied her left hand behind her back and made her write in cursive holding her fountain pen in her right hand.

When Rosa heard about her daughter's humiliation, she immediately contacted the mother superior—who also had a man's name, though Margarita could not recall it, and was slightly over six feet tall—and requested a meeting with her.

"In addition to being clumsy and uncoordinated, children who insist on writing with their left hands are the puppets of the

Devil himself," the mother superior had explained in a hoarse whisper, with her eyes fixed upon Margarita's from behind a massive mahogany desk. To Margarita, she seemed menacing and gargantuan in her dark habit and her floor-length veil, which cascaded from a corrugated wimple that crowned her forehead. She wondered whether the nun frightened her mother as well, for Rosa—who had railed aloud to her husband when she heard what Madre Juan José had done and threatened to pull both of her daughters out of the convent school—was as unnaturally quiet and subdued in the superior's office as the still that comes over the landscape before a storm.

"You see, it's more than simply a bad habit, Señora," the nun continued, in response, perhaps, to the worried expression on Rosa's face. "Nevertheless, it's a habit that can be broken with patience and persistence. Perhaps you should consider leaving her with us for a term. We could straighten her out in no time at all, Señora. It's simply a matter of willpower," she concluded, rising from her seat to signal that the meeting was over. As Margarita and Rosa stood in unison, the mother superior's arms disappeared into the folds of black linen fabric beneath her stiff white bib. Without a parting word, she turned her back on them and stared out the leaded glass window that overlooked the courtyard where Margarita's schoolmates were taking their recess.

For months afterwards, Margarita cried every night in bed, for she was filled with horror and fear at the thought that her mother might consider abandoning her to the nuns. She couldn't imagine for herself a more terrible fate, for it was rumored that the nuns forced their boarders to eat their supper on their hands and knees—like kittens—from metal bowls that were placed upon the floor, and that they made them kneel on shards of glass which were scattered across the stone floor in the chapel as they recited their morning prayers. To her great relief, Margarita eventually realized that she had fretted over nothing at all, for Rosa never once mentioned their visit to the mother superior's office, let alone acted on her suggestion.

The sound of the immense wooden door scraping open at the back of the cathedral interrupted Margarita's thoughts. A woman with a veil pulled over her face walked down the side aisle toward a metal cart that stood near the confessionals. The tiered shelves of the cart held rows of votive candles in red-and-blue glass cylinders. The candlelight glanced off the plush burgundy drapes that shrouded the confessionals. Margarita watched as the woman borrowed light from a neighboring candle with a thin taper and transferred the blue flame with an unsteady hand to an unlit wick. After lighting nearly half a row of candles, she dropped several coins into the locked metal box attached to the side of the cart. The metallic ring of the coins, hitting the bottom of the box, sounded like hollow laughter through the cloaked air.

The woman then crossed to a side altar and knelt on a prie-dieu that was placed in front of the wrought-iron gate that fenced in the nave where the statue of Our Lady of Mount Carmel usually stood. With outstretched arms the woman whispered barely audible prayers to the empty pedestal. As she sat motionless in the pew, Margarita wondered what she prayed for. She, herself, had never prayed for anything other than the things that the nuns at La Sagrada Familia had told her to pray for. In their stiff blue shifts and white cotton blouses she and her classmates prayed in one voice. Repeating after the nuns, they prayed for the salvation of their eternal souls and then they petitioned for the sick; they petitioned for the dead; they petitioned for the poor; they petitioned for the conversion of the heathens; they petitioned for the sugar cane; they petitioned for the rain; they petitioned for misplaced objects and souls; they petitioned for the Christians in purgatory; they petitioned for the unborn children in limbo. They always closed with a prayer for the seemingly endless list of dying nuns, whose wakes and funeral masses they would eventually be made to attend. But after all of those prayers, Margarita had never thought to pray for her own special intentions as, she supposed, the woman at the Virgin's altar was now doing, for she imagined that after a while God would grow tired of having people ask for things day in and day out. Even God needed a vacation, she thought.

Rising from the blue velvet kneeler, the woman crossed toward an oversized wooden cradle that stood nearby. She reached into her front pocket and withdrew a handful of flower petals, which she tossed into the cradle and then set it in motion. As she walked down the center aisle toward the vestibule, she raised her veil just above her eyes and threw Margarita a mournful glance that penetrated her to the quick.

Tata had told Margarita about the cradle long ago, though she had never actually seen it before. According to the calambucas, it had been carved by a local carpenter for his wife. After many years of waiting, the childless couple's patience grew thin. Soon they began to argue and grow apart, each blaming the other for their inability to produce offspring. As a last resort, the desperate couple traveled to Havana and presented the cradle to the bishop, who reluctantly blessed it—for the woman had long since passed her childbearing years—and sent them on their way. Soon after, the carpenter's wife grew large with child. Early one spring morning she gave birth to two plump, fat-cheeked boys, though she did not live long enough to see them grow into men and pass on their father's name to their own sons. And so during the first week of the carnival childless women came from as far away as Sancti Spiritus to set the wooden bed rocking in hopes of ripening their barren wombs.

"The carpenter's cradle fills with silver coins and white rosebuds, pale braided ribbons, and a wide array of satin slippers," Tata told her. "A week after the Virgin is taken from her nave it is emptied and returned to the cedar closet in the sacristy, and the old women who sweep the aisles and clean and press the priests' vestments and the altar cloths collect the coins for the nuns in the monastery—who were known to take in abandoned children from time to time—and throw the keepsakes in the trash bins that stand in the alley behind the cathedral."

Margarita sat in silence staring at the cradle, knowing that within a few days it would be emptied and put away. It continued to rock hypnotically back and forth long after the woman's footsteps had died away. As the bells in the monastery began to ring out, she suddenly noticed that the cathedral had grown dark. Even though the bells told her that it was midday, it was as if day had already passed into night.

Before she pushed open the cathedral door, Margarita hastily plunged her hand into the large baptismal font in the vestibule. Then she crossed her forehead and kissed her thumb, a habit Maita had taught her and Caridad. It didn't occur to her until she saw them the following morning at the funeral service that she had left the white lilies she had gathered from the roadside for the Virgin to wither on the pew.

A slow, wrenching pain issuing from somewhere deep within her abdomen turned Rosa's thoughts back to the birth of her child once again. Shifting onto her back, she attempted to control her fear with her mind by using the skills Tata had taught her when she was a little girl, but her lips continued to quiver. Unable to find a still point within herself, she concentrated on the fugue of voices that came to her from outside the courtyard walls.

The street vendors called out like goblin men and women advertising their fruits and vegetables and flowers. As their words

> *piña,   piña,   y mango*
> *piñe,   piñe*

echoed through the canyons formed by the tall pastel-colored houses on the avenida, they were in counterpoint with other voices

> *mamoncillo   y anón   anón*
> *papaya   mamoncillo*

calling out in other streets.

The vendors' songs were gradually drowned out by the voices of the serving women who worked in the houses that lined the avenida. They were squabbling like hens over the prices they were willing to pay for the produce. With the sweet fragrances of their flowers and fruits and their tempting songs, the vendors had lured the women away from their morning chores. As their voices rose and fell in the streets, Rosa visualized the women clamoring with outstretched limbs around the merchants, who balanced baskets filled with succulent, exotic fruits and brightly colored flowers upon their heads. The serving women were purchasing for their mistresses' pantries. Soon they would return to their kitchens with nets and baskets filled with bunches of flowers and produce. Afterwards, the vendors would separate the produce the servants had overlooked— perhaps because it was bruised or overripe—and at the end of the day they would distribute it among the children who wandered barefoot and hatless through the streets of Cienfuegos.

Rosa closed her eyes once again and listened to the voices of the women caught in the chaos and the fray outside the courtyard gates. For an instant she thought she heard Checha's voice among them. Just at that moment a nearby fight erupted in the street, causing the women and the children to begin to scream. The sound of the fight took Rosa back to the day she had seen the mayor of Cienfuegos dragged through the streets.

She had gone to the cathedral to see the mural of the martyred saint that one of the older schoolgirls had described in a whisper to her friends as they assembled for morning prayers in the chapel. Rosa, who was sitting directly behind the girl at the time, could not help but overhear. It had taken her quite awhile to locate the mural, for it was partially hidden behind an immense marble pillar toward the back of the cathedral. When she finally found it, she could not tear her eyes from the image painted upon the plaster wall, though it filled her with horror—the ripped veil and severed breasts, the thorny crown that pierced the saint's forehead, leaving a circlet of moon-shaped wounds across her brow. The saint's arms were untouched by the tonguelike flames that hungrily licked at her calves and reached up her skirts, though the points of her long, dark hair had already caught fire. With closed lips, she delicately balanced herself upon a pyre of burning embers as though she were about to take flight, and soundlessly allowed her pale flesh to be consumed by fire and pain. Among the burning embers was a hideous-looking snake, which she trod underfoot. As though contradicting her mutilated body, her eyes were filled with ecstasy and her lips curved ever so slightly into a mysterious kind of half smile that reminded Rosa of the laugh of the Gioconda.

Sitting in the pew across from the plaster image, Rosa stared into the red mouth of the serpent that was pinned under the saint's foot. It reminded her of the day Tata had slaughtered the black snake in the courtyard at Tres Flores:

It was early in the morning, long before the other servants had risen from their beds. Tata swore that she knew something was wrong, for the parrots in the dome-shaped cage were flying against one another in a frenzy and crying out with fear. The black snake had coiled itself into a knot on the hot tiles near the base of the cage as it lazily took the sun. (Of course, this wasn't the first time snakes had been seen in Paolo's garden—for they often made their appearance wrapped around long, thick poles that were balanced on the shoulders of the boys who caught them by the stream. From the safety of the balcony Rafaela would choose among them, selecting those with the shiniest skins, and a few days later the snakes would reappear at Tres Flores transformed into belts and pocketbooks and high-heeled shoes, along with a pair of shiny alligator shoes with which Rafaela would surprise Antonio on el día de los Reyes.) Certain that Rafaela would die of fear if she saw the huge reptile as big as life in her father's garden, Tata borrowed Graciela's sharpest butcher knife—a crime the latter would never let her forget for as long as she lived—and sliced the snake into tiny pieces that began jumping spasmodically across the courtyard as though each separate one had a life of its own.

No one ever discovered what Tata did with the remains of the snake, but before Rafaela had woken from her sleep, the serpent had vanished. If it hadn't been for Graciela's younger brother, Pito, who had witnessed the event from behind the screen door in the kitchen, not a soul would have guessed that anything unusual had happened that day.

In less than an hour, however, the boy spread the news like a hundred fires through the town. All morning long people lined up at the arch to catch a glimpse of the severed reptile. Fortunately, by the time they began arriving at her front gate, Rafaela had already left Tres Flores for her friend Ana Rubio's house to help embroider linens which the nuns distributed afterwards among the poor. Antonio, of course, was in the cane fields. In front of a sizable crowd, Graciela boxed Pito's ears when she discovered that he was charging each person a real to look at what he claimed to be the tail of the snake through a small hole cut in the top of a cigar box. No one seemed to notice or care that the box contained nothing more than one of Antonio's fat black cigar butts.

For months afterwards, Graciela wept with regret over having struck her brother in public and confiscated his earnings (which, someone later told her, he was saving in order to buy a guitar), for only a few days later Pito woke with a burning fever from which he never recovered. The servants were convinced that he had been poisoned by the snake in the cigar box, despite the fact that Tata assured them that she had buried the remains somewhere near the orange tree in the corner of the courtyard.

Staring into the serpent's mouth, Rosa had been reminded of the canción Tata always sang when she retold the story:

> "Sambala, culembe, sambala, culembe."

Sitting back in the pew, she shifted her head from side to side with the rhythm, and as she did so, the saint's eyes followed her just as the girl in the chapel had said they would.

That day, Rosa recalled, the cathedral was soundless except for the occasional breezes that caught in the ceiling vaults. Unexpectedly, a woman's scream shattered the silence. At first Rosa was convinced that the saint had uttered the cry. Covering her face with her hands, she shrank back into the pew in terror. When a second cry sounded, she realized that it had come from outside, entering through a rectangular pane of stained glass that someone had tilted open above the mural.

As she stepped into the street, Rosa saw women scattering in all directions, screaming out indecipherable words as they gathered children in their arms like broken flowers. After a moment all was silent except for the yelp of a wild dog chasing its tail near the fountain of dancing maidens. Then an unearthly clamor rose up behind her and she remembered running across the plaza, glancing back over her shoulder at a column of men who moved toward her like a wall. They carried sticks and guns in their hands, and at their heels was a second throng mounted on horseback. They all wore red bandannas tied around their foreheads and some wrapped chains around their arms. A heavyset man wearing a vest with red-and-blue stripes rode ahead of all the rest on an immense ebony-colored horse. He was missing three fingers on his right hand.

Rosa remembered dropping to her knees at the arch of a walled courtyard just across from the plaza. As the mob approached, she threw herself onto the pavement with her arms spread out from her sides, as though she had been crucified. Paralyzed with fear, her vision began to blur and a blue mist seemed to surround her. Embraced by the mist, she felt the presence of her grandparents and of her aunt, Sylvia, who had passed away only a few days before in Santiago de Cuba, though the news had yet to reach Tres Flores. Rosa instinctively began to pray to the Little Flower. As the sound of the horses' hooves thundered all around her, a pair of invisible hands lifted her from the pavement and carried her, still frozen in a curve, through the arch of the pink marble house on the corner just moments before the angry crowd reached the place where she lay in the street. She could still recall the acrid scent of gunpowder and perspiration that filled her lungs as the black riders passed by the arch in a cloud of dust.

Staring blindly into the corner of the ceiling in her bedroom, Rosa saw the face once again of the man the riders had dragged through the streets on his back. Years later she learned that his name was Esteban, and that he was the mayor of Cienfuegos. He was an immense man. His face was swollen from the beating they had given him and his neck and his chest were covered with dark, jagged gashes, as though he had been pulled by a strong current among the branches of coral in the reefs beneath the surface of the sea. She remembered her father mentioning the man's name once or twice, though she had never actually seen him in person before. A thick hemp rope was tied around his boot and then fastened to the horn of a saddle. The mayor's body, galvanized by the motion of the horse that pulled him, creased and crumpled like a ribbon of light. His arms were extended above his shoulders, as though he were trying to get hold of something just out of his reach. His face was turned toward her as he was dragged by the arch. He stared at Rosa with vacant eyes as rivulets of blood flowed from his open mouth and flaring nostrils like ruby-colored tears.

Two of the other riders carried with them the bodies of the chief of police and his assistant, whom they had also dragged into the street earlier that morning and shot in the head at point-blank range while they stood with their backs to the wall. They left the three men tied together like a bloody bouquet on the steps of the cathedral as a warning to "la aristocracia y las curas," they had scrawled on a piece of paper that was pinned to the mayor's pant leg. The people had grown tired, it said, of the corruption and the abuses that went unacknowledged by the mayor.

At the time it had all seemed like a dark vision of things to come. Though many years had passed since that day, Rosa could not erase from her memory the sorrowful expression on the mayor's face. She had never seen a dead man before.

As she recalled the event, Rosa suddenly realized that she hadn't recorded it in her journal, which she always kept in the top drawer of her escritorio. Before she had even learned to write, Tata gave her the green Morocco notebook, telling her to record her dreams each morning when she woke, for dreams, she claimed, were more important than the things that happened during the waking hours.

"You must also be sure to write down the stories that your abuela and your mother and your tías have told you," she had said as she watched Rosa unwrap the notebook with the empty cream-colored pages, "for one day your children and your children's children will need them when there is nothing left of the past but a heap of broken images and songs and a path of unhewn stones. They will need to learn their own stories, m'ija, in order to defend themselves against the stories of others—others who will try to rob them of their memories or turn them into lies. Believe me, the next time around the wheel will be no different from the others."

Though Tata's words baffled her, Rosa knew by the expression in her eyes and the tone of her voice that she wasn't joking. And so, as soon as she learned to write she described the way old

145

Chang laughed like a madman amid the pink-and-red lotus in her dream; the red door at the end of the alley; Tata kneeling on the hot clay tiles sowing leathery green-and-brown seeds into the dark, moist earth in the flower beds; Graciela bent over her black skillet frying fish without heads or tails; the white courtyard wall where the women gathered to weave together yarey leaves or shell nuts; her father sitting on the balcony pulling on a cigar; the smell of jasmine and gardenia that burned like incense during the hot summer nights when she lay on top of her bed linens bathed in perspiration; and the orange tree that her grandfather had carried with him from Spain and planted in the corner of the courtyard.

As the years passed her by, Rosa recorded these memories and more, stringing them together like pearls on a string. In between the stories that she had heard at her mother's and grandmother's knees, she practiced her school lessons and inscribed the dates of her birth, her Communion and first confession, her confirmation, and her wedding. On a separate page, dated only days after she had met Pedro for the first time, she practiced writing her new married name—*Señora Pedro Amargo de Miramar AMARGO Amargo Señora Amargo* **Rosa Amargo**—in various scripts and combinations. Then one by one she filled the pages of the green notebook with newspaper clippings announcing her engagement and wedding and the births of her children, the parties and the openings she had attended in Havana, and the deaths of her aunts and her parents. On a separate page she pasted a lock of hair from each of her infant daughters' heads and their first fingernail clippings. She also charted their growth, noting their heights and weights; recorded the exact times and dates of their births; the long list of gifts they received at their christenings; their favorite foods; the allergies they developed and the childhood illnesses they both contracted (and usually shared) over the years; the first time they really smiled (as opposed to passing gas), rolled onto their backs, stood in their cribs, took their first steps, began to teethe, lost their first teeth, spoke their first words, went to school for the first time, and on and on.

After Rafaela's death, Rosa spent an entire afternoon bent over her writing table recording all of the things she could recall about her mother, including the dress she was wearing on the day she died. When she had finished she noted, with great dismay, that she had summed up her mother's life in only a few brief paragraphs. Rereading her own words, Rosa realized that the image of her mother, which she had tried to recreate with words, was vague and disjointed, pieced together like a counterpane of memories and impressions that she was certain only she would understand. The following morning—with María and Tía Marta's assistance—Rosa filled in the pieces of Rafaela's life, creating a picture of her mother that was a bit clearer and more accurate, though still incomplete. Uneasy at the thought that her own life might also be left to silence or to the mercy of those who imagined that they really knew her, she began to write in her notebook every evening, just before retiring to bed, driven by the consciousness that too many things had already been lost . . . *swept down the dark stream of memory*, she wrote in her loose, wiry script, *like a photograph that had slipped, unobserved, from a picture album*.

Somehow—though she could not imagine how—she had forgotten to record her memory of the day the mayor was dragged through the streets of Cienfuegos. As soon as she finished her breakfast and had a chance to bathe and dress, she thought, she would write down the story.

* * *

The chiming grate of a porcelain cup chafing against a saucer drew Rosa's attention back to the bedroom. She spread her hair out across her face and arranged it on the pillowcase as though it were a flower floating on the surface of the sea, and waited for her husband to pass through the room on his way to the cane fields. After a while she heard the sound of Pedro's chair scraping back against the floor and then the sound became the hollow tap of leather on wood, then a soft pat upon the stone stoop and the marble tiles. She shut her eyes as he crossed the dressing room and the bedroom. Then the sound of his footsteps became the smell of coffee and almonds, the smooth sensation of newly shaved skin, the rough undersides of his fingertips as he brushed the loose strands of hair from her forehead, the press of his lips, and the wet warmth of his tongue as he dragged it across her neck and her eyelids and brows. She knew in that instant that he had forgiven her, though he never knew that she was awake—that she lay waiting for his touch.

* * *

Rosa lay still beneath the comforter until she heard the faint sound of Pedro's motorcar pulling away from the front entrance. Throwing off the bed linens, she ran to the balcony and hung over the railing with her hair falling over her face like black rain. She thought she might catch a glimpse of her husband sitting in the back seat as Francisco pulled out into the avenida, but the leaves of the framboyán tree screened her vision. Moments later she saw Margarita cross the courtyard and open the wrought-iron gate at the arch. And though she wanted to call out to her, something deep inside her choked off her words and prompted her to withdraw into the shadows. For months it seemed she had been watching the gradual changes in her daughter from behind a pane of leaded glass. Gone was the child who had once hung on her neck and pressed her kisses into her cheeks until they burned. As she watched her daughter glance in her direction and then disappear into the street below, Rosa sensed that in that moment Margarita was pulling away from her, widening the seemingly uncrossable distance that had already begun to divide them. Despite her impulse to protect her—to shield her child's eyes— to conceal her from the world—something inexplicable told Rosa that she would have to let her daughter go.

Tomás waited in the paddock with Pedro's white-skinned Arabian, who pawed her front hoof against the ground with impatience. At the sound of her master's boots she arched her head and pricked her ears forward. Pedro took the reins from the old man's hands and stroked Matagas's neck as he fed her a handful of raw sugar. After she had finished licking the sugar from his palm, he mounted her and gently spurred her sides with the heels of his boots.

The cane fields lay some distance outside of the town beyond the thick groves of fruit trees, the fields of white lilies, and the thatched bohío huts where the guajiros who worked his plantation lived with their families. As the Arab made her way undirected toward the canebrake, Pedro sat back in his saddle sucking on the tip of his cigar until it became moist and pliant. Then he cut the end of the cigar with his teeth and scratched a long wooden match against the side of his boot. Plumes of smoke escaped from the corners of his mouth and formed garlands around his head as he held the lighted match to the tobacco and drew with quick gasps on the end of the cigar. As he rode along, the fingers of the breeze pulled the smoke out like wads of cotton and stretched them into thin spectral streamers in his wake.

While the white horse cantered in an easy lope through the lilies, Pedro glanced over his shoulders at the town of Cienfuegos huddling on the far edge of the fields. As the band of white flowers widened between them, the town became an indistinct, quivering mirage that seemed as though it would suddenly collapse into the horizon. From such a distance it appeared to be small and insignificant—a white plaster maquette rising out of the ground. Pedro tilted his hat, causing the houses and the cathedral spires to vanish behind the brim. It was a game that he loved to play even as a child, when he stood on the sea wall along the Malecón waving at the ships and the ocean liners that left the harbor and blocking out the hot tropical sun with the palm of his hand.

*　*　*

As they approached the canebrake, Pedro pulled sharply back on Matagas's reins, causing the white horse to come to a sudden stop so that he could take in the scene that stretched before him. His fields were filled with men and women who had begun in early June to clear the land that had lain fallow of stubble and turn the blood-colored soil. Pedro watched as they tore at the soil with their sharp metal tools. As one person—a single human machine—the cane workers bent their shoulders toward the earth, moving their hips in synchronized rhythm to an unheard beat like some great prehistoric beast toiling in the heat. By the end of the month the limpia would be complete, then holes would be dug into the earth with hoes and planted with cane tops. Once they had grown to be over six feet tall, they would be harvested, Pedro calculated, in sixteen—perhaps eighteen weeks—depending on the rains.

In late November, Pedro thought as he watched from his horse's back, he would return to Cienfuegos from the city for the zafra. By then the red fields in the upper quadrant of his property would be divided up by tall rows of green tasseled sugar cane. Season after season, he had witnessed the harvesting. In his mind's eye, he could see the women and children following in the wake of the men, who hacked and flailed at the ripened cane stalks with their machetes and cutlasses. As the cane bent toward the ground, sheared at a lower joint by razor-sharp blades, the women pulled it to the ground and the children immediately began stripping the leaves, knowing that it would have to be transported to their patrón's mill within twenty-four hours or it would begin to ferment. After they had cut the cane into smaller pieces, the men dragged it to the end of each row, where the women and children gathered it into piles. As soon as the cane was stacked, the men loaded it into ox-drawn carts that carried it to Purísima Concepción, the sugar mill Paolo Moro had built upon his arrival in Cienfuegos long ago. There it would be ground and then boiled in immense copper vats along with the cane of several neighboring plantation owners, who were dependent upon Pedro, being that he had the largest and most modern mill in the entire province. The coarse brown muscovado would then be placed in cone-shaped clay molds in order to purge the raw sugar of molasses, which would later be sold or distilled into rum. The clayed sugar was processed at a nearby refinery and then sent by train to the market in Havana to be sold to foreign buyers.

With great pride Pedro beat his chest three times, recalling that he hadn't missed a single zafra since he first took possession of the land following Antonio's death. As he watched the cane workers it occurred to him that many of their ancestors had toiled on his land for generations, for most were descended from the first slaves Paolo had purchased from the Englishman who had settled on his land. Over the years, only their patrones had changed.

"Most of them are like helpless children," his father-in-law had insisted the very first time they rode through the cane fields together, "and I have been like a father to them. You know that when we gave them their freedom, most of our workers chose to stay on at Treinta Sierras. My father-in-law gave them everything they needed well before the government dreamed of giving them their independence. He allowed them to marry in the Church and if they managed to save enough money, they could even buy their freedom. But nowadays—now that they are legally free—they all want something for nothing," he said with obvious disdain and anger. "I offered them legitimate work in exchange for their beds and their meals, but just the other day Alfredo, my overseer, told me that many are dissatisfied. This is not the first time that I have heard them complain that their energies are wasted working for another man's benefit and their labor is completely without meaning, mind you. That's an old story. So go ahead, go buy your own land, I tell them. See if you can make it without me. But if you fall on your face, don't expect to crawl back here on your hands and knees and find your bed made and waiting. The minute you walk out the door, someone who is more than willing to give me an honest day's work will be sleeping under your covers and wearing your shoes. Imagine," Antonio would conclude with a shake of his head. "What more do they want from me? The moon?"

Although Pedro pretended to share his father-in-law's disgust, he knew that in reality working the cane was all that these people knew. He had followed the debates that raged in the papers in Havana over the workers' rights and the patrones' abuses. He knew that need and practicality, rather than a sense of obligation, prompted them to stay on at Treinta Sierras and during the slow time of the year the men went to work on other plantations or to tend the gardens of the rich plantation owners while their wives and children worked in their houses. Against her father's will, Rosa convinced Pedro to pay them for their labor. Once Antonio had retired and her husband had taken over his role, she convinced him to allow them to send their children to the grammar school run by the Spanish missionaries, where they could learn to read and write.

"You are very foolish, my son," Antonio used to tell him as they sat together on the balcony at night sipping rum that was distilled from his own cane. "You are only asking for trouble. They're naturally ungrateful, Pedro," he would add. "If you don't keep them in their place, they will demand all that you give them and more. My daughter has a soft heart. She doesn't understand these things. No woman does. What could she possibly know about business matters, anyhow? Business and charity work simply do not mix, my friend."

As he sat on Matagas's back, filled with emotion, Pedro laid his hand over his chest. His father-in-law had been wrong after all. His workers were completely devoted to him and to the Señora, as they called his wife. Somehow they were all inextricably linked together through the land, he thought, as he threw down his cigar and took the joint of sugar cane Checha had purchased that morning from his saddlebag. With a switchblade that he carried in his boot, Pedro sliced off the top of the cane stalk at the joint and stripped it of its swordlike sheaths and its woody husk until he reached the pulpy, ivory-colored guarapo within. As he did so his thoughts turned to the mulata—the little flower, he thought as he sucked contentedly on the sugar cane and watched the women bending in the fields.

Gazing momentarily into the angry white eye of the sun, Pedro suddenly realized that if he didn't hurry he would fail to accomplish all of the things he had set out to do that day. A wave of anxiety washed over him at the thought that his whole day had been disrupted because he had delayed his departure from Tres Flores. For that matter, his entire week had been thrown off all because Rosa had decided to return to Cienfuegos with the children unannounced. At the thought of his wife's indiscretion, his cheeks flushed with anger once again. Just then Matagas began to prance nervously, laying back her ears and tossing her head from side to side as though she sensed her master's agitation. Pedro dug his heels into her belly, causing the horse to bolt forward. As they moved along the border of the cane field he was gradually calmed by the soft rhythmic sound his field hands made as they scratched and pounded the earth with their metal tools.

* * *

Conscious of the presence of their patrón on his pale horse, the men in the fields began waving their straw hats and red bandannas in the air above their heads. Pedro noticed that most of the women turned their backs on him, refusing to bend their eyes in his direction.

"Why," he imagined them arguing with their husbands in the privacy of their own homes, "should we feel obliged to acknowledge him when our backs and our spirits are being broken for nothing? We are working for the good of the patrones and their spoiled children."

Dismissing the women's arrogance, Pedro acknowledged the men's presence with a quick nod of his head and rode on.

Rosa stood on the balcony for a moment, leaning over the wrought-iron railing. As she brushed aside a long strand of hair that had caught between her lips, it occurred to her that she never would have stood so exposed in the city. Whenever they returned to Tres Flores, her life in Havana seemed so distant and unreal, as though it belonged to another. No matter how brightly the sun shone there, it always seemed to her to be washed in the same sad colors—a dull haze that thickened and thinned according to the hour of the day, robbing the scenery of shadow and light—of difference—and causing her to retreat back into herself like a tortoise into its shell. Only the shadows of shadows appeared in the evening like night spirits, formed by the street lights that lit the avenidas and the yellow lamps that burned in the houses and cafés.

Everything about Cienfuegos was different from the city, she thought. When she first arrived at Tres Flores after months of absence, it took her days to adjust to the lush landscape. Here the sunset seemed to be more brilliant, the flowers more fragrant, even the air seemed opulent and verdant as the sun pierced through the leaves of the trees, sending shivering shadows and shifting ribs of yellow-and-green light dancing across the ground.

"In Cienfuegos," Tata used to tell her when she was a little girl, "you can throw down a seed and a banana tree will sprout at your feet."

Each year when they returned to the house on Calle Semilla, Rosa brought with her something that would remind her of Tres Flores—a flower pressed between the pages of her notebook, a shell she had discovered during her walks on the beach—any object that would help her sustain the image, the feeling, of Tres Flores, with its rhythms, and colors, and scents.

A sudden sharp pain that opened and closed within her like a fist tore through Rosa's thoughts and caused her to double over. With her arm cradling her belly, she lowered herself into the chair where Pedro had sat when he took his morning meal. She breathed in slowly and deeply until the pain gradually subsided. As she did so her eyes fell upon the silver teaspoon resting against the side of his coffee cup.

"Abuela Azul," she said aloud as she took up the spoon that had once belonged to her grandmother. Rubbing the curved handle between her thumb and forefinger, Rosa recalled the day she and María had given Mariela her nickname. It was the day that their grandmother's hair—which she always piled high on top of her head like a silver dome—turned blue. (It also happened to be the day that the two sisters received their first and only slaps across their faces, though Rafaela refused to believe that her mother would ever strike her only granddaughters.)

Rosa had not thought of her grandmother for quite some time. Caught in her memory was the image of Mariela just before her death—a short, stocky woman with feet so small one might have thought that they had been bound, and steely blue eyes that seemed to penetrate even the most intimate secrets and desires concealed in their young hearts.

"Abuela Azul, Abuela Azul," Rosa repeated in a chanting voice, as she recalled the morning that Mariela had purchased tonics despite Tata's warning, from a street vendor—a complete stranger who had never been seen at Tres Flores before and was never expected to be heard from again after the commotion he caused in the Moro household.

"Señora, Señooora," the vendor had coaxed her with a thick black cigar wedged between the two remaining fingers on his left hand and a syrupy sugar cane voice that Mariela could not resist. "Trust me. My tonics will wash the gray from your head and make you look like a young girl again."

Noting the way that Mariela leaned toward him and her eyebrows arched with curiosity, he felt encouraged and continued. "My tonics will make your husband's hair grow even thicker than mine." With these words he ran the palm of his hand across the top of his head and then down his greasy beard. "They are guaranteed to cure your rheumatism and give your caballero new vitality," he said, winking a bloodshot eye at Mariela and causing her to blush. "Trust me, Señora. Do I look like the kind of man who would go around fooling beautiful and intelligent women such as yourself?"

To prove his good intentions, the vendor gave Mariela a large black jar filled with his most expensive and popular face cream at no extra cost. He vowed that only one dab of the pink cream, applied on a daily basis, would smooth the creases from the corners of her eyes and blend in the liver spots on her neck.

That same evening Mariela and Paolo followed the instructions on the labels of the tonic bottles—handwritten in a delicate, flowery script—to the last loopy tendril and floret. Rosa and María took turns watching through the keyhole as their grandparents rubbed the oily liquid into each others' scalps. When they had finished, they carefully wrapped their heads, like sheiks, as they had been instructed with matching green-and-white striped cabana towels, which Mariela had also purchased from the vendor.

Early the next morning the pictures on the walls and the crystal goblets in the china cabinet rattled and shook with Mariela's screams. The girls followed Rafaela into their grandparents' bedroom and found Mariela sitting cross-legged, propped up against the quilted satin backboard of her bed pulling thick tufts of cobalt blue hair from her scalp. Rosa immediately noticed that her grandmother's nightgown was partially open at the collar, revealing the large, hairy brown moles on her neck and a wide array of holy medals and scapulars of all shapes and sizes that jingled together when she walked. Paolo, who slept just across from her in a twin bed (for they had long since reached the point where physical comfort had replaced desire), was wearing a pair of boxer shorts that yawned open at the crotch and a sleeveless ribbed undershirt that had grown threadbare and pearl-gray with age and use.

As Rafaela entered the room with the girls at her heels, Mariela instinctively pulled her cover sheet over her head and began shouting, "Por Dios, Rafa, cover their eyes!" At her words all eyes turned upon Paolo, and they noticed that not a single hair was left on his head. Unable to mask their mutual surprise, Rafaela and the girls clapped their hands over their mouths at the same time that Paolo clapped on the Panama hat that he hung on his bedpost each night before climbing into bed. At first it was hard to know what was more shocking, Paolo's bald head or the sight of his boxer shorts. Not only had Rosa and María never seen their parents (let alone their grandparents) in bed before, they had never seen a man's private parts. As a result, their eyes were riveted onto the long, wiry hairs that sprung like seaweed from the crotch of Paolo's shorts and armpits. Perhaps out of horror and embarrassment, combined with the comical sight of Mariela and Paolo—who were usually so stern and dignified and, in Rosa's and María's view, genderless—the girls simultaneously burst into uncontrollable fits of laughter, despite their mother's ferocious looks.

Knowing that she would never regain control of her daughters, Rafaela begged for her mother's forgiveness in their names, swearing that they didn't know what they were doing.

At her daughter's words Mariela began to bray aloud in a pitiful voice and pointed her finger toward the bedroom door. Terrified and completely discomposed, Rafaela herded the girls out of the room, though by that time both were doubled over with laughter that their mother knew would soon turn to tears.

Later that same afternoon, as Mariela bent over her granddaughters' shoulders to inspect their needlework (for every ten stitches that they embroidered she ripped out twelve), she took her revenge. Without the slightest warning, she boxed Rosa and María sharply on the ears. Too startled to cry out, they turned in unison and faced their grandmother in silence, only to receive one long slap that covered both of their faces and left ghostly white handprints on their scarlet cheeks.

"That's what happens to disrespectful little girls who laugh at their elders," she hissed, blowing her sour breath into their faces. "Now put your things away, both of you, and go to your rooms. I want you to sit on your beds," she continued in a menacing voice, "with your hands folded on your laps until Checha calls you for merienda. If you so much as move a single finger or a hair," she warned, raising her hand in the air as though she were about to strike them once again, "¡te voy a dar!"

The girls recoiled in their chairs, fearful that if they spoke back to her Mariela would wash out their mouths, as she always threatened to do, with the lozenge-shaped bar of black Spanish soap that she kept in a lacquered box on her dressing table for such occasions, or make them gargle with the imported French cologne their grandfather always brought back for her when he traveled on business to Havana. Without a word the girls placed their needlework in the workbasket by the sofa before hurrying from the sewing room to their bedrooms. There Rosa spent the remainder of the afternoon stretched across the bed crying as she snipped off all of the hair on the imported Madame Alexander doll that her grandmother had given her for her birthday—a doll that she took a disliking to the moment she saw her, for she had specifically asked Mariela for a fountain pen and note paper instead. Unlike her sister, María sat dry-eyed in silent penitence, with her hands primly folded on her lap just as she had been told to do until she was called downstairs to take her merienda.

The following morning as they sat in the back seat together while Francisco drove them to school, Rosa and María resolved to call Mariela "Abuela Azul" whenever their grandmother was out of hearing range, a nickname that even the servants caught on to and adopted—with great amusement—when they referred to their mistress among themselves.

For months afterwards the local authorities searched for the fingerless man with the beard and cigar, whom Mariela described as having sold her the miracle potions. Meanwhile, she fed her husband large doses of an evil-smelling, syrupy green liquid that their old friend Carlucho de Silva had prescribed for him to take before each meal, but not a single hair ever grew back on his head.

After several months had passed, Mariela finally felt able to speak about the matter. (She knew that sooner or later she would have to offer her female friends, who gathered in her parlor each Wednesday afternoon to pray the rosary together and exchange gossip, some explanation regarding the color of her hair.) She told them in a confidential whisper that she had agreed to try the tonics only because the love potions that she had purchased so long ago from a Spanish gypsy had worked so successfully on her husband. While she explained, her friends could not help but notice the carefully braided lock of Paolo's fine silver hair, which was encased in a large oval locket that Mariela wore around her neck, along with her holy medals and scapulars. The rest of his hair, which lay scattered across his pillowcase, was later gathered together at Mariela's request with a triangular whisk broom and a dustpan, and from that time forward every baby blanket and bootie that she knitted or crocheted for her granddaughters' hope chests or for the orphaned children, whom the nuns took in at the monastery behind the cathedral, bore at least three strands of the old man's hair, a tradition that Rafaela kept up in her parents' honor long after their deaths.

As she stared at the silver spoon in her hand, Rosa felt overwhelmed with sadness, for there was no one left who could remember the story except María, Checha, and Tata. (Though Graciela was still living, her memory had long since abandoned her like an unfaithful lover.) A sudden wave of melancholy swept over her and turned her thoughts to the multitudes of silent and forgotten—those who had held her grandmother's silverware in their hands as she did now—those whose names she didn't even know to remember, though they were inscribed on the family crypts and tombstones somewhere in the north of Spain—those whose lives were somehow bound to hers, though their throats were stopped and choked with ancient dust.

"It will outlast me, too," Rosa murmured aloud, as she lay the teaspoon down on the table.

You were always a fatalist, m'ija, just like your father.

Rosa raised her eyes and found her mother sitting across the table from her, shaking her head as she stirred the sugar that had settled at the bottom of her cup of café con leche. (Ever since Rosa learned that she was with child, Rafaela had managed to make contact with her daughter, for pregnancy, she insisted, heightened women's intuitions and dreams and made them more receptive to visions and visitations. For the first time, however, Rosa noticed that her mother drank her café from the same porcelain cup that had smashed into shards the morning she collapsed at the breakfast table and sunk into a comalike state from which she never woke.)

"Mami!" she called out like a child, with unmasked happiness and surprise. "You always manage to come at the right time. But where have you been? I really expected to see you sooner than this."

Here and there, m'ija, Rafaela laughed, casually dismissing her daughter's question with a quick flourish of her hand.

"I'm afraid this time, Mami," Rosa said, as the smile disappeared from her face.

Rafaela leaned across the table and squeezed her daughter's hand. *It will all be over soon, mi amor,* she said with a touch of sadness that left Rosa unconvinced.

"Is there something you're not telling me, Mami? I know . . . let me guess . . . it's going to be another long labor, just like Caridad's. But I suppose I don't need a ghost to tell me that, do I? Look at the size of me, Mami," Rosa laughed, rising from her chair and proudly displaying her belly in profile. As she turned to see her mother's reaction, she noticed that Rafaela wasn't listening, for she stared absentmindedly into her coffee cup. "But that's not it, is it?"

You're being ridiculous, chica.

"Are you positive that nothing's bothering you?"

I'm positive, Rafaela answered with growing impatience.

"Ok, well, then just answer one question. Is it going to be a boy or a girl?"

Rafaela shrugged her shoulders. *You shouldn't be tampering with destiny, mi cielo.*

"Tampering with destiny? Come on, Mami. Just tell me. That's all I want to know." Rafaela shook her head from side to side without responding. "But what if it's not a boy this time?" Rosa pressed.

Gazing at her daughter's swollen form, Rafaela sighed with contentment and pride. *You know, Tía Marta swore you'd never marry.*

"You're changing the subject, Mother. You can't pull that old trick on me."

Let alone be carrying for the third time.

"Isn't it more like you never thought I'd marry?"

Who ever told you a thing like that? In response, Rosa shrugged her shoulders just as her mother had done a moment before. *How did you know that?* Rafaela asked, realizing the moment the words left her lips that she had given herself away.

"I just do." As she said the words Rosa recalled the conversation between Tía Marta and her mother—the one she had overheard by chance in the courtyard, while she sat on a stone bench behind a screen of lavender and yellow azaleas writing in her notebook.

You were listening! Rafaela said in surprise, wagging her index finger at her daughter. *Shame on you. If you weren't so big—and when I say big I mean big—I'd put you over my knees and spank you,* she added with a smile.

"It wasn't my fault that you were talking so loudly," Rosa responded, sinking down into her chair with a pout. "It just so happened that I was there that day. That was the only place where I could go for some privacy. Do you know that I used to borrow books from Papi's study and read them behind the azaleas?"

Why didn't you just read them in the house? Rafaela asked, opening her eyes wide and raising her eyebrows.

"Because when we were little Abuela scolded us when we read. She said that too much reading ruined a girl's eyes for sewing and embroidery and filled her imagination with romantic ideas and idle thoughts."

Rafaela began to rock back and forth in her seat with uncontained laughter, showing a carefree side of her nature that Rosa had never seen before.

¡Oye! When we were growing up your grandmother told every one of us that reading would make us squint, and that if we started to

squint, no boys would ever dream of coming to call, let alone ask for our hands in marriage. She insisted that too much thinking ruined a girl's beauty because when you think too hard, you wrinkle your forehead, Rafaela said, barely able to contain the tears of merriment that ran freely down her cheeks and formed a pool at her feet.

"So?" Rosa asked.

So you get wrinkles, m'ija. Wrinkles. What man would want to marry a woman with wrinkles? Catching on, Rosa joined in on her laughter.

But getting back to the original subject, Rafaela broke in, *what was I saying to Marta that day when you heard us talking in the courtyard?*

Rosa detected a nervous quiver in her mother's voice when she asked the question. It was obvious that she really could not recall the conversation. "The two of you were walking down the path together—you were carrying a basket filled with cut flowers and Tía Marta was holding a pair of gardening shears. First, Tía Marta said something like, 'Where in heaven did Rosa ever get that dark skin? She looks like a guajira.'

" 'I'm sure it's not from our side of the family,' you answered."

I did not!

"You most certainly did. But you didn't stop there, Mami. You went on.

" 'Who knows whether María will ever marry.' "

That was Marta, not me. I'm sure of it.

Rosa shook her head. "No, Mami. Tía Marta kept telling you that you worry too much—that we would be fine. Then you whispered something that I couldn't catch. All I heard was, 'What's going to happen to my girls?' You said that right when you passed by the azaleas. You know, I dropped my notebook. I think Tía heard me because she kept turning around and squinting suspiciously at the bushes."

Did I say anything else? Rosa nodded her head. *What did I say? I can't remember now.*

"Well, you went on and on about how María couldn't sew a straight line or eat without spilling something on her blouse if her life depended on it and that she was a gordita and had begun to lose her looks because of all of the weight she'd put on . . ."

¡Mentira! Rafaela gasped. *I never said any such thing.*

"What can I tell you?" Rosa shrugged. "You were very ornery that day, Mami."

I honestly don't remember a thing about this so-called conversation. Are you sure you're not making this up?

"Now that I think of it," Rosa continued, ignoring her mother's question, "you were always talking about whether or not María and I would get married."

That's not true!

"The worst thing was when you told Señora Ramos that I wanted to become a nun."

What?

"I'll never forget that conversation . . . you told Señora Ramos that it was only natural to expect that María would marry first. When you said that, she looked at María and said,

"'She will bring you many grandchildren, Rafaela, just like my Amparo' (you know, she's Amparo Aragona now). Then she threw me a sympathetic look. 'Pobrecita,' she said, patting my hand, 'at fourteen you're still no wider than a needle.'

"As if that wasn't bad enough, she turned to María and said, 'But then again, Rosa will never have to worry about her figure.'

"Every single time that woman came to our house she insulted María about her weight and reminded me that I was the only female in the Miramar family who was not blessed with wide hips and a large chest. She always found a way to make me feel as though I'd already failed at being a woman."

Forget it, m'ija. You have two beautiful daughters now and another on the way.

Rosa went on as though she had not heard her mother's words. Rafaela could see that she was upset. "Anyhow, to get back to the story, that's when you told Señora Ramos that I wanted to become a nun."

I don't remember telling her that, Rafaela said with a sigh.

" 'Even though Rosa is still very young, Antonio and I think that she might have a vocation.' Those were your exact words, Mami," Rosa insisted, reading the skeptical look on her mother's face. "Señora Ramos was so impressed she hardly knew what to say. She congratulated you and told you how lucky you were to have a daughter who would pray for your special intentions."

Was Marta there? Rafaela asked. Rosa nodded. *Did she say anything?*

"She was eating a huge slice of melon. I remember, because every time Tía Marta spit out her seeds on the ground, Señora Ramos winced. If I'm not mistaken, it was Tía Marta's third piece of melon."

She never had to worry about her figure, Rafaela sighed. *My sister used to eat and eat and wouldn't gain an ounce. I would look at an avocado and gain ten pounds. I had to watch everything I put into my mouth,* Rafaela added with false modesty.

"I don't think Tía Marta really cared what anyone thought. Anyway, what are you complaining about? You've always been slender as a rail."

Yes, but I've had to work at it.

Rosa glanced across the table at her mother and saw the same sadness cloud Rafaela's face that she had seen the day she'd overheard the conversation in the courtyard. She knew that although Rafaela had always boasted about her daughters in public, in her heart of hearts she worried about their future prospects. She had been crushed when her husband gathered them together in the parlor and announced that Rosa would be the one to marry Pedro, not María, as everyone had expected. Even the servants were surprised, for the eldest daughter was the natural choice— "her first hope," Rafaela used to say when referring to María.

The two women sat in awkward silence for a moment. As Rafaela began to stir the sugar in her café once again, Rosa fingered the hem of her nightgown, recalling the time that her mother had gone to consult the espiritista, Blanca Nieve.

Rosa! Rafaela called out in surprise, interrupting her daughter's reverie. *How did you find out about that?*

"So, Mami, what did Blanca tell you?"

First tell me how you knew, Rafaela repeated.

"Tata told me. So what did she say?"

Rafaela shrugged her shoulders. *I really don't remember, corazón. It's been so many years.*

"Come on, Mami, you don't expect me to believe that, do you?"

Bueno. Bueno, Rafaela sighed. Leaning back in her chair in exasperation, she began to recount the story of the day she had consulted the well-known espiritista about her daughters' futures (editing only here and there the details she deemed inappropriate for Rosa's ears).

Against her husband's wishes Rafaela had gone, accompanied by Graciela, to Blanca's house early in the morning after Antonio had drunk his café and left for Treinta Sierras. A tiny old woman dressed in a white caftan and a turban opened the front door and, after asking them several questions that didn't seem to have any bearing on their visit, pointed them down a long corridor with doors on both sides. (Rafaela swore that she saw Emilia Ramos waiting in one of the rooms. It was rumored that she had taken Amparo to have her cards read by a fortune teller who had passed through Cienfuegos, but was asked to leave the tent after she repeatedly interrupted the medium while she was reading her daughter's fortune and insisted upon interpreting the tarot cards herself.)

The hallway emptied into a windowless inner sanctuary. To Rafaela's surprise, it was a spacious salon with a vaulted ceiling lined with a tentlike canopy of pink satin cloth. A round table surrounded by several high-backed chairs of darkly polished mahogany and upholstered with plush burgundy velvet were the only pieces of furniture in the room. The table was centered beneath a pendulous crystal chandelier and was covered with a crimson damask tablecloth that reached down to an Oriental carpet. In the middle of the table was a wine bottle filled with pink-and-red roses. The walls were painted a soft, fleshy color and behind Blanca's chair hung an oval pier glass with a cyclops-like, unblinking eye painted in the center. (Te Veo was handwritten just beneath the eye.) Beside the mirror was a shelf covered with unripe fruit and a plaster statue of Santa Bárbara. The air was still and heavy, perfumed with the scent of burning incense and roses, and the room was lit only by candlelight.

Blanca sat like a sphinx on her dark throne, rotating her flattened palms over the table in wide circles. Her eyes were only half open and she seemed to be in a trance. She was dressed all in white, just like the woman who had opened the front door, and her fingers, with their polished red nails, were covered with rings. Her arms were adorned with thin metal bracelets that clashed and collided together as she moved her hands through the air.

Rafaela and Graciela stood at the threshold. After several moments, Blanca gestured them toward the empty seats at the table with a wave of her hand. The two women waited in silence as she studied the cowries and nutshells she had rubbed between her palms and scattered across the tablecloth before her. After much deliberation, Blanca told Rafaela that the future did not bode well for her daughters in matters of love and that at best she could try giving María vitamins and cutting back on her portions at the dinner table. She recommended that Rosa soak twice a day in a mixture of crushed ceiba leaves and azucena, combined with equal portions of sea salt, bleach, and holy water from the baptismal font in the cathedral, in order to lighten her skin color.

"If none of these things works," Blanca said to Rafaela, as she watched her dig through her change purse and lay out ten pesetas on the red tablecloth, "bring your two daughters with you the next time that you come and I'll try blowing cigar smoke in their faces. It can't hurt."

That same afternoon, Rafaela sent Graciela to gather the ingredients for the solution Blanca had instructed her to add to Rosa's bath water. The old woman went to the cathedral, mumbling to herself all the way. Rafaela had instructed her to take a clay pitcher to Padre Rabia, explain the circumstances, and ask him to give them the holy water. She even offered to pay for it.

Unable to convince the old Jesuit, Graciela returned to Tres Flores empty-handed. (All the while Tata, who refused to take part in the arroz con mango, insisted that if Rafaela were willing to see a real santera, she would intervene. She also offered to bless the water from the well, but Rafaela would not hear of it.)

In desperation, Rafaela gave up the whole plan and began a novena to the Little Flower instead. Afterwards, when her novena also failed (after ten days she had yet to receive the flowers she had requested), she prayed to Saint Jude and Saint Joseph, convincing herself that her real mistake was sending Graciela in the first place.

Everything worked out in the end. My only regret, concluded Rafaela, *is that María has never married.*

"There's still time, Mami," Rosa said in an attempt to console her mother, though she knew full well that her sister would never marry.

¡Qué va! Rafaela responded, blowing air through her lips. *Who's going to marry an old maid?*

"At thirty-six she's an old maid?"

At twenty-five an unattached woman is an old maid, chica. You know that as well as I do. Besides, your sister's a pain in the you know what!

"Mother!"

You know, Rosa, Rafaela said with lowered eyes, *your father never forgave me for losing your brother. And Margarita will never forgive herself, either.*

Rosa studied her mother's face in silence, puzzling over her comment and wondering what had prompted Rafaela to think of the son she had never once spoken of in her daughters' presence when she was living, perhaps because the memory was too painful. It was only after Rafaela's death that Tía Marta had told Rosa and María about their brother. Only then did Rosa begin to discover the unacknowledged losses her mother had sustained over the years—stillbirths and miscarriages, twins to German measles—but she had never quite gotten over the death of her son—her only son and first-born child—the son who bore his father's name. When Tata found him in his crib, his little thumb was still in his mouth, Tía Marta told her. It was as though he was asleep, but by then he had already turned blue.

Doctor de Silva said that there was no explanation. For some reason he had just stopped breathing. Your father insisted that we never speak of him again, though he wanted the boy to be buried in a double grave so that he could be beside him when he died. He even insisted on being buried with his pearl-handled revolver so that he could protect your little brother.

"But he had me and María."

It wasn't the same, m'ija. The same thing happened to my mother. Imagine, she gave birth to seven girls, seven crystal goblets, one right after the other. Rafaela cupped her hands over her mouth and her voice dropped to a whisper as she uttered the next words. *When I was young, I once overheard my mother telling a cousin who was visiting that only boys are conceived in passion.*

"Do you believe that?" Rosa asked, unaware that she, too, was whispering.

Rafaela shrugged her shoulders. *All I know is that every time Mother talked about finding us suitable matches my father used to put his hands on his head like he had a splitting headache and say, "Seven daughters means seven weddings, Mariela! Seven weddings!"*

"What ever happened to the picture of Abuela Azul with you and your sisters?" Rosa asked, for her mother's mention of the Moro sisters recalled to her mind the black-and-white photograph that Rafaela had always kept on the night table alongside her pillbox and a filmy glass tumbler filled with water.

Abuela Azul? Rafaela asked. *Where did you ever get that name?* As Rosa pointed to her own hair both women began to laugh.

"So what ever happened to that photograph, Mami?"

Rafaela shook her head. *No sé, m'ija. I'm really not sure. My mother used to call us las siete estrellitas—her seven little stars.*

In her mind, Rosa pictured the photograph. Her mother and her sisters were all wearing sleeveless chinese silk dresses that were ankle-length and beaded. Long knotted strings of cultured pearls hung from their necks and they all wore pearl ear-rings that hung like teardrops from their earlobes. Vivian and Ketika wore live flowers in their hair—the others wore feathers or combs. Mariela, whose head was crowned with a diamond and sapphire tiara, reclined on a scroll-necked divan. She was surrounded by her daughters, whose bare arms were carelessly draped like white wings across her knees and around her neck and shoulders like necklaces. "You were all so elegant and love-ly," Rosa said out loud.

We were, weren't we? Rafaela sighed, conjuring up the same picture in her head. *Do you realize that that was the last time we had our photograph taken all together?* Rosa shook her head. *Your grandfather was a tyrant, m'ija. He drove all of my sisters away with his temper, except for me, of course, and Martika.*

"But where did they all go?"

Who knows? The last I heard, Vivian and Ketika married and moved abroad. Sylvia, whom you probably still remember, died in child-birth, and less than a year later Chi died of quinine fever.

"And Carmelita?"

She joined the Carmelites, of course. You know, the nuns in the monastery here in Cienfuegos. Mother said it was her destiny. I remember the morning that she left as though it were yesterday. In preparation for her departure she gave everything she owned away.

"What did she give you?"

Didn't I ever tell you this story?

"Never."

She gave me a jar filled with glass marbles, knowing that I had always wanted them—you remember, the ones I gave to Margarita and Caridad, the ones that look like cats' eyes—and all of her beauti-ful dresses—so many beautiful dresses that Mother had brought home from her shopping trips to Havana. Marta was put out because Carmelita only thought to give her a rosary my father had carved out of rosewood and blessed by Padre Rabia. I told her she was lucky to get that because she and Carmelita used to fight like wild dogs when they were children. Anyway, I hid under my bed when Mother and Father called us all downstairs to say good-bye to Carmelita. I can still hear her calling my name. I was too sad to answer, m'ija, although I'm certain her feelings were hurt. She left an envelope on my pillow scented with the lavender cologne she always used to wear. I found it that night when I went to bed. With her words, Rafaela slipped a tattered envelope out of her pocket and pulled from it a sheet of onionskin paper that had begun to tear at the seams, suggesting to Rosa that it had been folded and unfolded many times over the years.

"What did she say?"

She told me to be happy, m'ija. Too often in life, Rafaela began, reading her sister's words, *people create their own unhappiness— most people who I know are searching for something that won't really bring them happiness—in the search, they seem to lose sight of the things in life that can make them really happy. So, little Rafa, it's all very simple. All you have to do is choose to be happy. That's all that she said,* Rafaela sighed. *At the time I was certain that Carmelita was making a huge mistake, but after so many years with your father, I think that she might have made the better choice.*

Rosa stared at her mother in silence and surprise. Rafaela had never spoken so openly about her father before.

The day Carmelita left us, Rafaela continued, staring headlong into her past, *I knew I would never see or speak to my sister again. You know that the Carmelites take a vow of perpetual silence?* Rosa only nodded her head. *I suppose Father prepared her well for her vocation,* Rafaela added, with another small sigh.

"What do you mean?"

When we were children he wouldn't allow us to speak at the dinner table. "Young ladies should only speak when they are spoken to," he used to say.

"That's what Papi always told us!" Rosa cried, recalling the long, somber meals that they shared at the dinner table. She used to push her food around her plate with her fork, or spit it into her napkin after she'd chewed it to a pulp, hoping that her parents wouldn't notice that she had barely eaten anything at all. All the while, her father droned on in a monologue about the fluctuating price of rum and sugar cane.

He was just like my father, m'ija. I married a man just like my father.

"So did I," Rosa said with her eyes fixed on Pedro's empty coffee cup, which Casandra had left behind.

Ya lo sé, m'ija. Ya lo sé. But your father loved Pedro.

"And Pedro adored Papi."

Antonio once said that if he ever had a son of his own he imagined that he would want him to be just like Pedro. I don't know how many times he told me that he saw himself as a young man in your husband. What could I say, m'ija? I knew it was a mistake from the very beginning, but what could I say? What could I do? Rafaela said, throwing her hands up over her head. *Not that Pedro isn't a good man, mind you. He is. But he just wasn't the right man for you, corazón. You don't know how I have suffered knowing that I allowed your father to marry you off to Carita Huelemierda's son. There's no one else to blame but me.*

"Carita who?" Rosa asked, starting from her chair.

Rafaela clapped both of her hands over her mouth to suppress her laughter. *After the first time Marta met Josefina Amargo—you remember, the night of the disastrous dinner—your tía renamed your future mother-in-law for you.*

"Mother, I'm shocked," Rosa chided Rafaela, though her eyes were filled with laughter.

You have to admit, Fina always had that sour expression on her face, as though she had just stepped in . . . well, you know what . . . and smelled it. You have to admit that it's true, Rosa. Fina was so stuck up, m'ija. She had her nose in the air, all because her father was a doctor and her mother came from a wealthy family in Madrid. Your mother-in-law was the one with all the money in that family, although you'd never know it by the way Don Pedro strutted around like a peacock with a stick rammed up his . . . well, you know what I mean. I think the Amargos convinced themselves that they were Spanish royalty or something. She treated everyone, including you, Señorita, as though they were beneath her. At her words, Rafaela and Rosa burst into loud peals of laughter. As the laughter died from their lips Rafaela turned her eyes away from her daughter's. Searching her mother's face, Rosa realized that over all these years she had been oblivious to the depth of Rafaela's pain and suffering. "Poor Mami," she murmured after a moment, leaning across the table to touch Rafaela's icy-cold hands. "Why are you telling me all of these things now when there's nothing I can do to change the past? You should have told me long ago."

You wouldn't have understood then, m'ija.

"You never gave me the chance."

No one knows what I have suffered and endured, Rafaela responded, avoiding her daughter's gaze.

"Then why do you still wear his ring?" Rosa asked, as she leaned forward and spun around the silver band on Rafaela's finger.

I haven't taken off my wedding band since the day your father first put it on my finger, she answered with a touch of pride, pulling her hand out from Rosa's. *They wanted to cut it off the day you were born—my fingers were so swollen I thought they would burst. Doctor de Silva was afraid that he'd have to cut off my finger. Imagine! But the ring stayed on. I wouldn't let anyone take it off,* Rafaela added, as she contemplated the silver band around her finger.

When Rosa didn't respond, Rafaela took up her spoon and began stirring the sugar in her café con leche once again, occasionally shaking her head from side to side and gesturing with her hands as though she were carrying on a private conversation with someone invisible to Rosa's eyes. As she watched in silence, it struck Rosa that she had never seen her mother wear any other jewelry.

Except my pearl earrings, Rafaela corrected her, reading her daughter's thoughts. *These old things,* she added, pointing to the pearl earrings that hung like pendulous weights from the elongated holes in her earlobes. *I've had these on since the day I was born. Milagro, the midwife who delivered me on a pile of dirty linens right over there,* Rafaela said, pointing to the corner of the courtyard where the orange tree grew, *pierced my ears with an embroidery needle and thread even before Tata had a chance to bathe me in glycerin and rose water. He couldn't make me take these off.*

"Who?" Rosa asked.

Antonio. Your father. Don't you remember what he used to say to me?

Rosa rolled her eyes as she responded: "Of course, how could I ever forget? 'Jewels desecrate the cathedral.'"

No, chica, the cathedral needs no ornaments. Don't you remember? He couldn't bear to see a woman wearing any jewelry other than her wedding band.

The old anger that she had felt as a child—the anger that she had never fully understood—rose up like black bile in Rosa's throat at her mother's words. ". . . nor could he bear to hear women laughing too loudly or wearing makeup or having interests outside of . . ." Rosa stopped herself as her eyes fell upon her mother's face, for it was filled with anguish and humiliation.

But he gave me everything I could have asked for, Rafaela said in a whisper, without raising her eyes. *He gave me . . .* Her words suddenly fell off and she lapsed into painful silence.

"Like what, Mami? Tres Flores was yours and Tía Marta's. The house and the servants and the silverware and the jewelry Abuela left to you, not to mention Treinta Sierras . . . when it all comes down to it, everything was yours. But he wouldn't even allow you to choose your own friends."

That's not true, Rosa. There was Emilia Ramos.

"You know as well as I do that the only reason Papi allowed you to see Señora Ramos was because her husband ran his sugar mill. Your friendship with her—not that she was such a good friend to you, anyway—was good for business, Mami. You know I'm right. If Faustino Ramos hadn't been the overseer at Purísima Concepción, you wouldn't have been allowed to socialize with his wife. Besides, she wasn't your type."

I just knew you wouldn't understand. Everything that I had belonged to him, m'ija . . . Rafaela's voice trailed away, as though not even she was convinced by her words.

"I'm sorry, Mami. I didn't mean to upset you," Rosa quickly responded, pressing Rafaela's hand in hers once again. "You were a saint. Forgive me."

He gave me two beautiful daughters. Gifts from God, she continued, seemingly having forgotten her daughter's presence.

Rosa released her hold and turned her face away from her mother's, recalling the afternoon she had walked in on Rafaela in the front parlor shortly after her father's death. The room was like a museum filled with all the treasures Paolo and Mariela had carried with them from Spain. Closing her eyes, Rosa visualized every detail of the parlor, though much of its contents—the tapestries and the oil paintings, the Sèvres porcelain and the Persian rugs—were sold at her father's insistence to buy more cane fields. (Only later did they learn that he had gambled most of the money away.) Rafaela had fallen asleep in Antonio's tooled leather armchair near the front window—the same chair where she had spent so many restless nights waiting for her husband to come home. Her face was still moist with tears and though she slept, the corners of her mouth continued to quiver and grieve. Rosa had never seen her mother cry before, for Rafaela had always insisted that tears were a sign of weakness. But at that moment the slight little woman who was her mother—the same woman who sat before her now with fine, silvery angel's hair—seemed as fragile as a cut glass vase—she seemed like a defenseless child.

As she sat on the balcony looking at her mother in silence, Rosa realized for the first time that Rafaela was someone she had never really gotten to know. To her, Rafaela had always seemed so strong, so unassailable. She was a mountain, a cathedral in her daughter's eyes. Though it was too late to change anything, Rosa saw for the first time that her father had made his wife into a curio case, a vase of cut flowers. It was a sudden realization that she quickly dismissed to some dark corner of her mind for fear that it might threaten the fragile memory of her childhood and the idea of marriage she had worked so hard to preserve for herself and her daughters. As she looked at her mother once again, Rosa still felt as though she were watching Rafaela from behind a pane of glass like a fish swimming in a bowl, even though she was seeing her more clearly than she ever had before.

Carmelita was right. We always have choices, m'ija, Rafaela said, breaking the wall of silence that had thrust itself up between them. *Though we don't always seem to know it, do we?*

174

Rosa raised her bent head and gazed into her mother's eyes. *It's never too late, mi cielo*, Rafaela insisted. *Nunca.*

"There you are, Señora!" Checha called out in a shrill voice that sounded like the clucking of hens. "I was worried when I didn't see you in the bedroom. But then I heard you talking out here . . . all by yourself," she added, arching her thick eyebrows with apparent concern.

Checha's words startled Rosa. As she turned in her seat, her gaze fell upon the woman standing in the threshold holding a metal tray filled with dishes of cut fruit and a steaming cup of café con leche. Although she was a small woman, no larger than a girl of ten or eleven, Checha was thick-boned and sturdy, with strong muscular legs and powerful arms, high cheek bones and an eye left partially closed from a stroke. She squinted at Rosa with an odd expression on her face, as though she were afraid to approach her.

Sensing Checha's hesitation, Rosa gestured her toward the table and said, "Ven. Ven." With visible relief Checha approached her mistress. As she cleared away Pedro's coffee cup and spoon and arranged the plates of fruit on the table, Rosa unfolded the napkin her husband had left on the table and draped it across her lap. She had yet to realize that her mother had left her.

aving finished her café, Rosa gazed down upon the hatless young girls who had already gathered in the courtyard below. The older ones sat in a semicircle on three-legged camp stools. The younger children crowded together at their feet on handwoven blankets that were spread out across the hot clay tiles. Though she could not distinguish their words from the balcony, Rosa could hear them whispering and murmuring among themselves in voices that sounded like creek water passing over flat, polished stones.

Somehow the scene below her seemed incomplete—only gradually did Rosa notice that Tata wasn't present. Sometimes the old woman would abandon her place against the courtyard wall from where she watched over the girls, and sit among them telling stories as they cut the edges of pillowcases into scallops that they finished with satin embroidery thread or drew linen into lace with hair-fine needles. The little ones hung around her neck or draped themselves across her lap, and the ancient one, as they called her, seemed to have a thousand arms to hold them. Rosa could picture Tata in her mind, with her skirts spread out copious and full, suggesting that even more children might be hidden beneath them. Standing among the shadows, Rosa often listened to her stories, too. As the old woman recited her tales, her body and voice were transformed. Her hands became the gliding shapes of silver-skinned fish that wove between the coral in the reefs or the colorful birds that cleaved the air. Her eyes beamed forth with the light from the moon and the stars, and her voice sounded like the breeze that rustled through the canebrake.

As she gazed at the girls in the courtyard, Rosa knew that over the years when Mariela (succeeded by Rafaela) was the mistress of Tres Flores, the girls' mothers had come to expect the Señoras' gifts and favors. It was not that Rosa doubted her grandmother's and her mother's good intentions. How often had she heard Abuela Azul say that it filled her with pleasure knowing that she cared for those less fortunate than herself, and Rafaela had expressed the same sentiments. But even as a child, Rosa had felt as though there was something comically grotesque about the faces of the smudge-faced girls, with their large vacant eyes and dirty fingernails, wearing the imported linens and piqué dresses trimmed with lace and ribbons that never seemed to fit them properly. The garments hung sadly from their undeveloped forms, drooping and sagging in the tropical sun.

While she watched the girls in silence, Rosa recalled her grandmother's words as she called through the wrought-iron bars at the women softly protesting outside her archway . . .

"If you don't accept the things that I send with your children," she said in a voice that had grown shrill and reedy with age, "they will only go to waste or be given to others who will gladly take them. Do as you will."

And so the women weighted down their pride with ancient stones and reluctantly agreed to accept Mariela's charity for the sake of their children. They allowed them to be scrubbed behind the ears and bathed in scented waters in order to attend early Sunday mass with their mistress, even though she always sat them at the back of the church. They went along with all of it, knowing that their daughters would be clothed and fed at the Caballero's kitchen table after the services.

After Rafaela died and Rosa succeeded her as the mistress of Tres Flores, she began paying the girls small sums for their labor, much against María's advice, out of the pin money Pedro gave her each week. Her sister had always insisted that the girls much rather preferred the handfuls of hard candy wrapped in red-and-yellow cellophane that she stuffed into their dress pockets or tossed from the balcony. Rosa could still picture the eager looks on their faces as the children cupped their tiny brown hands together like the two halves of a clam shell in anticipation of receiving the showers of candy María threw down at them over the railing. She also noticed that the older girls refused to raise their eyes from their work, though their backs and heads were being pelted by the candies. Although Rosa had long since discouraged her sister from giving the girls candy anymore, convincing her with great effort that it was better to give them fruit rather than sweets, the memory of the young children scrambling across the clay tiles and fighting like small animals for the wrapped candy sickened her still.

* * *

As the servant girls bent over their needlework, the fat, bunchy morning shadows gradually stretched out across the courtyard toward the dome-shaped cage. Somehow conscious that it was close to noon, the girls folded away their cloth and needlework and carried their blankets and stools to the kitchen. After a moment, they crossed the courtyard with wicker baskets filled with freshly laundered bedclothes, which would be starched and pressed into smooth white rectangles and squares that would eventually end up wrapped in brown paper and corded with hemp on the shelves of the linen closet.

As it approached midday, the landscape—scorched and ravaged by the unforgiving tropical sun—appeared to be on fire. Pedro began to feel light-headed as his temples pounded with the heat like batá drums. Rubbing his papery lips with the back of his sleeve, he could not suppress the thought of a tall, beaded glass of sugar water. As his temples continued to throb, he turned Matagas around abruptly, thinking that perhaps he should return her to the stables and finish surveying the fields in the late afternoon after the sun had begun to sink toward the mountains.

Now that he lived in the city most of the year, he had grown unaccustomed to being directly exposed to the sun for long periods of time. The heat coming off the cane fields exhausted his senses, causing the landscape to swerve like a drunken woman before his eyes. Even the mountains in the distance seemed to shift from side to side like a great indigo-colored guajira dancing the rumba. The sunlight pricked at his back, prompting Pedro to pause for a moment to take a swig from his water sac and rub the red dust from the creases of his eyelids. As he threw back his head to drink, rivulets of water ran down the sides of his cheeks and across the front of his shirt. When he lowered the flask, black spots appeared before his eyes and the whole landscape began to bend and swerve, sweeping him up like a leaf in the swirling motion of a dance he could not resist. Focusing on the wall of blue mountains that arced and spun in the distance, Pedro felt the earth dilating and buckling beneath him and envisioned her opening her great jaws and swallowing him whole.

After he had splashed his face and neck, Pedro pulled down the brim of his Panama hat, though the barbs of white sunlight continued to pierce mercilessly through the woven fabric, etching an angular pattern on his cheeks. Feeling suddenly nauseous, he guided Matagas out of the direct sunlight into a shady grove of wild fruit trees.

Intoxicated by the sun, Pedro rested his chin on Matagas's neck and shut his eyes in an attempt to recover his senses. It was then that he noticed how still and silent everything around him had become. Not a leaf moved, not a bird called from the trees, and the air embraced him like a wet blanket, weighing upon his chest until his breathing became slow and labored. Even the insects had grown silent, as though they stood in waiting for some final judgment. Just as he began to feel as if he would faint, the image of his wife, undulating and fragmented in a liquidy pool, surfaced before him. The thought of her cooled the burning sensation in his chest and slowed the throbbing beat at his temples.

The warm breeze carried the salty fragrance of the sea to Rosa, mingled with the scent of bleached linen and soap. From the balcony she could smell the sizzling fragrance of the hot irons pressing down upon the starched wet linens.

Cupping her hand over her brow, Rosa scanned the sky and noticed that the sun had already climbed well above the spires of the cathedral. She closed her eyes for a moment and drank in the succulent breeze that came from the garden and the sea. The burning fragrance of jasmine, gardenia, and oleander was mingled with the scent of the linens and the smell of the saltwater. The smell of sunlight and rain.

Rain, Rosa thought to herself as she breathed in deeply. She was certain that she had caught the scent of the rain, though the sky was almost without clouds.

Opening her eyes, she gazed across the courtyard once again at the space against the white wall where Tata usually sat watching like a cathedral over the girls. In her place was Casandra, the mulata with blue-black hair, whom her husband had brought in from the fields like some war trophy. Rosa's gaze settled onto her. From the balcony, the girl looked like a dark medallion against the whitewashed wall and her face appeared to be without distinct features. From such a distance she could have been mistaken for almost any woman as she drew the milk from a coconut with a thin metal straw, seemingly unconscious of the infant wrapped in a richly embroidered mantilla, who nursed at her side. The child sucked and gasped loudly and greedily, grasping at the empty air and scratching the soft sides of his mother's dark breast. Their limbs were spliced and intertwined, as though the infant grew from her side.

The mulata was flanked by a band of walnut-colored women—the madrinas Tata called them—wearing colorful madras skirts that sank gracefully into the hollows of their laps. Their heads were wrapped in bright red bandannas, their arms adorned with thin metal bracelets that clashed and rang together as they worked. They arrived each morning long before the shadows had begun to form in the courtyard and took up their places against the wall that enclosed Paolo's garden. Sitting cross-legged or squatting over coarse reed mats, they sang a canción with words that Tata alone could translate. As with one pulsing throat, their soft trilling voices carried across the courtyard and into the street. In preparation for the Virgin's feast day celebrations, some shelled knotty, crescent-shaped nuts into earthen bowls that they held securely in the wells of their bent and folded legs. Others plaited frayed silvery palm fronds into wands, while a few made baskets and hats out of yarey leaves and straw. Although everything in the garden remained still, their untiring, misshapen hands moved quickly and methodically, causing their bracelets to collide like swift-beating drums, never ceasing. Though they appeared to be a mirage against the wall, together the women formed a kind of whole—a living mural— fixed yet fluid and eternal.

Rosa gazed back at the mulata, sensing all the while that the girl was keeping watch on her in Tata's absence. Yet somehow she seemed to disrupt the pattern the other women created and broke up the familiar composition of the garden. She was a riddle Rosa could not read.

Rosa's eyes slid from the woman's face across the surfaces—the textures—of the courtyard until they held the shapes of the nut-brown women once again. Amid the still-life of the garden, their moving shadows were thrown into sharp relief against the bushes and the plants that Paolo's gardeners had trained to climb the chalky white walls. The garden was filled with neatly clipped bushes shaped into boxes and balls and raised beds of brightly colored flowers with waxy green leaves, curling tendrils, and drooping lips and tongues—together, they formed a riot of shapes and colors.

Even as a child, when she entered houses and rooms Rosa could strip them bare with her eyes and read the hidden messages of the world. She could visualize them as nothing more than four walls enclosing green shadows and yellow shafts of sunlight. But as her eyes wandered over the garden, she could not imagine the courtyard emptied of these familiar shapes and textures.

Look for the space where the spirit can escape.

Rosa cocked her head, certain that she had heard Tata's voice, only to find that the door to the balcony was empty. Sounding a second time, the words seemed to come from somewhere outside the garden walls. Feeling like an abandoned child, vulnerable and alone, she swept the courtyard with her eyes. Perhaps it was the mulata who had spoken—she could not be sure. Then, almost instinctively, she sought out the opening in the pattern through the maze of haphazard shapes and colors until her gaze fixed upon the stone arch and the iron gate with the rambling rose pattern that Paolo had specially wrought for Mariela in Spain.

Sensing the weight of another's gaze upon her, Rosa turned and saw Casandra staring up at her, frantically waving her hands and mouthing meaningless words that were carried away in the jaws of the wind that had suddenly begun to rise. Just at that moment, a white electric pain that began at the small of her back shot down Rosa's legs and pierced upward through her side like a lance, causing her to bend toward the ground like a cut orchid. Sinking to her knees as though in prayer, she covered her face with her hands in order to suppress the cry that pushed its way like a clenched fist up her throat. She managed to grab hold of the wrought-iron table just before falling to the ground.

When he awoke, Pedro felt weak like a child, and all of his limbs were stiff and aching. He tried to swallow and found that his mouth had grown bitter and his tongue thick with the syrupy taste of the sugar cane. Too tired to open his eyes, he tried—to no avail—to conjure up Rosa's image once again. In the dream—he was certain that it had been a dream—she was walking behind him calling out his name as they climbed the side of a great mountain. He, in his anger, had turned his back on her. In vain he covered his ears to shut out the drumlike sound of her voice. She begged him in a desperate, pleading tone to turn around for a moment. Unable to resist her any longer, he turned and saw only her pale green eyes, hollow and filled with terror. Then she reached out arms that transformed into great, feathery wings. Despite all of their efforts, they could not reach one another, for their legs had turned to leaden columns beneath them. And then before his helpless eyes, she split apart—limb torn from limb—like an opening wound, and a great river of her blood flowed beneath him and swept him down the side of the mountain into the dark valley below.

It was all a dream, Pedro thought to himself, though the thought did not quell his agitation. Even in the shade the sun can do strange things to a person. A dream, he repeated inside his head, as he wiped the beads of perspiration from his brow.

"A dream," he said aloud. Though he could still feel the pounding of his heart at the back of his throat, somehow he felt unburdened and relieved. He had possessed it and reduced it—whatever it was—to something manageable, something he could name and control.

Once he had recovered some of his strength, Pedro rode Matagas out of the grove and was taken by surprise at the sight before him. The mountains behind the cane fields were surrounded by tall columns of menacing black clouds, and a great shadow had fallen like a final, dark curtain over the sun. The wind had also begun to pick up, agitating the leaves of the fruit trees and causing them to quiver against one another like cymbals, and the sky around him seemed electric.

Pedro gazed back at the distant mountains as he reined Matagas toward the stables. For a brief instant the sun reappeared, then irregular black clouds rushed toward it, obscuring it from view once again and causing the shadows to sweep across the cane fields and drape the mountains like dark veils. As he listened to what sounded like thunder rolling in the distance, Pedro recalled that when he had first arrived at Treinta Sierras less than two weeks before, Tomás had told him that they hadn't had a steady rainfall in Cienfuegos in months. It was the driest summer that they had seen for as long as he could remember.

"First the rains, then the dry season," Pedro murmured in a slightly uneven voice that caused the white-skinned horse to turn back her ears. Comforted by the familiar sound of his own voice, he continued, "Now the rains again—the rains are long overdue."

Distant hoofbeats interrupted his monologue. At first Pedro could not identify the sound, for it came like a faint throb from somewhere deep within his chest. As it grew louder and more distinct, he dismounted Matagas and lay on his belly with his ear pressed against the earth. As he did so his heart began to shudder uncontrollably, for the sound of hooves was unmistakable. He knew at once that something was wrong, for who would follow him out into the fields with a storm such as this approaching? In that instant Pedro recalled having heard that a mulato from a neighboring town, who had murdered his patrón and raped the man's wife for only a few silver coins and an ox, was hiding in the caves of the mountains surrounding Cienfuegos.

Pedro lay motionless on the ground, unsure of what to do. At that moment a great wind, which carried the rains, blanketed him. The rainwater beat like hammers against his back and penetrated his clothing like cold needles. Although the white horse was obviously terrified, Pedro decided that despite the storm he would try to make it back to the stable. As he remounted her, his hat was blown from his head and carried away by the rain-soaked wind. Seemingly unaware, Pedro dug his boot heels into Matagas's sides.

* * *

Matagas's hooves pounded the earth like summer thunderheads, displacing great clods of red clay in her wake. Twice she went down on her knees, skidding on the wet soil that had become glass, for it could not soak in the rainwater fast enough. Each time, Pedro dug into her sides and slapped her neck ferociously with the reins until she got back on her feet. Like a madman, he steered her through the wind and rain toward the stable at the edge of the lily fields. As she thrashed through the white flowers, her head arched and her tail was raised like a plume behind her. Her nostrils flared wildly and fatigue lathered her sides and her mouth into a froth. But still she could not move fast enough for her master.

A sorrel-colored horse bearing a solitary rider dressed in black appeared in the distance, blocking the path between the lily field and the stable. Pedro glanced up in alarm at the threatening sky that flashed all around him, knowing at once that he had no choice but to continue forward. There was no turning back now.

Leaning forward in his saddle, he whispered into his horse's ear:

"Trust me just this once, Matagas. If you return me safely to Tres Flores," he murmured with tears in his eyes, "I promise you, you will dine on pasteles and rum for the rest of your life."

As the two horses crashed through the field of lilies toward one another, the rain began to turn to white petals all around them. Pedro could barely see anything before him, for it was almost as though a great white wall had thrown itself up around him. Like a blind man, he pulled his knife from its sheath. Just as the two horses were about to collide, Pedro recognized Tomás as the other rider. Instinctively, he pulled savagely on Matagas's reins, causing the frightened horse to rear up on her hind legs. As she did so, Pedro twisted around in his saddle and saw Tomás turning his sorrel mare in a wide circle. Soon she quickly gained ground on Matagas, though the white-skinned horse refused to slow down and continued to race toward the stable that was now clearly within view.

As the space between the two horses narrowed, Pedro could hear Tomás shouting something into the air, though his words were scattered like unstrung pearls in the wind. All the while, he gestured wildly with his hands. Just as he leaned backwards, straining to make out Tomás's words, Pedro lost his right stirrup. With all his strength he pulled on Matagas's reins in a desperate attempt to turn her in a circle, but he could not slow her down.

* * *

As the two horses drew near to one another, a recognizable sound carried faintly through the air and reached Pedro's ears. "Señora!" was the last thing that he heard before falling from Matagas's back. Like the sun that had suddenly gone into total eclipse, Pedro involuntarily closed his eyes. Just before losing consciousness, he felt a blinding white pain enter his side.

S played across the balcony with her arms and legs spread wide and her hair espaliered against the floor like firethorn, Rosa felt as though a lifetime had passed her by. For as long as she could remember she had lain on her back, crucified, with her shoulders pressed against the wooden planks of the balcony. All the while, the rain lashed at the cords of her neck and tore into her calves and her thighs.

Suddenly conscious that her legs were exposed, she tugged frantically at the hem of her nightgown in an attempt to cover her thighs, but she could not unbend her knees to conceal them. Her legs had turned into marble columns when the pain invaded her body—her space—and nailed her to the wooden floor. As it gradually began to subside, Rosa realized that all of the cares and nuisances that plagued her each day were only relevant to this moment. Now nothing mattered to her more than the thought that the pain had ceased for an instant, that the pain had momentarily ceased to exist. But no sooner had she thought that than the white fire mounted within her, returning once more without warning, and she felt as though she were being torn apart.

Propelled across the balcony, she soundlessly clawed the wooden planks, and then her hands arced through the air like dying swans. With one great heave she emptied her womb, sprinkling her white nightgown with water and blood . . .

> *and she felt herself*
> *smothered*
> *she felt herself*
>
> *slipping away*
> *as softly as the wings of moths*
> *ancestral voices sounded in her ears*
> *and bits of charcoal-colored sky*
>
> *flashed by*
> *between the red chaos*
> *and the things that she'd meant to do*
> *and the things that she'd meant to say*

would go undoneunsaid
and when she tried to close her eyes
they would not close
and she felt herself being borne

away

catapulting
at a great speed through a narrow corridor
deep and dark
toward a point of violet light

Rosa stretched out her arms as though reaching after some retreating figure only she could see, and then her hands closed shut like night flowers on the invisible air. The scream that shaped itself on her lips was drowned out by the wind and the rain. Unable to find her way out of the fiery labyrinth of pain, her face froze into a mask of agony and rapture and she felt her heart beating faster and faster and then finally giving out.

* * *

Casandra turned her eyes to the place in the sky where the midday sun was going into slow eclipse. Already a great red river was gushing down the streets outside the courtyard wall, effacing the surface of the cracked clay that could not drink up the leaden waters fast enough and causing the ceramic jars in the four corners of the courtyard to overflow with rainwater. She slid her thumb into the corner of the infant's mouth to remove him from her breast and gently lowered the child into her lap. The dark nipple of her breast was red and distended, and a thin bluish liquid continued to weep from its center. Dampening the hem of her shift in a pool of rainwater caught in the French drain that ran between the clay tiles, she wiped the soft puckered underlip and the drooping corners of the infant's mouth. Drawing into a soft, warm ball, the child continued to suck in his sleep, undisturbed by the rain that glanced off the shiny leaves of the banyan tree and pricked at his forehead.

Raising her eyes once again, Casandra thought she saw the shape of her mistress ascend from the balcony and rise above the trees. With her child slung on her hip, she rose from her place against the wall and ran across the courtyard, shouting out Rosa's name. She shifted the child to her shoulder and paused to throw open the immense, dome-shaped cage. Then she clapped her hands together, making a sound like the shivering of gourds, until the birds within took flight. As though possessed, Casandra ran toward the house, nearly losing her footing on the moss-covered tiles made slippery with the rain, and made her way to the back steps that led from the kitchen to the second floor.

* * *

The air was filled with noise and crazed, wet movement as the oversized birds struggled for flight within the cage. The young barefoot girls who had gathered in a kind of organized frenzy at the wrought-iron gate ran through the stone arch. They screamed all the while in terror and joy, catching the black rain in their grateful mouths as they danced in the shadow of the sun. Undisturbed, the walnut-colored women sitting against the courtyard wall continued to work, never ceasing.

Margarita returned to Tres Flores much later than she had planned, for a tropical storm unlike anything she had ever seen before broke out over Cienfuegos. Señora Marazul, the old woman who lived in the large pink marble house across from the cathedral, had seen her crossing the park and sent her manservant, José, outside in the rain to bring her in. When Margarita refused to remove her wet clothing, fearing that the woman would discover that she was bleeding, Señora Marazul towel-dried her hair and wrapped her in a terry cloth robe. Then she offered her a cup of pineapple juice and a sweet roll to take her mind off the storm. Though she did not ask, she wondered why a child so young was out alone in the storm.

As the woman sat near her reciting the rosary and she sipped the cold, sweet juice—which made her shiver even harder—Margarita's eyes wandered from the glass case that bore the plaster statue of la Virgen Loreto to the casement window. She wondered whether the shoes that she had hidden under the plant outside the courtyard would be ruined in the rain. If they had, and her mother noticed, she'd have to make up some excuse to explain what had happened to them. Deep inside, she knew that the shoes were the least of her worries.

Outside the storm raged. Although the old woman encouraged her to close her eyes, Margarita watched with horror and fascination as the fountain overflowed like a waterfall and the palm trees in the plaza bowed down to the ground, sweeping their spiky crowns across the wet earth, and then snapped upward toward the spires of the cathedral as though they were made of India rubber. Large objects were swept up by invisible hands and hurled like paper swords through the curtains of rain that were drawn across the window. Margarita covered her ears to block out the deafening sound of splitting limbs, and breaking glass, and the locomotive howl of the wind.

After several hours, the rain and the wind began to subside. Like an unexpected wedding guest, the sun reemerged from behind

191

the swollen clouds and shone brightly on the plaza. Anxious to return home, Margarita politely thanked the old woman, whose name she had forgotten to ask, and headed for Tres Flores.

When she arrived at the house, she was struck by the fact that the wrought-iron gate had been left open. Broken palm branches lay scattered across the courtyard, and she noticed that all of the birds had flown from the hive-shaped cage. She passed through the kitchen and up the back steps unobserved, for all of the servants except for Graciela had retired to their quarters. The old woman stood in the same place she had been when Margarita left that morning, only now she was pushing thinly sliced plátanos across the bubbling surface of her wrought-iron skillet. She seemed completely unaware of the girl's presence. Margarita passed behind her once again without drawing her attention.

The door to her bedroom remained closed, and the down feather she had pulled from her pillow and placed in the door jamb was undisturbed. Margarita closed the door quietly behind her and stood in front of the mirror pulling her fingers through her wet hair like a comb. The room was still dark, for the storm had yet to fully pass. She was startled by the voice that came from the corner of the room, a voice that was thick with ancient sorrow.

"Do not be afraid, m'ija, the blood makes you stronger than any man, though it will one day bring you great sadness."

Tata rose up like a mountain out of the squatting position she had assumed against the wall. "Come with me to the kitchen. Graciela will make you a cup of warm tea with hierbabuena. It will soothe your pain."

At first Margarita did not respond. She could not imagine how Tata had managed to get into her room without disturbing the feather.

"But my mother . . ."

"Your mother knows that you are with me. Ven, mi cielo," the old woman coaxed, folding Margarita in her powerful arms. "Your old tata will take care of you now."

Tata extended her hands before her, reaching out for Margarita as though she were blindfolded. When she leaned forward and kissed her Margarita could feel Tata's wet cheeks on her forehead.

"Why are you crying?" she asked in a trembling voice, for she had never seen the old woman weep before. Gazing into Tata's eyes, she saw at once that they were glazed and empty. The sight of them filled her with inexplicable fear.

"I couldn't help her, niña. There was nothing I could do. Something—perhaps the vision—I should have listened to the girl."

Margarita looked into Tata's face and realized that emotion had stopped her words. In silence, she ushered the old woman into the hallway and guided her by the arm down the back steps to the kitchen.

18 February 1964

Querida Margarita,

Thank God that you have finally written to us. Do you know that we haven't heard from you in over three years? So many people have disappeared without a word, I thought that you, too, were hidden somewhere in the mountains or perhaps that you were dead. How did you know about Tata? Gracias a Dios, we found her in time—she was in the courtyard vomiting up black bile and blood. No one knows for sure what really happened. Our old doctor (Carlucho) swears that someone was trying to poison her, although I can't imagine who would want to hurt her or why. Anyhow, she has made a full recovery and as I write to you I can hear her humming in the next room.

Speaking of Tata, do you know that she knew you had given birth to a son even before your father's letter arrived? He must be very big and strong by now. Send us a picture whenever you can. In his letter, your father demanded that I strike your name from the Bible in the parlor. Of course I didn't do it, though I wrote to him saying that I did. Last week, we heard that he sent Manuel to the padres at the cathedral (you know whom I'm talking about) asking that he destroy your birth certificate and the records of your baptism and your Communion, so that he could tell everyone who asked that you no longer existed! ¡Qué malo es tu padre, Margarita!

Shortly after you left the island, Concha (the wife of our old doctor) told us that the new government officials had begun to detain all of the professionals—the lawyers and architects, the doctors, even the professors at the universities. Concha told us that her son (Ricardo), who is now a doctor somewhere in Oriente, and his wife (Teresita) sent their two teenage sons to the States, knowing that they might never see them again. They stayed behind, Concha told me, so that their house would not be confiscated—apparently Ricardo is convinced that he can defend their home and their land. In a year or so things will get back to normal and they will send for the boys. "It's like a long vacation." Those were Concha's exact words. Well that was almost two years ago, and now Ricardo and Teresita's house has been subdivided; they are living there with I don't know how many other families, without their boys of course. Concha says that Teresa could probably go if she wanted, but she'd have to leave Ricardo behind. They will never let him go, m'ija, his skills are much too valuable. That reminds me, about a month ago I ran into Dora. She looked terrible, chica. You know how elegantly she used to dress all the time. (I'm still convinced that that woman wore her pearls in the bathtub and high heels when she let the dog out at night!) Anyway, she looked like something Lobo had dragged in from the courtyard. Although we were never very close, she dropped her things and ran to meet me. She begged me to take her in. Apparently two party members came to her home early one morning last week and told her that she had half an hour to pack a small valise. When she told them that they had no business barging into her house (you know how imperious she can be!), one of the soldiers hit her on the back of the head with his rifle butt and told her that the house didn't belong to her anymore—it was the property of the Cuban people. Just like that, they took everything. She wasn't even allowed to take her picture albums, let alone any of her china or her silverware. She's here with us now, Margarita, helping Checha with her chores. La pobre, she has nowhere else to go. You know, she has only one brother, but she lost contact with him years ago when her father left her the house and the plantation, rather than him. What's even sadder, Margarita, is that there are thousands just like her. We're waiting for the knock on our door when they come to tell us that this house is not ours anymore. Tata insists that it will never happen, at least not while she's living.

Concha also told us that when Ricardo and Teresita arrived at the airport, the boys were taken from them by soldiers carrying guns. All of their belongings were searched and then tossed on the floor. They were forced to watch from a small room with large plateglass windows. First the soldiers ordered all of the passengers to take off their clothes. Imagine the humiliation they must have felt, Margarita, their children were standing not only among other children, but among men and women my age and older. The soldiers frisked the passengers in front of their families before allowing them to board the planes. There was nothing that Ricardo and Teresita could do—pobrecitos—other than stand there crying like babies as the soldiers led their sons away.

Concha said that it was the only way to keep them out of the military. We are losing our young ones, chica, like blood from a wound. Only the viejitos like me will be left—left to remember.

Please, Margarita, write to us again. Cariños, Tía

P. S. Fear keeps me from signing my letters or using the last names of our relatives and friends. We are told that the revolution has guaranteed all Cubans freedom of speech—qué chiste—so I trust that with a little help from a few friends here and there, my letters will reach your hands. Give our love to your new American husband and besitos for my little nephew. You know how my arthritis bothers me, but I promise to write whenever I can.

Checha has offered to write for me, corazón. She and some of the others have learned their letters. Nowadays everyone is being educated—except for me, of course. There are still some things that an old mule like me refuses to do. Why didn't you come to us, m'ija? You should have come. Did you doubt that I could handle your tía? You should have come to us with your son, Margarita; we could have helped you raise him and protect him. Although you are hiding it from your tía, I know that your heart is empty. In time you will learn to live without him. I am lonesome without you, mi cielo. Believe that I am always with you. Be strong.

Siempre,

Tata

21 November 1964

Querida Margarita,

Just after I sealed a letter to you, we received a call from one of your father's neighbors telling us that he had fallen and cracked a rib (his eyesight, which was never very good to begin with, is getting worse and worse). Tata traveled to the city alone (imagine!) to get your father. The long and the short of it is, she could not convince him to come back with her. He wrote to me last week saying that he would never return to C____. He's convinced that there are still going to be elections, even though the government continues to confiscate everyone's property. How can your father, of all people, be such an idiot? They've even begun to burn the cane—I think I told you about that in my last letter? In the local paper they quoted one official (I forget who it was—they're all the same to me!) as saying that they were burning the cane of the American imperialistas. Tata said that your father fought her like a león. It's people like him—people who have money—who put el cura in power, Margarita, not the guajiros or the negritos, as most people believe. And it's pigheaded people like your father who will keep him in power. He's as bad as the "come candelas," who claim to be unconditionally committed to the revolution— but to eat fire, you must wear a blindfold, no? Take my word for it, your father has been deceived and he will die alone and disillusioned, having lost everything that he treasures in life, including his daughters. (I'm half convinced that he really knows the truth—but pride keeps him from admitting that he was wrong!!)

and then he picked the number three! Can you imagine?

Even though the walls are invisible, our town has become a prison, Margarita. No one can come or go without the permission of the government officials (the vigilance, they call them) who guard every block—they are the eyes of the revolution. It's rumored that the military has established labor camps all over the island. Though I still don't know how she manages to come and go without getting caught, Tata has been to see your father several times now. Can you believe that she arrived at the house and found your father burying his mother's silverware under the rose bushes in the courtyard? They say that Cuba is filled with buried treasure now, like the Spanish galleons resting on the bottom of the harbor, and the mountains around the city conceal a king's ransom. Half of the people in Havana are burying their pasts, while the other half are fleeing the island with their fortunes sewn into their hatbands and hidden in their socks. After the fall, many believe they will return and reclaim their fortunes! Tata said that in truth most of your grandmother's belongings have already been confiscated and it's only a matter of time until they take the house. Gracias a Dios, Mercedes died in her sleep just before all of this happened. She was the last of the old tías to go, and with her a world, I fear, that is lost forever, except in memory. (Do you know that she would have been eighty-nine next month?)

Despite all of the evidence to the contrary, your stone-headed father still writes to me praising the new government. How can anyone be so blind? The truth of the matter is that your father is too proud to admit that he was wrong—that he, along with most of his friends, was deceived. After all of the broken promises, he still insists that there will be free elections. Imagine! Rey muerto. Rey puesto, I wrote back to him, el cura is just another king. He was so furious that he called me up and roared his nonsense like a madman in my ear for over half an hour. I almost hung up on him, but something in his voice made me listen—I must be getting soft in the head!

Abrazos,

Tía

2 December 1964

Querida Margarita,

Like a fool, your father refused to listen until it
was too late. They even took your silver baby cups
and spoons and slashed the portrait of Josefina and
Cuca that hung beside the family crest in the front
parlor. Needless to say, your father is with us now,
and he is still as thickheaded as ever. Before
Manuel could get him into the car, the soldiers had
already emptied the contents of his bedroom onto
the driveway and the front lawn, and the house had
been transformed into a barracks. I hate to say it,
but it serves him right. When I told him that, he
wept with rage like a child. I will write again soon
and let you know how we are getting on together.

Cariños,

Tía

Mi cielo,

I found your father sitting beside Manuel this morning on the base of the old dome-shaped cage in the courtyard. The things that he witnessed in Havana have driven him half out of his mind. In only a few months, he aged so much that I barely recognized him. Only Lobo (el tercero) knew him. The old dog was curled into a ball at your father's feet. At first I thought he was sleeping, but when I leaned down and touched him he was already cold, pobrecito. He was so devoted to your father, m'ija. Perhaps he died of happiness at the sight of his old master.

Siempre Tata

2 December 1964

Querida Margarita,

Like a fool, your father refused to listen until it was too late. They even took your silver baby cups and spoons and slashed the portrait of Josefina and Cuca that hung beside the family crest in the front parlor. Needless to say, your father is with us now, and he is still as thick-headed as ever. Before Manuel could get him into the car, the soldiers had already emptied the contents of his bedroom onto the driveway and the front lawn, and the house had been transformed into a barracks. I hate to say it, but it serves him right. When I told him that, he wept with rage like a child. I will write again soon and let you know how we are getting on together.

Cariños,

Tía

Margarita,

He told us that the Cuban people would bathe in milk, but milk is nowhere to be had. Perhaps he meant coconut milk, or perhaps we'll have to buy powdered milk—that is, if the shelves aren't already empty in the stores. Food is getting more and more scarce every day. Even though Checha and Tata wait in ration lines (sometimes for hours), they often come home empty-handed.

If you can imagine, your great-grandfather's courtyard is now filled with billy goats (who have eaten through most of the flower beds) and two baby pigs, and the old birdcage has been converted into a chicken coop. The entire neighborhood has changed, chica. Everyone, including myself, takes turns guarding the animals because meat has become a luxury. It's all we can do to keep the neighbors, let alone the santeros, away. In fact, last week two chickens and a goat were stolen right out from under our noses despite our vigilance, and it's rumored that people have even begun to eat their own housepets. Thank God, Lobo is no longer with us—nowadays even a flea-bitten bone of a dog looks good to someone who hasn't had meat in several months.

16 July 1964

Querida Margarita,

Wait until you hear what happened! Last night
Ignacio—Lucía's (from Varadero) husband, whom we had
all taken for dead—just appeared in the kitchen. We
all stared at him as though he were a ghost. Once
Tata had fed him, he told us a story that no one but
those who had witnessed would believe. He said that
each evening he used to go to the park near his
house to smoke a cigar with his friends and talk.
They were warned several times by the guardia who
patrolled the park, but that didn't stop them from
talking. When the news of the invasion at Playa
Girón reached them, Ignacio said that the rebel
soldiers arrived in Varadero by the truckload. Some
beat the people with clubs and rifles. Then they
ordered them to lie down in the streets, where the
soldiers continued to beat them and curse them.
Others, including Ignacio, were handcuffed and
arrested on the charge that they were enemies of
the revolution. Before blindfolding them, the soldiers
separated the men from the women and then loaded
them into trucks that took them to different camps.
When they arrived, the soldiers took off their blindfolds and forced them to strip down to their shorts.
Many were burned on their genitals with lit cigars or
beaten with leather thongs and joints of cane until
they collapsed, unconscious, in puddles of their own
blood. (In order to prove to us that he was not lying,
Ignacio raised his guayabera and showed us the scars
on his back, Margarita. They form a hideous labyrinth

with no beginning and no end, like the roots of the old banyan tree in the park at the end of the street.)

After several hours, which seemed like an eternity to the prisoners, Ignacio said, they divided the men into groups of ten and threw them into windowless dirt cells which were so crowded, Margarita, that they couldn't even lie down. They were standing for three days with no food and no water and nowhere to relieve themselves. (He called the cells the black holes of Calcutta.) Those who managed to survive were moved to cages where they were confined like wild animals. In the morning, they were given only a cup of water and un pedazo de pan. Ignacio said that he knew he was surrounded by his old friends, most of whom never made it out. He said that during the weeks that he was confined he never once fell asleep (though he must have but doesn't remember) because the air was filled with the stench of rotting flesh, and human waste, and the sound of the men's anguish.

Ten times a day, he told us, the soldiers threatened them with their lives, filling them with horror and fear. They swore that if the Americans advanced, all of those who had been arrested would be shot. After all that, they transferred some of the prisoners to the dungeons in El Moro. Ignacio was sent to La Cabaña. Early in the morning, the prisoners were forced to watch as they lined up groups of "dissidents" (that's what they call anyone who is even suspected of not supporting the revolution) against the prison wall. Sometimes, Ignacio told us, the soldiers would shoot their rifles just above the prisoners' heads to terrorize and humiliate them, for many of them dirtied themselves out of sheer fright. Other times they would open fire, murdering them in cold blood as a warning to the others. He told us that they shot the man next to him. He died crying out, "¡Viva Cristo Rey!"

Ten days ago—for no apparent reason—the soldiers blindfolded Ignacio once again and threw him in the back of a truck. They drove for what seemed hours, he said, then stopped the truck and left him sitting by the side of the road—in the middle of nowhere— just like that, as though no time had passed and nothing had ever happened. He has no idea why they let him go.

Ignacio was crying when he told us the story, as we all were. I could not look at his face. His words made me recall the stories Tía Marta used to tell us about the cimarrones who were pushed by the Spaniards through the trap doors in the dungeons of El Moro and fed to the sharks that were hungrily swimming beneath them. Although they keep telling us that the Cuban people have never been freer, in reality we are slaves, Margarita. Even though it may be impossible to locate her, we have begun to search for Lucía to let her know that her husband is here with us, alive and (for the time being) safe.

Besitos for you and your husband and son.

Tía

21 January 1964

Querida Margarita,

Your father is a broken man. Although I can never replace your mother in his heart, he relies on me now like a child. The other day he told me that when Rosa died, the whole world died with her. Back then, he said that there was nothing else to lose. Now he realizes that he has truly lost almost everything. At first, I thought he was talking about the house in the city. If you can find a small space in your heart, forgive him for the things that he said and did to you. Forget the past, Margarita. What is done is done. Your father has changed, I swear to you, the old dog has changed. We all have. Except for our memories and our sense of humor (and, of course, the palm trees and the sea), they have robbed us of everything.

Tía

6 March 1965

Querida,

The other day your father asked for you for the first time since you left. We didn't have the heart to tell him that you were gone. In his old age, your father needs the comfort of his daughters. Since you're not here, we sent Pancho to try and locate Caridad, but both the monastery and the cathedral have been stripped and shut down. (I can't remember if I told you, but Padre Rabia died a little more than a year or so after you left and Padre Morales just disappeared into thin air. No one knows what happened to him, el pobre. He's probably dead, too.) Anyway, a soldier with a bayonet was guarding the door at the monastery. When he asked the man if he knew of the whereabouts of the nuns, Pancho said that he just shrugged his shoulders and said, "No existe." Pancho asked a second time, but the soldier turned away as though he was invisible, sin vergüenza. We've been asking around, but no one seems to have any information about her. For all we know, she may be dead. In exasperation, I told your father that Caridad could not be located. Now he talks of nothing but you and his grandson. At the very least, send him a photograph of your son. Por favor, chica.

                            Tía

by the way.

I meant to ask you, do your American papers tell you that el barbudo keeps many homes so that no one but his closest advisors is certain where he is at any given time? We heard that your grandmother's house in the city was being used for that purpose. Your father would hit the ceiling if he knew. Your mother's old friend Amparo saw him at a rally last month. (She and her daughter Isabelita are very active in the revolution these days and Amparo has even volunteered to cut cane, though she is well into her sixties! "If everyone does their fair share," she told me, "we will reach our goal of ten million tons." I think she was trying to make me feel guilty for not contributing to "the cause." Can you imagine? You should see her—she looks like an old fool in her fatigues and her red bandanna!) Beard and all, el cura insists that he has no home, no wife, no family. Cuba is his home and the revolution is his bride (and, of course, the Cuban people are his children . . . ha! . . . one big happy family, no?).

Write when you can, and don't forget to send a picture.

Saludos a todo mundo,

Tía

Your sisters are together now, mi cielo. I saw them in a dream. Caridad, along with several of the other nuns in her community, have taken care of Violeta in your mother's place. Carmelita, la pobre, is sleeping peacefully with her sisters, mi amor. But Caridad and Violeta are now in hiding with a small group of Carmelites. Don't worry, the mountains will protect them, m'ija. There they will find everything they need.

Siempre Tata

7 October 1965

Oye Nena,

I am worried about your father. During the night he
cries with terror and hides himself under the bed. He
said that it's the only place where he feels safe.
When I try to coax him out, he screams that it isn't
his fault—No es mi culpa. No es mi culpa. Every day he
eats less and less. When I asked him why he wouldn't
eat, he said he was afraid that I was trying to poison
him—imagine! And his limp gets worse and worse;
when he walks, he drags his leg behind him. Manuel
carved him a cane from a branch of the orange tree,
but he refused to use it. You know what he did? (I'm
almost embarrassed to tell you.) He broke the cane
over his knee (your father's still as strong as an ox)
and, as if that wasn't enough, he ordered Manuel to
attach a chain to the back bumper of his old Chevy (if
you can believe it, that old tin can still runs!) and had
him tear out the orange tree your great-grandfather
planted—nearly a century ago—by the roots. No one
could stop him, m'ija. Your father is a very stubborn and
bullheaded man—he won't allow anyone except for Tata
to help him with anything. Even though he denies it,
he has all but lost his hearing and sight. (The other
day I overheard him telling Tata that now all he could
see were silhouettes and the shadows of shadows.) He
makes me repeat everything I say at least ten times,
even though Checha can understand every word I'm
saying from the kitchen.

From morning until night, he does nothing but sit
in the rocking chair by the window sucking on his

fingers and staring into the courtyard. Often, Tata and I find him nodding his head and whispering words that we can barely make out. He insists that he's holding long conversations with your mother and that just before she appears to him, the room fills with the scent of jasmine and sandalwood. He said that she was the one who told him to take you from Tres Flores and bring you to Havana, and that even though you didn't seem to be aware of it, your mother watched over you continuously. He is haunted by regret over the fact that he didn't kiss Rosa one last time before leaving for the cane fields on the day she died. The first time he told me these things, I made the mistake of laughing. Filled with rage, he told me that if I knew anything about anything, I'd know to fear the living more than the dead. It's almost as though a voice that only he can hear has sounded from somewhere deep within him. Most of the time Tata's the only one who knows what he's saying. Other times, his lips move incessantly, though   I can make out no words. He continues to ask for you and his grandson. The other day, when I asked him how he was feeling, he told me that your name was being consumed by the tongues of strangers. Your father is crazy, vieja, completemente loco.

Sometimes he lies in bed all day with his hands folded across his chest and his thumbs twirling, and he recites his prayers or sings old folk songs. Other days, he does nothing but laugh, although that always ends in tears. Last night as I stood at his bedroom door, I heard him calling out your mother's name in his sleep. When I came to his bedside, he thought that I was you. He began weeping with happiness. The night before, I found him crawling half-naked on his hands and knees across the marble floor. When I asked him what he was doing out of bed, first he told me that he was looking for your mother's hairpins. Then he said that she had lost her wedding band and he had promised her that he'd find it. (You know it's strange, Margarita, when we found your mother on the balcony, her ring was gone and we never did find it. What do you want to bet that mulata took it? She vanished not long after you did—I swear I saw her wearing your mother's ring. You can be sure that Checha gave it to her—I wouldn't put it past either one of them. You should have seen the way she made eyes at Padre Morales when he came to see me at the house. That mulata was bad news from the start.) Your father was so grief stricken that I didn't have the heart to tell him we can't find your mother's ring. When I finally got him under the covers again, he whispered that the wind had stolen his hat, and that a man without a hat was no man at all. If only you could come, Margarita, and help me through this nightmare. At least write to him. He makes me read your letters over and over again. Even though they are addressed to me, they bring him such comfort, m'ija. Forget the past, corazón. Your father is old and dying.

Tía

Don't worry about your father, m'ija. He has talked with your mother and soon they will be together again.

Siempre Tata

Margarita,

You should have come like you promised. Now it is too late. Your father is dead. Apparently the news of your father's death spread quickly because in less than a week some big galoot whom no one has ever laid eyes on before showed up at the front door and tried to kick us out of the house. He insisted that it rightfully belonged to him because he was your father's only surviving heir—can you imagine! We still don't know who he was—probably just some high-ranking big shot in the government who thinks he owns everybody. Anyway, he might have succeeded in throwing us all out if it were not for Tata. No one knows what she said to him, but the big black crow left without any gold in his beak. You should have seen him, running out the same way he came in—sin vergüenzas—with his tail between his legs.

    The government has divided up nearly all of the houses in the neighborhood, sometimes squeezing three or four families into one home like a can of sardines. (It's a mystery to me why they haven't divided up our house in the same way—it's almost as though we are protected by some invisible wall.) And they're not even nice families, if you know what I mean—they're low class, chica—our neighborhood is filled with a bunch of negritos who practice brujerías. All of the good families have either left or they've died out. Sometimes (though not very often), I walk to the corner to get some fresh air and it breaks my heart to see the balconies on the beautiful houses strung with clotheslines cluttered with underclothing and sheets. These people have no pride, Margarita—they hang their dirty linens and their underpants right out in the street so that everyone can see them. (Nowadays—if you can believe it—even underwear gets stolen right off the clothesline!) What's worse is that they slaughter their animals right in the middle of the solar. The other day I saw a goat hanging from a clothes pole. It was thrashing around, struggling to free itself from its noose. Who knows how long it had been hanging there, suffering in the sun. As I passed by, a big negra came out with a butcher knife and slashed the poor thing's neck. It was horrible, corazón. There was blood everywhere.

Most of the houses on the block, including ours, are falling apart. Materials to repair them are nowhere to be found. This morning I noticed that the ceiling in the entrance hall is beginning to cave in on us. One of the walls in Ada Pérez's kitchen did collapse. Gracias a Dios, no one was in the house when it happened. Before you know it the sky will be falling in. We have learned to save everything. Even the candle stubs and bits of paper and string. Though the sun continues to shine, our world is slowly coming unstrung and splitting apart. But I suppose we must learn to improvise.

Tía

5 January 1979

Margarita,

This morning Cuca (my old friend—we went to school together, remember?) was over and told us that her brother, Roberto, who lives somewhere in Pennsylvania, sends them packages of seeds, dry gravy, and soup every time he writes. (She gave us two packages of soup to try. It was surprisingly good, considering that it's not homemade. If you can, send us some Lipton Chicken Noodle; I think it's the best.) Apparently he presses them down until they are flat and then seals them in envelopes. She said that most of the envelopes and the packages that he sends arrive empty except for the sheets of carbon paper, which she thinks Roberto uses to conceal money. Considering that everything is tampered with nowadays, it's a miracle that any of the things he sends reach her at all. The other day Lourdes received a letter from her cousin in Toledo, Ohio—two sheets of carbon paper were left inside the envelope and the bottom half of a photograph of the family. The only one who didn't get her head chopped off was the dog!

I'm almost afraid to tell you, but we've had to sell most of the carpets and the furniture. (If we didn't, they'd be confiscated sooner or later, so why not make the money, right?) Even though we are told that everyone is equal here, the mayimbes and the pinchos—the new bourgeoisie—know how to work their way up in the system. Somehow they always manage to drive new cars and buy up all of the things

that we sell on the black market. Gracias a Dios
Mami didn't live to see the things that we have
been made to witness. She would be mortified if she
knew that some guajiro was eating off her china
plates and drinking from her crystal goblets. You
know, Margarita, I've often thought of leaving Cuba.
No one would care if I stayed or went—here, old
people like me (who refuse to be integrated) are
useless. But you know, every time I think of leaving I
forget the idea—I'm too old to start over again, m'ija.
Besides, you have your own life to live. All I would do
is get in your way. I suppose I will die here.

   Although you probably never hear anything about it
on the radio, it seems that el cura has even been
tampering with the sea. Pancho said that thousands of
fish wash up dead on the shore each morning.
Everyone is afraid to fish from the sea now. Luckily,
we still have the groves of wild fruit trees in the
hills outside of the town, though in time they too will
be stripped and left barren. Each morning before the
sun rises, Tomás goes with his pole and knocks some
fruit from the trees. Often, we eat it before it has
ripened because by the end of the month the pantry
is completely bare.

   As though these hardships aren't enough, there
are rumors circulating that our rations will be cut
back even further. Can you beat that! We have
become a race of foragers, m'ija, crazy with hunger
at the end of the month as we search for our next
meal. People have taken to hiding their animals in
closets and bathrooms, otherwise they will be stolen

or confiscated by some member of the comité for the defense of the revolution. Those who manage to buy a small chicken or a pig on the black market guard it like bullion. We heard that a neighbor's son got sentenced to ten years in prison for unlawfully killing a pig for Nochebuena—I'm not kidding—ten years! (We still haven't figured out whether he got arrested for killing the pig or for celebrating Nochebuena, for both are illegal!) Nevertheless, everyone keeps livestock hidden in their homes and slaughters their animals right in their back yards. Can you picture me butchering a pig in the courtyard? Probably not! (Although I did try to cut off a chicken's head, the smell sickened me, Margarita.) Sometimes, when I'm sitting out on the back porch, I can hear the high-pitched squealing of pigs being slaughtered—their voices are filled with terror and fear and they follow me into my dreams. Even small children are made to witness the slaughter. Most are forced to learn how to wring chicken's necks and boil them in pots of scalding water in order to pluck their feathers. (Some people are so desperate, they've taken to eating the birds they shoot out of the sky with slingshots. Others are stealing animals from the zoo—can you imagine! Just the other day they caught a ten-year-old boy stoning the flamingos. Pobrecitos!) I swear I can smell the scent of blood and burning skin issuing from my pores.

Soon we will be reduced to eating the dirt in the flower beds and the paint that peels off the walls. But I suppose I shouldn't complain, Margarita. In

221

many ways we are much more fortunate than others. We have heard that those who are sent to the camps are fed nothing more than sugar and water. When they finally released Andrea—after three years—the poor thing was so heavy she could barely fit into her husband's old clothes. Her husband, Juan, on the other hand, was nothing more than a skeleton. Apparently, they give you as much sugar water as you want. They told us that there are special camps for maricones (the government calls them military units to aid in production). Though nothing is ever said about it, Andrea told us that el macho líder will not tolerate them in his revolution. He thinks that a little hard labor will turn them into men. Pobrecitos, they can't help themselves—after all, God made them that way. Remember Julia's son, Eduardo (the one you had a crush on but wouldn't admit it)? We always suspected that he was one of them, but of course no one would ever have dared to suggest it. Don't you remember the light blue velvet suit he used to wear to mass on Sunday and the patent leather shoes with the silver buckles? And when he talked he waved his hands around as though his wrists were broken!

Anyway, that's how things are here. I can only imagine how busy you must be, but write when you can, corazón.

Cariños,

Tía

Last night I heard your father crying out your mother's name. I went to him right away and anointed his forehead with a kiss from you, m'ija. Though I hadn't said a word to him, he told me that he knew it was from you. Your mother was at his side the entire time, mi cielo, waiting patiently for him to come to her. They are together again at last, Margarita.

Siempre,

Tata

Margarita,

You should have come like you promised. Now it is too late. Your father is dead. Apparently the news of your father's death spread quickly because in less than a week some big galoot whom no one has ever laid eyes on before showed up at the front door and tried to kick us out of the house. He insisted that it rightfully belonged to him because he was your father's only surviving heir—can you imagine! We still don't know who he was—probably just some high-ranking big shot in the government who thinks he owns everybody. Anyway, he might have succeeded in throwing us all out if it were not for Tata. No one knows what she said to him, but the big black crow left without any gold in his beak. You should have seen him, running out the same way he came in—sin vergüenzas—with his tail between his legs.

The government has divided up nearly all of the houses in the neighborhood, sometimes squeezing three or four families into one home like a can of sardines. (It's a mystery to me why they haven't divided up our house in the same way—it's almost as though we are protected by some invisible wall.) And they're not even nice families, if you know what I mean—they're low-class, chica—our neighborhood is filled with a bunch of negritos who practice brujerías. All of the good families have either left or they've died out. Sometimes (though not very often), I walk to the corner to get some fresh air and it breaks my heart to see the balconies on the beautiful houses strung with clotheslines cluttered with underclothing and sheets. These people have no pride, Margarita—they hang their dirty linens and their underpants right out in the street so that everyone can see them. (Nowadays—if you can believe it—even underwear gets stolen right off the clothesline!) What's worse is that they slaughter their animals right in the middle of the solar. The other day I saw a goat hanging from a clothes pole. It was thrashing around, struggling to free itself from its noose. Who knows how long it had been hanging there, suffering in the sun. As I passed by, a big negra came out with a butcher knife and slashed the poor thing's neck. It was horrible, corazón. There was blood everywhere.

Most of the houses on the block, including ours, are falling apart. Materials to repair them are nowhere to be found. This morning I noticed that the ceiling in the entrance hall is beginning to cave in on us. One of the walls in Ada Pérez's kitchen did collapse. Gracias a Dios, no one was in the house when it happened. Before you know it the sky will be falling in. We have learned to save everything. Even the candle stubs and bits of paper and string. Though the sun continues to shine, our world is slowly coming unstrung and splitting apart. But I suppose we must learn to improvise.

Tía

We hear that the streets in the city and the countryside are spotlessly clean. Even the mountains and the jungles have been swept. In broad daylight, they arrest people in the street, though rarely do we see the violence—they save that for when they're behind closed walls. La limpia, the people call it. Although everyone knows about the firing squads, these are not the thirties when the undercover police left the singers in the streets lying dead in the alleys as a public warning to others. Now we are filled with such terror that no one dares to even hum out loud. Even without words, the music might betray you.

On a daily basis, unspeakable atrocities go on behind the windowless walls of the labor camps and the sanitariums. It is common knowledge that even the rumor that someone has spoken out against the cause or been involved in counterrevolutionary activities could send him or her to jail. Once there, they are experimented on and punished for their "disobedience" and many are either sent to the paredón or forced to spend their time weaving baskets and straw hats for the rich foreigners whom el barbudo has carefully selected and invited to visit his worker's paradise. Of course no one sees these things happen. But even the things that we do see with our bare eyes are denied. Either way, people live in fear in this new society—if they speak out, others will be punished, but if they don't speak out they risk their own lives and the lives of their families and friends.) Just the other day, a few old men were sitting in the plaza near the fountain playing dominoes—a dozen perhaps. Do you know that they were arrested for organizing an "unauthorized gathering"? The district vigilance in our neighborhood told us. We also heard that they are holding repudios at the universities (reviews or repudiations in which students are encouraged to report on one another and turn each other in. A family on our block has a daughter who is studying at the University of Havana.) Inquisitions—that's what some students call them—others call them limpiezas de sangre. You'd think we were back in the sixteenth century!

People are turning on one another right and left, Margarita. Luli told us that her niece was reported on by her ex-boyfriend. He told them that she had criticized the Young Pioneers. She insists that he's still angry because she dropped him for his best friend. Within a week the kid was sent from the chemistry lab to the cane fields. But these kinds of things don't just happen at the universities, m'ija, they happen everywhere. We heard that Luis, the boy who knelt beside you at your First Communion (you nearly got sick on him, remember?) betrayed his own mother. ¡Qué horror! Then we heard that Concha and Carlucho's daughter Mía and her husband Miguel were reported on by Amparo's daughter Isabelita (the little snitch!) The police detained them in jail and when they were released, both found themselves in the street with no jobs. Once you are marked, there is no chance of redeeming yourself. No one will hire you. People are afraid. Concha said that an old classmate of Mía's

offered to take them in. Nervous about her own
safety, she reported to her district officer so that he
would know what she was doing and why. Of course
she assured him that she didn't support their views,
but in the name of humanity, she felt obliged to help
Mía and Miguel out. Apparently he appeared to be very
sympathetic when she told him that they were out on
the streets with their two children, but the next
week Mía's friend was given notice and she, too, was
left to wander the streets. We heard that she has
taken to selling herself to wealthy tourists, along with
the doctors and dentists and teachers and nurses who
are forced to compromise their morals and lead a
double life simply because they cannot make ends meet.
It's true, Margarita, respectable people like Mía's
friend are becoming night jockeys in order to feed
their children. What's worse, the government is using
our beautiful young girls to boost tourism and breathe
new life into the economy, despite the official rhetoric
which denounces jineteras and insists that they are
like children being "tricked" and "corrupted" by
foreigners offering them capitalist vices in the shape
of caramelos.

Somos completemente limpios, Margarita, so clean
that we have lost even our most basic freedoms and
all of our dignity. Those who have managed to
survive the interrogations refuse to speak about the
terrors they have witnessed. But I am too old to care
what I say anymore—what does it matter if I die now
or later? As it is, we are all rotting alive like an
overripe mango left in the sun to spoil.

31 July 1978

Querida Margarita,

¿Qué tal, vieja? When are you coming? The government has inaugurated the family reunification program. Por favor, nena, ven con tu hijo—it's about time that your son met his family and started to learn about his roots. Are you teaching him to speak Spanish so he can converse with his old tía? I hope so.

Did I tell you that Arminda, Checha's daughter with Pancho, I think (you know how the servants fool around!) abandoned us long ago. As she was walking out the door she told me con una cara dura that now that she was educated and working for the government she could earn more money in a week than our family had stolen in three centuries. ¡Qué fresca! She's probably out selling herself on the street corner because nobody we know is allowed to have a lot of anything. You know I always said that the government made a terrible mistake teaching just anyone to read and write.

By the way, I meant to tell you when I wrote last month that Manuel died. It was like the fall of a monument, Margarita. Even though your father might not have approved, we buried them side by side. Manuel was so devoted to your father, chica, just like Lobo. He was almost like part of the family.

Tía

10 August 1979

Querida,

Remember the family I told you about in my last letter, the ones with the daughter (Anita) in Boca Raton (she's a lawyer and her husband's a college professor)? Well, the daughter was visiting last week and somehow managed to see her mother. The plan to reunite the exiles—the gusanos—with their families backfired, chica, because now the Cuban people know what they are missing. Eulalia's daughter said that in Miami everyone is saying that the government only instituted the plan to bring American dollars into Cuba, but now los gusanos se convirtieron en mariposas ricas— the worms have all transformed into wealthy butterflies. Here, the government is saying that we are witnessing the first free elections—that we have been given a voice—so what do you think is happening? Cubans are leaving the island in droves— they're voting with their feet. No words could express their feelings more clearly.

Tía

Querida Margarita,

In the cities they are organizing public rallies to denounce the maricones. Here being equal means that everyone has to be the same—difference is never tolerated. We also heard on the shortwave radio, which Pancho managed to trade with someone for a bottle of your father's rum (which he had hidden in the wine cellar), that many have fled to the States in the boatlift. Is this true?

Each of us is expected to take a turn at playing the inquisitor (that's what we call the vigilance). It's the revolution's idea of chaperoning! Tell me, honestly, can you see me marching up and down the street guarding our block? But I never let on about my real feelings—like everyone else, I have to wear a mask and recite what I think others want to hear. But the worst are those who don't even know that they have been conditioned to mouth nothing more than a string of meaningless slogans that fly in the face of reason— the true test of loyalty, no? The truth is, they have made us into machines, Margarita. Una negrita is in charge of the neighborhood committee in our district—can you imagine? She was a servant to one of the best families in town (people you knew very well) and now she has turned on all of us. She lives at the corner of our block—when you were little, it was pink (now it's yellow—in fact everything is yellow nowadays) and had two stone lions at the front entrance. Her son's position in the military won her the house and a car that she drives around town like an empress—we are nearly starving to death and she has a car, sin vergüenza! But that isn't the end of it. When she heard that Concha and Carlucho had petitioned to leave the country in the boatlift (I don't know if I told you, but Concha has been very ill and they have a granddaughter in Miami who has offered to take them in), la negrita walked through the streets waving a bright red bandanna and shouting for support—we closed our shutters so she would not think we were home. We heard that she gathered a mob together, and that they were all carrying sticks and torches. The crowd surrounded Concha and Carlucho's home. At first they threw stones, breaking all of the windows on the first floor. But then their fury grew into a frenzy—they sacked the house, dragging the old man out of his bed and into the street in his drawstring pajama pants and bedroom slippers. They beat him so severely, Margarita, that he never regained consciousness. Menos mal. He died the next morning, el pobre. A few of his old friends (who didn't have the nerve to defend him in public, mind you) buried him in the middle of the night in an unmarked grave just outside of town.

Concha was beside herself with grief. To have lived so long and to suffer such sorrow—it makes you wonder. She said that without Carlucho she had no home, no life in Cuba anymore. After she had secured her papers, she managed to bribe someone to drive her to Havana. (I think she sold that big amethyst ring Carlucho gave her for their silver wedding anniversary—the one she always wore on her left hand.) When she reached the dock, the soldiers denied her passage to Miami, even though she had been promised a place on the boat. She died only three days after she returned to her home. They buried her next to Carlucho.

Another neighbor who had also petitioned to go to the States (you wouldn't remember the family because they moved into the white house two doors down from ours after you'd left), told us that the boatlift is another one of Fifa's tricks. She told us that even though her family had been assured that they were free to leave if they chose to do so, the soldiers split them apart. They told Inés that she could go with their eldest son but that her husband, Rafa, had to stay behind with their other two children—one is only eight months old. (It will be interesting to see how he manages when the child is hungry, in light of the fact that women are being forced to nurse their children.) It is an impossible choice for anyone to make. Needless to say, they decided to stay, but only God knows what will happen to them now that everyone is aware that they wanted to leave. (Despite these tactics, people are fed up with it all. Rafael said he saw a group of people standing on a bridge, cheering out in the open and showering the boats that were carrying away their precious cargo with candies and flowers.) You know, Rafa and Inés's story reminds me of the way the government tried to split up families at the beginning of the revolution. René and Iraida's sons (remember the family with the eight

boys—we used to see them in church together?)
were sent to different military schools all over the
island. The oldest, Aristides, was selected to study
mathematics somewhere in Germany, and Dionisio was
sent to Moscow for music (do you remember the way
he used to play the piano? That boy was gifted.) Two
of the others (I can't remember which ones) were
sent to fight in Angola (did I already tell you this?)
and only one returned with his brother's empty coffin.
You'd think Iraida was the queen mother, listening to
her brag about her boys. The truth is, m'ija, there is
no choice but to send the children—when the
government tells you they're going they go. So Iraida
can brag all she likes, but the honest truth is that
she has lost her control as a mother. In this country
your children are not your own—they are instruments
of the state. You don't really have the choice to
refuse when you're told what to do, even though
everyone is free to make his or her own decisions
according to the official rhetoric. The only other
option for parents is to send their children out of the
country, a choice many people have already made. The
result is that we have a whole generation that is
growing old alone without the comfort of their
children.

Of course, I would never say a word to Iraida or
René. The revolution is their religion, or so it seems
(you never know whether people actually believe, or
whether they are only pretending to be integrated).
You know, Margarita, people like them who grew up
with the revolution (and so they don't know anything

different) don't seem to be conscious of the fact that their own children are born into slavery with chains on their feet and blindfolds over their eyes. All they see is red. As a result, they are like the little egg, ariquitico, in the riddle Tía Marta used to make you and your sister repeat after her, for they are born without wings and beaks (ariquitico no tiene ni alas ni patas, ni pico; pero los hijos de ariquitico tienen alas y patas y picos . . . remember?). It's as though differences as vast as the sea between us divide your generation from mine, m'ija. We were raised in a world that no longer exists for these children of the revolution.

You must tell your son what they have done to us, Margarita. You were raised at a time when life was good—qué suerte that you got out before anything really changed. You must tell your son what has happened because he has wings and a beak and feet. Everything must be told. There is no one left here to fight anymore. Only the old and the sick are left to remember, but no one dares to speak the truth. Besides, who would believe it, anyhow? The government keeps all of the foreigners away from us. When Ricardo (Concha and Carlucho's son) came to retrieve the few belongings that were left in his parents' house, he told us that the government workers make sure that the tourists spend their dollars in a Cuba that is nothing more than an illusion. They are herded around the city and the seaside resorts like ponies with blinders on. They even have special buses and currency for the tourists. Ricardo said that last week there was a dinner party in Old

Havana (held outside in the plaza in front of the cathedral). People paid a hundred dollars a plate to eat lobster and drink champagne under the stars while ordinary Cuban citizens looked on from the roped-off entrances to the plaza. The same thing happens at the hotels and beaches, chica. Unless you are an official worker or a musician, you are not allowed to enter the spaces that are reserved for tourists—we are all segregated by la soga now, regardless of our skin color. Can you imagine that? I never thought I'd see the day that I'd be on this side of the rope.

                                                    M.

and then there were seven, or perhaps it was eight.

Nevertheless, they continue to cut back our food rations, even though there is barely any food to be had. There are no choices—you take what they give you. Each month we are entitled to about four to five pounds of rice (the amount varies from month to month), about the same amount of sugar, a pound and a half of lard and coffee, about three pounds of beans, a bar of soap, and two rolls of toilet paper. Sometimes we are given a chicken or some cooking oil; other times we manage to buy some milk, though this is usually reserved for small children. Can you imagine that we are able to live on this? Though some people we know have socios who throw a few extra potatoes in their bags and then turn their eyes the other way (or get their sons out of military duty by signing a form that says that they are maricones or that they have bad eyesight), by the end of the month most people are desperate, m'ija. But if you try to start your own business—they either make it impossible to pay for a license, or they just cut off your water or your light (what am I saying—half the time there is no water or electricity anyway!). There is no incentive to work—and why should there be, if there is nothing to gain? Everyone goes from day to day, doing as best as they can to resolver—a fancy name, mi cielo, for stealing. But what can we do—we have to improvise and invent! Tata takes the cream and the fat from the top of the milk and whips it with a fork until it turns to butter. I don't know how she does it, but she has even figured out how to make sugar biscuits out of thin air. When we have potatoes and onions, we save the peels—Tata makes a delicious broth with the onions and the peels.

Late at night we listen to the shortwave radio. They say that the wealthy American tourists are treated, especially the famous ones, like royalty. Then they return to the States wearing the straw hats that the old people weave in the labor camps and the brightly colored bandannas that the vendors sell in the plaza. What's worse is that they tell their friends and the newspaper reporters who interview them that Cuba is a tropical paradise filled with show girls, rum, and big black cigars. Somehow they forget to mention the fifteen-year-old prostitutes. Isn't it funny that our libretos entitle us to a pair of shoes a year—yet there are no shoes to be found other than the canvas ones— there is no food to be found at the peso stores—yet certain people are walking around in the alligator loafers that Pablo, Magda's cousin, makes at the shoe factory in Santiago, and the pinchos are buying all the food that they want at the official dollar stores and the paladares. Meanwhile, the tourists stay out all night long—even though there are blackouts and no gasoline—and gorge themselves on our green papayas and yellow mangoes, our mamoncillo and anón, while the Cuban people feed on their rinds. They never seem to notice the empty shop windows or the endless lines. With one hand, they line the pockets of Fifa's party members with their American dollars, and with the other, they toss handfuls of worthless candies made

238

from their sugar beet to our children. They are like overfed parrots flying in and out of a glass cage with an opening the size of a needle. It's hard to ignore the irony, m'ija—we fought the war of independence to free ourselves from Mamá and what did we get? Mickey Mouse and Coca-Cola. So Fidel promised to give a puñatazo to the yanqui capitalists, and what did we get? The reds, who are using us like all the others. And mark my words, when things start going bad and they get tired of us, they'll abandon us with our pants down like a faithless lover. What will we do then? If he's still around, Papá Cucaracha will probably sell us down the drainpipe to all of the enlightened, "liberal-minded" tourists, who sip on Daiquiris in plastic cups as they stroll down the streets of Old Havana bargaining down the price of T-shirts with Che Guevara's picture on the front. They sleep a dreamless, uninterupted sleep with their heads buried like flamingos in our beautiful pink-and-white sand.

Escríbame pronto,

Tía

Margarita,

We are strangers in our own country, m'ija. We are a nation of foreigners—exiled in our own land. People are filled with such horror that they fear even to speak aloud in their sleep. Even the shadows are watching and the night has ears. But in my dreams I have seen words of protest scratched on the prison walls and scribbled on the trunks and the waxy green leaves of the trees. Even the wells are churning with blood and bones and singing with discontent. Before you know it, the bearded one will exchange his habit for a suit and a tie and the wings on his boots for wing tip shoes—but one day the cannibal within will consume him.

Siempre,

Tata

Querida,

I am an old lady now (almost sixty-two years old—imagine!). I never thought I'd live so long. I've grown so thin you wouldn't recognize me anymore. When I look in the mirror, I barely know myself. The part of me that you would know me by has long since been washed away—erased by centuries of wind and rain like the words on the broken stone cross that used to bear your great-grandmother's name. My bones have become so frail and brittle that sometimes I think they're made of glass. If you can believe it, I fractured a rib last month trying to make my bed. Tata wrapped me in old linens that nearly tore apart they were so threadbare—but there are no medical supplies available. (She already used all of the curtains and drapes to make me a few extra housedresses—now they are even rationing shoes and clothing, and it's next to impossible to get a needle and thread.) Today is the first day that I could sit up on my own—that's why I haven't written in so long.

This morning I had such a headache I thought my forehead would explode, but do you know that Tomás searched the neighborhood, going from house to house for over five hours and couldn't come up with a single aspirin? Thank God for Tata—she mixed together some kind of ointment and rubbed it into my temples—before I could count to ten, my headache was gone. The pain in my side still keeps me up at night, but Tata makes me sit up at least a few hours a day so that my lungs will not fill with fluid. Still, the pain robs me of the few moments of sleep and forgetfulness that are left to me. I sleep in the kitchen now on an old cot Tata set up in the corner where Lobo used to lie. I feel safer there because now I'm afraid that I'll fall if I try to go up the marble staircase.

We heard on the radio that there is a surplus of ice cream in Havana. Next week the people may have to eat the paint right off the walls of their houses. But soon he will fall, chica. He, too, is growing old. (Even cucarachas have to die sooner or later!) Some believe that when he does, we will sell ourselves like prostitutes to the foreigners who come like carrion birds to take the little that is left to us. (I think it's already too late, m'ija. I think it's already happened.) But there are still those who cling to the hope that never again will the people allow themselves to be betrayed. Never again? I can only hope that even though he has tried to make us into a people—a place—with no memory—even though he has changed the names of the buildings and streets, the towns and provinces, there are some things that cannot be erased, chica. Even if I am the last to remember, there will always be the sea, m'ija, there will always be the sea.

This may be the last letter that you receive from me, Margarita. It's almost impossible to even find onion peels, let alone paper and pens.

Te quiero,

Tía

All I see is darkness before me, m'ija. But still I write with hope—for all things pass, mi cielo, all things eventually pass. Surely nothing so terrible can last for more than one hundred years. I pray that one day you will return, if only because something deep inside of you will never let you forget that the sun once beat at your temples and that you can never wash the brine of the sea that surrounds us from your limbs.

Even as I watch Natasha (Tomás's granddaughter) recording my thoughts—she is my messenger now that Checha is gone—I know deep inside my heart that someday we will all be together again. Before long we will all wake on the other side of this dark night.

Never forget that you are always dancing in the shadow of that sun. Te veo, pronto.

Siempre

Part Two

26 March 1986

Margarita stood on the front porch with her two children, listening to the ocean pounding like a distant drum against the shore. Standing in her own shadow, she waited for her husband to open the front door. After he had pushed the door open they followed him into the hallway, straining to see in the half-light as he put down their suitcases and crossed the entrance hall. The air was cold and dry, sending a shiver through her that ended at the cold metal handle of the birdcage she gripped with two hands. She had covered the dome with an old linen sheet, but the tiny parakeet inside continued to spring nervously from bar to bar.

She'll break her wings one of these days, Margarita thought to herself as she listened to the muffled whirl that came from within the cage.

Meanwhile, her husband's shadow glided back and forth on the far side of the room. Margarita could hear the chatter of the flatware as drawers opened and closed . . . the rustling sound of papers being pushed impatiently from side to side . . . and then the clatter of the doors in the corner cupboard in the dining room, unwilling to yield to his touch. The sound told Margarita that the wood had swollen with the humidity and the salt air.

Like a blind person, she had always been able to identify noises in the dark.

"Damn. Why won't these cabinets open?" she heard her husband mutter under his breath. Then a drawer shrieked open and closed with a slam, startling Margarita and the children, who stood waiting together in the dark entrance hall. "Where the hell are the candles, Margarite? These drawers were filled with them."

"I think you threw them all out last summer, Joey. But check the bottom drawer in the cupboard anyhow—left-hand side," she answered in a calm, steady voice. He always called her Margarite (rather than her nickname, Daisy) when he was annoyed. After all these years she knew that if she tried to match his temper with her own anger it would only make matters worse. Besides, she was too tired to argue or respond. The sparks of rebellion had long since died out within her and turned to ash.

"*I* threw them all out? How could *I* throw them all out? You wouldn't let me. You never throw anything out."

"No, never," Margarita whispered, knowing that he was right. Ever since Lilly and Peter had been born she couldn't bring herself to throw anything away. Pressed flowers, bits of yarn and string, small swatches of material that she knew she'd never use, Easter palms (which she had promised Joey she would burn), Christmas cards, shoe boxes, buttons, old report cards, stacks of *National Geographic* magazines, empty peanut butter jars, and half-full bottles of Elmer's glue—these things and more cluttered her drawers and sewing boxes. She had lost too much already. Now fear and memory made her cling and clutch.

"Goddamn it."

"What's wrong, Daddy?" Lilly called into the darkness.

"I closed the goddamn drawer on my goddamn finger. Where the hell are the candles, Margarite? Where did you hide them this time?"

Margarita drew in her breath and refused to respond. She had grown tired of feeling as though she had to smooth over the rough corners of his temper—his impatience. Even a few months ago she would have felt obliged to answer him, but not now. Ever since she had received Lucía's telegram announcing her aunt's death, something had snapped within her like a branch caught underfoot on an autumn day. For years she had successfully held her memories at bay, but for some reason the telegram had brought her face-to-face with a past she had tried to bury. In one afternoon the life she had kept so tightly wrapped, like the leaves of her father's thick black cigars, had come undone. Ever since that day her thoughts had run recklessly over the years like a wooden shuttle crossing a loom, and with them the happiness she had worked so hard to preserve seemed to be tearing apart at the seams.

* * *

As long as I live, Margarita thought to herself as she closed the front door behind her, I'll never allow myself to get used to the way he speaks to me. Never.

"Ahhh, apparently you missed one," Joey said after a moment, interrupting her thoughts. The tone of his voice, the latent insinuation she sensed behind the words, rubbed her raw and caused her to flush with irritation. Still, Margarita didn't utter a word, though she stood in the doorway lashing out at her husband from across the dining room with her eyes.

Through the darkness she heard Joey strike a match, and the sound carried her back to the warm nights spent in the kitchen at Tres Flores. Margarita closed her eyes and saw the glazed tile countertops and the clay tiles on the floor, the Panama fans that hung from the cathedral ceiling, pushing the hot, humid air around them. An immense coal-burning stove with a brick oven that was perpetually in use stood against the back wall alongside a long porcelain sink balanced on thick piano legs. Once a week, Checha sent Pancho, with his red bandanna tied around his neck and his tan canvas shoes, to buy coal for the stove, which she stored in a heavy metal bucket beside the oven. The pantry, which was stocked with large burlap bags filled with rice, sugar, flour, and a variety of beans, was next to the kitchen. The door was always locked. Tata kept the key on a thin satin ribbon that hung around her neck like an amulet. (The entire household knew that the sight of the key was a constant source of irritation for Checha, though she never mentioned a word to Tata about it, for she, rather than the old woman, had overseen the kitchen ever since Graciela had been retired from her duties after leaving a pan of hot oil burning, unattended, on the stove.)

Large cast-iron cazuelas, ranging in size and shape, hung from hooks in the ceiling, and a long work table with a veined marble top ran down the center of the kitchen. There Margarita would sit with the servant girls. Amid the soft patter of beans and the comforting smell of perking coffee and baking bread Tata answered their questions and recited stories.

"You have to learn your own stories, m'ijas," she would tell them as she sorted lentils and black beans into separate piles, "so that you can pour them into your children's ears, where they will take their own shape like water in earthen jars."

Some of her happiest moments had been spent in the kitchen with Tata and the servant girls. As a child, Margarita had always envied the girls, not only because of their relationship with Tata but because of the freedom their lowly status gave them. How often she had resented them when she heard them laughing loudly together in the kitchen or saw them sitting in the court-yard, barefoot and hatless, exempt from wearing the frilly dresses she was made to wear in the hot afternoons and heedless of the endless number of rules by which she had to abide. But then everything had changed at Tres Flores following her mother's death and her father's departure. Margarita was allowed to join the girls in the kitchen, for no one except for Tía María (who was overruled by Tata anyway) seemed to pay attention to the rules any longer.

Margarita recalled the first time Tata had invited her to sit at the kitchen table among the girls. She watched as the old woman struck the red tip of a wooden matchstick against a piece of flint that she always carried in her apron pocket. Leaning on her elbows with her chin resting on her outspread hands like a flower blossom, Margarita stole quick glances at the others' stony faces, inwardly wondering whether or not she could withstand the pain as fearlessly as they. Meanwhile Tata, like a priestess, held the lighted matchstick beneath a taper for a moment, allowing the liquid drops of melted wax to drip onto a porcelain saucer. When they had formed a thick, glistening pool, she secured the candle to the dish and slid it toward the center of the table.

As the girls waited for their turns at the candle, Tata taught them to bend back their fingers until they touched the creases of their wrists.

"You must learn to be flexible, m'ijas," she would say as she paced around the table, pushing their fingers further and further back with every word. "You must learn to endure the pain." Though Tata always spoke to her in Spanish, the old woman often addressed the servant girls in a language Margarita could not understand.

One by one, the girls took turns passing their hands over the candle flame with their fingers pressed tightly together. Some of them cried aloud—Tata chased them from the room with her eyes. Those who remained silent cried inwardly. Margarita could read their anguish in their taut, quivering lips and the flared wings of their nostrils. Though she was visibly older than the other girls, the mulata with the blue-black hair who only appeared at Tres Flores during the evening after María had retired to her room, remained expressionless. She always sat across from Margarita like a chess opponent, with her pale-eyed boy sitting on her knee—the child, the servants whispered among themselves, who was the young priest's bastard son. She alone held her palm, unwavering, over the flame Tata set before her. She alone could mask her pain, though Margarita could see that it lay hidden deep within the wells of her eyes. But when she sensed Margarita's prying gaze from across the table, Casandra quickly lowered them to the ground.

Cringing within herself, Margarita wondered whether the palms of her hands would toast brown and salmon-pink like those of the servant girls. When her turn finally came, she cupped her hands together, shell-like, and whispered her worries into Tata's ear. Without taking her eyes from the flame, the old woman laughed her fattest laugh and said aloud,

"It is the light of the sun you must fear, corazón. Each morning he laps up the night like a paunchy yellow cat drinking dark milk from a bowl. But he can never drink fast enough, for there are always shadows left behind. The candle accepts the night like the moon, m'ija. She finds her way through the darkness by scattering it with her tears. She knows that the shadows are always there—day and night—no matter how brightly she shines. But she does not try to fight them. She accepts them, knowing that she will never fully understand. And still, she burns. You must learn to be like the candle, mi cielo, learn to be like the candle."

With these words, Tata leaned over the table and picked up the candlestick. She raised it high above the girls' heads saying, "But look at her. Look at her. She burns more brightly in the darkness than in the sunlight." Then she placed the candle in front of Margarita.

At first the pain seemed unbearable—it seemed to come from every direction.

It's too much! I can't take it anymore! Margarita heard herself scream in a shrill, half-crazed voice, but the unruffled expressions on the girls' faces told her that no one had heard the words. No one except for Tata. And then the old woman seemed to speak to her in a soothing stream of unspoken words that wrapped around her and bound her pain until the heat became cold.

Roll it over your tongue, she told her. Let it slide down the back of your throat. And when you have had enough, vomit it out as if it were venom. Then drink it up and swallow it once again. In time you will learn to swallow only the best part and spit out the rest. But remember, never forget the feeling of the first pain.

Gradually, Tata taught her to consume her pain. Though her skin burned and blistered, Margarita learned to withstand the heat like no other. There were even times when Tata had to pull her hand out of the fire. She would crow with delight, while the wide-eyed girls stared at Margarita in awe and disbelief. They were certain that privilege had robbed the Caballero's daughter of the strength and the endurance that they believed they alone possessed. Margarita could still recall the moment when she reached the point of emptiness the old woman had described so many times before—the vacant space within her. But that night at the kitchen table she learned to detach herself, sliding off the manacles of pain and emotion that had bound her since her mother's death. It was almost as though she stood outside herself—outside the circle of girls—watching the anguished, sloughed skin of herself writhe in pain. But it was no longer her hand, her fingers. They belonged to another.

The thought of her mother brought unexpected tears to Margarita's eyes as she stood shivering in the dark hallway of the shore house. Her loss had changed everything, wounding her so deeply that it reached beyond words and emotion. Now, in retrospect, she realized that in a single afternoon the world as she had known it had simply vanished and her childhood abruptly ended. Without warning, the old, childish anger she had felt at her mother for leaving her so suddenly began to rise up within her.

Reaching back into the shadows of her past to a place she had not revisited in over thirty years, Margarita could still recall the day they buried her mother. With her face pressed against the glass, she stared out the car window. On their way to the cathedral they passed two women sitting on a park bench laughing; a group of children playing with broken glass on the pavement; a man with a large straw hat smoking a cigar; a boy stealing a piece of fruit from a storefront window. Somehow Margarita had expected life to come to a standstill, but the people they passed in the street were all carrying on as though nothing had happened, as though it were just another ordinary day. They were untouched by her loss. Even the sun seemed to mock her sorrow by daring to shine.

Though her father wasn't present, they had buried Rosa within twenty-four hours of her death. The sight of the white lilies she herself had left to wither on the pew was a painful reminder to Margarita of the fact that the last time she had sat in this very spot her mother was still alive. María had given her and Caridad roses to place in their mother's casket just before their infant brother was laid at Rosa's side and the coffin lid was sealed shut. As she gazed at her mother's face, which was shrouded with a white tulle veil, it occurred to Margarita that unlike the lilies in the pew, whose edges had already begun to curl and turn brown, her mother would always remain young and beautiful in her memory. Sleeping peacefully in her satin-lined case, she would never fall out of blossom or bloom.

The return journey to Tres Flores following the solemn funeral mass was nothing more than a blur. Somehow invisible hands had guided her home to Tata, who waited for her at the door with a cup of warm goat's milk, sweetened with vanilla and sugar and a dash of rum. Then the only thing Margarita could remember after that was the shadows that glided back and forth outside her bedroom door, and the sound of whispering voices in the next room.

Gradually, even the whispering voices and the shadows were consumed in a thickening pool of darkness. The first thing Margarita saw when she opened her eyes again was the mountainous form of Tata, hunched over on the edge of the bed. The old woman's head was lowered and her long silver hair, which hung loose, partially covered her face. Between her hands she clasped the ebony rosary that always hung from Rosa's bedpost. The soft glow of the candles she had lit on the bureau and the nightstand cast gigantic shadows against the walls.

Margarita learned later that Tata had held a vigil at her side until the curtain of perspiration broke her delirium. Afterwards she encouraged the child to release her sorrow.

"You must cry, mi amor, you must cry," Margarita remembered Tata whispering in her ear over and over again, as she rubbed small circles into her back with the palm of her hand and held a cup of steaming liquid to her lips. Though she longed to cry out, Margarita stared mutely into her face. She could see the old woman's lips moving, though she could only make out a word here and there. It was as though Tata were speaking in a foreign tongue. As she stared at the old woman, Margarita noticed that her eyes had shrunken into her face—grown small with tears and sorrow. She remembered wishing that she, too, could cry, but she had already slipped inside of herself and the tears would not come, perhaps because of the years she had been trained to restrain them.

Syllable by syllable, Tata taught her to speak once again. When she had finally gained enough strength to come down to the kitchen for her meals, Margarita discovered that her father and Caridad had left her. In response to her questions, María would tell her nothing except that Caridad had returned to Havana with her father and that he had left instructions that she stay behind. It was Tata who told her that Pedro had sent her sister to the monastery behind the cathedral. He had begged the nuns to take both of his daughters in, but the superior refused his request, finally convincing him that Margarita was too young. When he suggested that they send her to the nuns at the boarding school, Tata turned on him like a lioness, causing Pedro to back down and agree to leave Margarita at Tres Flores in María's care.

"Why didn't Father wait for me? Why didn't he take me with him?" she had asked María in anger and disappointment when she learned the truth. "Why didn't he even say good-bye?" But María refused to answer her questions, abruptly changing the subject whenever Margarita mentioned her father and Caridad.

After discovering the truth, Margarita vowed never to forgive Pedro for abandoning Caridad in the monastery and leaving her an orphan. In her eyes it wasn't enough that he had waited outside her bedroom door for almost three weeks, sleeping in an old cot Tata had set up for him in the hallway. The thought that he had been dragged across the field of lilies and Matagas had returned to the stable with his boot hanging from her stirrup did not quell her anger. Thinking that perhaps she should confess to someone that the blind anger she felt toward her father still boiled like corrosive liquid within her, Margarita went to the chapel in the cathedral late one Saturday afternoon and waited in a long line with the calambucas to speak to Padre Rabia.

"Tomás was not able to stop the horse," she remembered the old priest whispering through the screen in the confessional, once he recognized the tearful voice that filtered through the darkness. "Your father was knocked unconscious when he fell. His right leg was trampled, my child, and he landed on a switchblade that he was carrying in his hand. It tore a moon-shaped wound into his side. It's a miracle that his back wasn't broken or that the blade didn't pierce his heart. In vain your father waited for you to ask for him. Finally he gave up hope. He left for Havana only after Carlucho de Silva assured him of your recovery. Why didn't you ask for him, Margarita? Why?"

Unable to respond, Margarita left the confessional without waiting for her penance or for the priest's blessing. Overwhelmed with shame and guilt, she never had the courage to tell her father that she had wanted him all along, but at the time sorrow had robbed her of her voice.

When Margarita finally reached the point where she was able to openly grieve for her mother, Tata told her that Rosa had given birth to twins, and that the boy had been strangled in her womb by the umbilical chord.

"Casandra was with your mother when she died, m'ija. She wasn't alone," Tata told her, answering Margarita's questions before they were even asked. "By the time I reached Tres Flores, she had already bathed your little sister and laid her in the cradle beside your mother's bed, along with her own son. She wrapped your little brother in her mantilla. When I found her, she was lying across your mother's body, protecting her from the rain. She had waited for me to arrive, insisting that I should be the one to close your mother's eyes. Together, we gave your mother her last rites and baptized the boy. While I sprinkled his forehead with the water from your father's shaving basin, Casandra blessed him with a prayer that she recited out loud. He was buried with your mother, Margarita, so that he wouldn't feel as though we had abandoned him too."

"And what about my little sister?"

"Since your father refused to have anything to do with her, your tía decided to name her Violeta Asunción, the name, she later told me, that she would have given her own daughter had she had one. She was beautiful, m'ija. I wish you could have seen her. Except for the little star-shaped birthmark on her forehead, she was a replica of you when you were first born. Your father said that María could call her anything she wanted to, as long as the girl wasn't named after your mother. At his insistence, Violeta was taken to the cathedral to be christened, and then Padre Rabia took her to the nuns in the monastery behind the cathedral to be placed with a good family. Even though we tried to resist him, your father had his way."

"The nuns?" Margarita had asked, with a puzzled expression on her face.

"Don't you remember hearing about that? The Carmelites found good homes for the children who were left in their care, m'ija. Your father never saw your sister's face, mi cielo. He couldn't. He said that every time that he saw Violeta she would remind him that your mother was gone."

"So he gave my sister away? Just like that?"

Tata shook her head. "He doesn't know that the nuns agreed to take her in, mi cielo—for Caridad's sake. Since he never asked, no one has told him. It's best that he doesn't know."

The next morning, Tata took Margarita down the alley behind the cathedral. Often, she said, the nuns came to pray and meditate after the early mass in the shadowy grottoes that branched off the paths in the garden behind the cloister. Hoping to catch a glimpse of Caridad, Margarita peered through the chinks in the monastery wall where the stones had come loose, but it was impossible to distinguish her from the others, for all of the novices wore the same formless white habits and veils.

They returned to the alley together each morning, and from time to time Margarita would see young girls cradling infants in their arms steal across the garden and swing open the revolving wooden door at the back of the cloister. The words

Nene Suárez Nene Sánchez

were painted in uniformly scripted letters above a moon-shaped basket that was fastened to the interior of the door. Once they had placed the babies in the basket, they would ring the doorbell and then quickly disappear into the shadows once again.

"What are they doing?" Margarita asked, as she watched from the alley.

"In order to remain anonymous, they leave their children to the nuns, m'ija; otherwise they will be eaten up by the shadows outside the monastery walls."

"Do the nuns keep them all?"

Tata shook her head. "No, m'ija. How could they? Every child," she whispered in Margarita's ear, "who is left in that basket is given the same last name. Suárez for boys. Sánchez for girls. They're named in honor of Padre José Suárez de Sánchez," the old woman added, "Padre Rabia's spiritual advisor. Then the nuns place the children with families who are willing to care for them and love them."

"So my sister is Violeta Sánchez?" Margarita had asked, thinking that Tata had been mistaken and that her infant sister shared the same fate as the children the young girls abandoned in the basket.

"Trust me, nena. Your sisters are here, together with your tía-abuela. Carmelita will see that Violeta and Caridad are taken care of."

* * *

The sound of the poker hitting the grate drew Margarita's attention back to her husband. He was kneeling in front of the fireplace tending the burning embers and the blue flames while Peter crouched beside him pressing sheets of newspaper from the magazine rack into loose balls. (Every spring when they reopened the shore house, they discovered burst pipes in the basement and the pilot in the old furnace wouldn't light. This year Joey had come prepared with matches and firewood, but he hadn't thought to bring a box of fuses.)

A pale burr of yellow light had already begun to spread into the chilly air, chasing the shadows into the far corners of the room. Lilly sat just behind them, silent and detached, with her arms wrapped tightly around her bent knees as though she were hugging herself. Gazing at her daughter in the firelight, with its soft shadows and false light, Margarita saw her mother sitting before her once again.

For years after her death Rosa came to her in her dreams. And though Margarita could not touch her or see her in the daylight, she always felt as though her mother were nearby, as though Rosa were still within reach. When she left Havana, Margarita stopped feeling her mother's presence, even though Tata had always insisted that whenever her thoughts turned to Rosa her mother was beckoning for her attention. Even the image of her mother that came to Margarita in her dreams had been swallowed up in the darkness that followed her departure from Cuba and her son's death. It was as though Rosa's living spirit had not been able to cross the watery passage that now separated them.

Though Margarita had tried to conjure up the idea of Rosa a thousand and one times over, she could not recall the sound of her voice, the sound of her laughter, despite all her efforts. Until Lilly's birth, she had ceased to imagine her mother's face as a whole. The image she saw behind closed eyes was always indistinct and blurry, like an object that had sunken to the bottom of a well. Then suddenly her image was summoned up in its totality, for Rosa's features had been repainted onto her granddaughter's face. Even Lilly's mouth curved in the same way, and she had Rosa's wavy black hair and green eyes—only her chin was stronger, her eyes deeper and clearer.

* * *

Standing in the doorway, just outside the circle of light, Margarita took account of everything in the sitting room. At a glance she knew that it would take her and Lilly several days to get the house back in order, even though they had left everything scrupulously clean at the end of the previous summer. She also knew without looking that the wind had blown sand and dirt through the window sashes and a thick layer of dust had settled onto the furniture and the mantelpiece. That was a given. In the dim light she could see that the brown house spiders had spun their webs over the tatted lace valances and into the corners of the ceiling. Otherwise, the room had lain undisturbed, as though time had stood still. She alone had changed, Margarita thought, in the months that had passed since she'd stood in the same spot.

The room was dotted with baskets of various sizes and shapes, which were filled with unfinished projects. Margarita's eyes rested on a basket piled high with gingham cloth that had been cut into perfect triangles and squares for a counterpane she had never gotten around to finishing. The sight of the cut fabric reminded her of the mornings and afternoons she had spent bending over the kitchen table with a ruler and a white sewing pencil, measuring the material out against the plastic quilting templates. She glanced at the immense blue-and-green woolen throw she had knitted for Joey when they first started going together. It was neatly folded across the arm of the sofa and beside it lay the cathedral window pillows her mother-in-law had taught her to make. Every time she looked at the pillows she heard her mother-in-law's voice: "An error of just a tenth of an inch will disrupt the entire pattern, Daisy."

After completing her fourth pillow, which won a blue ribbon at the county fair, even Adelaide reluctantly conceded that Margarita's measurements were meticulous.

"Well I'll be," she had stammered out when they announced the prizewinner over the loudspeaker. "Who would have thought that a little Latin girl would beat out a whole tent full of belles?"

The worn plaid cushions on the sofa were sunken in like hollow cheeks. To one side stood a magazine rack overflowing with outdated magazines and periodicals that Margarita and Lilly hadn't had time to sort through before the house was closed for the winter. On the mantelpiece she and the children had arranged colorful bits of coral they'd bought at the local five-and-dime. Propped up among the coral was a small stuffed alligator her daughter had given her for Mother's Day. It was dressed in a wedding gown and a veil. Though she never told Lilly, it had always reminded Margarita of the crocodiles they'd sometimes see from the windows of the train as they passed through the swampland on their way from Havana to Cienfuegos.

In front of the fireplace were long branches of bleached driftwood the children had dragged home from the beach their first summer in the house. As she gazed at the driftwood from the hallway, Margarita could still picture Lilly and Peter running back and forth across the sand like tiny leaves haphazardly blown about by the wind. She could almost hear the sound of their laughter as it carried on the wind. They would shriek with joy and anticipation as the ebbing tide chased them, like sandpipers, from the edge of the ocean. In her mind's eye, Margarita could see them sauntering across the beach together, Lilly stooping every few steps to pick up unbroken clam shells and scallops that lay half-buried in the gray sand and Peter ordering her to place them in his bucket.

At the end of the day, the children would reluctantly return home with their bathing suit bottoms filled with sand and the pockets of their beach coats filled with shells and tiny pebbles. Even though they were less than two years apart, Lilly insisted upon dragging the larger pieces of driftwood home, allowing Peter to take only those pieces that he could easily carry in his arms. When they reached the house they spread the driftwood across the pavement and left it to bleach in the sun. But once it was brought into the house and arranged in front of the mantelpiece, Peter and Lilly became frightened, insisting that even in the daylight the silvery wood looked like the skulls and bones of animals left in the desert to die. By moonlight, the bleached driftwood became dead arms that reached after them, they insisted, and followed them right into their dreams.

How easily they were both frightened as children, Margarita thought, and how easily she could comfort and protect them back then by simply wrapping her arms around them and turning on the night-light. Even though Peter now winced at her kisses and tried to escape from her embraces, she thought, as her eyes settled onto his crouching form, he still clung to her at bedtime and would not sleep until he'd said his evening prayers with her. It was Lilly who had changed—who had grown remote and distant. No longer did Margarita feel as though she could sound her depths.

As Margarita glanced around the room, she recalled that even the pine knots in the paneling had scared Peter their first summer in the shore house. In his imagination, the black knots were screaming mouths and vigilant, evil eyes that never slept. More than anything else, he feared the darkness. Every shadow in the room that he shared with Lilly, every piece of furniture silhouetted in the moonlight, became a snapping wolf or a slouching monster. When bedtime came around, he would cling to her skirt and begin to wail even after she'd fastened the closet door and pushed their beds close together and agreed to put a night-lamp in their room. Margarita could still recall the sound of Peter's voice calling tearfully through the darkness,

"Don't leave me, Mommy. Don't leave me with Lilly; I'm afraid."

How relieved she felt when he finally outgrew his night fears. His innocent words had filled her with terror, for they recalled to her mind the vision of her son waving to her from the back window of the limousine mouthing words she could not hear, as it slowly pulled away from the curb and he disappeared forever from her sight.

Margarita's gaze listlessly wandered to the coffee table. On it lay a Chinese checkerboard covered with the coveted cat's eye marbles that her grandmother had divided between her and Caridad. Beside it was an empty plate and a green fluted coffee cup with a filmy brown ring just below the rim. Margarita shook her head with anger at the thought that someone hadn't even bothered to put the dishes in the sink.

"You'd think I was the maid around here," she grumbled beneath her breath.

For some reason the sight of the dirty dishes caused her to wonder whether or not the sheets had been stripped from the beds. The thought was vaguely disturbing. She and Lilly had overlooked the dish and the coffee cup—who's to say whether or not they'd left the beds unmade, the linens unwashed?

"Mobs could sack the cathedral, the sky could collapse in on Xanadu, but beds had to be made," her grandmother always said. "Beds had to be made."

As a child, Margarita used to scoff at the idea, although she never actually had to worry about making her own bed—that was Checha's job when they stayed at Tres Flores and Bebita's when they were at the house on Calle Semilla. Funny that now she too insisted that the beds be stripped and remade at the shore house before it was closed for the winter, and it was Lilly who complained not only about the fact that Peter was never asked to help, but about the idea that they would have to rewash the linens all over again when they returned the following spring for Easter break.

The very thought of the chaos, the disorder of unmade beds and unwashed coffee cups, made Margarita feel agitated and uneasy. Perhaps it was generations of conditioning that had made her respond that way, even though she knew that Rafaela would be horrified at the idea that her granddaughter did her own washing and ironing. But who would have thought that she would one day exchange her turquoise-colored passport for a navy blue one? Who would have thought . . . ?

The more she thought about it, the more certain Margarita became that the beds had been left unattended. And then the possibility occurred to her that perhaps she had been the one to eat toast and drink coffee the morning that they'd closed the shore house and returned to their house outside the city. She alone may have been responsible for the disruption. How many times in the past few months had Joey caught her putting the half gallon of Breyers ice cream in the cupboard with the pots and pans or the Corn Flakes in the refrigerator?

Maybe I left the dishes on the coffee table, Margarita chided herself, with her eyes fixed on the cup. I can't seem to remember anything anymore.

"What are you doing out there, Daisy, all by yourself?" Joey's words startled her. Lost in her own thoughts, she had almost forgotten that anyone else was in the house.

"Nothing," Margarita answered, crossing the entrance hall and placing the silver birdcage on the hall table. Above it hung the small oval mirror with the rambling rose pattern she had watched her mother paint on the glass with a hair-fine brush.

Margarita stood at the mirror for a long while, mechanically smoothing her hair into place. Even though she was staring at her own reflection, she saw in her memory's eye the back of her father's head as he stretched to hang the mirror at the top of the staircase in her grandmother's house on Calle Semilla.

The day of her fifteenth birthday Pedro appeared unexpectedly at Tres Flores and announced that he had decided Margarita should live with him and his sisters in Havana. Peering down from her balcony window at the bald spot on her father's head while he searched his pockets for the key to the front door, it occurred to Margarita that she had not seen him in almost two years, though he always sent Manuel to Cienfuegos with an armful of white lilies on her birthday.

Though María was completely taken by surprise, Margarita had waited patiently all morning for her father's arrival with her mother's old valise packed and the oval mirror wrapped in a green-and-white towel. The night before, she had dreamed that he would come for her. (Neither Tata nor Checha was surprised when Pedro appeared at the house, for Margarita had long since established her reputation for reading tea leaves and predicting the future, tricks she learned from a traveling magician who begged shelter one night at Tres Flores and ended up staying the entire summer until María finally chased him out.)

In her mother's looking glass, Margarita saw herself clutching the oval mirror under her arm all the way from Cienfuegos to Havana. She and her father didn't exchange a single word. When they arrived at the house, he took it from her, and though she begged him to hang it in her bedroom, he refused. Months later, for no apparent reason, the mirror resurfaced. Margarita could still recollect their conversation as he hung the glass above the landing on the stairs:

"But Father, what harm is there in putting it in my room? I can't even comb out my hair without a mirror."

"The nuns do," Pedro had responded. At her father's words, Margarita imagined her two sisters kneeling over porcelain washbasins early each morning, combing out their hair as they watched their broken reflections ripple across the surface of the water.

"Mirrors only make your head swell," he continued as he drove a nail into the wall. "You shouldn't be so concerned about the way you look, Margarita. Don't you believe me when I tell you that you're perfect? You are your mother when she was a girl," he added in a whisper, as he glanced up at her reflection in the mirror.

Margarita could not meet his longing gaze. As she stood behind him with her hands folded in front of her, she recalled Bebita's words to her when they had first arrived:

"Watch what you say to him, nena. He cuts down everyone around him. Even his sisters agree that he has become a tyrant since your mother's death. Haven't you noticed that they only come out of their rooms when he leaves the house?"

The years that had passed since Margarita had last seen her father had dulled the memory of his sudden impatience and ranting, which had always filled her with fear as a child. All that remained to remember him by, aside from the smell of his cigars, was his black riding boot, which Tomás had brought to the house and left by the kitchen door, where it remained untouched for years after his departure from Tres Flores. But after only a few days in her father's presence the lost memories of him, which she had dismissed to some dark corner of her mind, recreated themselves and she soon grew accustomed to his ways once again. In only a short time Margarita learned how to fence out his bitter words and drown out the sound of his voice with the song of the nightingale—the song that the little bird sang, she imagined as Tía Marta described the way she beat her dark wings against the dead air, impaled on the fiery tip of the thorn bush. But it was his sorrow—the sadness that broke through the cracks of his anger—that she could not consume or combat.

Pedro turned and reached out his hand momentarily as if he wanted to touch her. But then he quickly withdrew it, turning his back on her once again. Ever since her homecoming, he seemed to avoid her company, even though he would come to her room nearly every evening to check her before he retired to bed. As she lay under the covers, she would wait for the soft pat of his leather boots as he crossed the marble parquet floor, and then shut her eyes, pretending to be asleep as he closed the bedroom door softly behind him. He would stand motionless at the foot of her bed for what seemed to her to be an eternity, listening to the slow rhythmic sound of her breathing. And then he would run his thumbnail across the arch of her foot to see if she was awake, but Tata had taught her to lie still, her face expressionless on the pillow. Convinced that she was asleep, he would brush aside her hair and kiss her gently on the forehead. After he left the room, Margarita remained awake, hoping that perhaps one day he would gather her up in his arms like a bunch of flowers, holding her tightly against his chest as he covered her face and her hands with kisses moistened by tears. Night after night she would imagine herself being caressed and cradled like an infant in his arms.

"Besides," her father added, breaking into her thoughts, "what do you want this in your bedroom for, Margarita?" His words were cold and neat like the carefully pressed sheets and pillowcases she had helped Bebita take out of their brown wrappers and stack on the shelves of the linen closet that morning.

"To comb out my hair, Father, just as I told you," Margarita responded, with growing impatience. "Or suppose I wanted to put on some makeup or something? Most of the girls at school have begun to wear makeup and bobby socks and saddle shoes. Suppose I want to wear rouge or lipstick?" she added, with her eyes fixed on the points of Pedro's wing tip shoes, in a voice that had fallen to a whisper.

As she stood before the oval mirror in the hall, Margarita could still recall the look on her father's face as he spun around and yelped at her in response, like a wild animal:

"No daughter of mine will parade around the streets with her face painted like a clown's. Is that clear? I forbid you to wear makeup. I made a mistake leaving you with your aunt, Margarita," he said, pounding his fist against the wall. "I should have left you in Cienfuegos with the nuns."

Though he spoke in a smooth, even voice, the violent tone that pulled like an undertow beneath the surface of his words drew the servants from the kitchen. Margarita sensed that her old aunts were listening from behind closed doors. Pedro paused for a moment to wipe the beads of perspiration that had formed on his upper lip with a handkerchief that hung from his back pocket.

"I have given you everything," he continued in a slightly calmer tone, conscious that the servants watched him from the shadows. "Your closets are filled with the finest things money can buy. And still you ask for more? What more could I possibly give you? What more could you possibly want? My father always said that women are never satisfied. We give them everything, but they are never satisfied. I should have listened to him then, but who listens when they're young? While I am still living, you will never walk out of this house with makeup on your face. Never!" he snapped, his anger visibly mounting with his words, but when he caught the expression on his daughter's face, her trembling lips and the fear in her eyes, his voice softened.

"You are my pearl, Margarita," he murmured. "You are all I have—the last remaining jewel. You are all that is left. I won't allow you to die . . ."

His words trailed off, as though he didn't have the strength to roll them from his tongue. At that moment Margarita realized why he had wanted to send his daughters to the monastery in Cienfuegos—why he had refused to see her all of those years. She realized in that instant that he was afraid of losing them, just as he had lost their mother. And all at once all of the stored-up anger she had felt toward her father turned to pity—but when she tried to speak to him, to tell him what she knew, her tongue weighed in her mouth like an uncut stone.

"Back to the kitchen, all of you! This is nobody's business!" Pedro yelled, suddenly recalling that the servants were watching. His eyes flashed for a moment and then there was silence.

Margarita fastened her eyes onto her father's, conscious that his had become dull and rheumy as though the fire within had suddenly extinguished. It was the first time she had the courage to meet his gaze, for in that moment it seemed as though he had aged a lifetime before her eyes. It was almost as if some invisible hand had raised itself against him and he had conceded his defeat with silence.

"Go to your room now, Margarita," he said, after a long pause, without emotion. Then he turned his back on her and pretended to straighten the oval mirror once again.

He had hung it so high on the wall that she could not see her reflection when she passed. As she closed the door to her bedroom, the sense of relief that her father had dismissed her from his presence washed over her like a cool wave. She could not help but feel that she preferred his anger to his sorrow. Somehow it was easier to confront.

After she had locked her bedroom door, Margarita opened her top dresser drawer and took from it the jagged piece of glass that she had hidden beneath her camisoles and slips along with a jar of cold cream and a tube of orangy-red lipstick she had taken from her mother's dressing table.

Although Pedro had strictly forbidden anyone to go into Rosa's bedroom before he had left Tres Flores, she had decided to enter the room one afternoon while María lay in her bedroom napping. Her mother's room was as dark as a nave in the cathedral, for the shutters were closely drawn, allowing only a thin rib of light to penetrate the sacred gloom. Margarita closed the door behind her and stood motionless with her back against the wall, feeling a kind of living pulse in the room.

As her eyes gradually adjusted to the dim light, she began to make out shapes around her. The room had remained untouched by the months that had passed since her mother's death. Though empty, it was preserved like a shrine. At a glance, Margarita could see that someone had kept the floors meticulously swept and mopped and the furniture dusted despite her father's warning. The air was embalmed with the scent of dusting powder and cologne— the scent of sandalwood and jasmine that recalled to Margarita's memory the times she and Caridad had lain on their stomachs across the porch swing with their heads resting on their mother's lap. Rosa would fan their faces and the back of their necks with a rice paper handscreen and glide them across the veranda while she and Tía María—and whoever happened to be visiting that day— wore away the hot afternoons with their conversation.

Margarita sat on the corner of her mother's bed, running her fingers over the flowers carved into the wooden posts and the bits of ivory and pearl inlaid into the headboard. It seemed to her that the bed was like a living, breathing thing—a garden, throbbing and pulsing—hewed and shaped in some wild workshop out of the trunk of an old tree.

Someone had carefully made up Rosa's bed with the purple comforter and the cut linen shams, which concealed the pillows where her mother's head had once rested. As Margarita fingered the large ebony rosary that hung from one of the bedposts, it occurred to her that although the room was unoccupied, it was prepared as though at any moment Rosa might return. Margarita could still recall the feeling of the rosary beads in her hand. They were soft and smooth to her touch, though the varnish had long since been worn away by her mother's, and her grandmother's, and her great-grandmother's hands. As she held them in her own hands, her eyes paused over the familiar objects on the nightstand by Rosa's bed—the lamp with the bell-shaped eyelet shade, which Mariela had beaded and trimmed with red silk fringe, and her father's favorite photograph of her mother when she was a young girl. In the photograph, Rosa wore a blue linen dress with two red roses growing from a single stem fastened to her collar. There was something serene, almost regal about the way she held her head, though it seemed to be bent with sorrow. Next to her mother's picture was a small filigreed frame with a photograph of Mariela and Paolo standing in the portico at Tres Flores. The frame was supported by a metal figurine of a black boy on bent knee. The boy, who was dressed and bejeweled like a Turkish pasha, was wearing a gold turban adorned with a gold tassel, small coral beads and seed pearls, and a pair of wide harem pants with black-and-gold stripes. Tight silver bands with serpents' heads and tiny jade eyes coiled around his ankles and wrists.

After she had rehung the rosary on the bedpost, Margarita crossed the room in order to explore the contents of the tray on her mother's chest of drawers, something she and Caridad had always loved to do as children. It was crowded with hand-painted porcelain boxes and colored glass bottles. At the center were several gold tubes of lipstick, along with the jar of pink cold cream that Mariela had purchased from the street vendor, and her lacquered Chinese box, which slid apart and contained a lozenge-shaped bar of black soap. Beside the tray lay her father's shaving glass and the large camel-hair brush that he used to paint shaving cream on his face.

Uncovering the porcelain boxes one by one, Margarita greedily examined their contents with her fingers and eyes. Most were filled with an array of cloth-covered buttons, holy medals, straight pins with colorful tips, large wire hairpins wound with dark strands of hair, cotton balls, pearl-tipped hat pins, and small rubber bands.

A satin-covered jewelry box that was also on the dresser contained an odd assortment of brooches and stickpins, a cameo pendant on a thin black ribbon, a locket that sprang open and contained a braided lock of silver hair, and a tangle of chains and medals.

When she had finished with the boxes, Margarita began rummaging through her mother's work baskets and opening and closing the drawers in her escritorio in search of Rosa's green Morocco notebook. After she had found the notebook buried beneath a pile of loose photographs, Margarita moved on to her mother's dresser drawers. Most were jammed shut—a mélange of nightgowns and undergarments. She pulled the top drawer out of the chest and lay it on her mother's bed. Slowly she sifted through the embroidered handkerchiefs, ribbons, nylons and garter belts, satin sachets and knotted loops of palm leaves until she reached the bottom of the drawer, where she discovered a tooled leather compact fastened shut with an S-shaped hook.

Certain that she'd heard someone calling her name, Margarita hastily pushed her mother's things into the drawer and fitted it back into the dresser. In her haste she knocked her father's shaving glass from the bureau, where it shattered into a thousand shards and pieces that scattered across the floor. She could still recall the startling sound of the glass breaking against the marble like hands suddenly clapping in an empty room.

Fearing that she would never make it back to her room unobserved, Margarita resigned herself to the idea that she would be caught. Momentarily frozen with fear, she listened to the muffled sound of footsteps on the stairs. There was just enough time to slide beneath her mother's bed before Graciela came shuffling into the room. The old woman paused for a few moments, surveying the mess in the bedroom Margarita supposed, and then left the room. She returned carrying a triangular whisk broom and a red metal dustpan that usually hung from a rusty nail in the kitchen closet. Through the fringe of the bedspread Margarita watched Graciela's misshapen salmon-colored feet sliding slowly back and forth as she swept the broken glass together into a heap. They moved in rhythm with the creaky groan her old hemp sandals made each time she shifted her weight. Her calves were like pillars and her yellow toenails curled over the edges of her toes like claws. Graciela grunted and complained as she bent over to pick up the larger shards of glass.

"Ay, Dios mío," she muttered as she swept the shattered glass into the dustpan. "Mi madre!"

Though only a few moments had passed, it seemed to Margarita as though she would never finish. Eventually Graciela left the room without a word. It wasn't the first time that something had broken without explanation in the room, the old woman later told María, who questioned her (in front of Margarita) about the disturbance. Without even raising her eyebrow, María accepted Graciela's explanation, for she herself had seen pictures fly across the room from their places on the walls and discovered, on several different occasions following her sister's death, that the furniture in the front parlor had been rearranged. It never once entered her head that her niece was responsible for the broken shaving glass.

With great relief, Margarita slipped out of her mother's bedroom unseen. On her way out she noticed that Graciela had overlooked a crescent-shaped piece of glass from her father's shaving mirror. From time to time she would take the wedge of mirror glass from the back of her dresser drawer and stare at her broken reflection, searching the depths of her eyes for her own spectral image—her death, Tata had once told her. Over the years, while María was napping, Margarita would sneak back into the room and confiscate her mother's belongings, including the green Morocco notebook and the compact, both of which she eventually carried with her to Havana and then to the States in Rosa's old valise.

T he small green bird in the cage began to flutter and cry. As she began peeling off her gloves, Margarita turned toward the sound, distracted from her thoughts. She winced at the sight of the splotchy purplish-white skin on her fingertips and palms and was reminded of the day that her father discovered them.

"You always know a lady by her hands," he had told her one afternoon as they sat on the patio in cane-backed chairs sipping their iced tea. The way Margarita drew back in her chair and concealed her hands under her thighs must have attracted his notice, for he leaned forward and turned them over in his. She could still recall the lightening bolt of fear that ran through her as she watched him stare, uncomprehending, at her palms, which she had seared in the flame of Tata's candle. It was the only time he ever struck her.

Convinced that his sister-in-law was responsible, Pedro broke his promise and forbade Margarita from returning to Tres Flores for the summer.

"As long as I have a say," he told her, shaking the letter he had written to María in her face, "you will never see your crazy aunt again, or that bruja who lives with her." His words were prophetic, Margarita thought, clenching her hands into fists that reminded her of the mountains surrounding Cienfuegos.

Gazing into the mirror, Margarita studied her own reflection in its depths. The person who stared back at her from the glass looked like a faded flower someone had pressed and forgotten between the pages of an uncut book. At forty-five, middle age had begun to settle down upon her like the quiet dust that gathered imperceptibly on the closet shelves.

A pale shadow of the original, she whispered inside herself. Despite the soft light, the distortions in the glass seemed to accentuate her features, ravaged by years of solitude and silence. Deep creases fanned out from her eyes and her mouth, and her left eye—her speckled eye, Joey called it because of the dark fleck near the iris—had grown noticeably larger than the other. Her hair, which had always been heavy and long, had begun to thin and turn the color of mother-of-pearl. She had never bothered to dye it, despite Joey's encouragement, thinking that it would have been vain to do so. Even her skin, which had once glowed with the colors of the tropical landscape, was sallow and loose. It too had begun to fade. She had grown shabby and worn, she thought to herself. Not a trace of elegance now—not a vestige of the woman she had once known herself by. Only the color of her eyes remained unchanged. Unextinguished. The color of the earth, her mother had always told her.

How could it be, Margarita wondered, as she smoothed her hair off her forehead, that she always managed to keep the flower beds weeded, she sewed buttons even before they had a chance to come loose, but somehow she hadn't found the time—or the desire—to care for herself? But maybe she shouldn't be worrying about the way she looked. Wasn't it foolish to wish for youth and beauty at her age?

Margarita hastily passed her fingers through her hair once again and pinched the apples of her cheeks to give them color. Unable to take her eyes off the person who returned her gaze in the glass, it struck her that the years had lacquered and sealed her up like one of the polished Chinese boxes on her mother's dressing table. The years had gutted her like the deer that Joey brought home from the mountains during hunting season on the roof of his car.

They are dry and filled with sand, she thought, as she watched herself run her hand lightly across her breast and pinch the hard nipple, which was raised with the cold, between her thumb and forefinger. "A seedless gourd," she whispered. Closing her eyes, Margarita dragged her fingertips over her wet eyelashes, her nose, over her lips, and into her mouth. She hadn't even noticed that she'd begun to cry once again

Yes. Father taught me never to waste time looking in the mirror. And even to this day, Margarita laughed inside herself, as she hastily wiped the tears from her cheeks, she avoided the sight of her naked body in the glass. But was it a sin to touch herself in this way? she wondered, pulling her hands away from her face and her breast and turning from the mirror. Hadn't the nuns at La Sagrada Familia taught her that her body was a holy vessel? A temple? A shrine?

*   *   *

Margarita watched in silence as the newsprint Peter threw into the fire curled into feathery ashes, consumed by unseen lips and tongues of flame. She could not help thinking that somehow her life was inextricably linked to the fire. Almost nothing had turned out the way that she had planned. Almost nothing. All of her dreams, all of her labors—the baskets filled with unmatched socks (which she had darned and pricked her fingers over) and the frightened cries of the children in the middle of the night (which she had always answered) crossed her mind—were consumed, reduced, to the charred remains of a coal that was slowly burning out.

As she stared into the blaze, Margarita suddenly saw herself sitting in the office on a hot summer day at the American Consulate in Havana.

"It will be easier to get a visa if you travel alone," the consular officer assured her. "After you find a job and establish residency you can apply for American citizenship. Then you can send for your son. You know and I know that the Cubans are hard workers, but the American people aren't so sure. Already there's a wave of resentment against the refugees who are arriving in Miami. People are afraid that the system will just be exploited again. Once you prove to the courts that you can be a productive citizen you won't have any problem. Just sign here, Señora."

Margarita sat in the red leather swivel chair in front of his desk, clutching her purse in one hand and a large ballpoint pen in the other. Although she wasn't going to argue with the consular officer now, she had no intention of becoming an American citizen. When she arrived in Miami she would wait out the revolution and return with her son after the fall. It would only be a matter of time.

"We'll be placing him with a good family, Señora," the consular officer added in a businesslike tone devoid of emotion, "until you send for him." The expression on his face told her that he sensed her hesitation.

"It sounds awfully complicated. Wouldn't it be better if I just stayed?" Margarita asked, twirling her mother's wedding band on her finger, which Tata had given her the day she left Tres Flores. She had told the man that she was a widow of the revolution. "You know my son's not a crate full of sugar cane, Señor. He's just a little boy. Now that I think about it, it would probably be wiser for me to take him with me. Haven't you heard what the soldiers are doing to the children in Russia? They're just stealing them from right under their parents' noses and sending them to military camps."

"The government here cannot legally claim your child if you sign this document, Señora. Besides, you'll never be allowed to travel out of the country with your son. You'll have to send him out ahead of you to live with complete strangers. It may take you years to locate him. I honestly don't think that's what you want. Even if you don't care about yourself, Señora, think about the effect this will have on your child. Although I know it's not the perfect solution, in the long run, leaving ahead of him and establishing yourself in the States is the best thing for both of you. Otherwise they will end up taking him from you. You can't do anything to protect him here. You'll have a better chance going to the States by yourself and then sending for him afterwards. If you stay behind, there's no way of telling whom your son will end up with or where he'll be sent. Trust me, Señora. Trust me. Placing him with the family we have in mind is definitely the safest route for both of you. Besides," the officer added in an offhand way, "this madman will never succeed. Once we cut off the sugar market he will fall like all the others. We're his lifeline. In no time at all, you will be able to freely return to your country with your child and sip a Daiquiri or a Cuba Libre in La Floridita—you know, the place where Hemingway used to go?"

Though Margarita stared directly at the consular officer, all she saw was her son's face. Mistaking her silence for incomprehension he added,

"You know who I mean—he's the guy who put Cuba on the map for the rest of the world . . ."

"And the family you mentioned . . ." Margarita interrupted as she focused back on the conversation.

"They're Americans with lots of money and connections, of course." Margarita nodded. "I've already contacted them—they're personal friends of mine—and they've promised to take excellent care of your son," he assured her, reading the doubt in her face. "Trust me, Señora, trust me."

Margarita continued to nod her head as she strained to understand the broken Spanish words that meant she would have to leave her son with complete strangers. When she asked the officer the family's name, her told her that it would be safer for both of them if she didn't know.

When she walked out onto the street, it was as though she had stepped into a dark vision. Tanks rolled past her followed by trucks filled with bearded soldiers in olive-colored fatigues and black boots and machine guns with bayonets slung over their shoulders. They were laughing and cheering and shouting slogans as people hanging out of the windows above their heads showered them with flower petals and candy. Their words—"VivalaRevoluciónVivaCastro"—echoed against the buildings on either side of the avenida and collided in the air above her head. Margarita paused on the corner, waiting for a break in the convoy to cross the street.

"¡Señorita!" she remembered a young man who looked like her lover call out to her over his shoulder from the back of a jeep, "if you value your life get off the streets at once!"

For weeks afterwards, she could not decide what to do. Though Lucía and Ignacio wanted her to stay, Margarita knew that the government had already begun separating families, enlisting teenage boys in the military, and sending the younger children to schools spread out throughout the island where they would receive free education and training to become "productive citizens" who would "pave the way for the future of the new society," the government promised. When Margarita told her cousin that she was thinking of leaving the boy behind, Lucía had offered to look after him.

Though Margarita weighed the possibility, she finally decided that if she were going to leave him at all, it would be safer to send her son to the American family recommended by the consular officer. The only other option, he had told her, was to send the boy out of the country alone.

As summer collapsed into fall, she heard story after story about children who had been sent to the States ahead of their parents with their names and addresses scribbled on tags their mothers had pinned to their shirts and jackets. Cristina Olivares, an old schoolmate of Caridad's, was made to watch through the "pecera," a rectangular picture window at Rancho Boyeros airport, as her two daughters and son were frisked by the soldiers and then molested. The Echeverrías, the family in the big yellow house on the corner of Almendra and Turon, had left all six of their children behind with their grandparents in Matanzas in order to establish themselves in the States before sending for them. Margarita was aware of at least ten families who had already separated. Others, however, managed to get their children safely out of Cuba and were already reunited with them in the States. Margarita knew that this was true, for her cousin's next-door neighbors, the Rodríguezes, had sent Lucía a photograph of their home in Coral Gables—a pink ranch house with a royal palm tree and a flock of plastic flamingos on the front lawn.

After weeks of indecision, Margarita finally went to her parish priest. After listening to her story in silence, he urged her to give the child, who was born out of wedlock, away. Margarita finally made up her mind to leave her son behind when she heard that the Olivares girls had been separated when they arrived in the States, and one of them—Nuria, Margarita believed, or perhaps it was Paula—had been placed in an orphanage. Fearing that she would lose her right to protect her child, Margarita finally gave in to the consular officer's pressure and allowed him to place her son. The sense of urgency and sincerity in his voice had convinced her.

Much to her surprise, it took her several months to secure a visa waiver for herself, for she had no one to claim her in the States. Margarita could still remember her thoughts as she stood in the long, snaky line at the airport with her mother's valise at her feet. She waited, without rest, for almost twenty-four hours. As the frenzied crowd pulsed all around her, her thoughts turned to her lover. She could not help but think of him with bitterness. After all, she had sacrificed everything to be with him—defying her father's wishes and giving up all of the comforts of the house on Calle Semilla, only to be betrayed. She could still hear his words:

"All that you and your family represent go against the ideals of the revolution, Margarita. Your father's money—your name— all of it is stained by centuries of exploitation and abuse. I simply cannot afford to be associated with you any longer."

They had met for ice cream at Copelia, an outdoor café in the center of Havana. In a voice quivering with frantic desperation, Margarita pleaded with him, heedless of the people who turned in their seats to stare at her. Despite her offer to change her name and conceal her identity, he had left her literally standing in the street with nowhere to go, knowing that she was carrying their child. When she implored him in the name of their unborn son, he turned his back on her and walked away. His parting words stung her like a sharp thorn in her side as he violently shook her off his arm, throwing her onto her knees on the pavement, and disappeared into the crowd: "Go back to your rich father. Eres una puta."

Because of him, she thought, she was forced to abandon their child to strangers. December 2, 1960: It was a day that Margarita would never forget. As she stood in line waiting to leave the island—unaware at that moment that she might never see its shores again—Margarita could think of nothing but the look on her son's face when she handed him over to the man from the embassy. Even though the officer had assured her once again that she was doing the right thing, as the long black limousine with the tinted windows and the small American flag on its hood pulled slowly out of view, she could not shake the feeling that she had abandoned her son just as her own mother had abandoned her and her father had abandoned Violeta and Caridad.

As she pushed her way toward the ticket counter, Margarita consoled herself with the thought that she wasn't the only woman to make such a decision. Hadn't Rosa told her that a woman's life was a series of losses and separations? First from her own family, and then from her children. At the time she hadn't really understood her mother's words. But now that she had given birth, their meaning was all too clear to her. She could still recall the feeling of union and androgyny she had experienced when she carried her son in her belly, and the shock of separation, the splitting apart, at the moment of his birth. But the separation—the sense of loss—was modified and quickened by the pain of labor and birth.

With her face pressed against the glass, Margarita stared out the window as the plane lifted into the air like a small winged insect, circled above the royal palms that lined the streets below, and then flew over the Malecón and past El Moro. Soon all she could make out were the narrow bands of white sand that separated the green foliage and the blue mountains from the sea. As the island collapsed into the horizon, Margarita stared blindly at her son's photograph. Too numb to cry, she assured herself that he would quickly adjust to his new circumstances and that in no time at all they would be reunited once again. Children are flexible, she told herself, they can adjust to anything.

Just a few weeks after her arrival in Miami, Margarita learned that the American embassy in Havana had closed and the United States had severed its ties to the island. She had barely made it out in time. She was introduced to the Maradonas at a New Year's Eve party—a wealthy Cuban family who had broken with Batista but had also anticipated the direction that the revolution would take and, therefore, migrated with most of their belongings to Florida only months before the 26 of July Movement took power. The next day they contacted her through the refugee center and offered to put her up until she found a job. Perhaps because her father had always boasted that he'd never relied upon the charity of others, Margarita's pride prompted her to refuse their offer. But when Señor Maradona begged her to stay with them, arguing that his wife (who had given birth to their fourth child only days after the march of the guerrilla troops from the Sierra Maestras into Havana) desperately needed her assistance, Margarita reluctantly agreed.

As the months passed, Margarita could not help but feel resentment at the thought that she was caring for another woman's children rather than her own son. Despite their kindness and the opportunities that they offered her, she felt isolated and remote, like a prisoner held captive against her will. Gradually her sense of curiosity and adventure turned to disillusion. Though she never mentioned her intentions to the Maradonas, in her heart she vowed to return to Cuba the first chance that she got, certain that she and her son would never adjust to life in America. Here, Margarita thought to herself every time one of Catalina Maradona's children spit beets across the kitchen onto her clean white apron or her wealthy American girlfriends paid her a visit, people have too much. In fact, everything that Americans do is too much. They laugh too loud; talk too much; eat too much; ask too many questions; have too many cars and too many pairs of shoes; drink too much coffee, too much soda, too much wine and beer. Even their music is too loud.

What shocked her more than anything was the way that Catalina's friends openly complained, often among strangers, about their personal relationships or the problems they were having with their children.

In addition to the fact that their children are spoiled brats, she thought to herself while she baked beneath the plastic hair dryer globe at the beauty parlor and listened to one woman complain about her daughter and another describe her husband's quirky bedroom habits to the beautician who teased out her bleached-blond hair, American women are shamelessly vulgar. More than that, they're shallow and unrefined, she thought, certain that if she even tried to talk to any one of Catalina's female acquaintances about the things she'd seen, the things she'd lost, none of them could even begin to appreciate or understand. It would be a wasted effort, like casting pearls before swine, she thought.

After several months of looking after the Maradonas' children, Margarita decided that it would be best to go out on her own in order to earn enough money to pay her passage back to Cuba. Though they had been more than kind to her, they paid her slightly less than minimum wage. Despite what she had heard about life in the United States, it took her months to find a decent-paying job outside of a private home. Aside from her halting English—one of the ugliest, not to mention most difficult, languages in the world, Tía Nélida always insisted—Margarita discovered early on that she was totally unprepared to support herself. She had no skills or special training and had never worked at even a part-time job before. Women of her class simply didn't need to work, Rafaela always insisted—all they need to know is how to look beautiful and flutter their fans in front of their faces when men passed by. More than that, it was clear to her that what the consular officer had told her was true—they were not welcome in south Florida, a notion witnessed by the signs in restaurant windows and on apartment buildings that made it clear that "Blacks, Cubans, and Dogs" were not welcome.

Eventually Margarita found a job at a Chinese restaurant in West Miami. Although they were disappointed to lose her, the Maradonas helped her find a cheap furnished room with a hot plate and a communal bathroom at the end of the hall at a boarding house only a block away from the restaurant.

Somehow Margarita managed to put away a small portion of the salary and the tips she received from waitressing at the restaurant several nights a week and from the occasional sewing jobs that the owner of a nearby laundry gave her from time to

time. But after only a few months, she was fired from the restaurant for throwing a bowl of hot won ton soup on the lap of man
who patted her buttocks while she leaned over the table to serve
him his appetizer. Too proud to return to the Maradonas,
Margarita decided to postpone her return and use the money she
had saved for her plane ticket to buy an old push-pedal Singer
sewing machine she had seen in the window of a thrift shop she
passed each night on her way home from the restaurant. She
imagined that it would not be any easier finding work in Havana
than it had been in Miami. By putting off her return for a couple
of months, she could go back to Havana with some money in her
pocket and they could live off her savings until she found a
decent job. As a result, during her free evenings Margarita took
in washing and ironing, and during the day she cut and pieced
together children's sundresses, which she embroidered and
smocked with pale satin thread. (To pass the long, hot afternoons, Tía María had taught her to knot embroidered flowers
and satin stitch delicate butterflies, and the nuns at La Sagrada
Familia had showed them how to cut out dress patterns and gather fabric into small, even pleats for smocking.) Mr. Chang, the
owner of the laundry, offered to sell the dresses for her to his
wealthy customers, most of whom came from Coral Gables.
Despite her protests, the old man took no profit for himself.
Somehow he seemed to sense her situation, and Margarita was in
no position to refuse his kindness. Finally she gave in to his offer,
convincing herself that it was no coincidence that her new patron
shared the name of the man from whom she bought ice cream in
Cienfuegos. Margarita was certain that it was a sign.

At first Margarita stuck with making children's clothing, but soon
she began to experiment with women's jackets and shawls. Using
Tía Marta as her source of inspiration, she began began to design
and embroider a menagerie of imaginery creatures frolicking in
tropical paradises, which she pricked into life with the point of
her needle. Although it took her some time to establish herself
in the neighborhood, gradually word spread about Margarita's

talents as a seamstress. Soon customers were coming from as far away as Boca Raton to purchase her dresses and shawls. Nevertheless her career as a seamstress was short-lived, for not long afterwards Margarita received a letter with an official seal from the American Consulate. Even the postman, who delivered it by hand, had been impressed. Margarita waited until she had completed the last stitches on a winged zebra before opening the letter. She skimmed over the words [WE DEEPLY REGRET TO INFORM YOU . . .] until her eyes [. . . TOOK YOUR SON FOR A WALK . . .] lighted on the part [. . . A SUDDEN OUTBREAK OF GUN-FIRE IN THE PARK . . .] that snapped her life [. . . BETWEEN CIVILIANS AND REBEL SOLDIERS . . .] into two halves [. . . AN UNIDENTIFIED PERSON WHO IS STILL AT LARGE THREW A GRENADE INTO THE CROWD . . .] which would never be whole again.

The following week, a periodiquito "dedicated" to the "defense of el país" credited the attack to a small splinter group of Cuban exiles who had been secretly training in the Everglades and called themselves The Freedom Fighters. In addition to the gunfire and grenades, they had planted a homemade bomb in the park that day, killing more than twenty people, most of whom were women and children. "We are in a war against Fidel Castro, fighting for the liberation of our country," one of the militants was anonymously quoted as saying.

In a single moment, Margarita's entire life had been blown off course. All of her dreams and hopes were scattered by the seven winds. The days that followed flew by like dark-winged birds. Margarita closed the windows and drew the shades, locking herself into her room—into herself—and worked like a woman possessed on her sewing. Refusing to take visitors or accept any phone calls, she shut out the indifferent world as though she was in a mausoleum. She wanted nothing more than to forget everything that surrounded her, including the palm trees and the sun and the sound of the tropical birds. During that time, she frantically tried to reinvent the events of her life, to make sense of the insane pattern she, Margarita convinced herself, was responsible for having created. She had wanted nothing more than to protect her son—to keep him out of harm's way—but in the process, she had fed him into the jaws of the earth with her own two hands. Now her memories of him were like spilt needles on a flowered carpet that pricked her when she tried to gather them together.

After months of silence and seclusion, Margarita decided to go to the early mass at a chapel only three blocks from her boarding house. As she knelt at the altar of a god who, she believed, had hidden his face from her and now seemed totally alien and unfamiliar, Margarita came to the realization that she would probably never return to Cuba again. She had lost her reason to return.

Although she reconciled herself to the idea that she would live out her life in this strange and foreign place, Margarita also knew that if she didn't turn her back on her past, she would die—alone. And so, from that day forward she vowed to cauterize her memory and give up trying to make out the justice of it all. She would use all of the skills Tata had taught her, she convinced herself, to consume her anguish and loss. The only way that she could do this, she decided, was to leave Miami—a city filled with painfully familiar scents and textures and rhythms. The only way that she would survive was to separate herself from all of the Cubans—the sculptors turned manicurists, the philosophers turned barbers—who prayed and waited and prayed and waited and prayed and waited for the fall—for the failure of the revolution—so that they could return to homes and professions that existed only in their memories and imaginations and resume the lives they had once lived again. They had destroyed her future, she told herself, now she would sever her connections and surround herself with the company of strangers. She would bury her past. And so Margarita decided to go without leaving behind a trace, a fragment, a shadow that anyone would know her by. She wanted nothing more than to blend in and thereby remain anonymous.

And so that same afternoon, she collected her week's earnings from the Chinese laundry and broke her lease. She left a note for the Maradonas with no forwarding address, telling them that she no longer felt safe in Miami—*People feel free to just enter your home and take what they please,* she wrote. *I can't sleep at night with the head-splitting shriek of the sirens in the streets. Nothing is sacred here anymore—not even human life. The city's too dangerous for a single woman like me to live alone, but there's no one whom I can rely on or trust enough to share an apartment with.*

Though she had vowed to destroy all remnants of her past and to set fire to the only remaining image of her son—the small black-and-white photograph randomly tucked into the green Morocco notebook—Margarita could not bring herself to leave behind the photographs or her mother's few belongings, and so she packed them in Rosa's valise once again. When she stepped onto the plane that would take her to Atlanta, she introduced herself to the stewardess as Daisy, a nickname, she told the young woman, for Margarite. Now I am a nobody, she thought with some relief, a stranger without family or country or past.

Once she had found a job and settled in an apartment, Margarita began taking English classes on her day off. Though she could barely suppress her longing for arroz con pollo or con-grí, and her disdain for chitlins and hot sauce, in the evenings she ate soggy vegetables and candied fruit out of tin cans with plastic utensils while listening to the voice of a little man with oversized glasses and a tiny Charlie Chaplin mustache reciting English words and phrases. In the mornings, as she waxed her mustache and her legs or dyed the dark hair on her arms and plucked her eyebrows, she sang along with the loud British and American music that played on the transistor radio she had purchased at Woolworth's until she managed to imitate the pronunciation of the words. She had decided to swallow her own tongue like the African slaves Tata had told her about who chose to die by their own hands rather than allow their patrones to work them to death on their plantations.

In no time at all, Margarita became a ventriloquist. By the time Marlene, her supervisor at the motel, introduced her to Joey Marasool (a salesman from Baton Rouge who was transferred to the "Dirt Cheap and Easy to Assemble Furniture Warehouse" in Athens), Margarita had already managed to distort her accent, though she still walked around as though her child was slung on her hip, and even when she stood in line at the supermarket she rocked back and forth, as if he were sleeping on her shoulder.

* * *

The memory of her son weighed down on Margarita like a stone. She had always meant to tell her husband about him, she thought as she watched him point the green baize bellows at the logs in the fireplace, but there never seemed to be a right time. Of course Joey knew that she had left Cuba under duress, and she had told him that in their haste to leave the island her family had scattered in all directions, leaving no traces behind. To her great relief, he never questioned her account—he assumed that her story was no different from any of the other political refugees', which he read about from time to time in the newspaper when a new wave of exiles arrived in south Florida. Never once had he pressed her about her family, her home, her history. He had accepted her lies without question.

"When in Rome, act like an American," he had responded in his lazy Southern drawl, when Margarita overheard his mother ask him questions about her future daughter-in-law. "What I don't know won't hurt me."

Since Joey never asked her anything, Margarita never volunteered any information. But from time to time she felt the sudden impulse to purge herself and tell her husband everything—she imagined herself marching in circles like the mothers of the Plaza de Mayo, waving her son's photograph in the air above her head. But during those rare moments, her courage always failed her. In truth, a part of her feared that he would reject her like her own father had when he found out that the reason she refused to marry Raúl Campogrande, the son of one of his business associates—the middle-aged man who used to bounce her on his knees when she was a child—was because she was pregnant with another man's child. In his eyes, she was indelibly marked. Stained. Spoiled, like overripe fruit. In his eyes, she was already beyond redemption.

Consoling himself with the idea that his daughter had been taken advantage of by their gardener's son, Pedro threatened to murder José Carpentier with the ivory-handled revolver he kept in his top dresser drawer hidden beneath his socks and handkerchiefs. "You've been watching too many novelas, Father," Margarita had responded in exasperation. "The father of your grandchild is one of the top students at the university. He comes from a very good family, Father, a family you regard with great respect," she added, knowing that she was rubbing sea salt into Pedro's wounded pride.

Despite his daughter's words, Pedro remained unconvinced. He kept insisting that poor, unsuspecting José—who punctually arrived at the house the following morning to help his father trim Josephina's roses and cut back her jasmine bushes and was greeted with the barrel of Pedro's revolver—was the culprit. Perhaps it was easier for him to believe this. (Gracias a Dios, José later told his friends at the bar over a tumbler filled with rum, Bebita had the good sense to hide the bullets!) Pedro became convinced of the boy's innocence only after his confessor, Padre Sinfuente (who also happened to be Margarita's confidant), assured him that the boy was blameless. Nevertheless Pedro hounded Margarita for the information he sought, but she persisted in protecting her lover's identity, eventually prompting her father—who couldn't bear the prospect of explaining his daughter's condition to his family and friends—to throw her out of the house. The calmness with which she packed her valise in the face of her father's anger surprised Margarita even still. But back then she had been certain that her lover would take her in—that they would marry, as he had promised her from the first time she had surrendered herself to him.

"Get out of this house, you worthless whore!" Pedro had roared from the landing, as Margarita dragged her mother's valise down the stairs past her tías' closed bedroom doors. "As long as I live you will never set foot in your grandmother's house again!" he yelled, shaking his fist at her over the banister while she took her mother's mirror from its place on the wall.

From the shadow of a palm tree across the street, Margarita watched her father throw open her bedroom window and savagely toss the clothing she had left hanging in her closets and neatly folded in her drawers across the driveway and the front lawn. (Through slightly parted curtains, Pedro's three sisters, along with all of the servants and the neighbors, watched the spectacle.) After it became clear that her lover no longer wanted her, Margarita called María and asked her to take her in, but her aunt refused to do "anything of the kind," claiming that if she allowed her niece to return to Tres Flores, "considering the circumstances," she had added, her brother-in-law, "with his ridiculous temper," was liable to kick them all out of Tres Flores. (Only afterwards did it occur to her that she should have contacted Tata first—she alone could have persuaded María to give her sanctuary.) In desperation, Margarita called Lucía, who was married to her father's cousin Ignacio (who eventually numbered among the disappeared during the invasion of Playa Girón, and was presumed dead when they found his horn-rimmed glasses in the park near his home crushed in a pool of blood). Having had a child out of wedlock herself, Lucía asked no questions when Margarita told her that she had been abandoned by her husband. Seven months later, Ignacio wrote to Pedro on Margarita's behalf announcing to him the birth of his grandson and promptly received a letter from a lawyer telling him that as far as Pedro was concerned, his only daughter was now living in a convent in Cienfuegos. For him at least, Margarita had ceased to exist. He had banished her just as he had banished Caridad and Violeta.

On the anniversary of her son's death, Margarita asked Joey to make love to her. Even in the darkness she could sense his hesitation and surprise. She had never initiated anything between them before, having been raised with the belief that it was her husband's responsibility to do so, not hers. But this time it was

288

different—this time there was a reason. She wanted a baby, she had told him—she wanted to have his child before it was too late.

"How are we going to manage with another mouth to feed?" she remembered him asking. "With only one of us working it could be pretty tough, cher."

"Babies always come with a loaf of bread under their arms," she had responded, recalling Tata's words. Inside herself, she told him that she needed *another* child—she needed to have *their* child. *Their* son. Somehow she had convinced herself that building an altar of remembrance in her heart would be enough—and that another son would somehow compensate for the loss of her first.

As the years wore away, Margarita suffered through one miscarriage after another. She consoled herself with the idea that if she lived long enough, time and age would make her forget her son—forget her island—forget even her own name. Almost ten years passed before she was able to carry beyond the third month. Only then did she allow herself to pretend that the little stranger who kneaded her side and rolled in the waters of her belly was the son she had left behind. On March 29, 1973—eight months later and four weeks premature—Lilly was born. (Margarita had chosen that name, she told her mother-in-law—who was obviously put out because her granddaughter wasn't going to be named after her—because Lilly was born on Easter Sunday.) She had arrived early, almost as though she had anticipated her mother's needs and desires.

Lowering her eyes to the floor, Margarita recalled the unexpected feeling of disappointment that had swept over her and consumed her joy when she regained consciousness in the recovery room and the nurse who had attended the birth congratulated her and told her that she had a daughter. She felt cheated and betrayed. Even though she sensed the woman's disapproval when she insisted that her breasts had run sour and dry, she could not bring herself to nurse the small infant who cried inside the incubator. Only then did she realize that there was no way to fill the void her son had left in her heart—the son she had banished after years of discipline and effort into the shadows of her past.

After they brought Lilly home, wrapped in a fuzzy pink bunting—an event which Joey documented with three rolls of Kodak film—Margarita found some comfort imagining that the boy she had named after her father lay sleeping in the crib at the foot of her bed. In the darkness she could fool herself into believing that the little head resting heavily on her shoulder, while she sang softly in Spanish and rocked slowly back and forth in the moonlight, and the arm that hung limply over her shoulder was his. But they were only short-lived moments, for the pain and loss would return like an unexpected visitor and Margarita would wake up each morning with a new burst of grief at the thought that she was still alive and he was not.

"You just don't understand," she had told her doctor, who tried to assure her that the severe depression she was experiencing was not unusual. How can I begin to explain, she told herself during the car ride home, to a man who knows nothing about carrying or giving birth to a child? "How can I begin to tell him that I am condemned?" she shouted, unaware that the woman in the yellow Mustang that waited next to her at the red light was staring at her. "Condemned to the fate of the Sibyl, who hung for what seemed to be an eternity with the knowledge that she had made the wrong decisions?" By the time she pulled into the driveway, she was convinced that she'd made another mistake and that perhaps it would have been better if the child had never been born.

"Never mind if you can't have any more," Miss Adelaide—the name that Joey's mother insisted everyone call her—told her as she stood in front of the nursery window at the hospital. She had mistaken Margarita's depression for despondency over the fact that her obstetrician had warned her against having another child. "How blessed you two are to have such a beautiful child! Such a quiet and content little girl."

Though Adelaide had intended to cheer Margarita up, her mother-in-law's words only increased her guilt, for she had already begun to hope for the day when her own memory would begin to falter and fade and her past would sink gracefully to the bottom of consciousness like a stone.

Just after her eight-month checkup at the obstetrician's office, Dr. O'Malley told Margarita that she was pregnant once again. "Congratulations, Mrs. Marasool, it looks like you're going to have another."

At the time, Margarita was speechless with surprise, but only a few months later her life seemed to be moving in a new direction when the nurse showed them the picture from the ultrasound and assured Joey that within three months or so he would be holding his son in his arms.

Margarita waited for Peter's birth with joyous anticipation. (Joey couldn't understand why she refused to name the child after him.) When he was finally born (almost three weeks after her due date), she woke at least ten times during the night to check his breathing, which sounded to her like the snuffling and sniffling of a puppy dog. The possibility of losing him filled her with a nameless fear, something that recalled to Margarita's mind the dread she had always felt as a child when she and Caridad bathed together in the warm waters of the private beaches in Havana. Though they knew that their father stood close by, and that they were surrounded by nets that fenced out the sharks that swam too close to the shore, somehow they always felt unprotected. They knew that from time to time one always managed to slip through the holes in the unseen barriers that enclosed them. Despite her intense love for her son, Margarita tried to no avail to hold him at arm's length, ever conscious that the thin silver thread that tethered them together could at any moment be sheared in half. Lilly, too, seemed to share her anxieties and fear. Even though she was only eighteen months old when her brother was born, she assumed her role as his protector, a role that she continued to fulfill even though she was nearly grown.

How patient her daughter had been over the years, Margarita thought as she gazed at Lilly, who remained half-hidden in the shadows of the living room, accepting her place in her brother's shadow with little complaint. Surely she was aware of Margarita's obvious preference for Peter. Feeling the sudden urge to wrap her arms around her daughter, Margarita moved toward Lilly, but at that moment the girl uncrossed her legs and rose from her place on the carpet.

Margarita watched as her daughter crossed the room and stretched across the plaid cushions on the couch. Despite the dim light, she could see that Lilly was on the threshold of womanhood, for her face had begun to mature and her body had begun to lose its baby fat and take on an hourglass shape. Even her gait had become slower and more self-assured. Margarita could not help thinking that her daughter was about the same age she had been when she lost her mother. Though Margarita was now facing middle age, somehow the young girl whom she had left behind on the island—with another life, another future—still existed within her. She had never been allowed to grow up.

As she remained in the hallway, silent and motionless, with her fingers woven together as if in prayer, Margarita wondered if she would ever have the courage to bridge the gap between them and speak to her daughter about the changes she would soon face. Her own mother had failed to do this, she thought, recalling that it was only after she'd had her third period—and convinced herself that she was dying a slow death—that she gathered the courage to confide in Tata and learned the truth. For years she had put off the thought of having such a conversation with Lilly, but now that the time was actually approaching—or perhaps she had already missed her chance—she felt certain that it would never take place. They had grown worlds apart from one another. Lilly seemed to misunderstand and misinterpret everything she did. They seemed to share no common ground.

Even at her age, Margarita thought as she stared at her distorted reflection in the silvery sea of the oval mirror, she still struggled to suture and mend the divisions within herself. How could she possibly heal those that she sensed were beginning to divide her own daughter? Middle age, which had thrust itself upon her unexpectedly, seemed to accentuate even more deeply the deficiencies in her life—the lack of accomplishment—and increase the nagging certainty that she had failed with Lilly. Though something inside her already proclaimed irreversible defeat, Margarita was filled with regret at the thought that she had shut Lilly out all of these years and denied her the knowledge that she needed to guard herself while searching for her place in a world of men.

Gazing across the room into her husband's face, Margarita longed for some sign that would let her know that he sensed the feeling of failure and loneliness that had suddenly descended upon her like a black veil. He was still squatting in front of the fireplace, seemingly unaware of her suffering. Then for no apparent reason he turned toward her as though he knew. Margarita stared at him mutely, conscious of the color rising in her cheeks. Instinctively, she lowered her eyes, fighting against the feeling of naked isolation that unexpectedly came over her. After a moment, she gathered the courage to raise her head once again, but when their eyes met she noticed at once that his were without rapture. He had divined nothing—nothing at all.

"Hey, little flower girl," he said, rising to an upright position and resting his arm around Peter's shoulder, "how about you and Lilly getting that shopping bag out of the car and fixing me and my man something to eat while we run over to the hardware store and pick up some fuses?"

Margarita began to laugh madly in response, somewhere deep within herself. "If you want," she responded, pulling on her leather gloves once again.

28 March 1986

With her fork poised in her hand, Margarita sat at the kitchen table watching Joey carve himself a second helping of the canned ham she had pierced with pineapple slices and cloves. (Rather than cutting up several pieces of meat all at once, he insisted upon cutting one slice at a time.) Margarita continued to watch as he resumed eating. Every evening he followed the same ritual. First he divided his food into separate portions on his plate. Then he ate counterclockwise at a maddeningly slow pace, moving methodically from the meat to the starches to the vegetables and the fruit . . . the ham to the scalloped potatoes to the peas to the applesauce and the pineapple, and finally back to the meat.

He divides his socks in his top drawer the same way my father did, she thought, separating them by color and weight. Even the paper clips in his desk drawer were sorted by color and size. Worse than that, he had begun insisting on labeling the cans in the pantry while she and Lilly unpacked the shopping bags, with the date that they were purchased.

Margarita knew that her eating habits annoyed him just as much as his bothered her. Joey often commented on the way she mixed her food together on her plate or dunked her buttered bread into her coffee cup.

"How can you do that?" he had asked the first time he watched her butter her toast on both sides, sprinkle it with sugar and cinnamon, and then soak it in her café. When they were first married she used to tease him by eating chocolate cake or cookies for breakfast or by having dessert before dinner.

"That's just not normal, Margarite, just not normal," he always said, shaking his head back and forth in disapproval.

Margarita watched him spear the last piece of pineapple onto the end of his fork. As he did so she noticed the raised tea rose pattern on his stainless steel fork. The nuns at La Sagrada Familia, she remembered, had taught her that a lady always leaves the last bite of food on her plate, no matter how tempting. From the first time they had gone out to dinner together she noticed that her husband never left anything on his plate. When he finished eating it was almost as though his china had been unused.

"You haven't eaten a thing, Daisy," Joey remarked as she lifted her plate from the table and scraped its contents into the brown paper bag in the wastebasket. Without responding, she stacked it on top of the dish Lilly had already scraped and left on the counter beside the sink.

"You can't live on thin air, Margarite," he persisted.

"I'm making up for all the Americans who overeat," she shot back at him without raising her eyes.

"Very funny, Mrs. Marasool. I bet you won't be laughing when the doctor sends you to the hospital for malnutrition. You can't live on cigarettes and coffee."

"Are you finished with these?" she asked, lifting the bowl of scalloped potatoes. Without waiting for his response, Margarita began to scrape the potatoes into the garbage. She refused to save leftovers despite Joey's protests, an old habit she could not shake after growing up in a place where even the fruit that hung like pendulous weights on the trees rotted and spoiled in the rain and the heat. When she had finished, she filled the porcelain kettle on the stove with tap water and clicked on the blue flame beneath the gas ring. Then she stood on the tips of her toes, reaching into the cabinet for the mint-green cups and saucers with the fluted edges that she had ordered from the Sears catalog with the money the girls at work had collected and given them as a wedding gift.

It seems as though everything is an effort these days, Margarita thought to herself, as she lazily grazed the rims of the cups with her fingertips. Even the simplest things ordinary people take for granted, such as opening their eyes in the morning or brushing their hair, seemed overwhelming to her and barely worth the effort. When Joey was on business trips, she didn't even bother to get dressed in the morning, never mind shave her legs or put on makeup.

The saucers chattered angrily as she paused in midair to brush a stray wisp of hair from her mouth.

"Do you want me to get them for you?" Joey asked, without raising his eyes from his newspaper.

"I'm not completely helpless, you know," Margarita snapped back at him. He just shrugged his shoulders. As she placed the cups and saucers on the counter she noticed that most of them were chipped or cracked. Still, she refused to allow Joey to throw them away.

Leaning against the counter with her dishtowel draped over her shoulder, Margarita measured two teaspoonfuls of Sanka into their cups and waited for the water in the kettle to boil. As Joey read the sports section of the paper, Lilly sat at his elbow, folding her paper napkin into various shapes, while Peter ushered his peas back and forth across his plate. Joey had pushed his dinner plate aside—she knew that he expected her or Lilly to clear it for him. Margarita picked up the cigarette she'd left burning on the rim of the sink. It had become one long gray ash, which she balanced like a juggler as she drew the filter to her lips. She often lit several at a time, taking a drag or two and then leaving them to burn out in an ashtray or a saucer.

As Margarita inhaled the cigarette it scorched her lips and throat, for the tobacco had already burned down to the filter.

Her gaze rested on her husband again, who was too absorbed in his reading to notice, and she recalled the night that he had proposed to her:

"You don't have to make any of that fancy stuff for me," he had assured her when she told him that she had never learned how to cook. Knowing that he came from a large family (all of whom still lived within a mile of one another), with a mother who could stuff boudin into its casing with her hands tied behind her back and whip up fried chicken or pralines in her sleep, she was certain that he would retract his proposal.

"I'm a simple man, Daisy, with simple needs," he told her as he cut off a large piece of prime rib with a steak knife. "Three square meals a day and someone to keep me warm at night—that'll do me, cher," he added, fingering a piece of fat into his mouth and then loudly sucking on his fingertips.

Though he was offering her an anonymous life in exchange for almost nothing, it took her three days to decide. The thought of making such a binding commitment to a man she had only been seeing for a couple of months filled her with fear and reservation. After all, she finally convinced herself (with Marlene's help), we both stand to benefit. He'll have someone to look after him, and I'll never have to worry about being deported.

Margarita finally accepted Joey's proposal in an Italian restaurant over a Chianti bottle filled with plastic roses.

"Come on Spanish eyes, marry me," he had said, as he took a small velvet-covered box from the inside pocket of his jacket. As he pushed the box across the table toward her, Margarita could not help but think of what her father would say when she noticed the dirt beneath his fingernails. She blushed with embarrassment when Joey pulled one of the flowers from the wine bottle and circled around her snapping his fingers with the gold rose clenched between his teeth. Knowing that it was useless to hold out any longer, she accepted his ring, telling him that she couldn't refuse a man with a name like Marasool. (Months later he admitted that he didn't know what she was talking about.)

The following weekend, they began shopping for a wedding dress together, even though Marlene insisted that Joey shouldn't see it before the ceremony. Margarita picked out an inconspicuous ivory cocktail dress with a handkerchief hem that Joey later spilled cherry punch on at their reception. He didn't seem to notice that she hadn't chosen white, though she was certain that her mother-in-law had. (Adelaide's abrupt silence, combined with the way she stared at her dress with raised eyebrows while they all stood waiting in the front lobby of the courthouse for Joey's older brother, Ray, confirmed her suspicions.) Even though Adelaide had protested, they were married by a justice of the peace, along with four other couples, in a small, stuffy office in the basement of the courthouse. And though the sun was shining when they left the house, it started raining when they arrived at the courthouse and didn't let up until halfway through the reception, an ominous sign for a bride, Joey's aunt, Miss Gladys (Glad for short), told her in the reception line. Marlene and Ray stood for them. (Although everyone was convinced that it was planned, Marlene caught the bouquet at the reception and Ray caught her garter. As the disc jockey played a striptease on the record player, Ray pushed it so far up Marlene's thigh that everyone could see her red polka-dot panties.) Meanwhile Adelaide, who had lost her husband when Joey was only eleven years old (in an oil rig accident on a platform off the Gulf of Mexico), cried at intervals throughout the entire ceremony and reception because it reminded her, she later told them in a letter, of her own wedding day. Somehow the rain seemed appropriate, she wrote.

When the ceremony was over, Margarita's girlfriends showered them with rice and birdseed on the steps of the courthouse. (Minnie, Joey's little sister, was poked in the eye by a piece of rice; and though everything turned out in the long run, Ray had to rush her to the emergency room!) Marlene had decorated Joey's old blue Plymouth with paper flowers and white crepe streamers that drooped and ran in the rain. She even tied a bunch of empty Campbell's soup cans to the bumper of the car and taped a "Just Married" sign onto the interior of the windshield.

On the way to the reception, Margarita insisted on stopping at a church so that she could leave a bouquet at the Blessed Mother's altar. Joey thought that the idea was ridiculous, but he stopped anyway, waiting in the car for Margarita while she ran in.

It wasn't exactly a wedding like the ones Margarita had read about in the bridal magazines at the drugstore while she stood in line to buy cigarettes or a candy bar, but at least it was a wedding, she consoled herself, complete with name cards and white matches with their first names hand printed in silver ink on the covers. Joey rented a tent that Marlene offered to put in her backyard for the reception, where a caterer served hors d'oeuvres and spiked cherry punch. On a small rollaway table there was a three-tiered cake with a plastic bride and groom standing under an arch of silk lilies of the valley. Together Margarita and Joey cut the cake and then smashed it into each other's faces, a peculiar ritual that she never quite understood.

After the reception, they spent the night in a small motel near the airport. As she unpacked her toothbrush and shampoo and the lacy red nightgown Marlene had given her for their first night together, Joey proudly pulled a pearl choker from his suit pocket and fastened it around Margarita's neck.

"You shouldn't have," she had murmured, knowing by the touch that they weren't real pearls.

"Anything for my girl," he whispered as he sucked gently on her neck, leaving a purple semicircle that she later concealed with a turtleneck and a silk scarf.

Margarita lay awake half the night, listening to the sounds of the airplanes taking off and landing at the airport. She could not help thinking that perhaps one of those planes was bound for Cuba. The next morning they left for Atlantic City, where she spent the weekend sitting at the bar drinking Pink Ladies and Joey gambled away the money his aunts and uncles had pinned onto her dress and wedding veil at the reception.

"Intimacy. We lack intimacy," Margarita muttered under her breath as she refilled the metal ice trays with water from the tap.

It was the word that she noticed on the cover of a woman's magazine at the hairdresser's under an article entitled "What Do Women Really Want?"

"Did you say something, honey?" Joey asked without lowering his newspaper.

Margarita shook her head, knowing that he wasn't looking. She squashed out her cigarette and began to light another. Gazing at her husband through the rings of smoke, she began to regret that she hadn't formed at least some close friendships after Joey was promoted to a managerial position and transferred to north Jersey. When they lived in Georgia, Margarita almost never declined Marlene's invitations to go shopping or out to lunch with her and her girlfriends. She had even accepted Marlene's invitation to join the women's auxiliary at the Baptist church. But when they moved up north into a development of houses (with wall-to-wall carpeting and vinyl siding) that had sprung up overnight like multicolored mushrooms, something inside her seemed to wither and die, even though Joey was convinced that they were living out the American dream.

Aside from her involvement in the PTA, Margarita rarely left the house without Joey, even to take a walk. Though she knew that her friends in Georgia had their faults and shortcomings, she found northern women cold and unfriendly. She could not help but compare their calculated reservation and smug arrogance to the warmth and hospitality of the southern women she had gotten to know so well, even though Margarita knew that their courteousness was sometimes false and masked their true thoughts and opinions. It rubbed her raw every time someone asked her, with obvious scorn and disdain, about life among the southern belles.

"In the south," she argued with the wife of one of Joey's supervisors at the company's annual Christmas cocktail party, "they at least try to preserve some sense of ritual and tradition, unlike you northerners, who think that lunch at the club every Wednesday is the height of social accomplishment."

"At least we can sleep betta at night, honey," the woman had snapped back at her in a mock southern accent, "knowin' that our fancy balls and comin' out pa'ties on't funded by money that comes from cotton picked on some ol' plantation."

When Margarita, who by that time had had one too many drinks, told the woman that her membership fees for the country club had probably come from trading the local Indians tobacco and alcohol for their land, the woman turned on her heels and left her standing alone by the piano. Needless to say, it was the last Christmas party she attended with her husband.

The following spring, Joey received a huge raise in his salary, something Margarita did not expect after the fiasco at the Christmas party. She suggested that they use the extra money to buy a house near the ocean, where she and the children could spend their summer vacations. To her surprise, Joey agreed, so the following weekend they drove down to the beach and met with a realtor. That same afternoon, they found themselves in his office, signing a contract. In her excitement, Margarita had told the man that she'd grown up on an island surrounded by the sea. "Hell," he laughed, taking the toothpick from his mouth and throwing his head back, "if you can't have the Caribbean, the next best thing is the Jersey shore!"

From that time on, they spent every summer at the beach. And when they returned to their other home, Margarita lost herself in the hectic whirlwind of raising two small children. As Lilly and Peter grew older and went off to school, she actually began to enjoy her solitude and the freedom her uncluttered schedule gave her to perform the mindless household tasks that she set out for herself to do each morning at her own pace.

After Joey would leave for work, she would sit in her bathrobe at the Formica table in the kitchen, sipping coffee and listing the things she wanted to accomplish that day. Margarita recalled thinking that even if she didn't have a chance to finish everything on the list, writing things down made her feel as though she had already accomplished something. At first, she always wrote her lists using the pen with the red plastic rose and the green silk petals that the man from Bell Telephone had given her as a complimentary gift when he installed a princess phone in their bedroom. Frustrated at the fact that she rarely completed the tasks she planned for herself each day, she eventually began writing with a lead pencil—that way she could erase any of the chores she hadn't had time to finish. Of course it was a silly thing to do, like cheating oneself at solitaire, but somehow the list of chores—which she had checked and crossed off—that she read off to Joey at the dinner table each night gave her a sense not only of accomplishment but of closure as well.

She could still remember how she had hurried to finish her housework by noon—straightening the cushions on the couch, emptying the ashtrays, going over the furniture with a feather duster (the wood and the baseboards were polished every other week) and running the vacuum over the rug—that way if Joey happened to come home unexpectedly for lunch, his house would be spotlessly clean. The days that he didn't come home, she'd set up the ironing board in the living room and press his laundry—usually a few button-down shirts and handkerchiefs, a pair of drawstring pajamas, and several pairs of boxer shorts and under-shirts—while she watched soap operas on the black-and-white TV. When she had finished, she would usually sit at the kitchen table listening to the morning talk shows on the radio while past-ing green stamps into the little booklets she had picked up at the A&P. (Even though Joey teased her about the stamps, she had managed to save enough to buy Lilly and Peter a phonograph so that they could play their 45s and an electric can opener for the kitchen.) Other days, when there was no ironing or pasting to do, Margarita would reorganize the things in the house. First, she began with small projects—the flatware in the kitchen drawer, the towels in the linen closet. Then she moved to the shelves in the medicine chest. Finally, she began rearranging the furniture and moving around the knickknacks and the photographs of the chil-dren in the living room and the den and rehanging the pictures on the walls. She stopped after Joey broke his toe one night on a sidetable that moved, "by itself," he muttered, from the living room to the hallway between their bedroom and the bathroom. Only then did she decide to take a quilting class at her mother-in-law's suggestion—she had already taken a class on flower arrangement and knew how to knit and crochet.

By spring, she and the children were ready to be liberated from their schedules once again.

* * *

How different the shore house seemed from their home in the suburbs, Margarita thought as she gazed into the living room from her place at the sink, with its bare wooden floors and uncurtained windows which let in the sunlight and the salt air and the colors of the garden that she tended with the children. At a glance anyone could see the difference between the two houses. Without a doubt the one in the suburbs was Joey's, with its straight lines and heavy insulated curtains, its dark shag carpets and formal living room furniture, which he insisted be covered with plastic protectors. (Though she had conceded to letting him decorate the house—knowing that the shore house was hers—Margarita had never grown accustomed to his hunting trophies. The moment Joey left for work in the morning, she would close the door to the television room, shutting out the fish and deer—not to mention the wild boar that had nearly gored his thigh on a hunting trip in Georgia—that he had stuffed and mounted onto the walls or made into lamps and ashtrays.)

Despite her insistence that everything be kept immaculately clean, the shore house had a comfortable, homey feeling about it, a feeling that their other home somehow lacked. There she and the children felt liberated from the cares and daily routines of their lives in the suburbs. During the week, while Joey was away or working in the city, they rose and retired with the sun, eating whenever (and whatever) their stomachs told them to eat and passing the time walking on the beach, tending the garden, and undertaking projects that kept them busy throughout the long summer evenings.

For Lilly and Peter, the end of the summer was marred by the thought that soon their feet, which had widened and spread with going barefoot, would be squeezed into stiff shoes that blistered the backs of their heels and refused to bend when they walked. For Margarita, it was the thought that she would have to set her alarm clock according to a schedule made rigid by early Sunday mass and the myriad school activities that they were required to attend. She found solace nevertheless in the large gray conch shell she had discovered—miraculously unbroken— during one of their long walks on the beach. Margarita kept it on the night table beside her bed and pressed it to her ear whenever she found herself longing for the sound of the ocean, even though Peter explained to her that it was only the sound of her own blood rushing through her veins.

While taking account of the living room, Margarita's gaze settled upon the quilted pillows she had measured out so meticulously and sewed. Though she had not realized it at the time, the life she had lived after they had moved from Atlanta had wrung her out and left her to dry. Somehow it had reduced her to following the forms and patterns others had invented for people just like her. Over all these years, she thought as she gazed at the intricate, flowerlike pattern on the pillows she had spent hours making, she had spilled herself away with endless distractions and now she had nothing to show for all of her efforts but a few quilted pillows and a throw. Even though she had everything a woman could want, something Marlene never hesitated to remind her about when they spoke on the phone from time to time, she felt as though she needed something more than Joey could give her. Something inside her had changed, and now she realized that she was no longer satisfied with the things he was offering her. But perhaps it was selfishness on her part. Hadn't her father said that she was never satisfied?

"I don't know what you want from me, Margarite," she remembered Joey saying the first time she had the courage to speak out and tell him that they needed to talk. "It's always so complicated with you."

Whenever she brought up the subject again, he'd begin to fidget and fuss and finally, without responding, he'd leave the room, usually going outside to read his paper on the back porch or smoke the Candy-Sweet cigars he bought at the drugstore.

Perhaps she expected too much from him. She was certain that her husband was doing the best he could. Hadn't he bought her this house so she could be near the ocean? Hadn't he been a good father to their children? she thought, recalling Peter and Lilly's laughter as Joey played the pony and jogged them on his knees or waltzed them across the kitchen floor on the tops of his shoes. He had even agreed to rub shadowy angels in the snow when they visited his "Yankee" cousins in New Hampshire, though Margarita knew that he couldn't stand the cold. He had been a good father, she told herself, with her eyes fastened on his face, though she knew deep inside that these things alone could not quell the feeling of discontent that had been simmering for months inside of her.

Lilly, who had left the room without attracting Margarita's notice, returned and sat beside Joey once again. Without protest, she allowed Peter to squeeze in between them and turn the pages of the newspaper until he reached the comic section. Feeling a twinge of jealousy, Margarita watched in silence as Joey and Lilly laughed at a cartoon Peter had pointed out to them. She could see how close they were in the way their bodies bent toward one another and their heads pressed together over the newsprint.

In a way, she thought, Joey had projected all of the love she had refused to accept from him onto their children. Now that Lilly and Peter were growing up, the fine silver knot that had once tied them all together would begin to come undone.

At that moment, Margarita glanced down and a throb of grief and pity surged through her, for she noticed the frayed elbows on the cardigan she had knitted for him when they were first married. Her eyes traveled down to the old, shapeless slippers he wore on his feet to the place where the leather had begun to peel back near the toes. Every evening he insisted on wearing the "same old sweater," she scolded him, and "the same old shoes."

"But I'm comfortable in them," he would say, stubbornly refusing to wear anything else.

A sign that he's aging, Margarita told herself. But how had she missed it? she wondered. Somehow, between the awkward silences and the years, he had begun to grow old and she hadn't bothered to take notice.

As she studied her husband, a sharp pang of sorrow and regret pierced through her, for she realized that Joey was about the same age as her father was the last time she saw him in Havana. It was right before she left the island, nearly three years after he had thrown her out of her grandmother's house. He was walking down the street, his pants hiked up to chest level, heading toward the same park where they had always taken their Sunday promenades together. Margarita knew that if she went there she would almost certainly see him. Only the most severe illness could prevent him from adhering to the habitual patterns he followed almost every day of his life. Even from a distance, she could see at once that he had aged a lifetime, for his raven black hair and his mustache had gone almost completely gray, he walked with a slight limp, and his shoulders had begun to hunch forward. Now he was little more than a broken wreck, a shrunken ruin of a man who barely measured up to the image she had looked up to and feared as a child.

Margarita watched as her father paused at an ice cream cart on the corner. Without looking, she knew that he was buying a cup of strawberry and chocolate ice cream—the flavors he always ordered, without exception. She noticed, almost immediately, the tremor in his hands as he took the cup from the vendor. For a split instant she was filled with pity and considered going over to him—leading his grandson by the hand and introducing them for the first time. But when he turned around she recognized the old anger, betrayed even from a distance by his gestures and the manner in which he clenched his jaw, and her courage failed her. Without a word, she shepherded her son in another direction.

Margarita's thoughts were scattered by the sound of the kettle humming on the stove. She imagined them mingling in the swirling plume of steam and dispersing throughout the room. She clicked off the burner and with mechanical precision began arranging store-bought raspberry pastries on a green plastic tray.

Dirty water, she thought to herself, as she filled their cups with boiling water. Agua sucia, and they call it café.

*   *   *

Once he had finished drinking his coffee, Joey folded the newspaper in half and threw it on the kitchen floor.

"It's late, Daisy," he said as he pushed back his chair. "Leave the dishes for tomorrow."

After all these years, she told him in her head, angrily pushing the Entenmann's pastries across the tray, you'd think you'd know by now that I can't stand the thought of finding dirty dishes stacked in the sink in the morning. Even a blind person would know, she shouted after him. Tearing at his back with her eyes, Margarita watched him leave the room with Peter following close behind.

Before going into the living room, Lilly helped her clear the table in silence. Though Margarita rarely acknowledged it, she could not help but notice that Lilly was the only one who seemed to care about the fact that she was always left to clean up after them. As Margarita stood at the sink rinsing the soap from the dishes, she listened to her husband checking the window locks in the living room and lowering the rusty Venetian blinds. Even when they were in their other house, Joey performed the same ritual every evening. Drying her hands on the edge of her apron, she watched him refold the green-and-blue throw and then methodically straighten the pillows on the couch where Lilly had settled, creasing and folding squares of brightly-colored foil and patterned paper into delicate origami birds. Peter sat across from her at a card table he'd set up in front of the fireplace clipping out decals for a model of a World War II tank he had bought at the hardware store. Just as he was about to drop them into a glass of water to soak, Joey turned off the light that stood nearby.

"Jeez, Dad!" Peter cried out with obvious annoyance.

"Tomorrow's another day," Joey responded without a glance backwards, as he adjusted a crooked painting and then began winding the wall clock that hung at the bottom of the staircase. When he had finished, Joey made sure that the front door was locked and then drew the chain. Though he did not seem to notice her doing so, Margarita gazed at his reflection in her mother's oval mirror.

"Ready to hit the hay, kids?" he called over his shoulder. "Don't forget to turn out the kitchen lights before you come up, Daisy."

Margarita felt as though she would scream, Things aren't the same, Joey. Can't you see that something has happened and things will never be the same between us again? Haven't you noticed that we lost one another somewhere along the way?

But the old familiar gestures that she was witnessing from her place in the doorway, the choreographed movements that she knew so well, silenced her.

"Come on, Daisy girl, it's been a long day," he said, pinching her lightly on the chin as he passed by the kitchen door.

"OK," she heard herself answer, in a voice that sounded strangely small and unfamiliar. She could feel her cheeks burning unexpectedly at his touch as she watched him move toward the staircase followed by Peter and Lilly. As she watched their shadows mingle and part on the stairs, she was reminded of the poem about the little shadow that she used to read to the children when they were young.

Joey paused for a moment on the steps to light the candle he had found in the cupboard, for the bulb in the upstairs hall light had burned out. (Though he had bought fuses at the hardware store, he hadn't thought to purchase lightbulbs.) "Coming?" he called to Margarita as Peter blew out the match and they vanished in a circle of light across the landing.

Margarita stood at the bottom of the staircase listening to the sound of the floorboards groaning above her head. After several minutes, there was only the tick of the clock and the sound of the ocean crashing against the shore.

They're lying in unmade beds, she thought, with surprising calm, as she lifted the silver cage from the table in the entrance hall and headed toward the stairs.

29 March 1986

Lilly waited in a pale ribbon of moonlight while her mother searched her purse for the silver key that would unlock the front door. With the moon at their backs, their shadows forked and stretched ahead of them, reminding Lilly of the poem she had made Margarita repeat over and over again when she was just a child. It was evident to her that no one had used the front entrance for years, for the cracked black-and-white floor tiles were impaled by spiky weeds and thick shocks of grass, and the portico was covered with a leafy canopy of creepers and knotted vines that twisted around the immense stone columns, knitting them together like yarn on a loom. Glistening with raindrops that beaded on their waxy green surfaces, they gave out a rich and loamy scent.

You're blocking my light, Margarita whispered. Lilly inched behind her mother until her dark image merged and then finally disappered into Margarita's, leaving her without a shadow. In silence Lilly watched from behind as her mother turned the key from side to side until the old, rusted lock finally gave way. She couldn't help but notice that since their arrival, Margarita had begun to transform, shedding the thickly varnished skin that living in a foreign place had wrapped around her. Her dark brown eyes seemed to be almost gold, though they were still etched by lavender semicircles, and her hair was threaded with iridescent strands of violet and green and blue, making it appear to be the color of mother-of-pearl. Margarita had absorbed the colors of the sea and the landscape and she glowed with an unearthly light.

As Margarita pushed open the front door, a muffled thumping noise sounded from somewhere deep within the house as though an army of small animals, momentarily disturbed by their unexpected presence, was scurrying for cover. Slipping her hand into Lilly's, Margarita led her daughter over the threshold into a world that seemed somehow immune to the ravages of the tropical heat, the decay, and the dust. Though she was filled with hesitancy, the steady pressure of her mother's hand gave Lilly courage as she trailed behind Margarita like a blind person.

Once her eyes had adjusted to the dim light, Lilly noticed that the floor in the entrance hall was covered with a thick carpet of moss and the walls were hung with what appeared to be immense tapestries composed of lichen and luminous, trumpet-shaped flowers that gave out an opulent scent. Birds' nests were woven into the spindles of the marble staircase and the leafy arms of the chandelier, and cloudy gossamer webs were spun into the corners of the ceiling. Just above their heads, a part of the ceiling had given way, allowing the rainwater that had gathered on the flat roof of the house to cascade into a shallow pool that had formed at the center of the hall. In it, long strands of algae waved lazily from side to side and red-and-white waterlilies bobbed gracefully on the surface of the water.

Though the house been almost completely reclaimed by nature and exposed to the elements, there was something soothing about it all. There Lilly felt the same serenity that she used to feel as a child when Margarita would lie down beside her in bed after she'd woken from a bad dream and could not fall back to sleep. Though the house was oddly comforting and familiar, Lilly knew that she had stepped into another world, like Alice through the looking glass, she thought.

311

She followed Margarita to a spacious room with a high, vaulted ceiling and windows that reached to the floor. Even in the half-light, Lilly could see that the room had once been beautiful, though few traces of its original elegance remained. A large oval mirror that hung over the mantelpiece—almost identical to the one that hung over the table in the entrance hall at their shore house in New Jersey—had become a swirling, silvery pool of mercury. The few pieces of furniture left in the room—a Victorian love seat with a broken leg and a scroll-necked divan—had sprouted green tendrils and leaves, and great, gaping holes were gnawed into the cushions and the upholstery. In one corner, a table and a chair with padded legs and clawed feet and what appeared to be a pedestal were covered with dingy gray linens. In the violet light, they looked like snow-covered mountains. Nearby stood a large embroidery frame with an unfinished canvas stretched across the surface like a drum. As Lilly walked toward the tapestry, something swooped past her and then the air was suddenly filled with small birds that looked like sparrows. The room had become an aviary.

Squatting down on the moss-covered floor, Lilly covered her head with her arms until the last of the birds had settled onto the furniture and disappeared from sight once again. All at once she became conscious of someone's gaze upon them. Slowly turning her head in the direction of the entrance hall, her eyes fell upon an old woman standing like a dark mountain in the doorway. Behind her were two other women, and standing behind them half-hidden in the shadows was a small boy. The women's heads were covered with red kerchiefs, and the older of the two was wiping her hands on the corner of her apron, as though she had just come from the kitchen. Though the facial features of the more youthful of the two women were obscured in the light, Lilly could see time repeat itself in her face, for something about the woman reminded her of a younger version of her mother. They were identical in all but the indigo-colored star on the woman's forehead, like the good sister, Lilly thought, in the story that Margarita had always told them, the sister who gladly shared her cheese sandwich with the talking fish.

Margarita followed her daughter's gaze, and when her eyes rested upon the three women and the boy, she cried out like a child and rose to her feet. Lilly watched in silence as the eldest of the three enfolded her mother in her arms and pressed her head down on her breast, as though she were a little girl. The old woman's shoulders seemed to be bent with the weight of a thousand years and her eyes were veiled with milky blue clouds.

We knew you were coming, she said, finally breaking the silence and fixing her eyes on Lilly. Under her gaze, Lilly felt as though the old woman could see right through her—as though she already knew everything about her.

The three women led Margarita and Lilly by candlelight up the staircase. Then they walked for what seemed an eternity through a maze of long, winding halls, over landings and passages that led to a series of interlocking rooms, until they stood at the end of a narrow corridor. There Lilly felt as though she had arrived at the very heart of the house. As she reached for the doorknob, some immense winged creature pushed past her through the shadows, knocking her to the floor and . . .

. . . waking Lilly from her sleep with a jolt.

Yawning aloud, with her arms stretched into a bow above her head, Lilly reached for the alarm clock that stood next to her night-lamp. Though a pale phosphorescent light had already begun to spread itself across the horizon at the place where the sky meets the ocean, the green neon hands on the clock told her that it was barely three-thirty in the morning. "It's got to be later than that," Lilly whispered to herself, as she raised herself into an upright position. "The sun's already coming up." Just then she realized that the minute hand was no longer moving on the clock. The electricity must have gone off again, she thought to herself, recalling that the power had been out when they first arrived at the shore house. "Hey," she said out loud, "today's my birthday!"

With flattened palms, she kneaded the small of her back, conscious of the almost imperceptible pangs that had begun to pull at her waist and the fluttering sensation, like the velvety movement of moths' wings, that stirred deep within her stomach. As she did so, her gaze locked on to the pale green eyes in the mirror that hung above her dresser, and in that glance she noted her resemblance to the woman in the photograph that had slipped from the pages of the faded green notebook she had discovered by chance in the bottom drawer of her mother's writing table—a graceful young woman in a blue linen dress with two roses fastened to her collar. She was accompanied by a man with a pencil-thin mustache and a tightly clenched jaw.

The notebook was jammed with yellowed newspaper clippings, an assortment of black-and-white rectangular photographs and thin, translucent flowers that someone had pressed between the pages and now crumbled at Lilly's touch. Knowing that Margarita never bothered with the contents of the drawers, Lilly had claimed the photographs and the notebook as her own, sensing that they connected her to a past her mother had, for some reason or another, denied her—an image of a past, she thought, that had begun to inhabit her deepest dreams.

Mundo Habanero

La Fiesta De Anoche

Deslumbrador. No se puede emplear otra palabra para expresar con la debida justeza, el aspecto que ofrecía anoche el amplio salón de Black Cat. Ese nuevo lugar de esparcimiento que gracias a felices iniciativas, desde hace poco tiempo cuenta la Habana. Deslumbrador era, en efecto, el golpe de vista del Black Cat con sus miriadas de luces eléctricas combinadas con verdadero arte, entre enjambres de flores que de los jardineros del gran jardín "El Fénix" transplantaron a pleno Prado, toda la belleza, aroma esplendidez que siempre reina en el jardín primoroso de Carlos III.

EN LA ELEGANTE RESIDENCIA del Señor Pedro Amargo de Mendoza, en la Calle de la Semilla tuvo lugar anoche una lúcida fiesta de arte en la que tomaron parte valiosos elementos.

Estas tertulias son siempre deliciosas. La de anoche, sobre todo, por la calidad de los que tomaron parte en ella fué de grato efecto pero los que allí se congregaron.

Velada interesante. Comenzó ésta con el nocturno de Chopin, por las señoritas Luisa y María de los Ángeles Martín, á mandolina y piano donde estuvieron admirables. La "Tarantela" de Gouchart fué ejecutada con habilidad y maestría por la señora Rosa Amargo de Miramar.

Campoamor, Anoche

La hija del circo llevó anoche teatro Campoamor a un numeroso público.

Todo estaba lleno.

Recordar, de entre lo selecto que allí acudió, a todos los damas, es imposible.

Pero citaremos entre éstas las señoras siguentes: Emelina Quevedo de Laestra; Margarita López de Muñoz; María Teresa Herrera; Josefina Duque Menéndez; Rosa Amargo de Miramar; Dulce Guzmán Baños; Juanita Rodríguez; María Luisa Mestre; Carmen Cabello de Alvaré; Aida Fumagalli; Flor Gallardo; Mercedes Belt; Olimpia Alegret; Cristina Masforrol; Blanca García; Carmen Andrea Teresa O'Reilly; Herminia Herrera de Alcaraz; Magda Cañizares; Chani Valdés; Adela Martínez; Carmen Teresa Herrera, Condesa de Fernandina. Señoritas: Silvia Delfín; Carmelina Quintana; y la graciosa y simpática Concepción Moreda.

Notas de Sociedad

LA HERMOSA FIESTA FILANTRÓPICA

Hermosa por todos conceptos fué la fiesta de carácter filantrópico celebrada ayer tarde en el "Roof" del Plaza, organizada por distinguidas damas de nuestra sociedad, y bajo el patrocinio de muchas que, por justos méritos, escalaron los primeros puestos entre las primer as del gran las almas a la más pura e ideal de las esferas.

Después de todo, al final de carrera insignificante de la vida, hay un acto solemne, definitivo, inevitable, que a todos equipara equitativamente; no por sus linajes y glorias de este mundo, sinopor su grandeza de alma y las virtudes que atesoran. Ojalá siempre mi pluma pueda reseñar, de manera pálida, estas fiestas que ensanchan los corazones y fortalecen los espíritus aunque María Teresa Paredes, Asunción de la Torre, Rosa Amargo de Miramar, y su hermana, María Esperanza Miramar, y la bellísima Lourdes de la Campa. Unas delicadas "signorinas" que estaban un tanto retraída, Carmen Cabello y Teresa Alvaré. Entra otras señoras: Presidíalo la elegante esposa del honorable alcalde de Boston, Mrs. Tyler, y la viuda de

Most of the photographs were inscribed with names and dates, some going back to the turn of the century. Lilly thought she recognized her mother in several (though Margarita was obviously very young) accompanied by two other girls. They were all taken in the courtyard of an immense white stone mansion—the one that had been overtaken by nature in her dream. Blending into the background was a dark-skinned woman—a servant, perhaps, with a stiff white apron tied around her waist. Though Lilly could not make out her facial features in any of the photographs, she seemed to be holding vigil over the three girls.

Lilly held the green notebook up to her nose and slowly breathed in the faint scent of jasmine and sandalwood. Spreading it across her lap, she leafed backward through the rough-cut vellum pages until she reached the first entry. The entire page had been hand-decorated with an intricate design etched in red India ink. Lilly's eyes wandered through the maze of soft circles and interlocking chains until they rested upon a flourish of letters that appeared to spell out someone's name:

Los sueños de Rosa Miramar.

Somewhere near the center of the notebook this same handwriting left off. It was replaced by what was obviously a child's cramped, awkward script, which several pages later gave way to what Lilly recognized as her mother's tiny, perfectly formed print. Turning over the pages filled with her mother's words until she reached the last entry, dated February, 1963, Lilly recalled the disappointment she had felt when she first found the notebook and discovered that she could only make out the long lists of names that appeared in the newspaper clippings and a few words scattered here and there, for all of the entries were written in Spanish.

Las Estrellas

Las conquistas de la ciencia han producido una trans-
formación grandiosa en el concepto que se tenia del
universo; nuestros antepasados no tuvieron idea completa
de la magnificencia de su belleza y de sus armonias. Las
estrellas eran para ellos clavos de oro fijos en una
bóveda, y pareciales que nuestra diminuto tierra constituia
por sí sola la creación y que son el universo de Moisés,
el de Pitágoras, el de Homero, el de Virgilio y el de
los Padres de la Iglesia comparados con los panoramas de
la astronomía moderna.

☙

20 de mayo

El 20 de mayo del 1902 fué un dia memorable para
todo buen cubano por ser un dia que se constituyó la
república de Cuba, después de tanta sangre y lagrimas
que costó, pues desde el año 1823 cuando se instituyó
aquella sociedad secreta llamada Soles y Rayos de
Bolívar, aspiraban los cubanos a restablecer la libertad y
tener patria, así vinieron sucediéndose las guerras con
intervalos de años, hasta que intervinieron los Estados
Unidos el 1 de enero de 1899 cesó en todo el

territorio de la Isla la soberanía de España y
comenzó el gobierno de la intervención, siendo
el primer gobernador militar el general John R.
Brooke.

⊙

La caña

La industria de la caña de azúcar es la major riqueza
de Cuba pues hay muchas en el país.

Hablaremos sobre el cultivo de la caña de azúcar
y la manera de sacar el azúcar de ella. El terreno
se ara en cierta epoca del año para ser sembrado,
esto se ejecuta dividiendo la caña en pedazos y
enterrándolas en la tierra; despúes de estar
completamente desarollada los agricultores la
conducen en carretas para ser molida, la quitan de
las carretas y la echan en el conductor que la lleva
a una gran masa que la aplasta y le saca el guarapo.
Éste va al tacho donde se cocina y convierte en
miel, que a su vez llevan en unos carritos, queda más
blanca y se convierte en azúcar. Entonces la llevan
en sacos a venderla, pero si se quiere que quede más
blanca y fina se manda á una refinería.

El azúcar es muy útil, pues sirve como ya sabemos para hacer los dulces que tanto nos gustan, y en las boticas se usa como jarabe para los medicamentos y en fin para muchas cosas provechosas al hombre.

Terminaremos diciendo que hasta en las cosas más pequeñas de la naturaleza se ve la grandeza y poder de nuestro Creador.

*

Juana de Arco y Cristóbal Colón

Juana de Arco fué la célebre guerrera que tanta gloria le dió a la Francia con sus hazañas.

Cristóbal Colón fué el gran descubridor de América. Nació en Génova donde se educó y pasó su primera juventud. . . . . Colón había oído hablar de que Marco Polo había descubierto las Indias, y que venía contando que aquél era un país delicioso donde todas las casas eran de oro y las calles de diamantes.

Colón era de un carácter muy noble y religioso.

Fin.

Re-examining the photographs one by one, Lilly tried to imagine the world beyond the serrated borders of the pictures. She could not help but feel as though she were standing just outside of a closed door—set within a stone wall she could not climb alone. She was certain that the stories that they gave out probably had little connection to the actual events that the unknown photographer had intended to capture. Overturning the photos like a deck of tarot cards, Lilly searched in vain for some clue, some hidden message. Given that her mother had taken a vow of silence about her past, she herself would be forced to fill in the blanks and the voids with her own imagination.

Margarita lay awake long after her husband had fallen asleep, pondering and rearranging, weaving and unweaving her past in order to stave off the knowledge that soon she would have to make a decision which, she had convinced herself, she could somehow avoid. Ever since she had arrived at the shore house, she lay awake night after night, examining her life like a deck of overturned cards. She felt as though her past self was bound in a violent struggle, shadowboxing with the other self she had created. One by one she reversed the events of her life,

I should

        never

                have had the child

        never

                        married

        never

left Havana

        never

    abandoned him to strangers

        never

have gone to the dance

        never

                have worn red shoes

. . . going further and further back in time...

if only

        he had left me at Tres Flores

if only

        Mami hadn't died

if only

                I'd gone

if only

        I'd never been born

until there was nowhere left to go but back to the start, moving her in the same restless circles once again. Despite the years of trying to mask and hide, a foreign sun continued to beat at her temples and a tropical breeze blew through her with every breath that she took. As she lay in bed, Margarita realized that perhaps the severed halves of her life would always remain separate and distinct from one another. They would never be reconciled. And though she could feel herself splitting apart like a wound that would not heal, in order to hang her life back together again she would have to keep living with the contradictions and ambiguities, juggling them like spinning knives over her head.

The whole night appeared to feel Margarita's restlessness. The rain beat out an agitated rhythm against the windowpane, reminding her of the drums she had heard the women in the courtyard play from time to time, and the wind whistled and howled, causing the window sashes to rattle loudly. Then the sound of the rain brought her back to the room, for it reminded her of the chimney leak the roofer had never managed to mend.

Listening to Joey snoring softly beside her, Margarita stared into the darkness, imagining that all of the world lay peacefully sleeping, and she alone was awake. As he shifted beneath the lavender comforter she could not help but envy his extraordinary ability to fall asleep regardless of what was on his mind.

Buses, trains, movie theaters, armchairs, even sitting on the sofa in front of the television, he can fall into a passionless sleep almost anywhere. And once he has drifted off, she thought, he's impossible to wake. A locomotive barreling through the room would have failed to rouse him, whereas she was cursed with the ability to hear even the softest of sounds, like the rustling of the oak leaves talking among themselves outside her window. But they weren't the only sounds she could hear. As a child, she was certain that she could hear people's thoughts, and often, when the house was very still, she could make out the voices of her grandparents and her mother whispering in soft tones that others always confused with the shifting of the palm trees in the breeze. More than once, however, Tata confirmed these visitations, for when they compared their experiences they both had overheard the exact same conversations. Though her powers had remained dormant for years, Margarita continued to be a light sleeper.

The sound of the clock chiming out the quarter hour came from somewhere deep within the house. Margarita raised herself into a lotus position and looked toward the window. This time Tata's remedy for insomnia—a cup of warm milk mixed with a teaspoon of sugar, vanilla, and rum—had failed her. Perhaps it was the dream that kept her awake.

For three consecutive nights she had dreamed of the bride who had been buried alive, though the newspaper story had been folded away in her memory for years. In her dream, she had been buried along with the girl somewhere in the Great Wall of China. Then the two became one and she saw herself crawling in her mother's burial gown toward her father's house. On her hands and her knees, she clawed and clawed at the back door until her fingers began to splinter and bleed, leaving bloody prints on the white wall and staining the wooden door red. The more she tried to raise herself up, the more she choked on the clay-colored dust that stopped up her throat and mouth.

The first night that she had the dream, Margarita awoke panting and moaning like a frightened animal. She was scratching at the quilted headboard of her bed and hooking the empty air with her fingers. The second night Joey shook her from her sleep. He said that she was screaming something in Spanish.

Margarita sat motionless in the darkness, spinning her wedding band around her finger as she tried to divine the message of the dream. The ring spun off her finger and rolled across the floor. In vain, she searched beneath the bed, groping about on her hands and her knees like a blind person. It had never fit properly, she remembered, as she crawled across the floor, and she had never bothered to get it sized. Now that she had grown so thin, she could hardly keep it on her finger. Half the time she ended up taking it off and leaving it in the soap dish by the sink for days at a time.

I'll never find it in the dark, Margarita thought, as she ran her palms across the cold floorboards. She decided to wait until the morning to search for the ring.

* * *

It had stopped raining. Margarita stood at her bedroom window shivering in her thin flannel nightgown while she watched the night withdraw, veil after veil being torn away before her eyes. Even though the window was fastened shut, she could still smell the scent of the ocean. As she slipped on her bathrobe, she noticed the split reflection of the moon undulating on the surface of the waves.

Reaching into the pocket of her robe, she pulled out a half-empty pack of cigarettes and a piece of paper with a list of chores she had composed at the kitchen table sometime during the previous summer. A pack of matches from a hotel she could not remember having stayed in before was tucked into the cellophane liner of the cigarettes. Although she scratched match after match across the flint, she could not draw a flame, for the matches had grown damp in the salt air.

Searching the top drawer of her bureau for a lighter, Margarita came across the telegram from her cousin and the packet of unopened letters that her aunt and somebody else (she could not make out the handwriting) had sent her over the years. Though she had consciously chosen not to read the letters, Margarita couldn't bring herself to throw them out. Somehow they seemed to preserve her link with the island—her link to a world that she was certain no longer existed. Though she still had not found the courage to open them, she had brought the letters with her to the shore house with the intention of reading them. Margarita groped toward the closet and grasped in the darkness for the cord. Switching on the bare bulb, she stared at the Western Union telegram that coldly announced, in impersonal blocklike letters, her tia's death.

MARIA IS DEAD. THOUGHT YOU WOULD WANT TO KNOW. LUCIA.

Margarita pulled off the thick rubber band that held the packet together and slipped out María's first letter, the only one she had actually read. Though she had vowed not to allow anyone to follow her out of her past, Margarita had been shaken from her sleep one night by the sudden knowledge that Tata was ill. Only then did she decide to break her vow of silence and write to María, for she knew that Tata had never learned to read or write. She could still recall that when she had received this first letter, she could not imagine what had come over her aunt. The last time that they had spoken, María had denied her sanctuary at Tres Flores. Perhaps, Margarita thought, her aunt had assumed that by writing to her after such a long silence, her niece was trying to reopen the door (though only partially) which María had closed long before. In her mind it was a second chance—an opportunity to forge a reconciliation with her sister's child and, in some small way, compensate for the fact that death had cheated her of the opportunity to do so with Rosa following their argument at the club.

Though she had continued to write to Tata and her aunt, Margarita had never bothered to open up the letters that arrived from time to time. Fearing that if she read them she'd be tempted to return to Cienfuegos—something she had vowed she'd never do—she had left them untouched and forgotten in the top drawer of her writing desk. She had read the first only to be sure that Tata had recovered. The others remained sealed in their envelopes and arranged in the order in which she'd received them.

After she had reread María's first letter once again, Margarita contemplated the next one in the pile, considering the possibility of opening it up. What does it matter now, she argued with herself as she thumbed through the remaining letters, if I open them after all these years?

As the night gradually passed into day she sat at the window on the same cane-backed rocker in which she had rocked Lilly and Peter to sleep when they were just infants, opening the letters one by one.

illy perched herself on the edge of her bed, trying to make sense of the mosaic of dreams that spliced together the photographs in the green notebook with inexplicable fragments of her unconscious life. Figuring out the first dream was simple, if only because she had just been looking at the photographs. But maybe that was too obvious, she told herself. She had read enough novels to guess that there was probably some complicated but obvious meaning to her dreams that was hidden from her view.

Rising with restless agitation, she opened the drawer of the nightstand in search of the tooled leather compact she had discovered alongside the notebook. With great effort she undid the S-shaped hook that fastened it shut with her fingernail, for the clasp had rusted into place. One side was lined with creased blue velvet and a mirror was on the other. At first she saw only her own reflection, but as she tilted the mirror from side to side, a pair of eyes that were not her own suddenly gazed out at her—then the bridge of a nose and the curve of a mouth came into view. Lilly drew the glass toward her to get a closer view, but the face vanished like a ghost. Startled at the sight of the unblinking green eyes that flashed up at her in the mirror, she dropped the compact on the floor—nearly breaking it in two—and then she began laughing at herself when she realized that they had been her own eyes staring back at her from the surface of the glass. For an instant, she hadn't recognized her own image.

Standing at the window in order to get a better look at the picture in the glass, she held the open compact up to the light, moving it from side to side until the ghostly image in the mirror came clearly into view. A stern-looking woman in a wide-brimmed hat stared out at her. She was sitting stiffly in a tall wicker peacock chair that was placed between tall potted plants. One of her arms encircled the waist of a little girl with long corkscrew curls—in the other she cradled an infant. Lilly guessed by the obvious age of the woman in the daguerreotype that she was probably her great-grandmother.

Cocking the compact sideways, Lilly saw her own reflection once again. This time only one of her eyes and the corner of her mouth were visible. As she turned it length-wise, both of her eyes came into view, outlined by dark tiaras of eyelashes and thick brows which were shaped into triangular arches that joined together like the wings of a bird at the bridge of her nose. Lilly began to move the mirror around in small circles, watching all the while as her triangular brows, her pale green eyes, her fleshy pink lips, cheekbones, pearl earrings, and wave of black hair flashed across the surface of the glass. Then gradually, she began to move the glass around faster—

triangular

arched pale green

lashes fleshy

—and faster—

pinkpearlwave

triangulargreenfleshypearlblacktriangulargreen

—until her features blurred and blended into indistinct shapes. Growing tired of the game, she held the mirror at arm's length until the living puzzle was pieced back together again.

*   *   *

Reclining with the green notebook spread across her lap, Lilly gazed with irritation at the maze of symbols that formed a kind of indecipherable palimpsest before her eyes. Shrugging her shoulders, she thumbed backwards through the pages once again in search of the place where she had left off writing the night before.

3/28/86

Mother, I've never told you this before, but when I grow up I want to be a writer. Maybe you'll think I'm crazy, but ever since I found this notebook I've had the strangest dreams. (This already reads like something out of an amateur novel, doesn't it!!!) Anyhow, in one dream I awake to the chattering of parrots in the trees. At first I have no idea where I am. After rubbing the sleep out of my eyes, I turn and notice that the place where you were reclining beside me is empty, even though the pillow still holds the sunken oval of your head. The air is heavily scented with the warm, humid incense of waxy plants and flowers and alive with the sound of tropical birds. As the heroine (A. K. A. me) takes in the unfamiliar fragrances and sounds, I begin to wonder why you left without waking me. (You never did like to say good-bye—even when we would go with Daddy to visit Granny in Baton Rouge!) That's when I start to get scared. Who knows? I think to myself. Maybe you sprouted wings and claws and a beak during the night and flew from my side—never to return.

It's then that I notice for the first time that the big white house—the one in the picture, with the tall columns at the front entrance—is silent as a tomb, and I suddenly become conscious of the possibility that I am alone. The thought that you might have abandoned me fills me with fear, Mommy. Just suppose that I wanted something to eat or drink? And what if I needed to call for help? Where would I go? What would I do? Looking at the pictures from the green notebook that you always kept in the bottom drawer of your desk has made me dream about these things. I've just begun to study Spanish in school—but maybe I'll never be able to speak your language well enough to defend myself in this place. I'd have to rely on my hands and my eyes to communicate—like playing charades. It is I who do not exist in this place in my dreams—I am the stranger in this house, not you. I, rather than you, am from the other side. (Despite all of this, I feel certain that this house is my home. Does this make any sense to you?)

But the dream doesn't stop there. I prop myself up in bed (like when Peter and I were sick with the mumps and you brought us a tray with hot tea without any milk and cups of consommé) and glance out the window that faces the back courtyard. The intensity of the sunlight that pours through the uncurtained windows makes me feel light-headed and drunk. (Yes, Mother, I've actually gotten drunk before, at an eighth grade graduation party at

Johnnie Mularkey's house. We buried a couple of six packs in the snowbank outside his basement and snuck beer through the window all night. His parents never knew!)

When I look out the window I notice that the long morning shadows in the courtyard reach toward a large hive-shaped cage. (The cage is also in one of the photographs from your notebook.) The door of the cage stands open on rusty hinges like a yawning mouth. The garden is a tangle, a wilderness, a riot of lush colors and shrill animal sounds. It's like a lost paradise, Mommy—like a travel brochure come to life. Lined up against the courtyard wall is a group of old women dressed in brightly colored outfits. Their shadows seem to knit and splice together as they sit, cross-legged and sphinxlike, braiding palm leaves into wands and shelling nuts into great wooden bowls that they hold between their legs.

Growing tired of watching the women, I rise from the bed and cross to the balcony window, which faces the front of the house. Gazing into the street below, I can see at a glance that the neighboring houses are in ruins from years of neglect. The weeds and the thickly tangled foliage seem to be swallowing them up and the large plaster patches that have fallen away from their pink-and-yellow walls make the houses appear as though they are diseased. Their windows have been broken and stripped of their wrought-iron bars, reducing them to hollow sockets. Balconies and porch roofs have sunken in and clay tiles that have fallen from the roof tops litter the pavements, which are cracked and split open with gnarled roots. The whole street seems to be rotting and decaying right before my eyes, the houses melting like candy in the sun, something like those funny-looking houses on the postcard Meghan sent me when she went to Barcelona with the Spanish Club. Though I can sense that they were once beautiful, they remind me of the old biddies who gather around the pool at the country club. They are like ancient elephants, mother, oblivious to the fact that their makeup is puckering and peeling off in the sunlight like a mask.

Though it too is overgrown with foliage, somehow the white house I am in does not seem as neglected and overrun as the others on the block. It's obvious that its foundation is intact, but it needs reinforcement here and there, and the cracks that have formed in the walls have been plastered and repainted. The dream usually ends with me at the window looking out.

N early halfway through the letters, Margarita paused. She stared down at the sheet of onionskin paper in her lap, reading and rereading her tía's words: You should have come like you promised. Now it is too late—your father is dead.

She felt so numb and weary, she couldn't even cry. Though she had sensed his passing the night the candles in the candelabra had extinguished—in unison—without explanation, Tía María and Tata's letters confirmed that her father was gone.

As she stared at the packet of letters, Margarita wondered how her aunt had managed to get them delivered. Over the years, they had arrived in her mailbox bearing the postmarks of various cities and towns all over the country—Desmoines, Miami, Denver, Buffalo. Several of the letters were duplicated by hand and mailed to different cities, in order to ensure that at least one copy reached her, she supposed. Somehow María or Tata had managed to bribe someone willing to take the risk and see that they were not intercepted—to see that they fell into the hands of those who agreed to forward them to her address in the States or smuggle them out of the country and mail them once they'd arrived. But the irregular dates on the letters and the sometimes confusing references suggested that not all of María's letters had arrived safely. Many had been lost along the way. Margarita couldn't imagine how Maria had managed to buy paper and pens. Perhaps she had sold Maita's jewelry to purchase writing materials and food through the black market.

Lighting another cigarette, though her last was still burning out in the ashtray on the bureau, Margarita inhaled the stale tobacco with quick puffs until the tip grew hot and red. As she blew smoke rings into the darkness, she recalled having written to María several times, promising that she would return and knowing all the while that she never had any intention of doing so. Over the years, she had seen various photographs of Havana in newspapers and magazines—some picturing only its decaying buildings and peeling paint, its crumbling statues and monuments, many of which had long since disappeared from sight, and others portraying the city as an edenic Caribbean resort, which looked to Margarita more like a Hollywood back lot than an exotic, primitive paradise. Perhaps because it had remained untouched by the modern world, parts of Havana undoubtedly still retained their original grace and beauty. But as far as Margarita could tell, the city had been reduced—diminished—to faded splendor and even the ancient beauty of the surrounding countryside was concealed beneath a thick veneer of neglect, and rape, and ruin. A city waiting like the sleeping beauty she thought, to awake from a spell.

Staring blindly into the dark face of the night, Margarita's thoughts turned back to her father. Perhaps the anger that still simmered within her wasn't natural. When she was in Miami, she was surrounded by families who had sacrificed almost everything they had to support their relatives back home. They simply would not give up trying to find a way to get them out. It wasn't uncommon to find a household composed of several generations. She couldn't begin to count the number of people she had met who had taken in cousins and neighbors and in some cases, the children of complete strangers. The revolution, they all responded with a shrug, had made all of the Cubans in exile family. But she, like a negligent mother, a thoughtless daughter, had not only abandoned her son, she had left her whole family behind without a second thought.

A cacophony of words and phrases, which she had memorized by heart since childhood

Familia . . . familia . . . la Sagrada Familia . . . through thick and thin . . .

Combined with her aunt's letters

. . . forget the past . . . what is done is done . .

rang out all at once in Margarita's head. Maybe Tía was right, she wondered, with her head resting on her arms. Maybe I was the bad one. The one with mala leche. The selfish sister who was so concerned with herself that she refused to give the little fish even a small bite of her cheese sandwich. The selfish one who refused to reverse the flow of time—the natural order—and care for her aging father.

"But I didn't choose to be your daughter—your Iphigenia," Margarita whispered aloud, as though her father were close by. "You were the stubborn one—the one who turned your back on me. You and Mother left us alone." As the words passed unexpectedly over her lips, Margarita realized that in spite of all the years that had passed, she was still being dogged by her father's memory and the loss of her mother. They were all bound together by nothing more than bitterness and regret. "A poor memory that works backwards," she thought, recalling the words from something she had read.

Margarita squashed out her cigarette and stared at the reflection of the moon on the waves once again. Only after she had regained her composure did she begin to unseal the unopened letters that remained in the packet.

taring out the window into the backyard, it occurred to Lilly that their shore house garden, which had grown wild in their absence, had also become part of her dream. Gazing into the garden, she remembered how her mother had always looked forward to planting the garden at the shore. She seemed to know everything about gardening. Maybe one of her relatives—her father or her grandfather, perhaps—had been a gardener in Cuba, and the house in the picture was the place where he worked, Lilly mused.

Of all of her childhood memories, the times they worked in the garden together were among Lilly's favorites. Perhaps restoring the garden made her mother think of her home, but why, Lilly wondered, did Margarita uproot herself—why had she shut everyone out and walled in her past, her story, with silence?

The more she thought about it, the more Lilly realized that she knew almost nothing of her mother's past. Picking up her pen, she began writing:

March 29, 1986

Here I am alone, Mommy, in this cold attic room, surrounded by the living presence of your past. Sometimes I imagine that an old woman whom I recognize but whose name I can't remember is sinking like a stone into the sea. Each wave pulls her farther and farther down until she is at neck level. (Other times, she is being pulled down the plughole of the sink—but it's always the same woman.) As she descends into the sea, she mouths inexplicable words to me—words that I cannot make out for the howling of the wind and the crashing of the waves upon the shore. Even though I can't hear her, I think I know what she is trying to tell me.

How I long to unveil the part of your life—my own life and past—that has been hidden from me. It's just not fair, Mommy. You have told me next to nothing. It's as though you have buried a whole lifetime, a whole world, inside the bottom drawer of your desk. The more I think about it, the more I am filled with anger, for now I know that you have intentionally deprived me of my memory. I feel as though I have been orphaned and betrayed. Emotionally abandoned. Even though I know next to nothing about the world that you came from, I feel as though the voices of my ancestors have begun to speak through me, Mommy, to push this pen across the page, only because their voices cannot be silenced forever. Do you understand what I'm trying to say to you? If I told you all of this face-to-face, would you think I was crazy?

I am surrounded by photographs of people who look oddly familiar, spread out across the bedspread like a deck of cards. In their faces I search for some clue that might heal the wound that has suddenly torn open inside me. As I stare at them, I cannot help but think about a story I once read—in

National Geographic, I think—about a group of women somewhere in Mexico who leave their homes and their villages to venture into the mountains with their daughters. Sometimes they journey from their homes seeking nothing more than solitude. Other times they go to the mountains to give birth. As they climb the mountain path together, the women overturn branches and stones along the way. Their daughters follow in watchful silence, knowing that when it comes time to return, they will be responsible for remembering where the branches and stones lay. Only they can find the way home. As I stare at these photographs spread across my comforter, I feel as though they are indecipherable stones—as indecipherable, Mommy, as the Rosetta stone—as indecipherable as you. Yes, you, Mommy, you are as indecipherable as the sphinx's riddles—but maybe you think the same thing about me, too. Among these faded and torn photographs—of houses and palm trees and people whose names I may never learn to pronounce—there is no familiar mark with which I can identify myself except perhaps in my resemblance to the woman in the blue linen dress with the roses pinned to her collar. Who is she, Mommy? One day I will have the courage to ask you out loud.

Of course I always knew that you were born in Cuba. Even though your English is perfect, a shadow of an accent still pulls just beneath the surface of your words when you speak. It was something I hadn't really noticed until a classmate (Violet Flounders—the girl everyone teased and called purple fish) made fun of the way you spoke the first (and last!) time that she spent the night. (I can still remember you occasionally confusing words like sheet and ship and shit). I felt so ashamed of you then— please don't be angry, I just didn't want to be different from anyone else. Later that same year my second grade teacher, Sister John Marie, asked the class if anyone had parents who had immigrated to the United States. When I told her that you were from Cuba, the old nun said that she had heard about the exotic nightclubs. Then she humiliated me in front of the entire class by asking me to stand at the chalkboard and teach everyone some Spanish words. (I was too embarrassed to tell you about this— like the time that I wet my underpants in third grade—Sister Sean Elizabeth made me sit on the radiator in the music room until my bloomers dried. No one—I mean no one—wanted to sit near me for the rest of the day, probably because I smelled like a pee-pot!) The only thing that I could think to do was count to ten, something I had learned, and luckily remembered, from Sesame Street. When I finished counting, Sister asked me if it was true that the women in Havana wore grass skirts and walked the streets topless.

Never mind, she said, in response to the puzzled expression on my face. I had no idea what she was talking about. Then Suzanne Leone started telling the class about a story she had read somewhere saying that people in Cuba had to live in houses on stilts so that snakes and scorpions wouldn't crawl through the cracks in the floorboards and the walls and into their beds at night. She said that in some places people greased down the legs of their babies' cribs and stood them in cans filled with oil so that poisonous spiders and scorpions wouldn't crawl up the sides and bite them while they slept. Sister told me to ask you if you knew anything about such things. Thank God, she forgot all about it the next day.

The honest truth is that until I found this notebook, I had never seriously envisioned you as a separate person, a person with a life that tunneled deeper and wider than mine, Mommy, probably because you never speak about your past. Whenever I thought of you, I only saw a thin, graying woman with a gingham apron tied into a bow at the back of her waist, waving at the doorway as the school bus pulled away from the curb. Until now, I'd never even seen a picture of you taken before the wedding picture you keep on your dressing table. Though maybe I never could have known it before, I am beginning to realize that some other woman—a woman who once belonged in the place of palm trees and sun in the photographs spread out across my bed—still resides somewhere within you like a silent tenant in an abandoned house. But I also know that she is someone whom I may never see or know. I've always felt somewhat neglected by you, Mother—made to take second place to Peter—and now I feel—even more than ever—that there is an ocean between us.

* * *

The thought of Peter made Lilly flush with anger. Laying the notebook aside, she stretched out across the bed. Even as a child, she had resented the manner in which Margarita expected her to watch over him, even though they were so close in age. She resented the fact that somehow she, rather than Peter, was expected to do all the chores, and she was always held responsible for the thousands of things that went wrong in a day. Broken vases, spilled milk, mud-prints tracked across the living room carpet, and cartons of ice cream left on the kitchen counter to spoil—the list went on and on.

"Shame on you, Lilly. You're older, Lilly. You should know better by now."

She had heard the words a thousand and one times over. In retaliation for all the misunderstandings and injustices, Lilly pinched her brother under his armpits and pulled the hair at the back of his neck when Margarita wasn't looking. Whenever she got the chance, she'd lock him in the linen closet while her mother was working outside in the garden or down in the basement folding laundry. She remembered telling him one time that he was a gypsy orphan whom their parents had found wandering in the streets and adopted out of pity rather than love. She refused to let him out of the closet until he swore never to tell Margarita what she had said.

Over the years, Lilly recalled with a touch of guilt, she had tormented her brother with the idea that he wasn't wanted or loved, taking a kind of sadistic pleasure in seeing him whimper and cry. Until he was bigger than her (and beat her up with no effort at all), she had taken advantage of every opportunity to taunt and terrify him with stories about wolves that crept under their beds when the lights went out and watchful goblins and demon men who peered at them through the knots in the paneling, waiting to steal away their souls. At the time, it seemed like the only way to lash out at him—to make up for the fact that he was her mother's favorite. It was the only way, she thought, to make up for the anger and the resentment that boiled within her like a poison-filled cauldron and the loneliness and sense of isolation she had felt from the time that she was a little girl.

The clouds hung like dark tents in the sky. A narrow ribbon of light appeared just above the horizon as though an invisible hand had stripped a piece of the sky's pitch-colored flesh, leaving behind a pale, jagged wound. As the sun thrust itself above the horizon, the creased shadow of the thorn bush began to stretch across the backyard and bend upward toward the window where Margarita stood holding María's and Tata's letters.

The last letter in the packet was postmarked during the fall of 1984, but with this letter María had failed, for the envelope was empty and the bottom had been sliced open with a sharp object like a bloodless wound. Perhaps her aunt had run out of things to sell, Margarita wondered. Perhaps she had grown careless or had trusted the wrong person. She would never know for sure. All she knew for certain was that her aunt's correspondence had suddenly ended, and now María was dead. Skimming over her aunt's final words, she smiled at the thought that amid her sorrow and pain, María still fibbed about her age—Margarita was certain (though her aunt, like her grandmother before her, refused to reveal her real age) that she was at least seventy-five or seventy-six, not sixty-eight as she claimed.

As she stood shivering at the window, Margarita realized that there was no way of knowing whether Tata and Tres Flores were still standing. Even if she returned to Cuba now, she thought, it would probably be a homecoming without a home. On the other hand, if Tres Flores was still standing, it was impossible to say who might be living in the house. She probably wouldn't be able to get past the front door. (Perhaps some poor guajiro and his family had moved in with nowhere else to go. She knew that she wouldn't have the heart to send them packing despite the fact that Tres Flores legally belonged to her.) But if Tata were still living—by some remote chance—she, like a priestess saying mass at her altar, would never have abandoned Tres Flores, even if it was burning to the ground. Margarita's only hope was that if Tata was dead, that the old woman had died peacefully in her sleep. But again, there was no way of knowing. The chances of even being able to locate her family's graves was remote. There was probably no one in Cienfuegos left to mark them or remember them. Besides, she had read somewhere that the Cuban government had claimed all of the land where the cemeteries lay and exhumed all of the graves. And her sisters—who knew if they were still living? It was anyone's guess. If they were alive, they could be almost anywhere. For all she knew, they could have washed up on the shores of Miami along with the thousands of balseros who had fled Cuba in their flimsy makeshift rafts over the years.

Gazing into the garden she and the children restored at the beginning of every summer, Margarita was reminded of the joyous ritual that they had shared together from the time Lilly and Peter were children. First, they dragged the soggy brown leaves and the pebbles out of the beds with a stone rake, and then, on their hands and their knees, they pulled, and pruned, and cut back a year's worth of undergrowth. When they had finished, they loosened the dark, moist soil—Lilly and Peter with brand new silver spades, and Margarita, with an old, silver-plated serving spoon with a rambling rose pattern she had found while browsing in an antique shop and bought (though she paid too much for it) because it reminded her of her grandmother's silverware. Preferring to feel the earth with their hands, they refused to wear the padded gardening gloves that Joey bought for them at the hardware store each year.

Even as small children, Lilly and Peter dug in the garden with such diligence, Margarita recalled, as though they alone were responsible for uncovering the hidden roots and the pulse of life that lay buried just beneath the topsoil. And then they lovingly sowed into the earth the packets of seeds they'd chosen together at the store while Margarita planted the mimosa seedlings that she'd nurtured through the winter in rusty Hills Brothers coffee cans. For days afterwards Lilly and Peter held a silent vigil, checking the beds each morning for the first signs of life and then showering them with water from a large metal watering can that they filled with the outside hose. To the children it seemed like a lifetime before the first seedlings thrust their hooded brown heads through the soil. By mid-July the beds were brimming over with tangled vines and flowers. Margarita smiled at the memory of the tulip bulbs they had planted at the end of the first summer they spent at the house when Lilly was only five years old. The flowers never came up, they later discovered, because Lilly had planted the bulbs upside down in the soil.

Nervously fingering the packet of letters in her hand, Margarita studied the garden as one might a familiar face. It was a jungle—a chiaroscuro of light and shade. From her height she could just make out the boundaries of the flower beds. The wooden fence that enclosed the yard was laced with thin vines that were covered with withered berries. Nightshade, she presumed, for honeysuckle didn't have berries. She could see that the painted fence had begun to blister and peel in the salt air. Shocks of silvery grass shot up haphazardly across the yard and black stubble pierced through the thick layers of leaves that the wind had blown across the grass.

The untended garden, Margarita thought, so forlorn and abandoned. And yet, despite its desolation, she could sense the life that had already begun to throb and swell beneath its surface and almost envision the wild growth that would soon break through the chaos of winter stubble. It had been an unusually mild winter and spring had come unexpectedly and unannounced. The crocuses and the hyacinth the children gave her every Easter had already begun to bloom in the corners of the yard, and the crooked thorn bush that stood at the center of the garden had begun to bud. Rarely did she remember seeing so many signs of life so early in the season.

"Gethsemane," Margarita whispered as she turned to light another cigarette and her gaze fell upon the watermarks on the ceiling by the chimney. They had formed a great, dark continent and a series of tiny islands, silent and mysterious. The oversized cabbage roses and the rambling, leafy vines on the wallpaper had paled and faded, and a long strip of paper had come loose and lay pleated on the floor. Margarita's eyes wandered back and forth from the wallpaper to the lavender comforter. When they settled on the dome-shaped bird cage on her bureau, she realized in a sudden flash that despite her efforts to erase the landmarks of her past, to pull out her memory by the roots, she had unconsciously reproduced the landscape of her childhood in the clapboard house by the ocean. And in the process, she had reduced her past to nothing more than a heap of pale images.

A cheap imitation. A forgery, she thought to herself as her gaze skipped wildly across the lavender comforter and the wallpaper, out the window and across the yard, and then settled on the expressionless, gray surface of the ocean.

* * *

The chirping of birds nesting outside her window drew Margarita back from the dark void into which she had fallen. She had no idea how long she had stood staring out the window. Like a woman possessed, she suddenly began gathering together in her arms the clothing she had folded and laid on the chest at the foot of the bed the night before. With her eyes fastened on the strip of wallpaper, she stood in the corner of the room, partially hidden from her husband's view in case he happened to wake, pulling on her skirt beneath her flannel nightgown.

Pain had made her try to obliterate her past, she thought, as she lifted her nightgown over her head. Now pain alone would allow her to unearth and claim as her own the sorrow and grief she had denied herself over the years.

T aking up the notebook once again, Lilly searched for the story she had begun writing shortly after finding it in her mother's bottom drawer. For months she had been unable to finish the story. The ending just wouldn't come. Then in a flash, the photographs held between the leaves of the green notebook broke their silence and the story seemed to write itself out word by word:

As the procession arrived at the water's edge, a group of men lifted the statue from its dais and placed it in one of the larger fishing boats. An armada of small skiffs escorted the Virgin to a floating platform anchored just off a thin strip of land that jutted out of the mouth of the bay into the sea. The fisherman and devoted townspeople followed in her wake, scattering flower petals into the water from the backs of their boats.

The old woman, accompanied by two others, watched in silent detachment as the bobbing knot of fishing boats launched across the bay. With her eyes she traced the haphazard pattern of the crowd, spread out unevenly across the shore. Some waved their straw hats and bandannas over their heads; others waded through the water after the fishing boats while flower petals undulated around them like colorful wreaths. Once having lost sight of the statue, the crowd gradually began to break off into smaller groups, making their way toward the deserted town, which lay in ruins.

Just as the last seams of violet light began to thread through the evening sky, those who had accom-

panied the statue to its floating island returned to
the shore. With great effort, they dragged their empty
boats through the flower petals that had caught on
the puckered lips of the sand and abandoned them on
the beach. Soon the sound of distant laughter and
music reached the women's ears. They closed their eyes,
allowing the day's images to parade through their
minds, listening all the while to the strain of guitars
and the soft, throbbing rhythm of distant drums—
the rhythm that the people had been denied for so
many years.

The carnival lasted well into the night, ending with song and dance and loud, drunken quarrels. And as the town at the base of the mountain slept, the three women remained upright and motionless. With their legs spread out and folded beneath them, and the palms of their hands resting on their knees, they resembled three dark flowers on a single stem.

Daisy stood on the portico with her daughter in a pale ribbon of moon-light, searching for the large silver key that had sunken like a weight to the bottom of her purse. With the moon at their backs, their shadows intertwined and stretched ahead of them. She turned the key from side to side until the old, rusted lock reluctantly gave way. As the red wooden door swung open, she

But their vigil was interrupted by the sudden knowledge that she had returned. Filled with unexpected joy, they pulled themselves to their feet and began making their way through the darkness along the steep path that sloped down the side of the mountain toward the sleeping town below. reached for her daughter's hand and together they stepped into a world she had left behind for what seemed to her a thousand and one lifetimes. . . .

* * *

Interrupting her thoughts, a muffled sound like an animal crying out in pain, suddenly caught Lilly's attention and drew her to the window that faced the ocean.

Prickly brown burrs clung to the hem of her skirt as Margarita crossed the backyard, picking her way through the withered cactus in her bare feet. When she reached the thorn bush she thrust her arm deep within its branches and wrapped her hand around a large, dark thorn, pressing its fire into her palm until the tears streamed down her cheeks and into her parted lips.

As the slow but mounting pain rose within her, Margarita began to weep over all the times she had never asked for anything for herself—the years she had denied herself the best portions—placing everyone's needs, everyone's desires, everyone's lives ahead of hers; and then a long litany of offenses and grievances followed. In silence, she began to recall the names and faces of all the people she had lost over the years, repossessing them one by one, until she reached her father.

"Father," she whispered aloud, into the salty wind, which swept her words like unstrung beads toward the ocean, "Please forgive me. I forgive you. I forgive you. I forgive both of us, so that we can both be free."

With these words, Margarita withdrew her hand from the thorn bush. She sank to her knees and covered her face with her hands like a cage. And as the pain slowly began to subside within her, she felt as though she had been awakened from a dream. Something had come unstopped—a waxy seal had suddenly broken. She realized that the chase was over. Throwing her head back, she unleashed a scream that sounded at the back of her throat like laughter, and with one great heave she released Pedro and unearthed the anger and the grief that lay buried deep within her. It was at that moment that her gaze fell upon Lilly, standing with outstretched arms at the attic window.

M argarita paused just outside Lilly's bedroom door, listening to the distant sound of the waves crashing upon the shore. Though she had already knocked twice, Lilly refused to answer. After a moment, she turned the brass knob and discovered that the door was unlocked.

Lilly stood with her back to her mother in the same position Margarita had seen her from the garden. Sweeping the room with her eyes, she recognized her mother's green notebook lying open among the photographs scattered across the bed. She crossed the room and picked up the notebook.

Pressing her face against the cold glass, Lilly looked out the third floor window and saw her mother crossing the backyard, picking her way through the withered cacti and the prickly grass in her bare feet, running in a delirium. She saw her mother reach into the thorn bush. With her arm thrust deep within its branches, Daisy had wrapped her hand around a sharp thorn, pressing it into her palm. Unmoving, Lilly watched while the tears streamed down her cheeks and into her parted lips.

At long last the pain forced Daisy to take notice of her body. As she withdrew her hand from the ebony branches—unaware that her blood stained the ground beneath her feet and the sharp thorns tore into her sleeve, leaving a swirling mazelike pattern on her arm— Daisy threw back her head and saw her daughter gazing down at her from the attic window with her arms extended from her sides and her head slightly twisted as though she hung from a crucifix.

Raising her eyes to her daughter's motionless form, Daisy wondered whether or not she had arrived too late. Perhaps she had already lost her.

"Happy Birthday, honey," she said after a moment, breaking the silence.

"Why did you leave Cuba?" Lilly asked without turning around.

Margarita paused for a moment, uncertain as to how to respond. Then a voice seemed to speak through her: "If I hadn't left, I wouldn't have you, would I? "

Lilly slowly turned her head around and they stared at one another in silence, unable to speak because their hearts had suddenly filled beyond expression. But in the pause of that moment, the pained look in Lilly's eyes pried open her mother's lips and arms. In a rushing torrent, they both began to speak at once, and it was as though they were calling out to one another from a great distance. Their words crowded thickly on top of one another, pressing together, knotted and tangled. And in the confusion they began to laugh and cry all at once in a single voice like schoolgirls. There was a sterling quality to Lilly's laughter, and in that sound Margarita heard her own mother's voice once again, distinct and unmistakable.

As the laughter began to sink in her throat, Lilly sensed a presence behind her. She glanced in the mirror hanging from the back of her closet door. Though the hallway was dark, she was certain that they were watched, for she could feel the weight of someone's presence among them. She knew that her mother had sensed something too, for she had reached out her hand as though she were trying to grasp some retreating figure only she could see. When Margarita turned, their eyes met in the glass, and though they had become silent, traces of their laughter still lingered at the corners of their mouths.

As they embraced one another once again, Margarita drew Lilly onto her knees and began rocking her gently back and forth like a child, rubbing spirals into her back with her fingertips all the while. With her daughter draped across her lap, like the

Virgin Mother holding her dying child in the cradle of her arms, she felt as though time had stood still, for Lilly was an infant once again. She felt as though she had retraced her steps and retrieved a lost blossom, a lost pearl which she had carelessly tossed into the furrow of a wave.

Tell her a story, several voices seemed to whisper, as though from one throat from the shadows of the hallway.

"Yes, tell me a story," Lilly repeated, opening her eyes and pulling herself into a sitting position."Then I have something to tell you."

"Did you grow up in this house?" she asked, pointing to a photograph of the front portico at Tres Flores.

Margarita stared at the image for a long while, seeing in her mind's eye everything that the camera had failed to capture. "Yes," she murmured. "But that picture doesn't give you much of an idea of what it was like. In fact it doesn't tell you much of anything at all."

"Then you tell me what it was like," Lilly said, crossing her legs and folding them beneath her.

Lilly listened in silence like a disciple as Tres Flores began to reconstruct itself around them at the sound of her mother's voice.